Warrior Queen

Guinevere
Book Four

Fil Reid

© Copyright 2022 by Fil Reid
Text by Fil Reid
Cover by Dar Albert

Dragonblade Publishing, Inc. is an imprint of Kathryn Le Veque Novels, Inc.
P.O. Box 23
Moreno Valley, CA 92556
ceo@dragonbladepublishing.com

Produced in the United States of America

First Edition July 2023
Print Edition

Reproduction of any kind except where it pertains to short quotes in relation to advertising or promotion is strictly prohibited.

All Rights Reserved.

The characters and events portrayed in this book are fictitious. Any similarity to real persons, living or dead, is purely coincidental and not intended by the author.

ARE YOU SIGNED UP FOR DRAGONBLADE'S BLOG?

You'll get the latest news and information on exclusive giveaways, exclusive excerpts, coming releases, sales, free books, cover reveals and more.

Check out our complete list of authors, too!

No spam, no junk. That's a promise!

Sign Up Here

www.dragonbladepublishing.com

―――

Dearest Reader;

Thank you for your support of a small press. At Dragonblade Publishing, we strive to bring you the highest quality Historical Romance from some of the best authors in the business. Without your support, there is no 'us', so we sincerely hope you adore these stories and find some new favorite authors along the way.

Happy Reading!

CEO, Dragonblade Publishing

Additional Dragonblade books by
Author Fil Reid

Guinevere Series
The Dragon Ring (Book 1)
The Bear's Heart (Book 2)
The Sword (Book 3)
Warrior Queen (Book 4)

Chapter One

SILVERED WITH AGE and long use, the ancient round table occupied the central space in the lofty Council Hall of Viroconium. The ornately carved, high-backed wooden seats assigned to each of the many kings of Britain encircled it, all but one of them occupied. The largest and most splendid. Being round, the table possessed no head, but this chair, a throne, occupied what might have been that place.

Pressed back against the plaster-covered walls of the hall's ground floor, and jammed in shoulder-to-shoulder, each king's followers crowded close, eager to observe the momentous proceedings.

Dressed in a vivid, dark red gown, and with my chestnut hair flowing loose to my waist, I stood with Merlin alongside our men of Dumnonia. A few paces in front of us, my husband, Arthur, had not long ago taken his place at the table. He now sat motionless in one of the chairs, beside his older cousin, Caninus. Only the back of his dark head, with the slender gold circlet of rank resting in his curls, was visible from where I stood.

In the galleries that overhung the hall, the locals jostled for position. The lucky few who'd managed to fight their way inside strained against the not-very-robust-looking rails put there to prevent them from toppling onto the flagstone floor below. The babble of voices rose to the rafters, and an unwelcome stink of hot, unwashed bodies permeated the stuffy air.

Caninus, King of Gwent, and son of the man who'd once held the title of High King himself, had called this Council the moment he'd heard Arthur had succeeded in drawing the sword from the stone. The stone that had stood for nearly three years in the forum at Viroconium, where any man who dared, young or old, rich or poor, had been able to try his hand at taking it. Many had tried, but until Arthur came, all had failed.

"The words written on the stone might say that you're High King because you've been able to draw the sword," Caninus had said to Arthur, when we'd arrived at his capital of Caer Went bearing the sword. "But it will take a meeting of the Council to ratify this. And they'll want to see you do it for themselves."

Wise words.

We stayed with Caninus while he sent out urgent messengers in every direction to all the kings of Britain, bidding them to come as quickly as they could to an extraordinary meeting of the Council. And now here we were, standing in the Council Hall, where Caninus had dropped the bombshell of what had happened on his fellows.

I glanced at Merlin. His thin face still bore the marks of the beating and torture he'd received at the hands of Morgana's henchmen, the bruises yellowing now, and the cut above his right eye scabbed over. I didn't need my woman's intuition to know his internal scars must remain raw and unhealed.

The cause of all this stood on the far side of the hall, at the front of her brother Cadwy's faction, beside Cadwy's dowdy wife, Angharad. The Princess Morgana, sister to Arthur, Cadwy, Morgawse and Cei, beautiful as ever in a long cream gown, her slender waist girdled with the chain of delicate gold links as was her habit. She wouldn't be able to wear that for much longer, now she had a child growing in her belly. The child she'd stolen from Merlin with her guile. Maybe even her magic.

I fixed her with my best hard stare. If there was anyone I'd like to see brought down, it was her. When necessity called, I could be as bitchy as the next woman. And as the next woman was Morgana, that was saying something.

She didn't look my way, but kept her eyes fixed on her oldest brother's broad back. Even from here, I could see Cadwy's face looked ten times worse than Merlin's. Both his eyes remained puffy and swollen, and probably bloodshot. His lower lip bore a huge dark scab, and shades of yellow and purple blotched his cheeks from where Arthur had gained the upper hand in their fight just two short weeks ago.

Cadwy had certainly borne the worst of it. But then, Arthur had been fighting not only for the return of Merlin, but also for the sword in the stone itself. Cadwy had lusted for it, still lusted for it probably, and the power it could bring him, just as he'd lusted for me and the power he thought I held. He'd schemed to gain it by any means, but he'd failed, and lost. At the last, Arthur had drawn the sword for himself, to replace his own, broken in the fight.

On the far side of Merlin stood the burly, red-headed Cei, Arthur's other half-brother, both his seneschal and trusted friend. He met my eyes, and his for-once serious face softened into a smile of encouragement, his blue eyes twinkling. It went a small way to calming my twisting stomach.

The legs of Caninus's heavy seat grated as he shunted it back across the flagstones and rose slowly to his feet. Gazing around the hall, lips pressed together in a stern line, he held one hand above his head, commanding silence.

A spare, ascetic man, he nevertheless possessed a quality of leadership and a deep voice that commanded attention: the voice of an orator.

Silence fell in the hall, as every man's eye, and every woman's, too, turned toward Caninus. As the son of Ambrosius, and great grandson of Constantine III, the last Roman Emperor recognized by Britain, he affected the old-fashioned, classical Roman style. Over his rich, dark-purple tunic, he'd draped an off-white gown that could have been described as a toga about his body, and he wore sandals on his feet.

When not a sound could be heard in the hall, and he'd gathered in the attention of every person present, he spoke. "Fellow kings." His voice rang out as his gaze ran around the table, lingering a moment on each man's face – on the old and the young, the bearded and the clean-shaven, the curious, the hostile, the openly expectant. "We are gathered here today for one reason only. Some of you will already know why. Rumor travels at speed even to the far-flung corners of our island, and others of you have been encamped here long enough to have heard the story."

Even though I knew exactly what had happened, I found myself hanging on his words. In another time, he could have been a theatrical actor.

"A little over two weeks ago, something momentous happened here in Viroconium." He paused, his gaze taking in the crowded masses in the galleries before dropping to the men of rank, and the few women, pressed back against the walls. Did I imagine it, or did his eyes linger on Morgana, standing defiantly beautiful at the head of Cadwy's faction?

Moving on, Caninus swiveled on his heel so as not to leave out the audience behind him, which included Merlin, Cei and me. "The Sword of Destiny has been drawn from the stone."

A hushed gasp whispered around the hall, of a thousand voices inhaling in wonder, even though most of them already knew this, and many of the townspeople had seen it happen for themselves. Caninus had a flair for the dramatic.

On the far side of the table, Cadwy glowered as much as his damaged face would allow, lowering his head like a bull about to charge. His bushy black brows met in a heavy scowl, thick lower lip jutting from within the nest of his tangled, graying beard. Although he must only have been in his mid-thirties, ten years older than Arthur, he had the look about him of an older man. Life in the Dark Ages wasn't kind to warriors. Or women, for that matter.

He'd wanted that sword badly. Enough to aid Morgana when she'd seduced Merlin and lured him into her power. Enough to have Morgana and her cronies fruitlessly torture Merlin in an effort to make him release the sword from the stone. Enough to agree to fight Arthur in hand-to-hand combat for Merlin and the sword.

He must have been convinced he'd win, and both Merlin and the sword would have been his. He hadn't. With his own sword broken in the fight, and Cadwy lying beaten to a bloody pulp, Arthur had stepped up to the stone where it stood in the forum – the stone they'd been fighting around. The time had at last been right, and in front of not just his own men, but those of Cadwy, and the watching population of Viroconium, the sword had slid out of the stone at his touch.

I had to shoulder the blame for the sword even being in the stone to start with. Merlin had set it up in the forum because of something I said. I'd once made the mistake of telling him he would be the one to make Arthur High King, and how it would happen.

In legend.

Thanks to me, that legend had now become reality, and had left me with a morbid fear of doing the same again. My biggest worry here in the Dark Ages was that my knowledge, gained from an upbringing by my Arthurian scholar father, was unreliable, and that I daily risked changing the past, and with it, the future.

Caninus, from his place beside Arthur, laid a hand on his cousin's shoulder. "And this is the man who drew the sword."

I hadn't thought Cadwy's expression could get any more malevolent. I'd been wrong.

Arthur got to his feet. As was his habit, his almost black tunic bore only minimal decoration around the neckline, cuffs and hem, and his dark braccae had been tucked into his everyday, mud-spattered riding boots. The simple gold circlet resting in his thick dark hair gave the only hint to his status as king of Dumnonia.

He turned on the spot allowing everyone in the hall a good look at him, his gaze pausing for a moment as his dark eyes met mine, the glint of triumph sparkling in them. Tall, with a horseman's slim, athletic build, my husband was the handsomest man in the hall by far. Shoulder-length, dark hair framed a clean-shaven face that could hold the respect of any man he met, and charm any woman. The fact that he only had eyes for me sent a warm glow cascading through my body. He certainly possessed the famous Pendragon magnetism.

My lips curved into a return smile, and his gaze passed on.

"Show them the sword," Caninus said.

Arthur put his hand to the sword hilt that protruded from the scabbard at his side, the only weapon allowed into the hall. For a moment he paused, as the thick air charged with tension. Then, in one swift movement, he drew the sword – the one we'd waited nearly three years to see. It slid from its scabbard as easily as it had from the stone. Raising his arm, he brandished it above his head. The light shafting in through the high windows glimmered on its blade.

It had never been a fancy sword. More the sword of a soldier – a warrior. The hilt was plain and unadorned, the grip bound with well-worn leather, the pommel burnished bronze. But every man and woman in the hall had seen this sword close up while it had been encased in the rock, and many had tried to pull it out, unsuccessfully. Now someone had succeeded, every eye fixed on the gleaming blade, and the man who'd drawn it, in open fascination.

As did the eyes of every king seated at the table.

King Caw of Alt Clut was first to speak.

Unsurprisingly. A little under a year ago Arthur had marched north to Caw's hilltop stronghold on the banks of the River Clyde and breached its defenses. Caw had been causing more than just a bit of trouble north of the Wall, raiding lands belonging to his neighbors and bringing in reinforcements from even further north in the form of the wild Dogmen, a tribe of fearsome, blue-painted Pictish warriors. Arthur had put a stop to that and, to maintain the peace, had taken Gildas, Caw's youngest and favorite son, south as hostage. No wonder Caw wanted to make known what he thought.

He rose to his feet, not a tall man but a wide and powerfully built one, aggression oozing from every pore. "How do we know he really did it?" he asked, his heavily accented voice reminiscent of a modern Glaswegian.

Arthur gazed at him implacably. This wasn't a man, or an opinion, that bothered my husband. Not for the first time, I wished I could see more of Arthur's face from where I stood.

"Aye." Meirchion the Lean, King of Rheged, got to his feet as well, a few places down from Caw, his sworn enemy. The man he'd refused to fight against when Arthur had asked for his help because he thought himself safe within the stone walls of Caer Ligualid. "D'you expect us to believe this convenient story?"

Of course, he'd be one of the first to object – not a man who wanted to help anyone to something he fancied for himself. Two and a half years ago, there'd almost been an election for High King after Arthur's father Uthyr died. Meirchion had been one of the candidates ignored when Arthur became Dux in place of having a new High King.

Impossible to see Caninus's face, but his firm-set shoulders and upright stance told me a lot. "Not to believe," he said, his voice carrying around the hall. "To witness for yourselves. We'll go outside now, into the forum, and you may all see the truth in what I've told you."

Arthur slid the sword back into the scabbard on his hip, his head turning as he surveyed his audience, his face betraying no sign of trepidation.

Caw leaned forward, his meaty hands resting on the silvered wood of the table. "That's right. Put it back in that stone, and let's all see if he can truly take it out." His voice rolled out across the table, echoing around the hall. His angry gaze rested on Arthur.

A chorus of ayes came from the listening kings, and a mutter of agreement rustled through the audience.

Caninus, his face a mask of calm seriousness, nodded. "We'll do just that." He gestured to the surrounding supporters of each king. "If you'll lead the way outside and leave a goodly space around the stone?"

Merlin caught my arm as I made to move. "Not us, Gwen. We'll wait for Arthur to go out and follow him."

The warriors and churchmen from each kingdom filed out of the hall, the sound of their voices rising in intensity as the prospect of what was to come occupied them. They were followed by the townspeople, shuffling down the stairs from the galleries above our heads, the hall emptying slowly around us.

At the round table, Arthur remained standing beside Caninus, but Caw and Meirchion resumed their seats. A few of the kings leaned toward one another in low conversation, their faces either alight with excitement or heavy with mistrust, or even anger. Arthur was one of the youngest kings here. Perhaps the thought of him ruling over them irked these older men.

At last, our turn to process out through the wide double doors of the hall arrived. The kings went first, in solemn single file, led by Arthur and Caninus. When the last one had departed, Merlin, Cei and I followed.

A wall of noise hit us. The forum thronged with people jammed in like the salted pilchards in a barrel we sometimes had brought up from the west country to Din Cadan. An endless blue sky burnt down on bare heads, helmets and hats, the sun already high and not a cloud to be seen.

Cadwy's palace guards were in the process of forcing the crowds back far enough to leave a circle of space between the doors of the hall and the empty market stalls. In the center stood the large, flattish rock that had appeared there overnight nearly three years ago. Devoid of any sign that it had ever held the sword.

Merlin's hand on my arm brought me to a halt just outside the hall doors, and Cei encircled my waist with a protective arm, drawing me closer, his nearness offering support. My heart thundered, clammy sweat prickled my skin, and by my sides my hands balled into fists. With careful precision, I straightened my fingers and drew a deep, steadying breath.

The kings formed a semi-circle around the stone in a long row of opulence – of brightly colored tunics, gold jewelry, crowned heads. Like birds of paradise, they'd come in all their finery.

Caninus stepped out of the row and up to the stone, gesturing Arthur to follow.

I chewed my lip.

Silence fell again, broken only by the loud cawing of a few rooks as they flew overhead. Despite the heat, a cold chill had settled in my stomach. Just because Arthur had taken it out once didn't mean he'd be able to do it again, did it? Even though I knew the legend, doubt festered, in my heart and in my head, that reality did not echo legend every time. If at all.

Arthur stepped onto the rock. For a moment, he stood still, gazing around at the watching people. Then he drew the sword from his scabbard once again, and held it high for all to see. In one sweeping movement he plunged it back into the stone. That it went into solid rock at all must have surprised most of the watchers, even though they knew it had come out of there. It surprised me a bit, too. I'd been wondering if once drawn it might refuse to go back, which would have been awkward.

A gasp rose toward the sky.

"See," Caninus said, voice raised to carry around the forum. "The sword goes back from whence it came." He nodded to Arthur.

My hands fisted again, the nails digging into my palms, as Cei's arm around my waist tightened. He must have been as tense as me. I glanced at Merlin. His battered face held no expression at all, and it wasn't Arthur he was watching. It was Morgana, standing off to one side with Cadwy's men, one hand on her flat belly as though to deliberately remind him she carried his child. *Witch.*

Arthur gripped the worn, leather-bound hilt, glanced slowly around, then pulled the sword out of the rock once more. He raised it above his head, half man, half glorious statue of a warrior king.

A cheer went up, but it died as Caw pushed his way forward, resplendent in his deep red robes. "Easy to pull it out once it's been drawn," he rumbled, like the lion of a man he was. "Any man could do that. Put it back, and let me take it out. Then we'll see who's High King here."

Although not a tall man, his wide, muscled shoulders and chest suggested great strength. Had he ever tried to pull it out before? Most of the kings here had at some time had a go. Cadwy the most embarrassingly, announcing before his attempt that it had been put there especially for him.

Without a word, Arthur slid the sword back into the stone and stepped down, his face impassive. But his eyes, as they shot to meet mine, sparkled with mischief. My nervous heart responded with a leap of excitement.

Caw took Arthur's place on the stone, settling his booted feet slightly apart. He glanced toward his followers, where some of the sandy-headed, thickset sons I'd seen last year stood watching with his men, and grinned, showing uneven, yellowed teeth. Wolf's teeth. Then he set his right hand only on the sword hilt and pulled. Nothing happened.

I could probably have told him that.

Inside, I grinned with delight, but dared not show it. A small part of me had worried Caw would be right, and that once Arthur had loosened it, any man might have drawn it. This wasn't a fairytale or legend – this was real life. I couldn't rely on the stories I knew being true.

A frown making his brows heavier than ever, Caw set his other hand alongside the first, settled his grip more surely, and gave an enormous heave. The sword didn't budge an inch. Undaunted, he heaved again. If the sword could have laughed at him, I swear it would have.

His frown turning into a scowl, Caw stepped down from the rock. "Let Pendragon try again. If it won't move for me, it won't for him."

You think?

Still impassive, Arthur took the empty place on the rock, and with one hand drew the sword once more from the stone, as easily as from the scabbard on his hip.

A cheer went up again, then fizzled out as another king stepped forward. Owain White Tooth, king of Gwynedd, a distant cousin of Arthur's through their joint descent from old king Cunedda of Guotodin. Since I'd been here, I'd become familiar with the internecine connections. Most of the kings here could boast Cunedda's widespread bloodline to some degree.

Owain was a few years older than Arthur, shorter, more thickset, with a mane of chestnut hair and a beard streaked with auburn. A good-looking man, his abnormally white teeth, glinting as he grinned around at the other kings, gave him his nickname. "I'll try this as well. Shove it back in the stone."

Arthur slid the sword back into its strange rocky scabbard. The hilt stood up like a cross, plain but impressive. With a glance at Caninus, he stepped out of Owain's way.

Owain tried and failed. A few more kings tried as well. Of course, all of them failed, but that didn't stop others wanting to try their hands, convinced that because Arthur had succeeded, maybe one of them could as well. They couldn't.

Then another man stepped forward.

I'd seen him at the table and not recognized him from the one Council I'd been to before. I'd assumed he was one of those rulers who didn't always answer the call to attend. That, I'd been told, often happened with the more far-flung kingdoms.

A man of Arthur's own build, he was slim and dark, his somewhat sallow face long and narrow with a prominent nose. Clear blue eyes gazed calmly out from beneath straight dark brows, and he wore his thick brown hair in a single braid to beneath his shoulder blades.

Merlin leaned toward me. "Cerdic of Caer Guinntguic," he whispered in my ear.

My breath caught in my throat. A man for whom my husband had no love at all. The man who'd killed Arthur's boyhood mentor at Llongborth and would have killed Arthur, too, had Merlin not intervened. And only this spring Arthur had met him in battle at Caer Guinntguic, when Cerdic had returned to claim the throne of that kingdom from his nephew Natanleod.

The fact that the childless Natanleod now lay dead, and Cerdic ruled in his place, and that Arthur had been forced to accept this as the only alternative to lawlessness, rankled my husband. If I'd known Cerdic's identity earlier, I'd have been watching him more closely.

Cerdic nodded to Arthur and Caninus as though no enmity existed between them, as though most of the kings here on the council didn't look on him with a suspicion born of his having a Saxon mother. As Cadwy also did, and no love was lost on him, either.

"Let me try," Cerdic said, his accent guttural, but clear.

Arthur's right hand shot to where his sword should have been hanging at his belt. Luckily, it wasn't. Killing another king during the Council, or even raising a sword against him, would have been a terrible crime, and would probably have ensured he never became High King despite his possession of the sword.

Caninus nodded. "All are free to try."

Cerdic stepped onto the rock. Caninus's restraining hand went to

Arthur's arm, his fingers closing tightly about it above the elbow. He probably had a good idea of how his cousin felt about this new king on the Council.

Cerdic didn't beat about the bush. He seized the sword hilt with both hands, set his feet on either side of it, and heaved. The tendons in his neck bulged, his face reddened, but the sword didn't budge. Releasing it, he straightened up, then stepped down off the rock and approached Caninus and Arthur. Caninus's fingers tightened further on Arthur's arm, the knuckles whitening.

Cerdic dropped to one knee. His words rang out around the forum. "I, Cerdic of Caer Guinntguic, acknowledge Arthur Pendragon, King of Dumnonia, as High King of all Britain." He bent his head in supplication.

Caninus's fingers relaxed. Arthur stared down at the man who'd killed his boyhood hero, his face working for a moment as he clearly struggled to control himself.

Common sense won. He stretched out a hand and touched Cerdic's bent head. "I accept your homage."

With a rustle of clothing, almost every king did the same, even Caw. Like barley flattened by the wind, their assembled retinues followed suit. All around the forum, the townspeople sank to the ground as one. They had a new High King.

Merlin nodded to me and Cei, and we three also knelt.

Finally, Caninus released Arthur's arm and took the knee as well.

The only ones left standing were Cadwy and Morgana, his face dark as a storm cloud, hers cold and calculating, her hand rubbing her belly.

After a long, pregnant moment, Caninus got to his feet. "All hail the new High King." His voice rang out as he surveyed the sea of bent heads. "All hail High King Arthur Pendragon."

A huge cheer rose from the throats of all the watching people.

My heart, that had been hammering with nerves, swelled with pride until it felt as though it might burst.

Chapter Two

Two days later we took the road south toward Arthur's stronghold of Din Cadan, capital of Dumnonia. The weather continued to favor us. Under a blue sky patched with only occasional white clouds, we rode through a countryside where farmers and their families labored in the sunshine. In the fields, the blades of sickles flashed, rhythmically cutting down an abundant hay crop. Behind them, the drying grass lay in fat swathes, and little barefoot boys and girls, waving long sticks and helped by scrawny farm dogs, chased off cattle and sheep looking for an easy meal. The scent of the newly made hay sweetened the air around every farm we passed.

Protected by stone walls and grassy banks, the wheat, oats and barley were turning slowly from green to gold as a blush of gilding crept across the fields. In the scattered stands of trees along the river valleys, and the denser tracts of forest, the pale green of spring buds had changed to the richer, darker hues of midsummer.

We followed the old Roman road that would be known as the Fosse Way in my day. Most likely it had been a road long before the Romans came, but they'd turned it into an engineered marvel, with layers of stones and finally a thick covering of gravel that made our journey far easier than riding across country would have been. Although, of course, we rode our horses on the rough ground beside it most of the time, to spare their unshod hooves.

Fifth-century Britain was nothing like the one I'd grown up in, fifteen hundred years into the future. It abounded with as yet undrained wet and boggy areas, especially in valley bottoms. The river crossings mostly had no bridges worth mentioning and were often only fordable in summer. The wild stretches of primordial forest in between the towns, fortresses and farms might harbor wolves, or worse, brigands. Roads were by far the best and safest way of traveling, and the Romans had kindly left a good supply.

Arthur's army – his *combrogi* – consisting not only of our men of Dumnonia, but also warriors supplied by almost every kingdom in Britain, followed behind us in a long snake of armored riders that no brigands would dare attack, the sunlight glimmering on the scales of their well-oiled mail shirts. Before becoming High King, Arthur had been Dux Britanniarum, and had put this highly mobile cavalry at the beck and call of any kingdom that needed his help.

"Now you're High King, will you still carry out all the same duties as when you were Dux?" I asked, as we rode side-by-side at the head of the column.

He'd been staring up the road ahead in silence for a while, his distant expression telling me he was deep in thought. Now, he turned his head, his eyes taking a moment to focus. "Will I what?"

His dark brows knit together in a frown, giving him a saturnine look not altogether unlike Cadwy. "Oh…yes. My duties as High King are not far different from those I had as Dux." He rubbed his stubbly chin and conjured me a smile. "It's more a title than an obligation. But at the Council, what I say will go. The other kings are duty bound to listen to me, to take my opinions seriously. And if I call on them, to follow me into battle against our enemies."

I frowned. "Why so much rivalry for the position, then? It sounds almost an empty title. I don't quite understand."

His smile widened, lightening his face and giving him back the boyish charm he sometimes showed me, and I felt the familiar leap of almost unbearable love in my heart for this man. "You can trace that back to the days of the legions. And you've Merlin to thank that I know the history. He was – and is – an excellent teacher. Not just reading and writing, but history and rhetoric, something of politics. As much about the world as he knows."

"And magic?" The only way I could have got to this world was by magic – Merlin's magic. He'd left a gold ring in the tower on the top of Glastonbury Tor for me to find. When I'd picked it up, it had whisked me back fifteen hundred years in an instant, and I'd somehow been able to understand the languages spoken here like a native. I glanced down at the ring on my finger, glimmering in the sunshine. I'd once taken it off, hoping doing so would whisk me back home again. It hadn't, and now I had no inclination to go. A lot served to anchor me here in the fifth century.

Arthur laughed. "Nothing of magic. He saved *that* for Morgana."

I didn't want to think about that cold-hearted, scheming bitch, still less talk about her. I steered the conversation away. "What does the need for the post of High King have to do with the Romans?"

"Theirs was a hierarchical society." He chuckled. "That's a direct quote from Merlin, by the way, not my words. Layers of greater and greater responsibility stopped with the Governor of a province. Here in Britain, before they left, many of the positions of command were taken by locally born and bred men."

"Just men?" I said, raising an ironic eyebrow at him.

He grinned. "Yes. Just men. I know you think women should be allowed to hold positions of power. It was as impossible then as it is now."

I grinned back. "I'm teasing you." No need to remind him of all the women in history who'd played important political roles. He knew them well enough. Or at least the ones I'd deemed relevant – like Boudicca, Cleopatra, and Helena, the mother of Constantine the Great.

"I know."

I reached across and touched his arm, partly to jog him into continuing with his explanation, partly just because I wanted to touch him. Sometimes, even now, I had to pinch myself to believe the life I was living as King Arthur's Queen. "Go on. I want to know."

His fingers brushed mine, his touch warm and promising. A glow started somewhere near my navel and descended. Even after nearly three years together, he still had the power to render me breathless, like a teenager suffering from her first serious crush. Annoying, sometimes, especially when I wanted to be cross with him, but the rest of the time…most enjoyable.

Alezan, my skittish chestnut mare, interrupted where my thoughts were taking me as she curvetted sideways, and I had to put both hands on the reins to control her. "Steady, girl." Laughter escaped me.

He chuckled again, probably aware of the way he'd made me feel. "Alezan's jealous. She wants you to herself."

There was definitely something about the Pendragons that drew people to them like bees to a honeypot. Morgana possessed the obvious magic, but Arthur had something more – a charm, an attractiveness that not only drew women, for obvious reasons, but also men, who just wanted to offer him their allegiance and service.

Tapping Alezan with my left leg, I pushed her closer to Llamrei, Arthur's gray. She laid her ears back in threat, but I had her under control. She was a very mareish mare. "Keep going. I want to know more."

"It goes back to when my great-grandfather, Constantine, declared himself western Emperor from Britain. If he'd stayed safely here and held onto the power he already had, he'd have survived. But he didn't. Greed took over. He gathered all the legions under his command and sailed off to Gaul to expand his share of the empire. For a while, he succeeded, and was even made joint Emperor with Honorius." He paused, thoughtful. "He truly wore the purple of his rank."

Ahead, a gangly boy clutching a long stick herded a gaggle of geese across the road toward the gates of a farmstead, probably afraid we'd want to steal them. Wise boy. Roast goose would be delicious, and there were a lot of us.

Arthur watched him for a moment or two before turning back to me. "He left his son, my grandfather, in charge here. When Constantine fell from power and was executed, my grandfather took the title Emperor in his turn. But he was wise enough to remain in Britain. An overlord was needed here, not an absentee Emperor. The people accepted him. And what had not long before been one Roman province, devolved in just a few years into many smaller kingdoms with him at their head – High King in all but name."

He watched the boy as he closed the farm gate behind his rescued geese, and tipped him a mock salute. The boy gave him the finger and ran away.

"I knew that bit," I said, preventing Alezan taking a sideways swipe at Llamrei with her teeth.

Arthur chuckled. "She's in a bad mood today. Where was I? Oh, yes. Merlin told me the tribes that still existed, from before the legions arrived, had already begun reassembling themselves into the kingdoms you see today, long before the legions left. In Dumnonia, we'd never lost our noble families – always been next best thing to a separate entity from the Roman ruled province. But the newly formed kingdoms still needed an overall leader. A hand to guide the ship."

"And that was your grandfather?"

He nodded. "For a while, before he was overthrown. Britain was as insecure then and as rife with rivalries as it is now. I can't say how good he'd have been at it – better than the man who took his place, I'd swear. Guorthegirn the Usurper shunned the title 'Emperor' and styled himself the first High King. He told the people the days of the Empire were well and truly over. They wanted to hear that. The Empire had let them down time and time again. Even the ones who saw themselves as Romans had lost faith in help ever coming from

Rome. They preferred a leader with a British title – not a Roman one."

I knew about Guorthegirn. He'd exiled Arthur's grandfather to Armorica, modern Brittany, where Arthur's father, Uthyr, and his older brother, Ambrosius, had been born. They returned to serve Guorthegirn as young men, long after their father died – probably poisoned on Guorthegirn's orders.

Arthur grinned. "When my Uncle Ambrosius overthrew Guorthegirn in his turn, and burnt him to a crisp in his stronghold, he kept the title the Usurper had made for himself. Having a High King fitted a Britain now separated from the old Empire, which was crumbling. We were independent, but we needed the structure the legions had given us. Far better to work together against a common enemy, rather than warring amongst ourselves."

That sounded the sort of policy that worked better on paper than it did in practice, but I didn't say so.

Instead, I squinted into the distance, where the dark shadow of forest clung to rolling hills, and modified my reply. "That doesn't always work though, does it? Look at Caw of Alt Clut. He put his own greed above his duty to Britain as a whole."

Arthur nodded. "There'll always be men like him. But think how many of the kingdoms have sent me their young warriors. They did that because they agree with me, at least in principle. My men are like the legions – ready to fight for any kingdom, not just one. And when we've lost men, the kings have sent replacements. That shows their will to work together. To defeat the Saxons."

Optimist.

"But what if our kings have Saxon lineage and mixed loyalties? You still have the men Natanleod sent you, but if one of them is killed, will Cerdic replace him? Send his men to fight against his mother's people? What if he sends you Saxons?"

He inhaled deeply, his voice taking on a discernible bitterness. "It remains to be seen where his loyalties lie."

"He bent the knee to you. The first to do so."

A scowl crept across his face. "I know. That had me puzzled. I don't know what he meant by that. He's not a man I'd trust. He fought side-by-side with his mother's people to win Natanleod's kingdom. They raised him. Despite his appearance, he's more a Saxon than a man of Caer Guinntguic. The people tolerate him because he's old Elafius's son and all they've got since Natanleod left no heir."

My lips made a thin line. The temptation to reveal what I knew of Cerdic welled up inside me. Living in the Dark Ages had already presented me with multiple occasions where I'd been tempted to reveal my somewhat dubious foreknowledge. However, after the mistake of telling Merlin about the sword in the stone, I'd learned to hold my tongue. Most of the time. But that didn't stop me wanting to spill all. It was like having a huge, exciting secret that could never be revealed to your friends – multiplied by about a thousand.

Supposedly, Cerdic would establish the kingdom of Wessex, and as such become the legendary ancestor of the English royal family. The key word there, though, was "supposedly." Of course, as with so much of the history of the time I now lived in, nothing was certain. Yet here he was, ruling a British kingdom, plonk in the middle of where Wessex would one day lie. The more I saw of the fifth century, the more I recognized the truths that lay behind many of the legends in my old world.

"Might it be a good idea to make him an ally rather than an enemy?" I asked. "He seemed to want that when he bent the knee."

"Never trust a man with Saxon blood in his veins," Arthur snapped. "I've made that my policy and so far, I've seen no reason to change it."

Considering plenty of Saxon blood probably ran in my veins, I chose not to comment on that.

Probably his relationship with his older half-brother, Cadwy, had prompted his reaction, though. Cadwy's mother had been a Saxon princess, married to Uthyr in a wedding arranged between Guorthegirn and Hengest, the Saxon leader who'd been Guorthegirn's magister militum – battle leader. For battle leader, read controller. In his later years Guorthegirn had fallen ever more deeply under the influence of the Saxons he'd first brought in as foederati – mercenaries – and who'd bit by bit taken ever more land in the east for themselves.

"Cadwy didn't bend the knee," I remarked.

Arthur grimaced. "Didn't expect him to. There'll be snow at midsummer before he forgives me for drawing that sword and taking the title he sees as his by right." He grinned. "And for marrying the Ring Maiden."

I ignored that. "Neither did Morgana."

"She's a different basket of eels." He glanced over his shoulder at where Merlin and Cei rode side-by-side behind us. "Do you think Merlin's going to be all right?"

This was such an unlikely insight from Arthur that my eyes flew wide open. He was always inclined to dismiss anyone's troubles as something they'd get over if you left them to it. But then again, he'd known Merlin since his early childhood, an ever-present force for good in his life. Perhaps he had more fellow feeling for Merlin than for anyone else.

I shrugged. "I don't know. He's very quiet."

"I tried to get him to tell me what happened while he was her prisoner, but he shut me off." He paused. "Something tells me he needs to talk, or it'll fester in his heart. Maybe you could try to worm it out of him. He likes you."

"Goodness," I said. "You're very perceptive today."

This made him chuckle. "I know. I'm quite shocked myself. But Merlin's my closest friend. Cei's my brother, and I love him. But Merlin is something different."

On an impulse I leaned towards him. We were close enough that I could plant a kiss on his stubbly cheek. "I do love you, sometimes."

He raised an eyebrow. "Only sometimes?"

"You know what I mean. I love you all the time, but sometimes you surprise me, and I feel an upswelling in my love for you. Like right now."

He grinned. "Remember that for tonight then. I could build on that."

I laughed. "Not if we're camped with all your men surrounding us!"

>>><<<

As dusk fell, we made our camp in a wooded valley beside a small river. The men were expert at this, and soon had sentries posted and a number of scattered cook-fires sending glowing embers spiraling up into the night sky to join the full moon, like little would-be stars. We always carried dried meat with us, along with hard cheese, and dark bread that by now was dry and stale. But by the time the designated cooks had reconstituted the meat in a stew with a few dried mushrooms and some ale, the bread could be softened in the gravy, and we had a good meal. When you're on the march, every meal tastes good.

Afterwards, in a darkness lit only by the flickering flames of their fires and the full moon overhead, the men gathered in smaller groups, telling jokes to one another, and singing songs. Bedwyr began the recital of a tale about a long-gone king of Gwynedd called Llew Llaw Gyffes, in a singsong, lilting voice that held his fellows enraptured and drew others to where he sat, even though they'd probably all heard it a hundred times before. The magic of his words held them in his thrall.

"Oak that grows between two banks:
Darkened is the sky and hill.
Shall I not tell him by his wounds,
That this is Llew?"

Arthur got to his feet, stretched, and put a hand down to me. "Come, I've heard this story too many times. Let's walk along the riverbank in the moonlight together. I need to stretch my stiff legs."

I scrambled to my feet and, hand-in-hand, we threaded our way between the groups clustered about the cook-fires, each one of them occupied in the same way as the men about ours. The words of a dozen songs, plaintive, martial, comic, twisted between the trees around the camp, floating away into the night air, sending us on our way.

The uneven ground sloped downhill through sparsely scattered trees. In the valley bottom, the dark river sang its own gentle tune as it wound south toward the distant sea, and, between the inky tree-shadows, moonlight silvered the rippling surface of the water.

A narrow deer-trod ran along the bank, leading our feet downstream in the quiet warmth of the summer night. The songs of the camp died away, the glow of the cook-fires diminished to nothing, and somewhere on the far bank a nightjar chirred.

Arthur's fingers laced between mine, warm and strong. He didn't hurry, and as we left our camp well behind, the feeling of being quite alone draped itself about my shoulders like a pleasant veil.

Ahead, a dainty roe deer sprang through the trees, disturbed by our approach, its white rump bobbing for a few seconds before disappearing into the gloom. An owl called, and another answered. Wings soared silently above our heads, just their shadowy shapes alerting us to their presence. The feeling that this quiet valley held some special magic couldn't be denied.

The riverbank, that had at first overhung the water by several feet, now dropped down to a gravely beach as the river curved in a meander. Small stones crunched. Arthur halted and turned to face me, his features thrown sharply into planes of light and dark by the moon's pale glow. "I've been wanting you to myself all day."

I gazed up at him, at the face of the man I loved. The man for whom I'd given up my whole world. My heart twisted with the intensity of my feelings, a physical ache forming in my chest. I'd never believed it possible to feel so strongly about someone – to put him above all else.

His hand caressed my face.

The same desire I'd felt earlier reformed in my belly. I stood on tiptoes and kissed him gently on the lips. "And now you have me."

He nodded, eyes twinkling. "It's deep enough to swim. Do you fancy a dip?"

My turn to nod. The thought of the cool water after the heat of the day, and the chance to wash the dust and sweat from my body, was intoxicating.

We retreated to the grassy bank. Arthur unbuckled his sword belt and laid it on the grass. As we undressed, I watched him out of the corner of my eye and caught him watching me back. The shadow of the bruises from his fight with Cadwy still marked his body, and on his thigh the knotted scar from the stab wound he'd received last autumn stood out more than I would have liked. But I laughed, and so did he.

The moonlight dappled our skin with her pale kiss as we negotiated the gravel on wary bare feet. Cold water lapped my toes, and I hesitated. No such thing held Arthur back. He leapt into the deepest part of the river, immersing himself and swimming a few long strokes away from me.

Throwing caution to the wind, I did the same. In an instant, icy water gripped my body, depriving me of air, and I floundered in breathless panic. Arthur's strong arms caught me, and the air came rushing back, making me gasp and splutter. He pressed me against his chest, laughter shaking him. "Best to keep yourself warm by swimming."

The river wasn't huge, but it presented us with enough water to swim energetically for a few minutes, which we took full advantage of. Arthur dived a few times, his feet flipping up in the air, as at home in the water as a fish. Where had he learned to swim? Perhaps in the River Severn. Wary of hidden currents, I kept to where I could touch the silty bottom, swimming a leisurely breaststroke in small circles near the bank.

"Watch out for leeches," he called from further out.

"What?"

"Leeches in the mud. They latch onto your skin and won't let go – and suck your blood."

Leeches?

Splashing wildly, I beat a path toward the bank, but before I got there, he came up behind me and swept me into his arms.

I clung to him in a panic. "Do I have leeches on me? Do I?" I could put up with a lot in the fifth century but not muddy river creatures sucking my blood.

Rivulets of water ran down our bodies as he carried me out of the river, staggering a little under my weight. "I'll need to inspect you all over to check."

He laid me down on the grassy bank, and I clung to him, shivering, but a lot cleaner despite having had no soap. His dark silhouette loomed over me in the moonlight, his long hair dripping water as, with a hand on my chin, he turned my head to left and right. "No leeches on your face."

My hand shot up to touch my cheek and he chuckled softly.

His hand slid down to caress my throat. "I don't *see* any leeches, but I might need to inspect you more closely…" A sensuous finger trailed from my jaw toward my belly, and goosepimples of arousal prickled. Now my shivering had more to do with his touch than the cold.

"My legs?" I whispered into his hair.

That teasing finger ran down first one leg then up the other, sensitive, gentle, tickling my skin, then paused where my legs joined my body. "Leech-free so far."

The need to have him touch me there sent a new shiver running through me, as an inner fire stoked my molten desire.

Teasing still, he bent and lightly kissed a nipple. "Better?"

For answer, I buried my fingers in his wet hair and turned his face up to mine. "I will be in a moment."

I pulled him into a kiss, my lips opening willingly under his insistent tongue. The kiss deepened, and the fire inside me blazed brighter, warming me from the core. We were naked. We were alone. And the night was warm.

"You naughty boy," I whispered hoarsely in his ear as my hand slid down his body to find him more than ready to satisfy my mounting need. "You had this planned all along."

His breath warmed the skin of my throat, and his wet hair trailed across my cheek. "I might have done," he murmured, his lips brushing my skin and traveling south toward my breasts, his hands hot on my hips.

A few lumps that might have been stones or tree roots poked into my back, but I didn't care. I lifted my legs and wrapped them around Arthur, drawing him closer. With the lack of privacy in a marching army's camp, I'd missed this very much.

Chapter Three

We reached Din Cadan a few days later, with light rain falling from a cloud-crowded sky. The welcome sight of the huge hill rising from the plain, and the columns of hearth-fire smoke mingling with the mist of drizzle, warmed my heart. After nearly three years here in the fifth century, this felt like coming home.

Maia was standing on the platform in front of the Great Hall with Amhar in her arms. At almost two years old, he was changing fast from a baby into a little boy, a small clone of his father, with curling dark hair, wide brown eyes and longer eyelashes than any male should be allowed.

I slid down from Alezan and, thrusting her reins into Arthur's hand, sprinted up the slope from the stables, brimming with excitement at seeing my son again. Maia set him down and he ran to me, proving that his bandy-legged, wobbly, toddling stage had almost passed.

I swept him up and hugged him close, breathing in the warm smell of little boy. "My, how you've grown!" I kissed his chubby cheeks, then, settling him on my hip, carried him sedately back down the hill to where Arthur was now coping with two horses. As I approached, he shouted to a stable boy who came and took them from him.

"Papa," Amhar exclaimed, holding out fat little arms, tanned golden from playing outside in the sun.

Arthur took him from me, swinging him up above his head, making him screech with excitement. "More, more, Papa."

Arthur lowered him gently, then threw him back up into the air, and Amhar squealed with delight. Who'd have thought fathers played at airplanes hundreds of years before they were even invented?

"You're heavy," Arthur said, after a third lift, and lowered Amhar to sit astride his hip. "And I think you're big enough to walk."

I laughed. "Be happy that he's pleased to see us. This is a better homecoming than the one we had a few short months ago."

After a year in the north of Britain, fighting beyond and along the Wall, we'd ridden home this spring to find Morgawse and her little son Medraut ensconced here – along with that witch Morgana. They'd already been here a week, and in that time, Morgana had charmed my son so thoroughly he wanted nothing to do with us. I'd been happy to see Morgawse, less so to see Medraut with the terrifying future his existence foreshadowed. But Morgana – well, no words could express how I felt about *her*.

She'd not only charmed my son, but she'd then done the same with Merlin, right under our noses. And while Arthur was away trying to help Natanleod defend Caer Guinntguic, a task that proved fruitless, I gave her the ultimatum of leaving or being thrown out. She went, but she took Merlin with her. The one consolation was that at least she hadn't tried to snatch my son, as well.

Arthur set off up the slope toward the Great Hall, still carrying Amhar despite his declaration that he was big enough to walk, and I followed. Amhar seemed contented, his chubby fingers playing with the bead necklace around his father's neck.

Maia bobbed a bow. "He do have another tooth, Milady," she said, pride in her voice. Still young and unattached, she loved Amhar as though he were her own. "One of they pokey ones at the side that do cause trouble in arrivin'."

"That's called a canine." I'd been educating her on the names of teeth, amongst other things. Being a girl, and lowly born, no one had ever thought to teach her much more than household skills, which she was far better at than I was. However, she'd also proved to possess a sharp mind that her manner of speaking had camouflaged well. She knew all her letters now, and could count to a hundred. The next thing we'd be starting was reading – when I'd sourced some paper I could write on.

It was times like that, when a search for paper had proved useless, that I most missed my old job as a librarian, constantly surrounded by beautiful books for every occasion…and lots of paper.

Running footsteps sounded. Llacheu, Arthur's nine-year-old son by the woman who had been his mistress before he met me, came running up from the horse pens. His face was liberally smudged with dirt, and his long hair, in which someone had threaded tiny, rattly beads, flew out behind him. "Father!" He stopped short, as though perhaps suddenly aware of his dignity, and that of his father.

Arthur passed Amhar to me and held out his arms to Llacheu. The little boy beamed and ran into them. As he'd done with Amhar, Arthur swung the boy up into the air, grunting a little with the effort. Llacheu was tall for his age and already sturdily built. "You grow any more, and I won't be able to do this." He grinned at me as he set Llacheu down. "My oldest son's nearly big enough to be a warrior."

We'd only been away a few weeks. Llacheu couldn't have grown that much, but Arthur's words had the desired effect. He puffed out his narrow chest and poked his chin into the air in an effort to look taller.

I smiled. The same pride shone out of Arthur as he beamed down at the boy. But then my smile died, as the cold hand of fear closed around my heart. Llacheu was nearly ten, and Arthur had been a warrior at thirteen, and already a leader of men. Did this child, whom I loved like my own, have only three more years before he'd be plunged into the dangers of battle?

Theodoric the Goth hurried past on his way from the stables toward the house he shared with his wife, Morgawse, who'd chosen to remain here when I'd booted her sister out. Theodoric was here with Arthur as much as he was with his fleet of ships, so it must suit her well. The door banged open, and Theodoric disappeared inside.

I frowned. I didn't much care for Theodoric, with his predilection for ladies of ill repute while away from his pretty little wife. Hopefully she'd never find out.

From one of the other houses in the courtyard that backed onto the Great Hall, my best friend Coventina emerged, her own baby on her hip. Reaghan, the miracle child. Our midwife had snatched her from Coventina's womb in a makeshift Caesarean section that for some lucky reason hadn't killed her mother. From that shaky start, Reaghan had blossomed into the chubbiest baby I'd ever seen. At more than a year old, she wasn't even crawling, never mind walking, or she hadn't been when we'd left.

As if in answer to my thoughts, Coventina beamed and set Rheaghan down on the dirt. On her feet. Our hall cat, a sleek tabby, trotted past the baby, who took three wobbly steps after her before dropping to the ground. Coventina swept her up and carried her over. "See, she can do it," she crowed, holding out her free arm to enfold me in a hug.

I hugged her back. So much had happened in the short time we'd been away, it felt like a lifetime.

Cei came up from the stables in a shambling run, and Coventina released me and held her baby-free arm out to her big, red-headed husband instead.

Cei enfolded both her and Rheaghan in a bear hug. "He's High King," he said into her hair, voice high with excitement. "He drew the sword from the stone. Not once, but several times. First, just for all of us – and Cadwy. Then again, a good few times, for the Council of Kings."

"High King?" Coventina, a tall, homely young woman, born a simple farmer's daughter, turned to stare at Arthur. "Do we have to bow and call you sir?" She smiled. "Do you get to wear a bigger crown?"

Arthur grinned. He'd known Coventina since he was a child Llacheu's age, and loved her as much as I did. "I'll let you off this once. If we can go inside and get something to drink, that is. My mouth feels like I've been eating the sawdust from Devin's wood-working shed."

BEING HOME AT last, after so many wanderings, gave me a deep sense of peace and belonging, and a wish never to have to leave the safety of Din Cadan's high walls again. Seeing Amhar and being able to play with him without fear of Morgana's malevolent influence gladdened my heart. And with Arthur having beaten his older brother and taken the sword in the stone for himself, and with it the title of High King, my world had turned full circle and was complete. The prophecy had come about – Arthur was where he was meant to be – High King of all Britain.

I refused to allow myself to think of what might lie ahead – of what I *knew* lay ahead, if the stories from my time were correct. Instead, I concentrated on enjoying life.

The summer wore on. Harvest time came, and in the tawny fields below the fortress the farmers worked from dawn till dusk, their sickles rhythmically swinging as they cut through the tall stalks of wheat, oats and barley. Their women and children followed behind them binding the stalks with quick fingers into bundles to stand in stooks to dry in the late summer sun.

In our orchards, the fruit swelled until it was ready to pick, and I realized I was doing some swelling myself. I was with child again. Counting back, I realized it had been that wanton night of love we'd spent beside the river on the way back from Viroconium. A river child.

Arthur was overjoyed. "A brother for Amhar. That's what he

needs. He loves to play with Medraut, but Morgawse might be going back to Caer Legeion with Theo for the winter." He paused, counting the months on his fingers. "He'll be born in the spring. A good time, when the animals are giving birth."

Did I detect a note of relief in his voice – that this child was a baby no one could claim as theirs in order to spite him? As Melwas had done before he died.

I wasn't quite so pleased. "I'm going to be huge and fat again."

He grinned. "Not fat – beautiful."

"Easy for you to say," I retorted. "You don't have to swell up like you've been inflated with a bicycle pump."

"Like I've been what?"

I sighed. "From my old world. I don't feel like explaining right now, but believe me, it's not good."

We were sitting on the wall-walk, legs dangling over the edge. Down in the practice area, the older boys were galloping their ponies at a line of targets, light lances tucked under their arms. Llacheu was easy to spot, astride his beautiful black cob, Saeth, charging with more ferocious gusto than any of the others each time his turn came.

Arthur tightened the arm he had around my shoulders. "But I do think you're beautiful when you're with child," he said, his other hand taking mine. "How could any man not love his wife for giving him another son."

I humphed. "This one might well be a girl."

"I'll ask Merlin–"

I stiffened and widened my eyes at him. He'd done this with Amhar which had annoyed me a lot. "No. That's cheating. And he could easily be wrong, anyway. And besides which, I don't want to know. Let it be a surprise."

Arthur made a wry half-smile. "He probably wouldn't tell me anyway. We've hardly spoken since we returned from Viroconium. He's been keeping himself to himself. Not coming to the hall in the evenings to eat, even."

I nodded. There wasn't much I could say. Merlin had been avoiding me as well. He hardly emerged from his house except to ride out alone for hours at a time, shunning all offers of company. Llacheu had told me he'd offered to ride out with him, and been briskly brushed aside.

"You said you'd talk to him for me," Arthur said, slight reproach in his voice.

I threaded my fingers through his, my thumb caressing the back of his suntanned hand, rubbing the scar from the wound he'd had the first time I met him. "I've tried. He's so elusive. Whenever I've approached him, he finds an excuse to get away from me." I paused. "He looks so sad, and he's got so thin. I just want to give him a hug, but I think he'd have a fit if I tried that."

"No hugging of other men, thank you. You're mine."

I poked him in the ribs. "Stop being silly. You've no need to feel jealous of Merlin. He's like a brother to me."

He chewed his bottom lip. "I can't help it. If any man looks at you... since Melwas... I feel an urge to beat them to a pulp." His hand in mine tightened. "I wish I'd done that to him, not killed him with a sword. It felt so good doing it to Cadwy."

I heaved a sigh and rubbed his hand again. "It's probably a good thing you beat Cadwy with your fists. If you'd not broken your sword, and you'd killed him, you might not be High King now."

Arthur shrugged. "He meant to kill me. He needed me to draw the sword for him, but after that I'd have been of no further use. I'd have been dispensable. Maybe you as well."

I shivered. "Don't say that. I don't want to think of what might have happened." How safe would Amhar and I have been if Cadwy had defeated Arthur and taken the sword? My only way out of this world lay on Glastonbury Tor, and although only ten miles lay between Din Cadan and the Tor, over a hundred miles stretched between it and Viroconium. *If* that doorway still functioned. For all I knew, the one time I'd tried to use it to return to my world had been the only time it would have worked. Maybe my decision not to go back had sealed it forever.

"Well ridden," Arthur called to Llacheu, who'd just succeeded in knocking one of the targets flat with a smashing blow from his lance. As he trotted back to rejoin the queue waiting for another tilt at the targets, he waved his white-painted shield at us, a big grin on his face.

"I've been thinking about Gildas," I said, at not quite the tangent Arthur would assume I'd take. "I thought maybe I'd ride over to Ynys Witrin to visit Abbot Jerome and see how his new pupil is getting on."

Gildas was our hostage and the youngest son of the belligerent Caw of Alt Clut, held to secure his father's peaceful cooperation beyond the Wall. Although how long that would work remained debatable. I'd befriended the lonely boy during our winter's incarceration at Vindolanda and discovered he was glad to be away from his father. He didn't want to become a warrior like his older brothers. Instead, his ambition was to become an educated man. In the Dark Ages that meant monasticism, so on our return to Din Cadan, we'd dispatched him over to the marsh-enclosed island of Ynys Witrin and the abbey, something that had pleased him immensely.

Arthur raised his eyebrows. "That surly boy? Really? I was glad to see the back of him. He's safe enough on Ynys Writrin. No one there'll show him the way out."

"He's hardly older than Llacheu," I persisted. "And in my world, that's a child. He's far from home, even though he didn't like it much when he was there, and now he's been left with a bunch of men he doesn't know. I'd have visited him sooner if we'd not had to go to Viroconium. I feel bad for abandoning him there."

Now I'd put it into words, the enormity of what we'd done to Gildas sank in fully – in my old world it would have been a shocking thing to do to a vulnerable boy.

He shrugged. "I suppose you might as well go. But don't expect me to join you. Other than his use as a hostage for his father's good behavior, the boy holds no interest for me."

I smiled to myself as the thought of the book Gildas would one day write leapt into my mind. From his lack of mentioning of Arthur in it, no doubt Gildas felt the same way about my husband.

"I could take Merlin," I said. "If you order him to escort me, it might give me chance to talk to him. He can hardly slope off to his house if he has to ride by my side there and back." I grinned. "I'll make him talk."

Arthur's eyes lit up. "A clever idea. I should have known you weren't offering to go just to see the boy. It's a long enough ride to get even Merlin to open up to you."

I sighed, but didn't put Arthur right. As far as I was concerned the reason for my trip was Gildas, not Merlin, although the fact that I could get the latter to myself was an added bonus. "I'll go tomorrow," I said.

Chapter Four

Accompanied by the eight warriors who were to keep me safe on my journey to Ynys Witrin, I rode Alezan down the steep cobbled track that circled Din Cadan. Just ahead of me, Merlin sat astride his horse, head down, lost in a world of his own. Somehow, I'd have to persuade him to talk once we reached level ground.

Easier said than done. As the road wound between the farmsteads that dotted the plain below the fortress, I edged Alezan up beside Merlin's horse, a bay mare he'd been randomly allotted from the stables. His own horse had been killed under him beyond the Wall, and as yet he'd not bothered to take the time to choose another.

Maybe he'd not had the heart to. Losing your horse was like losing a friend, even in my old world, so here, where horses were such an integral part of the life of a warrior, it was ten times worse. He'd been riding whatever was available, often not the best of mounts.

Alezan, ever mareish and contrary, laid her ears back at the little bay, who did the same back to her. Annoyed, I tightened my reins and pushed her closer in until my knees knocked Merlin's. He kept his head turned away, whether on purpose or because he simply hadn't noticed my proximity, I couldn't tell.

A young dog, scarcely out of gangly puppyhood, ran across the road ahead of us, pursued by two laughing little boys.

I touched my fingers to Merlin's knee.

He didn't turn his head, but his knuckles whitened on the reins.

"Merlin?"

Alezan took another sideways swipe at his horse, and I had to yank on my reins one-handed to stop her. Merlin still didn't turn his head.

I tapped his knee. "Look at me. Please."

His shoulders stiffened, but he did as I asked. Always a spare man, slighter than most of the warriors, now his face betrayed how much weight he'd lost. Dark circles shadowed his eyes, and although the bruises had gone, his cheeks had that hollow, undernourished look I'd seen in the beggar children of Caer Baddan.

I smiled – a forced, false smile.

He regarded me out of eyes that held pools of sadness, red-rimmed from lack of sleep. Several days' stubble shadowed his jawline, and his hair hung limp and untended. For once, he looked much closer to his true age – far older than Arthur and me. Perhaps in his depression, the magic I suspected he'd channeled to preserve his youth no longer worked. Or perhaps he'd only done it because of his unrequited love for Morgana, and now, after what she'd done to him, he no longer cared to appear that way.

My attempts to console Ummidia after she and her daughters, Albina and Cloelia, had been raped leapt into my mind. I'd been so useless, she'd gone on to slit her own and her daughters' wrists in the bath house of the villa where we'd taken shelter. I'd have to tread very carefully with Merlin.

A wagon loaded with sheaves of corn creaked past us, drawn by a pair of sturdy oxen with two men walking by their heads. The men tugged their forelocks in respect, and I nodded in return. In the fields to either side, small birds fluttered – corn buntings, finches, linnets – gleaning the corn left behind when the stooks were gathered in. A flight of swallows swooped down after the insects disturbed by all the activity on the ground.

Where to start? With practicalities. "You look thin. Thinner than usual, that is. Have you been eating properly? We haven't seen you in the Great Hall for weeks."

His sad eyes wandered over my shoulder, staring at nothing, most likely.

I squeezed his knee. "We all care very much about you, you know. We hate to see you like this." Why did everything coming out of my mouth sound like meaningless platitudes?

His gaze returned to me. "You don't feel the need to gloat that you were right?" The bitterness in his voice shocked me.

I shook my head. "I wish I hadn't been. I wish she'd really loved you."

He sucked in his lips, compressing them. "But you *were* right, and I was wrong. You'd think with my gifts I'd have seen it coming, wouldn't you? But I didn't."

Alezan tossed her head at the swarming flies. I patted her shoulder. "Love blinded you. It numbed your senses and stopped you seeing what I saw."

He tilted his head to one side, narrowing his eyes. "You think? How perceptive of you. I'd never have worked that one out for myself."

Ignoring his sarcasm, I touched his shoulder in what I hoped was a comforting gesture. "I want to help you. Just let me in, and I'll do my best. You need someone to talk to. Talking is the best way forward."

His lip curled in a sneer. "Is that what you do in your world? Talk about everything? Does it make everything better? Does it make the pain go away?" He shook my hand off. "If I talk to you, will everything that happened just disappear?"

Well, at least he *was* talking, even though he didn't seem to think he was.

I nodded. "Absolutely. If you lock things away inside your head, they stay there, festering. You need to get them out in the open, tell someone how you feel. It'll help you work out how to move on." If only I'd studied psychology instead of English at university. That might have been of some use. Conscious I was parroting things I'd heard in TV dramas, I closed my mouth.

"Maybe I don't want to move on." He looked away from me, at our escort riding just out of earshot. Four men behind, four in front.

A change of tack was required. "I tried to save you from her," I said, feeling lame and inadequate. "Because you're my friend, and I – I *love* you."

His head whipped around. For a moment something flashed across his face, an emotion I couldn't name.

My face heating, I ploughed on. "You're my best friend. My best friend who's a man, that is."

In the distance, the distinctive shape of the Tor reared out of the mist that so often surrounded it, as ethereal as its reputation. No wonder local people thought it the entrance to some sort of otherworld. Only they were right, and it was, wasn't it? Because I'd come through a doorway on the summit, from a world other than this one. Who knew if that door might take me somewhere else entirely if I ever tried to go back through it, instead of to my old world. I'd considered that possibility a few times.

Merlin shrugged. "I can't say the same about you, I'm afraid."

I smiled. "I know. Arthur's your best friend. He told me you were his. He's worried about you – about his friend. His mentor. The man who taught him so much. The man on whom he relies for the soundest advice."

His lips twitched. "I'm sorry."

I shook my head. "You don't need to be sorry for anything, Merlin. None of this was your fault. She used whatever powers she has to fool you. She knew you loved her. All of us knew you did."

His cheeks colored. "Was I so obvious?"

I tried another smile. "When someone's in love, it's nigh on impossible for them to hide it. Especially when they're faced with the object of their love. I realized the way the wind was blowing the first time I laid eyes on her and saw the way you were looking at her – at Uthyr's deathbed. Anyone who couldn't see it written clearly on your face back then would have to have been blind."

He stared ahead again, biting his lower lip. Maybe he'd thought he'd hidden it well. How like a man to be so unaware. Even men of magic had their weaknesses, it seemed.

Ahead, the forest had drawn closer as we talked, the dusty road dipping down into the trees and heading toward the lower-lying, marshy ground. This way would lead us to the lake village to take a boat across to the monk's wharf, as Arthur and I had once done…a lifetime ago.

Alezan swished her tail, and I swatted flies away from my face. Although it was autumn and the nights already chilly, the still-warm daytime weather kept them far too numerous. "Morgana would have seen it too. A woman doesn't miss a man in love with her." I paused. "And some, like Morgana, would use it to their own ends. There are many women like that in the world."

For a moment, the thought came to me that maybe Merlin, despite his age, was fairly ignorant of women. I'd never seen him with any woman at Din Cadan, nor heard whispers that he'd had any kind of liaison. At Caer Luit Coyt, when we'd stayed the night in what had turned out to be the next best thing to a brothel, he'd gone off with the men to the bath house, but had he partaken? He'd been the first to return, luckily for me. Maybe he was too innocent, and too naïve, to have ever guessed Morgana's intentions when she'd come to Din Cadan this spring and told him she loved him.

This image of Merlin as an innocent abroad shocked me. Somehow it didn't fit into the context of the fifth century, and yet it seemed to chime with what I knew of him.

"Women can be wicked creatures," I said. "Me included. I've got secrets I keep even from Arthur. Things I can't share, even if I wanted to."

"I thought you had. Secrets about the future." He shook his head. "But that's not the same as what she did to me. How she lied. You're just keeping things back. If he came out and asked you, you'd tell him, wouldn't you?"

Would I? I swallowed. Now was not the time for honesty about my secrets. "Of course I would," I said, not sure if it was the truth.

He seemed satisfied, and we rode on a little in a slightly more companionable silence. The lake village lay on the far side of the forest, and we'd be there before long.

Merlin broke the silence. "Do you think she has…*had* any feelings for me?"

Oh dear. Love, unrequited love, is such a painful thing. I again weighed up being honest or not for a moment. The fact that he'd probably be honest with me if I asked him a question won. "No, I don't think she ever did. Not the sort you'd want her to have, that is."

He didn't look surprised, thank goodness, although perhaps he'd been hoping I might have answered differently. "Never?"

"No. Never. I don't think she's a woman who's ever loved anyone but herself. She tolerates Cadwy, but really, she despises him." A small smile curved my lips. "To be honest, she'd fit in very well in my old world in the boardroom."

"The boardroom?"

"It's like the Council of Kings, but they have one to organize every business – type of work – and it's very cutthroat." I could see Morgana in a power suit with her raven locks scraped back in a tight bun from her beautiful but cold face. She'd have Louboutins on her feet and an expensive Hermès handbag on her arm, but explaining *that* would have been very hard. "Take it from me – there are ruthless women just like her in boardrooms all across Britain in my time."

He sighed. "I'm very glad I don't live in your time, then."

Our road twisted between the trees, the sunlight dappling down through the gold-tinged, leafy branches. Our escort rode closer, making private conversation difficult.

I watched Merlin. How had he come to this, that love of a woman had brought him so low? My heart ached for him, but what could I do to stop him feeling this way? Nothing I could think of. Maybe he needed a woman in his life who would love him back – perhaps not quite in the way he craved, but someone uncomplicated and kind and good? Sharp contrast to that bitch Morgana.

Anger at her welled up. Even though she no longer had Merlin, she'd done a good job of taking him away from us even when it seemed we had him back.

"Your pupils are missing you," I said. "Llacheu told me their other teachers aren't so much fun."

This did bring a smile, albeit a small one, to Merlin's face. "Really? You'd not think it to see their long faces when I make them read aloud in Latin, or tell me the names of the constellations, or medicinal plants. Or recite historical facts."

I chuckled. "Maybe you're the lesser of two evils. And I want you back teaching because before long Amhar's going to need you... and Medraut." My voice lowered as I thought of that little boy, now almost three years old, and what he represented.

"What's wrong with Medraut?" Even in this state of mind his brain remained sharp as a knife.

I bit my tongue, regretting letting my feelings for that small boy show. I stayed silent, but on reflection that wasn't the best thing to have done.

He frowned. "I thought we'd had that out last year?"

He meant my suspicions that Medraut might have been Arthur's child by incest – just like the legends. He'd put me right on that – it would have been a physical impossibility as Arthur hadn't seen his sister for years before Medraut's birth. I'd come to the conclusion that this particular story was an invention of some medieval pervert.

"We did," I said, then my unruly tongue ran away with me. "It's something else."

What was I doing? I'd sworn to myself never to mention anything I knew about the future again, after sword-in-the-stone-gate.

Merlin pressed his horse in close, with a glance over his shoulder at our guards. "Go on."

I shook my head. "I can't. Not here. We could be overheard. I'll tell you when we're alone."

Why couldn't I just shut up? But now I'd lifted the sluice gate an inch or two, relief was making the water pour out, and I wanted nothing more than to confide in someone. And Merlin would be the best, if not the only one I could tell. At least it might take his mind off his own problems.

※

THE LAKE VILLAGE nestled close to the southern shore of the perpetually flooded marshes surrounding Ynys Witrin. Not quite a lake, as a current flowed, and one day, when drainage of the Somerset Levels was in place, it might well shrink enough to become the modern River Brue.

Over hundreds, if not thousands of years, an island of rocks and the debris of its previous incarnations had accrued under the rickety platform the village sat on. Nearby, on the shore, the villagers' barns and animal pens clustered, and a narrow, uninspiring walkway led across the water to the village.

We found old Nial, the village headman, winnowing wheat in the largest barn with some of his men, the clouds of dust billowing out into the autumnal air warning us of their presence. Merlin sent one of our escort to winkle him out.

Nial emerged, covered in bits of chaff, with a thick layer of dust in his thinning brown hair and a big smile on his face. Probably more than happy to be dragged away from such an unpleasant, itchy chore.

"Milady the Queen. Milord Merlin. Good day to ye both." He made an elaborate bow, confirming his delight at being disturbed.

Merlin swung down from the saddle and handed his horse's reins to one of our guards. "I've brought the Queen to visit the abbey. We need someone to ferry us across – I was hoping you'd oblige."

Nial bowed a second time and ran a hand through his sparse thatch, sending bits of chaff fluttering off into the breeze. "I'd be honored, Milord. Will yer men be stoppin' 'ere a while?"

Merlin nodded. "If you can find somewhere to tether our horses and provide food and drink for my men, I'd be grateful. Not too much to drink, mind. I don't want to find them rolling drunk on our return. You know what warriors can get up to when they're bored." Just for these few minutes, he sounded like the Merlin I knew and loved.

I dismounted and passed Alezan's reins to one of our men. I wasn't looking forward to the next bit – negotiating the narrow, wobbly-looking causeway to the village. Merlin must have guessed from the look on my face. He held out a lean, tanned hand, and I slipped mine into it. We followed Nial along the plank bridge, me doing my best not to look down into the murky water beneath its spindly legs.

The village platform was just about circular, with a hotchpotch of houses jammed in side-by-side to the very edge, reminding me of a picture I'd once seen of a place where a patchwork of colorful houses had overhung both sides of a sleepy river.

A tall, crudely carved, wooden post stood at the village center. Fishing nets waiting to be mended hung from its high hooks, and the women of the village sat cross-legged around it, their grubby, bare-bottomed children playing within the circle they made.

The women's curious eyes followed us as we threaded our way between the houses to the far edge of the platform, but their horny fingers never ceased the threading of their shuttles through the nets. At a makeshift jetty, a cluster of flat-bottomed boats bobbed in a row on the current, like the fringe on a child's homemade cowboy costume. They didn't look any more seaworthy than they had three years ago.

Undaunted, Merlin hopped into the one Nial indicated, making it rock alarmingly. With reluctance, I took Merlin's outstretched hand and stepped into the boat, conscious of the inch or so of water that slopped in the bottom, alongside Nial's fishing rod.

With practiced fingers, Nial undid the rope tethering us to the jetty, and stepped lightly onto the stern, picking up a long, weathered pole from beside his rod. He used a foot to push us off, and we drifted out into the current, leaving the safety of the village behind.

The waterborne journey to the monks' wharf took less time than I remembered, and, before I knew it, Nial was tying his boat fore and aft to the single jetty, and getting out his rod. A row of wooden cider barrels stood to one side, as though ready for shipment, or possibly newly returned to be refilled, but no one was about except a few sheep drinking at the muddy watering spot just beyond the wharf.

"I don't know how long we'll be," Merlin said.

Nial shrugged. "That don't bother me. You takes yer time. I'll be happy with me rod and not havin' to winnow in all that dust." He gave a conspiratorial wink.

I thanked him, then Merlin and I turned away from the little wharf to head inland. We walked in silence for a while, until we'd left the wharf and Nial well behind, and the rows of farmed apple trees I remembered began. A few monks, the skirts of their long habits tucked out of the way into their belts, moved between the trees gathering windfalls into large woven baskets, but they were far enough away not to hear anything we said.

Merlin halted, and I stopped beside him, my heart doing odd leaps and bounds of apprehension. Did I still have the inclination, or the courage, to tell him about Medraut? Considering I'd asked him to bring me here so I could get him to talk, the tables seemed to have very much been turned.

"Now," Merlin said, taking me by the shoulders. "Tell me what it is that's worrying you."

I pressed my lips together, searching for the words I only half-wanted to utter.

Merlin sighed. "I feel a strong responsibility for you, Gwen. It's because of me you're here. I saw you in my visions, and deliberately went to your world to find you. If there's something wrong, you need to tell me so I can help you."

My own troubles had certainly loosened his tongue. He was definitely talking now.

"It's Medraut," I muttered.

"What about him? I thought we'd sorted out your silly worries?"

Ignoring his dismissal of my other worries as having been silly, I licked my dry lips. "I knew the moment he was born. When Morgawse told me his name."

"Knew what?" His brows furrowed in what was probably a mixture of puzzlement and frustration.

"What he'll do." My voice sounded small and insignificant in the silence that pressed all around me. Even the birds seemed to have fallen silent, listening.

He stiffened, his grip on my shoulders tightening. "*What* will he do?" His voice had gone as still as his body, low and urgent, almost as though he sensed what was coming. He did have the Sight, after all.

"Have you not seen?" I asked, blurting the words out in a hurry. "You told me once that you saw me with Arthur to the end. Then you said, '*If there is one.*' What does that even mean? Did you see his end or not? Did you see how it will come about?"

"I…" He hesitated, his mouth working as though he sought the right words. It seemed he had as many secrets as I did.

I stared into his eyes. "Well?"

He shrugged, his fingers like a vise on my shoulders. "I can't be sure." His voice shook. "Nothing was clear to me but you. You were there. At the end."

I swallowed. "And was Medraut?"

He stared. "What do you mean?"

"Was Medraut there too?" My voice rose with urgency.

Behind us the monks edged closer with their baskets. Still out of earshot, but maybe curious.

"I – I don't know."

"Well, he should have been," I snapped. "You should have seen him there. Because he will be. It'll be he who brings Arthur to his final battle – to Camlann. He's the one who'll cause Arthur's death."

There. I'd said it. The words hung between us as though someone had etched them in words of fire, blazing unquenchably.

His fingers dug into my flesh. "How?" Just one word. No other question, no words of reassurance that this couldn't come to pass. Nothing.

I couldn't tell him. Most likely it wasn't true – another medieval fabrication. My whole being recoiled from the thought, disgusted. From the story that said Medraut would seduce Arthur's queen. That I, Guinevere, would betray Arthur with his nephew.

I shook my head. "That's just it. I don't know how. All I know is that the legends say Medraut will rebel against Arthur. They'll meet in a final battle – at Camlann. Medraut will die, and Arthur will be fatally wounded."

Merlin's eyes bored into mine. He believed me. If my heart kept on beating this fast, I was going to die of a heart attack pretty soon.

"Well," Merlin said. "We'll have to make sure that never happens."

Chapter Five

We'd come all this way for me to check Gildas was all right, so after my revelation to Merlin, I forced myself to go on, even though what I really wanted to do was head straight back home as a nervous wreck. But Arthur, for all his lack of interest in the boy, would be bound to ask us how we'd got on, so I had to have something to tell him. Besides which, I owed it to the poor child we'd consigned to a bunch of strange men. The thought of how incorrect this would have been in my old world wouldn't leave me.

The abbey lay on the flat land beneath the slopes of the Tor, built within the footprint of the later stone-built version I'd known in the world I'd left behind. Greedy old Henry VIII had seen about its destruction in 1539, when he'd broken from Rome, destroying a line of religious houses stretching back well over a thousand years.

What I was looking at here might well not even have been the first incarnation of the abbey. Maybe many other wattle and daub buildings with thatched roofs had preceded this one, long before stone would take their place. According to legend, Joseph of Arimathea himself had founded the original abbey in the first century, and planted his staff on Wearyall Hill, from which the holy thorn tree had grown.

After the design of a Roman villa, these humble buildings surrounded a central, cobbled courtyard, with the little, thatched church facing the double-gated entrance. The remaining buildings held the accommodation for the monks, the storehouses and kitchen, and offices for the abbot, the prior, the sacrist, the treasurer, and whoever else needed one. I'd never been inside, only stood lost and afraid in the courtyard on the day I'd fallen back in time.

The memories of that day flooded back, as a monk – was it Brother Mark? – hurried to find the Abbot, who came quickly. After all, I was a queen now, so not to be kept waiting.

Abbot Jerome hadn't changed at all. Tall, thin, with a long aquiline nose and the crown of bushy dark hair around his tonsure perhaps more liberally sprinkled with gray than the last time I'd seen him. But his eyes remained the same – heavy-lidded, intelligent, and kind.

"My Lady the Queen." He made a small bow. After all, an abbot was a person of great importance and, as such, owed a little less deference to me than an ordinary man would. That he owed me deference at all felt odd and brought heat to my cheeks.

I held out my hand. "Abbot Jerome, I'm very pleased to see you again. In far better circumstances than when we last met."

He'd had to intercede between Arthur and Melwas to secure my release when I'd been kidnapped, and prevent Melwas sending me back to my husband piece by piece – starting with my nose. For that, and for his kindness to me on the day I'd arrived here, I owed him a great debt.

He took my hand in his. As before, his palm felt rough, and his nails showed the dirt of hard work. This was a man who wasn't afraid of laboring in the fields alongside his monks. This time, however, ink stains also showed on his long fingers.

He smiled. "You are most welcome here, my lady." His eyes slid to Merlin. Did I detect a momentary flash of hostility there? Perhaps. After all, Merlin had once expressed his doubts about the Christian religion, so maybe the Abbot knew this. Whatever it was, he hid it swiftly. "My Lord Merlin, you too are most welcome."

Merlin took his proffered hand. "My Lord Abbot." The frostiness seemed to be on both sides. Merlin's eyes had gone hard as pebbles.

Jerome's calm gaze returned to me. "Perhaps some refreshment after your journey?"

"That would be lovely. Thank you."

He led us through a door halfway down one side of the courtyard and into a square chamber. The wattle and daub walls had been washed a creamy white, with only a carved, dark-wood crucifix as decoration. A hefty table, scattered with scrolls, an ink pot and several pens, occupied much of the room, with a sizeable, high-backed wooden chair, not unlike a throne, behind it. Jerome gestured to two lesser seats set before the table and took the throne for himself.

I sat down, sensing hesitation in Merlin. After a moment, he took the second seat, leaned back and crossed his outstretched legs at the ankles. I wasn't fooled – he was nowhere near as relaxed as he'd have had me and Jerome think. Did he feel uncomfortable in a house of God? My father, a non-believer, had said he felt a sizzle coming on whenever he had to go inside a church.

Folding my hands in my lap, I waited while Jerome rang a bell to summon a monk and order refreshments. When he'd poured us goblets of wine, he too sat back in his chair, his fingers steepled. "What is it I can do for you today, My Lady?"

"I've come to see your pupil, the boy, Gildas, whom I sent here in the spring."

Was that a twinkle in Jerome's eyes? "Ah," he said. "I wondered if that might be the reason for your visit. Shall we send for him?"

I nodded. "Thank you."

He reached for the bell again, but I held up my hand. "Before I see him, could you tell me how he's getting on?" I felt as though he were the teacher and I the worried mother at a school parents' evening. Not that I'd ever been in that position myself, and nor was I likely to be, but I remembered my father moaning about how he hated them. Not because of me, as I'd been a model pupil right through school, but because of my twin brother, who'd been anything but.

Jerome lowered his hand. "He is a diligent boy." He licked his thin lips. "When he came to us in the spring, as you were aware, he knew very little. His letters, something of numbers, but nothing more. He'd had a somewhat deprived childhood – starved of the things he craved the most. Books. No one had cared to give him what he needed."

Poor boy, brought up in a house where becoming a warrior was deemed the pinnacle of achievement. He must have fitted in there like the proverbial square peg in a round hole. How he'd ever become his father's favorite puzzled me. Perhaps by guile, and by concealing his true wishes. Who knew? He had about him the air of a plotter. But even though we'd become friends, he'd never confided in me about that.

A smile raised the corners of Jerome's mouth. "Here he has devoured everything that's come his way. He learned to read in a few short weeks and surpassed the other boys very swiftly. The boy has a sharp intelligence, but more importantly, he has an overwhelming desire to learn. I've been most impressed with his progress, and so have his other teachers." He paused to sigh. "Unfortunately for him, not so the other boys. We've had a number of instances of violence. He has no patience when one of his fellow scholars is slow. He's not an easy boy to get along with."

Didn't I know it? Gildas was probably his own worst enemy amongst a group of boys his own age, especially if none of them could match him intellectually. Back in my old world, the gifted children were often the least contented, their intelligence setting them far above their classmates. Gildas had probably never been a boy others liked.

Hadn't he told me how unpopular he'd been with ten of his brothers, and only the oldest had taken the trouble to watch out for him? The brother Arthur had executed for his part in the northern rebellion.

"I guessed as much," I said, glancing sideways at Merlin but finding his face devoid of reaction. "I made a friend of him on our journey south, but the only other friend he made was a lad much older than him – Prince Drustans of Cornubia."

Jerome pressed his lips together and nodded. "He gets on well with the older novices and monks, but amongst the boys his own age he stands out as different. His intellect exceeds theirs, and they know it. And he still clings on to his old identity – he's unwilling to let them forget he was born a prince no matter how many times he's been told that we leave our old lives behind us when we enter here."

Merlin snorted. "A lesson many boys find hard to learn."

He spoke with such vehemence it startled me. I stared at him for a moment, but he'd gone back to straight-faced indifference again. I knew nothing of his past. Was it possible that as a boy he'd been placed inside an abbey to be educated? Now I thought about it, the possibility seemed very likely. He must have gained his education somewhere, and perhaps not enjoyed it. Which might account for his hostility to Christianity.

"I'll send for the boy," Jerome said, and rang the bell.

The same monk who'd brought the wine for us went scuttling off to fetch Gildas. It didn't take long. A few minutes later, a knock came at the door into the courtyard.

"Enter," Jerome called.

The door swung open, and Gildas stepped into the room.

He'd grown, as boys that age are inclined to do, and probably would have matched me in height had I been standing. Still an ugly, rawboned boy, he now had a look about him of the man he'd one day be, with more than a hint of his dead older brother. His shaggy, sandy hair had been chopped off short, by a blind man with garden loppers by the looks of him, and the dark robe he wore left his bony ankles and wrists poking out. Time for a bigger size. But his face held an inner light I'd not seen before, radiating from his pale eyes, despite the purple bruise on his left cheekbone.

He halted on the threshold, eyes widening as he saw me. "Gwen!"

An inner battle raged, easy to see, as he shifted his weight from foot to foot, clearly trying to decide whether he was allowed to run up to me and take my hand, or maybe hug me. He'd never done that before, but I sensed that seeing a face he knew after so long in the abbey had brought that inclination to the fore.

"Come here," Jerome said, forestalling any action the boy might have decided to take. "And close the door behind you. The day is chill."

Gildas shut the door and approached the table, halting to one side of it, his ink-stained hands clasped in front of him. Had his sleeves been long enough he could have concealed his dirty hands in them, but they weren't.

Jerome fixed him with a gimlet stare. "This is the Queen – your Queen now. You do not greet her by her proper name. That is for her husband alone. Now, greet her correctly."

"Milady," Gildas muttered, keeping his eyes lowered, his bottom lip beginning to jut. He had the full and fleshy lips of his father and dead older brother, good for looking sulky.

Jerome tapped the table with his long fingers. "And you can take that look off your face, young man. The Queen is here in her capacity as your guardian, to find out about your progress."

Gildas looked up sharply, his eyes darting from Jerome to me to Merlin, then back to me. The jutting lip vanished, and a small smile twitched at the corners of his over-large mouth.

I returned the smile. "I have it on good authority that your progress is more than could have been expected. I'm very pleased." I paused. "But that's not all I came to check." I shot a glance at Jerome, but he remained impassive. "I came to find out if you are happy."

Gildas's pale eyes flew open wide. Perhaps no one had ever cared to ask about his happiness before. "I–" he began, then stopped, his eyes flicking back to Jerome, who gave him a slight nod.

Gildas swallowed. "I'm happy with the learning. I love it. It's what

I always dreamed of." A snort from Merlin distracted him for a moment. "I work as hard as I can, and my teachers seem pleased with me…"

I nodded. "So I hear. But that's not what I asked. Are you happy? Do you have friends? You're a child. No, whatever you think, you *are* still a child. And children need friends."

"*I* don't," he blurted. "*I'm* happy just being me. If they'd let me."

"Who? The other boys? How many are there?"

Again, a glance toward Jerome, asking for permission to continue. He'd been well-trained in obedience by someone. Jerome nodded.

Gildas looked back at me. "Five – and I make six. They're idiots, all of them. They try to find any excuse to get out of working. They don't want to learn. They play tricks on our teachers and get angry when I tell on them. They play tricks on me too…" His voice trailed away as he took the full force of Jerome's stare.

The abbot cleared his throat. "That's no way to describe your fellow scholars. They may not be as quick as you at their work, but they are *not* idiots."

"Yes, Father Abbot." Gildas hung his head.

"Oh dear." Poor boy, he had no idea of how to get on with anyone. A thought crossed my mind – might he, in my time, have been diagnosed as high-functioning autistic? He had many of the attributes – the obsession with what he wanted to do to the detriment of all else, the lack of empathy, the yearning to be alone. I'd known a few people diagnosed with that back in my youth, and the challenges they'd faced had been similar to this. But how to help him lay beyond my knowledge.

Jerome tapped the table again, beating a tattoo with his fingers. "The only thing I can see to do is to move him from the boys' quarters to a cell of his own," he said. "But that will single him out even more as being different, and these are boys who will one day be monks with him. He may well become an abbot if he continues to work this well, if not here, then elsewhere. But he needs to learn how to get on with people if that is to be his destiny."

I nodded. "I think separating him from the boys who dislike and tease him would be a good idea, at least for some of the time." I glanced at Gildas again, standing bolt upright beside the table, his pale eyes flicking between our faces. "My husband and I would be prepared to pay for him to take his lessons apart from the other boys. Maybe if they don't see how far ahead he is, they'll treat him better." Optimistic words. Boys are unforgiving creatures.

Beside me, Merlin snorted again, but made no comment. Maybe he was thinking Arthur wouldn't see this investment in the son of one of his enemies as suitable expenditure. Most likely he was right. I'd cross that bridge when I came to it.

Jerome nodded. "As you wish. I'll have Gildas's belongings removed to a spare monk's cell. And I'll undertake his education myself."

Gildas's broad, ugly face split into the biggest smile I'd ever seen, his usually somber eyes dancing with excitement. "Thank you, Gw…*Milady*."

Hopefully I'd done the right thing here. This was the boy who would one day be known as Gildas the Wise, and who, as a man grown, would write about the kings of Britain in a work called *De Exidio et Conquestu Britanniae*. This would end up being the only work available in my time that was anywhere near contemporary to Arthur. And Gildas wouldn't mention Arthur in it even once, an argument often used to suggest Arthur had never existed.

Perhaps, if I became this boy's mentor, I could change that, and the world would know there really had once been a King Arthur.

Chapter Six

M Y DAUGHTER ARCHFEDD was born in the spring. As far as births went, it was an altogether more enjoyable event than the birth of Amhar nearly three years before. At least this time I didn't have Bretta, the girl from Caer Baddan, spitting curses at me. She'd been married off to a farmer from toward Caer Pensa, the old Roman town on the road west, and I hadn't seen her in a long while.

Llacheu's mother, too, had at last been found a man of her own – the tanner who lived and worked in the village at the foot of the hill. Now, at least, she wouldn't be endlessly hanging around the Great Hall ogling my husband. Llacheu, who now slept in the hall with some of the other older boys, and visited his mother from time to time, told me she was expecting a little brother or sister for him in the summer, and was happy with her tanner.

"My family just keeps on growing bigger," he said, as he led Amhar around the paddock on Seren, the little gray pony that had once been his. I leaned on the fence watching them, with Maia just behind me holding the sleeping Archfedd. She was a contented baby who spent much of her time asleep with her thumb in her mouth. I did wonder sometimes if she'd suffer from not having enough stimulation, but Donella the midwife told me to count my blessings and not to worry. A baby that slept as well as this was hard to find and should be valued.

Amhar hung on tight to the horns of Seren's saddle. Nothing like the sort of saddle I'd used in my world, this resembled a Roman cavalry saddle with four horns, one in each corner to wedge the rider in a stable position for fighting. I'd helped provide even more stability when I'd introduced the fifth century to stirrups. However, Amhar's legs were too short to reach them as yet, so the horns were needed to keep him safe.

He loved riding Seren, and Llacheu, who'd now turned ten and grown so much over the winter that the top of his head reached my nose, took pleasure in helping him. Today, he'd insisted Amhar should wear his little leather belt complete with its scabbard and wooden sword, although I'd put my foot down at him taking his small round shield. "He needs both hands to hold on."

Amhar loved that sword as much as he loved his other, in my opinion more conventional, toys. Devin, the fortress carpenter, had made him lots of playthings to my specifications, from sketches I did on the thin slivers of wood that stood in for paper. None of *that* available within the confines of the fortress, and what parchment there was, Arthur wanted for maps. He'd been delighted to exploit my knowledge of British Isles geography.

But every time Amhar picked up his wooden sword to play-fight with his older cousin Medraut, that familiar ball of fear and trepidation settled in my stomach. Camlann. Would these two little boys end up on opposite sides there, the one fighting for his father, the other aiming to kill him?

Merlin and I hadn't spoken much about my revelation since we'd returned that day last autumn from Ynys Witrin. We'd gone back to see Gildas a couple more times before I'd reached the stage where riding was too uncomfortable, but since the birth of Archfedd we'd not been at all. Gildas had ridden over just after Archfedd's birth, with a piece of parchment he'd decorated for her. On it he'd simply written her name, but he'd illuminated the letter A with scrolls and a carefully drawn painting of a doe by a river. I'd put it away carefully to give to her when she was older.

Strident shouts from the maze of pathways that ran through the horse pens disturbed us. Medraut came running down the slope with Morgawse in hot pursuit. His short legs pounded the ground, and his long dark hair blew out behind him. A larger version of Amhar. The Pendragon children were all very similar in looks, although now Llacheu was older, something of his mother Tangwyn had emerged in him.

Medraut crashed into my legs and for a moment clung onto them. "I want a ride too," he almost bellowed, the only thing moderating his vocal cords being his lack of breath after the run. "Amhar said I could ride his pony."

Morgawse arrived, also panting. "Good heavens, I couldn't keep up with him once he spotted you all down here."

"I want a ride," Medraut persisted. "Now."

I laughed, but a tiny nub of unease at his demands formed at the back of my mind. I pushed it aside to be attended to later. "You shall have a ride after Amhar's finished. Llacheu's just leading him round the paddock one more time."

Medraut's lower lip jutted, and he folded his arms across his body, head down, brows lowered. "Not fair. I want a ride – *now*." He stamped a small, booted foot. Several times.

Morgawse put a gentle hand on his curls. "You shall have one shortly. Let Llacheu lead Amhar round once more."

Llacheu and Amhar were on the far side of the paddock. He'd tied up his black cob, Saeth, by the gate to stop her following Seren and being a nuisance. Now, her soft nose nuzzled at me, probably hoping for a treat.

Morgawse turned to coo over Archfedd in Maia's arms.

Medraut stared hard at me. "I want to ride *that* horse." He pointed at Saeth.

I laughed. "She's far too big for you. Llacheu only got her last year when he was nine. You'll need to grow a bit before you're big enough to ride a horse her size."

Medraut glared. "I am big." He tried to stand up taller, stretching his neck and head and standing on tiptoes. "I'm big enough to ride Saeth. Why should Llacheu get to ride her when I can't? He's only a base-born brat."

Little monster.

I sighed, unsure what to do, and glanced at his mother to see if she was going to reprimand him for his words. My nephew was fast turning into a rebellious, rude child, even though he wasn't yet four years old. And as he was still an only child, Morgawse gave in to his demands too easily and tended to spoil him. But she was my sister-in-law, and I liked her. She'd elected to stay on here in Theodoric's house even when he'd returned to Caer Legeion and his fleet. Especially when she'd discovered I was pregnant.

However, she didn't appear to have heard what Medraut had said, or she'd decided to ignore it altogether. She held out her arms to Maia for the baby. "Here, let me hold her." Reluctant, Maia passed over the blanket clad bundle, watching her like a hawk from beneath drawn brows. She was of the opinion that no one could look after my children better than she could. Not even me.

Medraut tugged the wide sleeve of my tunic. "I *said* – I want a ride – *now*."

It was on the tip of my tongue to tell him off for his rudeness, but the last time I'd tried that, Morgawse had been deeply hurt. I glanced her way again, but she was deep in a cooing conversation with my baby, not paying her son any attention. Which might account for his perpetual bad behavior.

Llacheu walked back up the field toward us, Amhar beaming with delight. He stopped beside the gate, well clear of Saeth.

"Again!" Amhar shouted, banging his chubby fists on the saddle horns. "Again, Lachy. Again."

Medraut strode up to Llacheu. "No, it's my turn now. *I* want a ride."

From his position on Seren's back, Amhar regarded his cousin with some disfavor. "No. Seren's mine. I'm ridin' her."

I dithered. No help was coming from Morgawse. I didn't want to give in to Medraut's ill-mannered demands, and I didn't want to upset my son. Llacheu looked at me for help.

Inspiration came. "Seren's too tired to be ridden again today. You can have a ride tomorrow, Medraut." I turned to Llacheu. "Give me Amhar, and you can take her saddle off. She needs a roll after so much hard work." I winked at him.

Medraut stamped his foot again. "That's not fair. I don't care if she's tired. I *want* a ride." He kicked the nearest fence post. "I want it *now*."

I lifted Amhar out of the saddle and set him on the ground. "No, Medraut. She's tired."

Over Medraut's head, Llacheu met my gaze, his eyes full of adult understanding. He'd had the brunt of Medraut's bad behavior before. With quick fingers he undid the girth and slipped Seren's saddle off, then freed her from her halter. With a shake of her head, she trotted off to her favorite dusty rolling spot.

Wham. Medraut pushed Amhar over. My son sat down hard in the dirt and burst into tears. "Stupid baby," Medraut spat.

Furious, but trying hard not to show it, I scooped poor Amhar up in my arms and held him tight. "That wasn't a nice thing to do, Medraut," I said, fighting to keep my voice level, when what he needed was a good smack on the bottom. "And for that you shan't ride Seren tomorrow after all. She's Amhar's pony, and you've behaved badly today. Bad behavior never wins rewards."

Medraut's angry face crumpled, and he burst into floods of tears. Now we had two howling children. Llacheu unfastened Saeth's halter and set her free as well. She cantered off down the paddock to join

Seren, probably relieved to get away from the racket.

Morgawse hurriedly shoved Archfedd back into Maia's more than willing arms and bent down to her blubbering son. "Medraut, what is it? Are you all right?"

He couldn't get the words out he was sobbing so hard. She gathered him up in her arms and turned to me, her voice accusing. "What happened?"

Irritation coursed through me. The little brat was about to get away with it – again. "He was behaving badly, so I said he couldn't have a ride on Seren tomorrow. He'll have to wait." Why did I feel so defensive?

Her eyes flashed. "Isn't that a bit mean? He's only a child. And Amhar needs to learn to share."

"He pushed Amhar over," Llacheu put in, turning from closing the slip rails into the paddock.

Morgawse bristled like a mother hen. "I'm sure it was by accident. He'd never do anything like that on purpose."

Deluded woman.

Llacheu bristled back. He wasn't about to let this drop. I held up my hand, and he closed his mouth, his brows meeting in a scowl worthy of his father.

I stepped in. "He was behaving badly, Morgawse, and that's all there is to it. I don't want to reward him for his behavior. If you don't like it, I'm sorry. But I won't be spoken to like that by a child."

Morgawse's lips came together in a thin line. "Yes, well, look how you've upset him. I'm taking him back to my house." She shot an angry glare at Llacheu. "I'll leave you with my brother's bastard then, shall I?"

We watched her go, striding up the slope with the hefty Medraut still wrapped in her arms. He'd stopped crying and was regarding us with angry eyes over his mother's shoulder.

"I don't like him," Llacheu said. "I know he's only a little boy, but he's horrible. He's never nice to Amhar, but Amhar doesn't even notice most of the time."

As Amhar, too, had stopped crying, I set him on the ground again.

Maia stepped up closer with Archfedd. "I doesn't like 'im much neither. That boy, he's got a black heart."

I peeped at Archfedd's sleeping face. "That's a bit melodramatic. His mother's right – he's just a child. Albeit a very spoilt one."

Maia made a harrumphing sound indicating her disagreement. She'd been my maid since I'd first arrived at Din Cadan nearly four years ago, and she and I were more like friends than mistress and servant. She knew she could speak her mind.

"Maia's right," Llacheu said. "He may be little, but I don't trust him, and I don't think he'll grow up to be a trustworthy warrior. I wouldn't want him under my command. He's not a follower. And he doesn't have the skills to be a popular leader, either."

A shiver ran down my spine. What if they were right? What if even now Medraut was morphing into the sort of person who would rise in rebellion against his uncle one day? Could you see the man a child would become at that age? And how far away did that battle lie? The last four years had sped past. In no time at all these little boys would be warriors like Cei's son Rhiwallon.

He was thirteen now and training with the youngest warriors, instead of the boys. From being Llacheu's best friend, and spending time with him on boyish pranks, he'd turned into a young man overnight, one who'd rather drink a flagon of ale with his new friends and talk about girls than play-fight or climb trees with Llacheu.

⸻ ❖ ⸻

SUMMER HAD TAKEN Arthur, Cei, and Merlin away from the fortress to patrol the Dumnonian borders and the coast, and just when I felt I needed support more than usual, I had no one. I lay alone in bed that night thinking about the little scene that had unfolded with Medraut, and wishing I could talk to someone about it. But the only one who might understand was miles away with Arthur.

I finally fell asleep, only to be woken some time in the middle of the night by Maia bringing Archfedd to me to be fed. The baby slept in a cot in Maia's room so she could get her back to sleep for me after her feeds and leave me to get my rest.

As I sat with my daughter at my breast, an idea formed; one I could put into practice the next morning. One that didn't require either Arthur or Merlin.

After the morning feed, I left the slumbering baby in Maia's experienced hands, and, leaving by the side door, made my way across the courtyard to Cei and Coventina's house, taking Amhar with me. Secure in the knowledge that Cei was away with Arthur, I knocked sharply on the silvered wood of the door.

After a moment, Keelia, Coventina's maid, opened it with her latest baby firmly attached to her left breast. Seeing it was me, she made a hasty bow much hampered by the hefty baby. "Milady." She stepped back to allow me inside.

Cei's house, like most of the other dwellings, owed almost nothing to Roman influence and everything to the legacy of pre-Roman Britain, although instead of being round, it was rectangular in shape. Blackened beams sat on shoulder-high cob walls holding up a steeply angled reed-thatched roof. The smoke from the fire in the central hearth twisted up to filter between the reeds, pooling a little at the apex. As in all houses, the smell of damp soot hung heavily in the air.

Coventina's little daughter Reaghan sat quite naked on a rush mat near the fire, playing with a stack of wooden bricks just like the ones I'd had made for Amhar. Her mother perched on a nearby stool, finishing off a bowl of porridge. She looked up as I came in, and her face broke into a welcoming smile.

Amhar yanked his hand out of mine and ran to join his cousin in her games. Big enough now to wear braccae instead of just a shirt, he seemed very much a little boy next to the chubby toddler.

"Excuse me bein' still eatin'," Coventina said, putting the empty bowl behind her on the table and wiping her mouth on the back of her hand. "It do take such a long time to get Reaghan up and fed of a morning, what with Keelia having her own new baby to care for too, I don't know where the time goes." She made to get up, but I waved her down. She still suffered some nerve pain that would probably never go away from the operation Donella the midwife had performed on her to save her and her baby, and I didn't want to set it off.

I sat beside her on another stool, watching the two children play. Although Amhar was the older by nine months, there was none of the bossing about that happened when he played with Medraut. He seemed content to stack towers for Reaghan to knock down, laughing uproariously with her every time they crashed to the floor.

"They do get on well," I said.

Coventina shifted a little on her stool, perhaps easing whatever pains she felt from her scar. "They do that. 'Tis a pleasure to watch 'em."

I sat in silence for a while, wondering what I should say. At last, I couldn't hold my tongue any longer. "Not like when Medraut joins in." There, it was said.

Coventina shot me a sideways glance. "Not quite…" Wariness leant an edge to her voice.

Silence again. Clearly it was up to me to bring this into the open. "Do you feel anything is… different… about Medraut?" Probably I wasn't phrasing myself properly.

She turned her head, puzzled. "Somethin' different? Like what?"

Had I been imagining it because of what I knew about him? No, not what I *knew*, because I couldn't know for sure – more what I *suspected* I knew. "That he's…different to the other children?"

"Like how?"

This was getting harder by the moment. She sounded as though she had no idea what I was talking about. I drew a deep breath. "He always wants everything Amhar has. It's getting worse. Yesterday he pushed Amhar over and made him cry because he wanted to ride Seren."

Her brow furrowed. "I don't know. Does he? I can't say as I've ever noticed. He's a very… bossy little boy, that's for sure. But he's three. Well, nigh on four, and children aren't easy at that age. Rhiwallon were a demon, and Llacheu – I remember how naughty he could be. Although I didn't see so much of him as I'd've liked. I always thought it were his mother what let him get away with things so much. Because of who he was. He's turned out fine though, now he's ten." She smiled. "Don't you think?"

I nodded. Llacheu was a lovely lad, and had been from the moment I'd first met him when he was only six. So like his father in almost every way – with more than his fair share of the Pendragon charm. I frowned. "But there's something about Medraut that's not like a normal naughty child." Hadn't I seen enough of them when I'd been a librarian? I knew a thing or two about badly behaved children, even though that time was long gone.

"I don't see him enough to give you an opinion," Coventina said, with a sigh. "I daresay you see him oftener than me, he and Amhar bein' so close in age an' both bein' boys. But if he's naughty, it'll be because he's overindulged at home. Morgawse needs another baby, like you and me. Then he'd *have* to behave himself." She chuckled.

I sat back, staring past the playing children into the embers of the fire. Perhaps Coventina was right. Perhaps I was overly cautious because of what I thought I knew. Maybe Medraut was just that – a naughty, spoilt child. And maybe he'd grow out of it as Coventina seemed convinced he would.

Arthur was away all summer, and, with a young baby to look after, I was left at Din Cadan, worrying. Having been away from Amhar for such a long time while he was so little, I didn't want the same estrangement I'd felt from him repeated. But it was hard to remain at home, worrying about Arthur, and I was glad when autumn turned to winter and he returned, bearded, thinner, and with one or two fresh scars.

With him, he brought unwelcome news. Morgana had given birth to Merlin's child in Viroconium last winter. A girl, as she'd predicted. When I asked him about it, he seemed unwilling to talk, but I pressed him anyway.

We were lying in bed while an early winter storm raged outside, buffeting the stout thatched roof of the great hall and rattling the shutters in our chamber. Inside, the brazier on its bare patch of flagstones belched out heat, and the rugs Maia had hung in front of the shutters shifted in the draft.

We were naked, in that languorous afterglow good sex can give you, tangled in one another's limbs, my right cheek pressed against his chest, the curling dark hairs tickling my skin. Like any man after sex, he was dozing off. A good time to tackle him – with his guard down.

"Does Merlin know about the baby?" I asked, my fingers tracing his nipple with a deliberately light touch.

Arthur grunted. "He does."

I didn't need to look up to know his eyes had closed.

"How did you find out?"

His chest rose and fell in a sigh. "Do we need to talk about this now? I was nearly asleep."

I tweaked his nipple in admonishment. Quite hard. "We do. I have a feeling it's important."

His arm tightened around me, telling me I had his attention, and he was no longer dozing off. "You and your feelings. You're as bad as Merlin."

"We women usually have good gut instincts."

A little chuckle shook his body. "And men don't?" His head moved and his breath warmed my scalp. "You and your feminine desire for superiority."

I pinched him again. "Not superiority – equality."

"Ouch, but you can do that again – I liked it."

I stopped, of course. "How did you find out. You haven't told me yet."

His free hand snaked up my side and found my left breast. Now I'd woken him up, it seemed he had other things in mind than talking. "One of my men, Barra, is from Viroconium. He had news from home, from his sister who works in the palace. She told him, and he told me. Me in preference to Merlin. Barra was there last year when I fought Cadwy. He knows what Morgana did to Merlin. He didn't think it wise to share the news with him."

There was no doubting that what he was doing to my breast was distracting. I tried to concentrate. "Who told Merlin then?"

"I did." He kissed my hair. "Do we need to talk about this now? I can think of something else I'd like to do."

I wriggled. I could too, but I needed to know more about this baby. "Do you know what she's called it?"

His hand migrated down my stomach and past my navel. "I can't remember." His voice had taken on the same huskiness it had held when we'd first retired to bed that evening.

"Well think," I whispered. "Didn't your informant happen to mention, for example, what she's named her daughter?"

His fingers were now being most distracting, and a little gasp of pleasure forced its way between my lips. With no direction from me, my own left hand slid down his belly and found he was more than ready for what he had in mind.

"What's her name?" I persisted.

He wriggled around, slipping me out from under his arm until he was leaning over me, his face close to mine, illuminated by the golden glow from the brazier like a man cast in bronze. His long hair tickled my skin. Without thinking, I slid my legs apart in invitation.

"I have it," he whispered, mouth descending toward mine. "She's called Nimuë." Then he kissed me.

Chapter Seven

Nimuë. The name of the Lady of the Lake, according to legend. Yet this was an ordinary human baby, even though her parents both had the Sight. Not that I believed in fairies or whatever the legendary Nimuë was meant to have been. This wasn't some romantic fantasy. Far from it, considering the way that child had come to be born. In my baser moments, I wished very hard that Morgana had suffered a difficult birth as reward for the way she'd treated Merlin.

But here was yet another secret for me to keep. Although I hoped the coincidence of her name was just that, an awkward coincidence and nothing more, at the back of my mind lurked the nagging worry that it wasn't. That one day, little Nimuë would have a part to play in the tragedy I feared was looming ever closer. My one consolation was that as many of the players were so young, that tragedy must lie far into the future.

Hugging my fears to myself during the long winter nights when I sat feeding Archfedd, watching my sleeping husband's face, set a nasty nagging canker growing in my heart that I couldn't excise. I loved Arthur so much it hurt. And yet one day, a day that would arrive much sooner than I could imagine, he'd be taken from me. Unless I could set in motion events that would change history. Change his life. Change the legend.

He surprised me one night, as I sat in bed silently crying over Archfedd's downy head, the tears running unhindered down my cheeks.

"What's wrong?" His gentle voice made me jump.

I wiped my eyes, sniffing to clear my nose. "Nothing."

He sat up in bed, moving closer. "Rubbish. I can see there is." By the soft candlelight he peered at our baby, milk-drunk and nearly sated, eyes only half open, my nipple slipping from her rosebud mouth. "Is it Archfedd? Is she sick?"

I shook my head and sniffed again. "She's fine. Just asleep."

He put out a finger and stroked her soft cheek. "Then what's caused these tears? Has something happened to upset you?"

"No. Nothing." My brain frantically scrabbled for a good excuse. He wouldn't understand if I told him it was my hormones. Another of those *"if you can't see them, then they don't exist"* things.

His arm slipped around my shoulders. "Come here then." He dropped a kiss on the top of my head. "Has someone said something to hurt you?"

I shook my head again, inspiration arriving in the nick of time. "I'm just sad she won't always be a baby, cuddled in my arms." I peeked up at his face. "One day she'll be all grown up and off to marry someone far away, and I might never see her again."

He smiled with a touch of indulgence for a silly emotional woman. "That time's far away. She'll be ours for a long time yet." He removed his arm and got out of bed. "Here, give her to me. You're exhausted. I'll take her back to Maia, and you can lie down and get some sleep."

Considering he was naked, I thought that might give Maia a bit of a shock. Despite my tears, a smile twitched my lips. "You'd better put something on then."

He chuckled. "Can't have her screaming if she finds a naked man in her room." He pulled on the braccae he'd discarded last night on the floor. "Here, pass her over."

I snuggled down in bed, watching him carry our child toward the door into Maia's room, part pleased and part ashamed that I hadn't shared with him my worries about Morgana's daughter.

WITH THE FOLLOWING year came the Irish into Gwent and along the south coast toward Dyfed. In a wet spring, Arthur marched away north in the direction of Caer Gloui, to take the road west from there into what I still couldn't help but think of as South Wales. Ironic, as Wales was the rather cheeky name the Saxons would give that country long into the future – meaning it was the country of the *"wealas"* – the foreigners. And by that they'd mean the native Britons.

Merlin, left behind at Din Cadan, gave me a short history lesson and together we constructed a map of Wales as best we could, marking on the kingdoms where he thought they lay in relation to one another. This proved a harder task than I'd imagined, especially as I didn't have the luxury of a pencil and eraser.

"In the north, Gwynedd for sure," Merlin said, waving a vague hand over the quite detailed outline of Wales I'd drawn. "By the western sea. And Cadwy's Powys of course, to the east of Gwynnedd. A bit lower down. Owain White Tooth holds Gwynedd. Never trust a man who smiles as much as he does."

My pen hovered over the map.

Merlin leaned forward. "And this must be Ynys Mon, I think... the old Isle of the Druids. Of course, they're long gone now." The Isle of Anglesey on the northwest tip of Wales.

I raised my eyebrows. "Still known as the Isle of the Druids even now? I know the Romans had a big problem with the druids and attacked Ynys Mon – but that was hundreds of years ago."

He shrugged. "There might still be one or two there, I suppose. In hiding. I'd heard they died out years ago. No need for them now Britain's Christian... allegedly."

I smiled at his reference to Christianity in Britain. On the surface it was as he said – Christian. But scratch that surface and the more ancient beliefs would be revealed: the corn dollies, the festivals like

Beltane and Samhain, the ancestor worship... the taking of heads in battle.

I wrote the name *Ynys Mon* on the map in small capital letters, then sighed. "Well, I can put Viroconium on, for sure." I drew a small circle and inked it in, then wrote Viroconium beside it. "And Caer Legeion, and Caer Went, in Gwent." I added those two southern towns which I'd visited on numerous occasions with my father, thanking him mentally for my thorough education in things even he had never known would come in so useful.

"Moridunum in the west," I said with undisguised glee, and marked in Carmarthen, another place I'd been to. "Um, you weren't born there by any chance, were you?"

We were standing at the table in my chamber, the children playing on the floor around our feet. Merlin looked up at me, face puzzled, and shook his head.

I smiled. "Just that in my world it's called Carmarthen, and a legend says it's called that after you – because you were born there. Caermyrddin. Merlin's town."

He chuckled. "That's funny. No, I wasn't born there."

My curiosity rose. "Where were you born, then? Where are you from?"

He shrugged. "I'm from... nowhere."

I set down my pen, careful not to make an ineradicable blot that only scraping with a sharp blade would remove. It was made of a long wooden cylinder with a curl of metal round it that acted like a cartridge, making a receptacle for the ink. Using it was a hard to acquire knack, and I still found it difficult not to produce the sort of blotchy writing a drunken spider with a nervous tic might make. "That's a funny thing to say. You must be from somewhere. What about your parents? Do you know where they were from?"

The sudden urge to make him reveal more of his past swept over me – curiosity and plain nosiness, I suppose. I was a woman, after all. I smiled at him winningly. At least, I thought I did.

"I don't know where my parents were from," he said, with a wry smile. "Nor who they were. And I don't come from anywhere because the people who brought me up were wanderers."

My eyebrows must have shot up. "They weren't your parents, then? The people who raised you?"

He shook his head. "No. They weren't." His suddenly abrupt tone told me he wanted to drop the matter, so I turned back to the map, even though I itched to keep him talking. No wonder Guorthegirn's advisers had seized upon him for their sacrifice as the "boy with no father." I'd have to worm it out of him another time, when he was in a more forthcoming mood.

Merlin prodded the westernmost limit of South Wales in what would one day become Carmarthenshire and Pembrokeshire. "Dyfed, that's an Irish kingdom. They've been here generations now, and cause no trouble. The king styles himself with a Roman name and title – Agricola the Protector – and thinks of himself as British. You'll have seen him at the Council of Kings. A tall man with silver in his red hair. They say the Irish tend to be ginger – like Cei."

He laughed. "For all we know Cei's father Gorlois had Irish blood, coming from Cornubia as he did. He was a redhead as well. They say men with that coloring make good warriors. The Irish have ever raided and raped all along our western coastlines, so there's likely to be a lot of Irish blood in the men of the west."

I tentatively marked in Dyfed in capital letters across the area he indicated.

"Then north of that is Ceredigion – the king there is descended from Cunedda in direct line. A hundred years ago, when the old king came down from Guotodin, beyond the Wall, to fight the Irish in Gwynedd, he brought all his many sons with him. His great grandson Ceretic rules there now, but he's getting old."

I thought of Caw and all Gildas's many brothers. It seemed men from beyond the Wall were in the habit of getting themselves lots of sons. Maybe there was something in the water.

"If Dyfed's Irish already," I asked, "where are the Irish raiders raiding? Not their countrymen, surely?"

Merlin tapped the map with a long finger. "All along this south coast, most likely. They'll have no reservations about attacking Agricola. He's no longer Irish in their eyes, and his lands of Dyfed are rich pickings. In the hills he has gold mines. Dug by the Romans, but still producing some wealth for him."

At my feet, Archfedd stuffed one of Amhar's bricks into her mouth, dribble running down her chin from where a tooth was pushing through. An amiable baby, she didn't seem all that bothered by anything. Her hair had come through lighter than Amhar's, more like mine, but she'd inherited her father's curls, which clustered about her head in a pretty profusion.

"Watch how big a tower I can build," Amhar said, stacking bricks one on top of the other, while firmly holding the lower ones to stop his little sister sabotaging them.

"Excellent building skills," I said, just before Archfedd managed to knock the tower down. He glared at her for a moment, then started again with a sigh, a bit further away. He'd probably forgotten she could crawl now, and even teeter a few steps on her own.

I bent back over my map. "These are mountains." I sketched in the Brecon Beacons and the Black Mountains, the valleys of South Wales where one day coal would be mined, the smaller Preselis in Pembrokeshire, and the mountains of North Wales. I put a cross where I thought Snowdon lay. "And this is the highest point."

Merlin knew a few places I didn't, and by dint of careful detective work I managed to divine where they were meant to be and marked them on. Then I stepped back to admire my work, wondering where on this map Arthur was and if he was still safe. If I kept myself busy, I occasionally forgot to worry. In idleness all my fears came rushing back.

Merlin must have read my mind. "He won't die," he said as he removed the wooden bricks we'd used to hold the scroll down and rolled it up. "You're worrying unnecessarily."

I sat down on one of the chairs. "Easy for you to say that. I mean, I know you think you know, but experience has taught me that firstly you can't always see things, and even if you do, it's not always clearly. Then secondly, not being dead isn't the same as being unharmed. Look how bad that wound he took beyond the Wall was. Did you see that coming?"

In an ambush by the wild Pictish Dogmen, Arthur had been targeted and stabbed in the thigh, a wound that had taken a long time to heal and even now gave him trouble. Naked, the slightly wasted muscles on that leg were apparent. He still walked with a limp when tired.

Merlin shook his head. "All I can tell you is he won't die fighting against King Illan and his Irish raiders."

If the stories I knew were right, I could have told him that.

Amhar was fishing in his toy chest and setting out the wooden animals Devin had carved for him. A few of them were of Merlin's own making, all of them solid and easy for a child to grasp. Archfedd started across the fur rugs toward him in a fast crawl, an acquisitive expression on her face.

I huffed out a long breath. "That's of little comfort to me as I sit here twiddling my thumbs all summer."

He sat down on one of the other chairs. "I'm sorry. That's all I can say."

In companionable silence, we watched the children play for a few more minutes. Amhar was big and sturdy now, and every time I looked at him, I was struck by his similarity to his father and Llacheu. A good thing, considering the doubts cast over his paternity by that evil king Melwas who'd tried to claim I'd slept with him while I'd been his prisoner. The very thought made me shiver with disgust even now.

Merlin tapped his fingers on his knee. Was something going through his mind that he wanted to say? I sat and waited. I didn't mind. I never tired of watching my children play, which they mostly did very nicely. Unlike when Medraut intervened. He was such a trouble-making child, always wanting what the other children had. He'd even tried bossing Llacheu about on the few occasions all four of them had been together. Luckily, Llacheu was now a sensible eleven-year-old, and Medraut's bad behavior slid off him almost unnoticed.

Merlin's mind must have been running along the same lines as mine. "I've been watching Medraut," he said, after a while. "Paying him close attention. Now he's nearly five, he's begun a few lessons. He's a clever boy, and finds them easy. His teachers have to keep him working else he causes ructions with the others. Morgawse especially asked for him to begin early as he was bored at home – she said."

I kept my eyes on my children. Amhar was setting out the animals for Archfedd to play with. "What do you think of him?" I asked.

He shrugged. "It's hard to say of a child so young. Some boys are made to follow – a few to lead. Medraut seems to possess all the qualities of a leader, not a follower. He's bossy, autocratic, intelligent, and has good ideas that often the other boys want to copy." Llacheu had said something along these lines to me last year – only he hadn't seemed to think Medraut would make an inspiring leader.

"Do the other boys like him?"

Merlin frowned. "I'm not sure." He paused, the frown deepening. "If anything, I'd say they were afraid of him."

Now, wasn't that a strange thing to say of so young a child? But it matched more with Llacheu's opinion of his cousin. A good leader doesn't keep his men in line through fear. Arthur's men loved him with a deep, admiring pride.

I chewed my bottom lip, thinking. "When I first met his mother, when she was in labor with him, and I had to help her, she told me

Morgana had said her child was very special – important even. I can't remember her exact words. She said Morgana had given her things – medicine maybe – for sickness and any aches and pains she had."

Merlin's eyes narrowed. He usually avoided all talk of Morgana, for obvious reasons. Not for the first time I wondered if he still nurtured a secret love for her. Who knew what her powers were. She could easily have used something on him to kindle a lasting devotion. Five years in the Dark Ages had left me ready to believe most things, and I couldn't see any other way she could have caught as clever a man as Merlin.

"What are you saying?" he asked, his voice wary.

I hesitated. "Do you think…? Could she know something of what…of what frightens me?" I swallowed. "She has the Sight, the same as her mother, and just as you do. Have you ever… since I asked you, have you ever… been tempted to look and see what lies ahead of Medraut?"

A long silence stretched between us. The children played on, giggling together as Amhar made his animals climb a row of steps he'd built using his blocks to allow access into the wooden ark that went with the animals. "Two by two," he sang to Archfedd. "The animals went in two by two, the elephant and the kangaroo. Hoppity skip. One, two, in you go."

Eventually, Merlin heaved a deep sigh. "Yes," he said. "I have been tempted."

My breathing seemed to have suddenly become labored, as though the very air had thickened and was resisting my efforts to inhale. "And?" I whispered.

"Thassa camel," Amhar said to his little sister. "See his hump? He's from Afric'. They keeps water in their humps 'cause it's so hot in Afric'."

Merlin shook his head. "I've looked, but every time I've tried, my way is clouded."

"So you haven't seen anything?"

He shook his head. "When I see nothing, it's because nothing comes to me. It's been different with Medraut. I do see something, but it's misty and unclear. Vague shapes move in the mist, and I hear muffled sounds. Nothing I can make out. I've tried many times, but it's always the same. As though there's something there to see… but I'm being prevented from seeing it."

The voices of the children receded as though at the far end of a tunnel, echoing unclearly. My heart pounded, loud in my ears, and goose pimples prickled up my back. I shivered.

"There may be nothing *to* see," Merlin said, but I could tell he didn't believe what he was saying. "I'm not always right, you know. No one is. Morgana makes mistakes too, as Arthur's mother did."

I stared at him, eyes wide.

He met my gaze. "She didn't see what would happen if she crossed Uthyr, did she? Didn't see herself banished to Din Tagel. Separated from the child she loved the best."

True. I stayed silent.

Merlin nodded. "If she'd seen that coming, would she still have faced Uthyr down? Probably not. Did the fact she faced Uthyr down and lost her son create the future she feared? In all likelihood. We can't know what the consequences of our actions will be. I'm given a glimpse, from time to time, but it's only what *might* happen, not what will… I think…" He paused. "And I can't even be sure of that…" His voice trailed off.

I bit my bottom lip. "If you were me." I kept my voice low. "And you knew the future, or what it might hold, what would you do? If you feared, like I do, that if you acted on what you knew, it might make it more likely to happen, but that if you didn't, it still might happen anyway?"

He gazed back out of troubled eyes. "I don't know. Do any of us really know? Do even I know if what I see is true? Since… since

Morgana, I've doubted myself so much. I didn't see through her. I let her fool me. What kind of a man of magic does that? Was I... am I so weak that a smile from a beautiful woman and the offer of her body robbed me of all my senses?"

"This one's a lion," Amhar said. "Rrrroar. Thass what a lion says."

"Raaahh!" Archfedd copied her brother with relish, banging the lion on top of the ark.

I slid my hand across the table and covered Merlin's. "She used her arts on you. That's certain. But what bothers me right now is has she used them on Medraut? Before he was born? Could someone with the Sight do that? Could she influence an unborn child to bend to her will?" I fixed him with a hard stare. "Could *you* do something like that? Is it possible?"

He ran his free hand through his hair, pushing it back from his face. "I can't answer that because I don't know. I've never tried, and I never want to. It would be wrong."

I squeezed his hand. "*She* wouldn't see it as wrong, though, would she?"

He met my gaze. "No, I don't think she would."

Chapter Eight

IT TURNED OUT that I had very little time to dwell on what Merlin and I had discussed, because hot on the heels of our midsummer celebrations, half a dozen armed horsemen arrived at Din Cadan.

Late on a day so heavy with summer rain that not even the forest on the plain remained visible, they came riding their tired horses up the cobbled road to our gates. With Arthur absent, our guards were especially vigilant with strangers. They kept them standing waiting in the rain until someone from the hall came down to find out where they were from and what they wanted. Only then did they allow them through.

Of course, I saw none of this firsthand, and only heard it later, as I was playing with the children in my chamber with Morgawse and Coventina, while Maia sat sewing in a corner. Medraut, as usual, was ruling the roost. Amhar seemed quite happy to let him, something that irritated me, but then, Medraut *was* the oldest. Despite Medraut's bossiness and sometimes downright bullying, that Morgawse seemed blind to, Amhar took it all in his stride and looked up to his older cousin with something uncomfortably like hero worship.

At the back of my mind, I'd been half-looking for a reason to suggest Morgawse and her son should return to their home in Caer Legeion. However, the need for me, and Merlin, to keep an eye on Medraut had won over, and so far, I'd done nothing. Even though he was only five, I felt a need to keep him near enough for close scrutiny.

A knock on the door into the Great Hall disturbed us.

I glanced around. "Enter."

The door swung open to reveal Gwalchmei, Prince of Guotodin, a slight young man whose love of music overrode his love of fighting. "Milady." His gaze took in all three of us women. "Mi*ladies*. Riders have arrived from King Coel Hen, bearing news. They asked for the High King. I told them he's not here. And Merlin neither – he rode out this morning with his hawk before the rain began."

I scrambled up from where I'd been sitting cross-legged with the children. "I'll come."

"From King Coel? From Ebrauc?" Coventina said, getting up as well, with a slight grimace. "These men have ridden a long way – what can they want?"

"Ebrauc's in the northeast, so they'll be after help against Saxon raiders," Morgawse put in, still seated on the floor with Archfedd cuddled on her knee. "The same thing messengers from other kings always want. Help in battle. They'll be out of luck this time."

I smoothed my crumpled skirts and followed Gwalchmei.

Six men stood in the body of the hall, dripping wetly onto the rushes that covered the flagstones. All wore glittering mail shirts over their tunics, leather braccae on their legs and soggy woolen cloaks. Each carried a helmet tucked under his arm, and at their hips hung swords and daggers. But to my surprise, all were graybeards, their faces lined and wrinkled like last year's apple found forgotten at the bottom of the barrel. Wet, grizzled hair hung to their shoulders in tangled dreadlocks.

I stepped onto the low platform the high table occupied.

One of them, the oldest of the bunch, his white hair stained yellow by smoke, and with a thin, tired face, stepped forward. He made a low bow. "My Lady Guinevere."

"Good day to you," I said, my gaze sweeping over his fellows. I'd visited Ebrauc, King Coel's capital, two years ago on my way north to the Wall, but so briefly that I didn't remember seeing any of the faces before me.

The old warrior straightened with difficulty, as though his joints pained him. Probably he suffered from arthritis and had nothing much to treat it with.

He cleared his throat. "My name is Cadman, my Lady, warrior and close adviser to King Coel. I've come here to petition the High King for help. We six volunteered to bring our lord's message to you because of our extreme age. We're all old and less use in the defense of the kingdom than our sons and grandsons. Our quest is of the most urgent."

Redness ringed his bloodshot gray eyes, and dark circles shadowed them. It must have taken a lot for Coel, a proud old man, to admit he needed the High King's help. And nearly as difficult for these ancient warriors to stand before a mere woman and ask for it. I might still be nurturing my twenty-first-century ideals in secret, but I knew exactly how this world worked.

"My lords, you will have been informed, then, that the High King is not here," I said, conscious of the dignity of this situation. These faithful and weary old warriors deserved my respect, even if they balked at having to address their petition to a woman.

Cadman nodded, hope kindling in his faded eyes. "We have been. When is he expected to return?"

I wished I knew. What to say to them? They'd traveled such a long way to no avail. "I'm afraid I can't tell you that," I said, choosing my words carefully. "He's been gone some time, west into Gwent and Dyfed, where the Irish have been raiding this summer." The urge to say "Wales" was great, but they'd have had no idea where I was talking about.

"Then we must go after him," Cadman said, his bony shoulders sagging. "Our need in the north is great. My king charged me not to return unless I brought the High King and his army with me. If we don't get help, the north will fall, and after that… who knows? We are sore pressed by savage raiders who want only to pillage our city and torch our rich farmlands."

A brave old man. From the appearance of him and his fellows, the ride down here must have been a torture for their aging joints.

"No," I said. "You won't need to do that. You must rest here for the next few days before returning to your king. We'll see you, and your tired horses, well looked after. I will send my own men to search for my husband and tell him of your need. He will come to Ebrauc if he can." I paused, pleased with my decision, although not certain Arthur would see their request as more important than protecting South Wales's kingdoms, which were a lot closer to Din Cadan than Ebrauc, from the Irish.

However, I smiled with fake confidence. "Now, tell me everything so I can put it in my message to him."

Cadman squared his shoulders and stood up straighter. "Bryneich is in flames, Milady. And Ebrauc may well burn with it."

His tale echoed many I'd heard before. Since spring, isolated attacks by Saxon ships down the east coast of Britain, south of the Wall, had been on the increase. Coel's kingdom of Bryneich ran all along that east coast between Linnuis and the Wall, with the old Roman city of Ebrauc as its capital and miles of exposed coastline to protect.

"Of course," Cadman said, shaking his grizzled head, "the fishing villages were attacked first. The raiders burned the small boats that were the people's livelihoods, and either killed the fishermen and their families or took them as slaves."

Coel had sent out warriors to defend the long shoreline, but under sail with a fair wind, or under oars, the enemy's ships proved quicker than mounted warriors. With all the miles he had to guard, keeping the villages from harm had fast become impossible.

With his army divided north and south of Ebrauc, almost up to the Wall itself, Coel's central hub had been left poorly defended, perhaps as the invaders intended.

Cadman heaved a deep sigh and hung his head. "A huge force of Saxons landed due east of the city and marched inland. Only the timely return of our armies from the north and south saved a defeat from becoming an annihilation."

The fact that the Saxons had not followed up their victory by chasing Coel's army back to Ebrauc implied they had no taste for siege warfare. But Coel's severely depleted army still had an extensive coastline to defend, as well as the city, and all the inland settlements and farms.

Cadman didn't say, but his king must have reached the end of his tether. Otherwise, he wouldn't have decided to ask for help. No king would be keen to look weak by demeaning himself, in his own eyes, and begging for help. They all wanted to maintain a façade of invulnerability.

Cadman's shoulders sagged as he neared the end of his recital. "Every able-bodied man is needed in Ebrauc and along the coast to man the defenses. It was my idea that we old warriors should be sent south to the High King, leaving the young to fight. Thirty volunteered – we are six of the oldest." He stared into my eyes, his own anguished. "Without help, the East will fall, Ebrauc will be no more. And if that happens, the rest of the North will soon follow."

I stood straighter, drawing in a deep breath. "This was a brave thing to do. I honor you for it. Now, Gwalchmei will take you to our guest quarters, and find help for you with your horses. You, and they, need rest and food." I indicated the mutton roasting on a spit above our hearth fire. "You will be our guests tonight and for as many days as you need. You've delivered your message and have no need for haste. It grows late. I will see your message is sent on to my husband first thing in the morning."

Cadman and his fellows bowed again, relief as well as exhaustion in their bloodshot eyes. Gwalchmei stepped down from the platform where he'd been standing just behind me. "This way, my lords."

The drenched old men followed him out.

I perched my bottom on the high table, staring down the hall, empty now of all but the cook's boy, busy making himself small and insignificant beside the fire. The scent of the cooking meat, and the nearness of the time to eat, set my stomach growling, but I had other more pressing things to do. Where on earth was Merlin when I needed him? Surely not still out hawking in this weather? Impossible.

After a few minutes of deep thought, I returned to my chamber. Coventina and Morgawse were still there, playing with the children. They looked up as I sat down at the table, thinking still.

"What was it?" Coventina asked, after a moment. "Did they want what we suspected?"

"Just as Morgawse said," I replied. "Help for Ebrauc. Their situation sounds worse to me, and potentially more dangerous for all of Britain, than that of the people being attacked by the Irish. Yellow Hairs, intent on ransacking Bryneich and no doubt expanding the territory they already hold in the north."

I rubbed my temples. "I've told them I'd have their message sent on to Arthur. They're old men, every one of them, and exhausted from their long ride south. They wanted to go and find Arthur themselves, but by the look of them, it might have finished them off. I've said they should stay here and rest, but I doubt they will. They may be old, but they're also proud. Most likely they'll head back north tomorrow to their king." I paused. "We'll make sure they have fresh horses if that's what they decide."

"Who will you send to find Arthur?" Morgawse asked, smoothing Medraut's curls. "Do we have enough men here to dispatch more warriors to him?"

I nodded. "We do. Don't worry. I won't leave us poorly defended. We have our craftsmen, our older warriors and our boys. But I think Arthur will need all the men he can get for this." I paused, setting my jaw in determination. "I've decided it should be me who takes the message to Arthur."

Two sets of eyes flew wide open. "You can't," Coventina gasped. "It's too dangerous for a woman to go."

I shook my head. "You forget. I've killed a man with my own hands – sword – and I took part in the defense of Vindolanda. I'm not some fancy lady who sits and sews all day."

"You can say that again," Coventina said. "But just because you're bad at sewing doesn't mean you should be leading an army."

I gave her my best hard stare. "And just because *you* couldn't do it, doesn't mean I can't. Where I come from, women do all sorts of important jobs – and some of them fight in battles."

"Like the Amazon women," Morgawse put in. "I read about them once, in a book that came from Gaul." She frowned. "They had one breast removed to better fire their bows. You won't do that, will you?"

A chuckle escaped my lips. "No. That's a bit drastic, don't you think? And Arthur would have something to say about that. But I've got my chain mail to wear, and I'll take a helmet and shield… and my sword. I've no intention of fighting, just of finding Arthur, and being able to defend myself if I have to." I encompassed them all in my gaze. "Archfedd's big enough now for me to leave. And I know you two will care for my children."

In the corner Maia's head shot up from her sewing. I backtracked in a hurry. "I mean, help Maia look after them. She's as good as another mother to them." A satisfied smile crept over Maia's face, and she resumed her stitching.

Coventina's eyes clouded. "Will you be taking Rhiwallon?" He was fourteen now and nearly as tall as his father, but still willow thin and gawky with it.

"Do you want me to?"

She bit her lip. "He wanted to go with Arthur, but Cei said he couldn't. He's bursting with wanting to be part of the army – to take part in his first battle. I don't know if I should stop him. I feel as though it would be unfair."

She paused. "Both Cei and Arthur had already been blooded by his age – he keeps on telling me that." A little smile drifted across her face. "But to me he's still my baby, even though I have Reaghan now." She put a gentle hand on Reaghan's red hair, an exact match for Cei's and Rhiwallon's. "I shan't be having any more, not after last time. I don't want to lose my firstborn. My only boy."

"You have to let them go," Morgawse said, with a sigh, her eyes wandering to where Medraut was organizing the boarding of Noah's Ark, in a loud and strident voice. "We're women and mothers. From the moment they're born, we know they're only ours temporarily. That one day all too soon they'll suddenly be their father's, their king's, their friends'. It seems only the other day Medraut was on the breast, and now he's already on the path to becoming a warrior."

I dragged my gaze from Medraut and returned it to Coventina. "If you want me to, I'll take Rhiwallon. But if you don't, you only have to say."

She twisted Reaghan's rag doll in her hands, eyes brimming with indecision. "I daresay as how I can't keep him at home with me much longer. He'd not forgive me for it. He's always wanted to follow his father. So, yes. I think he'd best go with you. Other boys his age will be, won't they? His friends?" She laid the doll on the floor. "Those that didn't ride off with Arthur in the first place."

Morgawse nodded. "And if Gwen's intent on going, then there's no reason for Rhiwallon not to go too. He's probably a sight better at fighting than Gwen is."

⸻ ⟫⟫⟫⟨⟨⟨ ⸻

I ROSE BEFORE dawn the following day, a sense of eager excitement upon me. That I'd be finding Arthur after so long apart loomed largest, the delivering of the message taking very much second place. As I pulled on my leather braccae, it felt almost as though he were here with me, getting ready to ride just as I was. Hugging that thought to my aching heart, I stepped out into the Great Hall in my mail shirt and with my sword hanging by my side.

Elen, the wife of Riacus, magistrate of Vindolanda by the Wall, had taught me how to use my weapon, a thing I'd be eternally grateful for. She and I had slain a Dogman who'd somehow managed to survive the fall from the town walls and escape into the streets. There'd been no time then for shock about what we'd done, and after, when the siege was over, we'd had other things to think of.

In my own world, having had a hand in the deaths of two men would have singled me out for prison, or at the very least, counseling. Here, it made me confident I could look after myself, and brought me up to an almost level footing with my husband's warriors. They might not have agreed, but I didn't care.

The heavy rain of yesterday persisted. Not an auspicious start to my journey. Merlin, who'd returned disheveled after nightfall with no explanation as to where he'd been, already sat astride his horse, his cloak drawn close about him, hood up and shoulders hunched.

Cadman and his five fellows were strapping their saddlebags to the saddles of fresh horses. I'd been right – they didn't intend to take the offered rest. Brave warriors, all of them.

"We thank you for your offer of hospitality," Cadman said when I walked over to see them. "But my king has need of every able-bodied man, and although we are old, we still have arms to bear weapons and legs to carry us into battle." His gaze ran over my military outfit. "And I see the stories I've heard of King Arthur's queen are not all the works of fevered imaginations."

Was that a hint of respect in his eyes? Did he see me differently now I was dressed as a warrior queen?

I smiled, wiping the rain out of my eyes. "If a king cannot go, then a queen must."

"May God go with you, my lady." He made a deep bow, and, turning to his horse, mounted up.

My men had already assembled. Last night I'd called them to me in the Great Hall and explained my plan. Surprisingly few of them looked upset that I intended to lead them. Even Merlin, when he finally turned up, offered no objection. I was the Luck of Arthur, after all.

Llacheu brought Alezan from the stable block. She skittered across the cobbles, tail swishing and ears back, at her most mareish, but he was a good handler, and he held her firm.

I took her reins. "Thank you."

He grunted, then added a deep sigh. "I wanted to get her ready for you. The next best thing to coming, I suppose."

"You're eleven," I retorted. "Not even you can say that's old enough to be a warrior."

He scowled, the image of his father. "Rhiwallon gets to go, though." A jerk of his head indicated where his one-time friend stood laughing with three older boys, all of them mounted and ready for the off, their helmet straps hanging loose.

"He's considered a man now," I said, hating the words as they came out of my mouth. But this was the Dark Ages, and fourteen was no longer a child. Arthur had led an army at that age.

"It's still not fair," Llacheu muttered, keeping a hand on Alezan's bit to steady her as I struggled to mount.

I tightened the reins to stop her swinging around, and swung up into the saddle. "Can you fetch my shield? I left it by the door into the hall."

One-handed, I fastened my helmet straps while Llacheu trudged to retrieve my shield, his every step illustrative of his dejection. The shield was a light one. Those carried by the men would have been too heavy for me, and at my request Arthur had commissioned an especially light version, with my golden dragon ring painted on a dark background. Llacheu brought it, and I hooked it on one of my saddle's four horns, next to my saddle bags.

Coventina and Morgawse emerged to stand on the platform in front of the hall, sheltered from the rain by the overhanging thatch, with the children gathered around them. Maia stood a little back holding Archfedd, who was sucking on a wooden giraffe. When I'd shown my drawing of this animal to Devin, he'd scoffed at me and said it was a creature of my imagination. Arthur, too, had expressed doubt, even when I'd tried to explain to him about Africa. Amhar, on the other hand, believed every word I told him, and had an interesting collection of animals he'd most likely never see in the flesh.

He and Reaghan stood holding hands beside Coventina, my son's little face alight with excitement at being allowed to watch the army's departure. I'd already said my goodbyes inside, but the sight of them tugged at my heart, bringing tears that had to be dashed away with the back of my hand. Warrior queens don't cry. With my love for Arthur tugging me one way, and my love for my children the other, I walked a precarious path between the two.

At last, we were ready.

"You're in charge," Merlin said, coming up beside me. "You should lead the way." He swept his hand toward the gates.

With a final wave to my family, and a lump in my throat, I threaded Alezan through the throng of men, Merlin following close behind. Nowhere near as many men followed us as Arthur had taken when he left, but nevertheless, I'd mustered a formidable number. Now and then a warrior reached out a hand to touch me as I passed, taking on the luck they believed I brought them.

In the west, a few patches of blue showed between the clouds, and the rain lessened a little. At the head of my warriors, I rode through the double gates and onto the narrow, curving pathway that led down the hill and onto the plain.

Chapter Nine

"WE CAN RIDE up to Caer Gloui where there're still a couple of bridges across the river, or we can take the ferry across the estuary," Merlin said, as our horses clattered down the road toward Caer Baddan, our nearest large town. If you could call it a town, considering its state of extreme dilapidation. I'd been shocked the first time I'd seen it, but now I knew most of the old Roman towns were in a similar state, thanks to a systematic depopulation that had been going on for over eighty years.

"The ferry?" My voice rose in doubt. I'd had experience of that ferry across the wide River Severn before, and it hadn't been something I'd wanted to repeat. Ever.

He nodded. "The ferry would be much quicker, even if it has to go back and forth several times to fetch all our men over." He had the hood of his cloak thrown back, and a slight breeze ruffled his hair as well as mine. A relief from the sultry summer heat that had descended as soon as the rain stopped. "If we take the road west from Caer Baddan, we'll reach the ferry tomorrow. Instead of crossing straight over, the ferryman can let his boat drift downstream to Caer Legeion."

"What?" My eyes shot wide open at the very thought of what he was suggesting. I'd had a morbid fear of water from the time I'd fallen in a neighbor's swimming pool as a small child. "Drift miles down the river? Down the *River Severn*? It's practically the sea."

He nodded again. "The Sabrina River. Worth the risk to save several days riding and get to Arthur all the quicker."

I shuddered. I might be the brave warrior queen inside my head, but that did *not* extend to risking my life again in a rickety and very unseaworthy-looking ferry across one of the most dangerous stretches of water in the British Isles. "No, thank you very much. I think we'll go by the bridges at Caer Gloui."

Merlin's dark brows knit – probably in frustration at my contrariness. "It's nigh on a hundred miles to Caer Gloui, and once we're over the bridges we'll have to double back to Caer Went. That's another thirty miles. A good three days of extra riding. And that might not even be where we have to head…"

I glared at him. "Quite frankly, I don't care. Nothing is going to get me back in that leaky, wobbly old ferry." I shivered as the memory surfaced of how we'd had to lead our horses over the makeshift gangplank. "King Coel will just have to wait that little bit longer. We go by Caer Gloui – and the bridges."

Merlin shrugged. "If you're sure…"

I glanced at the column of men behind us. "Yes, I'm sure."

"YOU MIGHT HAVE warned me," I said to Merlin, my voice brimming with accusation. We were standing with our backs to Caer Gloui's tumbledown city walls, staring at the prospect before us. The city, or what remained of it that hadn't been carted away to build field walls, houses and barns, sat on the eastern bank of the River Severn – Merlin's Sabrina River. Its main west gates, behind us now, still stood, mostly in situ, although the upper levels had already been partly looted.

Before us stretched the low-lying lands that surrounded Caer Gloui, the city the Romans had called Glevum and that would become Gloucester in my time. Now I could see the reasoning behind that nursery rhyme my mother had sung to me as a child – *Dr. Foster went to Gloucester in a shower of rain. He stepped in a puddle right up to his middle, and never went there again.* It had been raining on and off for several weeks, and if Dr. Foster had happened along, he'd most definitely have been up to his middle in a lot of places.

Across this expanse of very wet wetlands rose a couple of uninviting wooden bridges. Well, to be fair, stone supports and wooden superstructures. But in between them the raised causeway, the *agger* the Roman road ran on, in places lay submerged under what could well be several feet of murky flood water. But it was the state of the nearest bridge I was berating Merlin for. From where we stood, the fact it had seen far better days was glaringly obvious.

The wooden guard rails either hung askew or had vanished altogether. Perhaps taken for firewood by the locals. Who knew? And the boards on the actual roadway appeared to have sizeable gaps in them. The sole consolation here was that the bridges only stretched over the river's normal channels. Not that you could easily tell where they were, other than by looking at the position of the bridges.

I glared at Merlin. "Is anyone who lives here brave enough – or stupid enough? – to use these bridges?"

He had the grace to look a little guilty, as well he might. "Last time I was here, they weren't in such a bad state." He shaded his eyes, squinting into the distance. "I think they're crossable, if we take it carefully."

He had to be kidding. "With warhorses weighing half a ton? *Lots* of warhorses, to be exact. Really?"

He flashed me a look of annoyance. "Do you want to go back and take the ferry, then?"

For a minute we sat in silence, our horses content to wait for our decision. Maybe they, too, didn't fancy a dunking.

"How far upriver to the next bridge?" I asked, eventually. "Or a ford. Is there a ford anywhere?"

He shrugged. "Not one we can use while the river's in spate like this. With all this rain, any ford will be dangerous, if not suicidal."

"And this isn't?"

Another shrug. "Your decision."

Irritation coursed through me. Yes, I'd said I'd lead the men, and yes, my decision should be final. But this was something I didn't know enough about. And my fear of water had resurfaced with a vengeance. He didn't need to know that, however.

From behind us came the murmur of voices as the men chatted together, unperturbed by what lay ahead. I was the Luck of Arthur, and they had a touching faith in me I didn't want to lose, even though I didn't share it myself.

However, we didn't have time to find another crossing place, even if one existed. The people of Ebrauc were depending on me finding Arthur and sending him to their aid. And if he'd come this way, then so could we.

I gathered Alezan's reins. "If you think we can do it, then that's what we'll do," I said, setting my jaw in determination even though my heart had started pounding in overtime. "Walk on." I squeezed my horse's flanks and she set off down the slope to where the floodwaters began. Luckily, she didn't suffer from the same phobia as I did, and stepped out boldly into the water, kicking it up behind her.

A moment later, Merlin brought his own horse in by my side, a grin on his face. "Nothing ventured," he said, and winked at me.

My annoyance burgeoned a little more. How could he be so off-hand? This wasn't a game. The first bridge looked anything but safe, and if any of it gave way beneath our not inconsiderable weight, someone was likely to drown. What would Arthur have done? Had he really come this way himself?

I twisted in my saddle to face the men behind me – *my* men. "The bridge isn't complete. We need to keep to the sides if we can, and leave a good gap between each rider. Just in case." I took a deep breath. "I'll be leading the way."

A ragged cheer went up. No doubt they believed the bridge would be safe for me, and that if they followed in my footsteps, they'd all be fine, too. Fingers crossed. I could only hope they were right.

Alezan splashed along the causeway, the water rising to knee deep, the fields to either side a vast lake. Ahead, a fast brown current tumbled through the bridge's stone supports. At least *they* appeared sturdy and unlikely to collapse. Most likely there were floods like this every year. I'd certainly seen the area around Gloucester flooded in my old world.

The causeway rose to meet the first bridge's eastern abutment, and Alezan's hooves no longer splashed in the floodwater. The start of the bridge was stone cobbles, the gravel topping presumably washed away, with robust stone parapets to either side that hid the view of the drop into the turbulent maelstrom. But all too soon the stone underfoot gave way to wooden planking.

On the far side, the hazardous woodwork became stone again, the distance at once short, and yet at the same time incredibly long. With the biggest gaps down the center, we'd have to walk at the side of the bridge and try to keep our horses' weight over the hopefully sturdy supporting timbers. But with no railings, and only a narrow width of planking to walk on, the way was precarious and foolhardy.

I drew in a deep breath. If Arthur had brought his men this way, then so could I.

Heart pounding ever more frantically, I turned my face away from the drop, which, although the water level had risen considerably from what must be the norm, seemed huge. Unfazed by the danger, Alezan stepped out across the untrustworthy timbers, her neat hooves picking their way so close to the left edge I wanted to slide off her and lie flat on the ground, hanging on for dear life and never moving again. Only it wasn't ground, but timbers that might be rotten with age. So not such a good idea.

I dared a peek over my shoulder to find the men had taken my advice and spread out, following with no sign of fear. Such was their touching faith in me, charlatan that I felt. Merlin, a full horse's length behind, gave me an encouraging grin I had to force myself to return, my jaw wobbling.

As Alezan's hooves hit the stone-built descent from the bridge, I realized I'd been holding my breath for far too long. I gulped in air as she splashed down into more floodwaters and headed for the second bridge. Behind me, the noise of many hooves doing the same, and no panicked screams, told me my men had negotiated the first bridge unscathed.

The water deepened, running muddy and opaque, with a strong current dragging along bits of greenery and small branches. But horses are heavy creatures, anchored by a leg at each corner, and now we bunched up together, riding three abreast, supporting one another against the pull of the water.

"Just one more bridge to go," Merlin said. "Then we'll be home and dry."

Had he guessed my terror? I probably wasn't hiding it all that well.

I kept my eyes fixed on the second bridge, as that was the only thing keeping us to the line of the causeway. My stomach twisted with a new fear. If I wasn't careful, Alezan might miss her footing and slip off the road's raised agger into deeper water. If anyone did that, they'd be washed away and lost.

My poor heart still hammering so hard a heart attack seemed imminent, and my breath coming in short pants, we reached where the road rose out of the water toward the stone-built abutments of the second bridge. A sigh of relief sneaked out – until I saw the state of this bridge.

The first one had been bad enough, but this was worse. Great empty spaces over the rushing brown waters gaped across the bridge, some of it with only a few feet of planking remaining on one side. And it was longer than the first one had been, over a wider channel of the river.

I swallowed the hard lump of fear that had risen in my throat. We couldn't go back now. We had to go on. I kept my legs on Alezan's sides, and she stepped onto the dark wooden planks. They creaked under our combined weight, and my heart did a leap that sent my stomach twisting into knots. Ahead, a wide gap stretched. I mustn't look down. I mustn't. The roaring of the water filled my ears.

Alezan kept going, either unaware of my fear, or so confident she didn't care. Usually, nerves communicate themselves to horses, and if you're afraid, they are too. Maybe, after all, I *was* doing a good job at hiding my terror.

From behind me came the creak as Merlin's horse trod the same dodgy planks as Alezan. I didn't look back. Fixing my eyes on the far abutment of the bridge, determined to ignore the huge temptation to look down into the raging waters, I urged my horse forward.

The narrowest bit lay ahead. Broken planks jutted into thin air. I kept my eyes on the path I wanted Alezan to take, my breath coming so fast I was in danger of hyperventilating. The planking groaned. Was that the crack of splintering wood? I fixed my gaze on the bridge abutment, willing myself to get there. Alezan's hooves trod stone.

We were across.

In a moment Merlin was beside me. Heaving an enormous juddering breath, I turned my head to look him in the eye, and found admiration there. But the men were still on the bridge. We hurried down the slope and back into the floodwaters to give them space, heading to where the land rose in the distance, and the road emerged from the water.

We hadn't lost a single man or horse, but there was no way I was coming back by this route.

CAER WENT LAY thirty miles southwest of Caer Gloui and our precarious river crossing. My one consolation was that a ferry crossing with the river in spate like this would have been impossible, so taking the road to the ferry would have cost us time. I'd made the right decision to come the long way around, terrifying as it had turned out to be.

We crossed the River Wye, that Merlin called the Guoy, by an altogether more robust construction, to my relief, late in the afternoon. Evening was drawing in as we approached Caninus's town of Caer Went, and its high, many-towered walls, a place I'd last seen straight after Arthur had drawn the sword from the stone.

The sturdy double gates remained firmly closed until we were within hailing distance, and only when the guards were satisfied of who we were did they swing one side of them open and allow us to enter. This was a place, along with Caer Legeion, ten miles distant, that I'd visited more than once with my father. Hard to believe he'd driven our battered old Land Rover down the very same road our horses were now taking – fifteen hundred years from now.

As with so many Roman towns in Britain, now their builders had been gone nearly a century, change had eroded the old way of life, and the pre-Roman Celtic traditions, which had been lying dormant, had largely taken over. Where once houses had stood in every carefully laid out quadrant of the town, small fields had taken their place, green with growing vegetables, fruit orchards and even some wheat and barley. A patchwork of different textures.

Thanks to the lateness of the day, not many people were still about, and those that were paid us scant attention. They had work to do – tending livestock, weeding vegetable patches, sweeping the streets in front of their homes.

The old forum and ruins of the once enormous basilica came into view, occupying the central and most important spot in the town. Once, the basilica must have stood sixty feet tall with several floors and been the center for administration of this part of the Roman province. Now, though, the roof had gone, and the walls had crumbled to half their original height. Through the entrance, I glimpsed empty market stalls around the sides, beside boarded up entrances to what might have been shops, and heaps of rubbish. Undulating flagstones covered the ground, vigorous weeds poking up between them. A reek of sad decay assaulted my nostrils.

Merlin headed to the left, down a side road, and within minutes we were standing in the courtyard of a mansio – the equivalent of a modern motel. At the end of the short street, a bricked-up gateway marked the abandoned southern entrance to the town.

"We should settle our men in here, then pay our respects to Caninus," Merlin advised. "His guards will have told him of our arrival already, no doubt."

I slid down from Alezan, gladder than I'd have admitted to have the ground beneath my feet again. It was a wonder all warriors weren't bandy-legged.

Down one side of the courtyard stood a row of open-fronted, thatched stalls, a few tatty horses already tethered in their shelter. Roomy enough for all our mounts. I glanced around at my men, all dismounting as stiffly as I'd done. However much you were used to riding, day after day of long hours in the saddle left you stiff. Even young Rhiwallon and his friends looked relieved to have their feet on the ground.

However, our horses' needs came first. A cavalry is no good if its horses aren't well looked after. I tied Alezan up in one of the stalls, untacked her and set about rubbing her down, greasing her tack, and giving her water and fodder. All along our horse lines every man did the same.

With my horse settled and eating her hay, it was at last time to attend to my own needs. Carrying my helmet and shield, I followed Merlin into the cool interior of the mansio, where an elderly man, wearing a too-short tunic over bandy, skinny legs and with a fluffy fringe of hair circling his otherwise bald head, lay in wait for us.

"My lords," he began, then did a double take, his voice rising to a surprised squeak. "I'm so sorry. My *lady*." He bobbed a not very neat bow.

Merlin set his helmet on the long table of what appeared to be the inn's dining room. "This is Queen Guinevere, wife of the High King." No beating about the bush here.

The man's jaw dropped, his expression going from disbelief to shock. The sweeping second bow he made revealed the liberally freckled top of his head. "At your service, M-milady." His voice was muffled, as he managed to say this while examining his feet.

"Do get up," I said. "What's your name?"

"Ewyn, Milady." He straightened, eyes wide – probably at seeing a queen dressed like a warrior. It seemed his fringe of fluffy gray hair had gone into shock as well, as it now stood out around his head like a dandelion clock.

"Well, Ewyn," I said. "My men and I are tired and sore after our long journey. I need to visit my cousin, your king. But first we all need rooms. And I need hot water for a wash. A bath if you have it."

Being a queen had its advantages. Within a very short time I'd been given a small but comfortable room equipped with a bed, a chair and a rickety table. Three servants brought a wooden bathtub lined with a linen sheet and some buckets of steaming water. I removed my mail shirt while they fetched more water, then kicked my boots off, watching the steam rise tantalizingly from the bath. The days since leaving Din Cadan had made me sweaty, dirty and smelly.

Six more buckets and the tub was full enough. I sent them away and, having struggled out of the rest of my clothes, dipped a grubby toe into the water. Warm enough to make me jump straight in. I lowered myself into the tub, the hot water creeping up my body. Too small for submersion, but better than the bucket of tepid water I'd once had at a similar establishment, while the men all went off to the bath house. A location that had turned out to be next best thing to a brothel. Hopefully this mansio, in the austere Caninus's town, wouldn't turn out to be similar.

Half an hour later, glowing from my ablutions and wearing the one gown I'd brought with me, my wet hair neatly braided, I knocked on Merlin's door.

After a few moments he appeared, his long hair as wet as mine and slicked back from his thin face. Those servants must have been kept very busy carting hot water.

"Food first," Merlin said. "Then we go to Caninus's house."

Nerves twisted my stomach. Might this king know where my husband had got to?

Chapter Ten

CANINUS'S HOUSE LAY in the western quarter of the town, on the main street. Once, it must have been the home of a wealthy Roman merchant, perhaps the town magistrate, but now it had become the royal palace.

Merlin and I, shunning the offer of guards, chose to walk there alone along a twilit, tatty street that reeked of animal excrement, household rubbish and urine, empty now of all but a few people. On the corner, we passed a tavern where lamplight spilled out onto the dirty cobbles through unshuttered windows, and the sound of merrymaking came tumbling from the open door.

The main road, the Ermine Way, was in a slightly better state, its cobbles swept clean by the individuals who lived there…or their servants. Light peeked from the cracks around firmly closed doors and shutters, and the tang of woodsmoke fought to overpower the baser town stink that came creeping in from the backstreets.

Word had gone ahead announcing our arrival, and the two armored guards standing by the main doors of the palace stood back to allow us entry, smartly saluting as we passed. In common with the rest of the town, an air of ongoing decay clung to the genteelly shabby building.

In the center of the torchlit atrium, a fountain played in a small square pool, beneath a roof opening that let in the cool night air. Shabby, ochre-painted pillars supported this roof, and underfoot a geometric mosaic decorated the floor.

Two more guards stood just inside the doors, hostile eyes fixed on us, and for a moment my stomach did a nervous twist. I'd been here before, not so long ago, but that had been in Arthur's company. Just because Caninus was his cousin, and had appeared friendly at the Council of Kings, didn't mean he would be in his stronghold.

The sudden clatter of a chair being pushed back drew my attention, and I turned toward the sound. A door stood open onto an antechamber. Inside, a grizzled warrior was getting to his feet. Unlike the guards, he wore no mail shirt, but a sky-blue tunic, decorated at the neck, hem and cuffs with embroidery, that marked him out as a man of importance. His swarthy, heavily lined face broke into a smile of recognition as he spotted Merlin.

He stepped forward to meet us. "Merlin, well met. And this is…?"

Merlin made the smallest of bows to the stranger, as though he were an equal. "Macklyn, may I present Queen Guinevere, wife of the High King." Last time we'd been here it had been with such a force that we'd had to camp outside the walls. Only Arthur and Merlin had gone to the palace.

"Milady." The man made a deep bow, and, straightening, stared curiously into my eyes. His were nearly as dark as Arthur's but half-hidden by folds of wrinkled skin. "Welcome to Caer Went and the king's palace. I hope your accommodation in our town is to your liking."

I smiled at him and held out my hand. He took it in his ink-stained fingers, and, bending again, to my surprise kissed not my hand but the ring on it. A bit like when people greeted the pope in my old world.

"We're lodged in the mansio by the south gates," Merlin said. "I judged that the best place to stay, rather than impose ourselves on you here in the palace."

"Most wise," Macklyn said, leaving me wondering why this should be so. But he didn't give me much time for speculation. "I assume you're here to see my master?"

Merlin nodded. "The Queen seeks an audience with King Caninus."

Macklyn turned toward the atrium's interior doors, closed now night had fallen. "This way."

He led us into a large, gloomy courtyard. Around the edge ran a colonnaded walkway with uneven flagstones underfoot and tall pillars supporting the overhanging roof. Steps led down into a sunken garden in the center, the scent of aromatic plants heavy in the warm night air.

However, Macklyn kept to the shelter of the walkway, so reminiscent of the palace at Viroconium that it brought back unpleasant memories of the time I'd had to hide from warring soldiers in its kitchens, and help Karstyn, the cook, deliver Morgawse's son. We passed from dark shadows into pools of light created by the few torches set in iron brackets on the pillars, their smoke curling up into the night sky.

Macklyn halted outside a set of ornate double doors embossed with heavy carvings and a hint of what might have been gold leaf still clinging on. Two more stern-faced guards stood sentry, swords on their hips and the butts of their tall spears resting on the ground beside them. As we approached, they swung their spears in front of us, making a cross to halt our progress.

"At ease, men," Macklyn said, and they swung their spears back out of our way. He pushed one side of the doors open, and stood back to let us enter.

We found ourselves in a shadowy, lamplit anteroom of some kind, with bench seats down one side and a long table down the other. Another mosaic covered the floor, this time depicting a sea monster surrounded by fishes, undulating a little as had the flagstones. Subsidence, no doubt. A man sat at the table, writing. He raised his head to look at us.

If I hadn't met Caninus before, I'd have taken him for a secretary.

He wore only a long, cream tunic, unadorned by even the smallest amount of embroidery, and when he got to his feet, just a plain leather belt showed, cinching his narrow waist. No sword, no dagger, and no braccae either – only a pair of rather skinny legs, and bony feet in open-toed sandals.

A spare man, older and not as tall as Arthur, he perhaps favored his late father, Uthyr's older brother, Ambrosius. Close-cropped, graying hair clung to his head in a tightly curling cap, and a shadow of dark stubble, speckled with gray, covered his square, determined jaw. He might not be so physically impressive as either of his cousins, but about him hung an aura of latent power that filled the room.

He came around the table and held out his hands to Merlin. "Welcome to Caer Went."

Merlin clasped his hands for a moment before stepping to one side.

Caninus's eyes settled on me, where I stood a little behind Merlin, still in the shadows. "Queen Guinevere, if I'm not mistaken." Even here, in private, he spoke with the deep, melodious tones of a stage actor. A voice I could have listened to even if he were only reciting a shopping list.

"My Lord King," I swept him a curtsey, even though I knew they wouldn't be around until the time of Henry VIII. A long gown cried out for one, so why not?

"Call me Caninus, please."

"And I'm Guinevere."

He grinned. I'd only ever seen him at the Council of Kings, when he'd been busy conducting the council, a position afforded to him due to his late father's status. Then, he'd seemed austere and aloof, a man very conscious of his responsibilities. Now, his almost boyish grin transformed his face, giving him a look of his cousin Arthur in the best of moods. "Welcome to my palace, Guinevere."

I couldn't help but smile back. "Thank you, Caninus."

He gestured to the seats around the table, and we all sat down, not quite close enough for me to be able to see what papers he'd been working on. I saw so little of the written word here, naturally I was nosy.

"What can I do for you both?"

"We're looking for my husband," I said, coming straight to the point. "He's needed in the northeast. We've had messengers from King Coel of Bryneich." While Merlin sat and listened, I recounted everything Cadman had told me, finishing with, "Do you have any idea where Arthur is?"

With obvious regret, Caninus shook his head. "Not now, I'm afraid. He *was* here, of course, but not for long. There's been trouble with the Irish all along the south coast between here and Dyfed. Even at Caer Legeion, well defended as it is. The Irish raiders swooped in and managed to set fire to some of the fleet. I marched to the coast with my army, but they'd already fled. That's our biggest problem – in their ships they can strike anywhere they like, and are away before I, or any of the kings, have time to react. On Arthur's orders, Theodoric has taken the rest of his ships to sea to try to follow them. But the sea is large, and ships are small…"

He shook his head. "Arthur rode west from here, trailing them along the coast, but that was weeks ago. I've heard nothing since."

Much as I'd feared. South Wales stretched over a hundred miles west, and finding Arthur, despite the size of his army, would be like finding the proverbial needle in the haystack. I glanced at Merlin for help.

He rubbed his chin, the sound of his stubble scraping loud in the silence. Then he fixed his eyes on Caninus. "We don't know this coastline well. But you must have men who do. Can you send out scouts to see if they can locate him? That would be better than us marching further west where we might completely miss him by just a few miles."

Caninus leaned forward, elbows on the table, eyes alight. "I do indeed have such men, and stations where they can get fresh horses. I'll dispatch them at first light. It's possible his army may be as far west as Dyfed, though. Agricola's lands are rich and attractive to raiders, but his coastline has high cliffs and rock-infested waters, as well as being well-defended. Let's hope Arthur's not gone that far."

Merlin nodded. "Thank you. That would suit us well. The Queen's men are tired and in need of a day or two of rest. As are we."

Caninus glanced at me. "Are your men installed in the mansio?"

I nodded. "Very comfortably. We are as well."

He got to his feet. "Nonsense. You'll be staying here for the next few days whilst we await the return of my scouts. I'll not take no for an answer."

⸻

I HAD TO admit the rooms allotted to me in Caninus's palace were a lot larger and more comfortable than the cell-like room I'd had in the mansio. And the bed much more comfortable than the one Meirchion of Rheged had given me when Arthur and I had stayed a night at Caer Ligualid at the western end of the Wall. But I felt a bit guilty at abandoning the men I was supposed to be leading. However, they didn't seem to feel the same, and it took Merlin to point out that without me to watch over them, they'd feel a lot freer to enjoy the fleshpots of Caer Went.

How typical.

"I do hope they don't take Rhiwallon," I said to Merlin, as we stood in the walkway outside our rooms, which were side by side. "He's only fourteen."

Merlin chuckled. "High time he became a man then, in more ways than one. If he's old enough to fight, then he's old enough to drink and whore."

I clamped my lips together to keep down the reply itching to burst out. A lot of things about the fifth century went against everything I'd been brought up to believe. And growing up too soon was one of them. Although probably becoming a warrior at fourteen and being initiated sexually by some stranger was better than working in a cotton mill or down a mine in the nineteenth century. Was it only a modern idea that children should remain children for such a long time? Maybe I'd better say goodnight to Merlin before I said something I'd regret.

I went into my room, closing the door behind me with more energy than it required. But he probably didn't get the message.

⟫⟫⟫⟪⟪⟪

WE REMAINED AT Caer Went for three long days. The men seemed to be taking full advantage of the pleasures of the town, both in the taverns and in the brothels – which very handily occupied a side street only a stone's throw from the mansio. Probably by design. I made no enquiries about what Rhiwallon and the other boys had been up to, so I wouldn't have to lie to Coventina if she asked me.

Late on the third day, the first of the scouts arrived back, and Caninus asked Merlin and me to come to his office.

He was seated at his long table, with two mud-splattered and travel-weary young warriors standing before him. We took our seats beside the king, and he indicated to his men to repeat what they'd discovered.

The first young man cleared his throat. "I rode as far as Moridunum, at top speed as you said. Changed horses as often as I found new ones. The same on the return. But the High King hadn't been there. Nor had any of the innkeepers where I took food and changed horses seen him or his army."

The second man, younger and slighter, with a shock of short, upright-standing ginger hair, stepped forward. "I had better luck. I took the road southwest, skirting the coastal settlements. There's been much raiding down there – villages burnt and people slaughtered or snatched. I was able to follow the High King's trail west. I found not just fishing villages destroyed but farms inland raided, as well. And the heathens had desecrated the churches and murdered the priests. But everywhere I went, I found the High King had been there first. He left me a handy trail of dead Irishmen to follow. Those who survived in the villages had hung the raiders' bodies from their gallows trees."

My hopes rose. "And did you catch up with him?"

He shook his head. "I returned to you when I discovered he'd struck north, pursuing a great army of Irish raiders heading inland. Perhaps toward Viroconium itself."

Merlin's eyebrows shot up into his hairline. "They dare to take their army inland? To the very heart of Britain?"

The young man nodded. "It's a huge army, so I was told. Perhaps they think their numbers make them safe. I returned as fast as I could to warn you."

I stared at Merlin. "Viroconium? Arthur's gone to help *Cadwy?*" For a moment the thought that my husband had gone mad occurred to me. Then common sense cut in. It wasn't Cadwy he'd be helping – it would be the people of Powys. He couldn't let an army of foreign invaders strike at the beating heart of Britain. Even if it did mean helping, or even saving, the brother he hated.

I swallowed. "We need to march north to find him. He's going to need our reinforcements. And we have that message to give him."

Caninus transferred his gaze from the two young men to Merlin and me. "I can furnish you with extra men to take to my cousin, but I can't leave my town undefended. For all I know there could be more raiders waiting out to sea, ready to land their currachs on our foreshore."

I stood up. "I understand. Thank you for this news and for sending scouts. And for the offer of your men, which I accept." My eyes met Merlin's. "We should march north for Powys tomorrow and try to join up with Arthur."

Merlin didn't rise, but sat very still, his dark eyes unreadable. Viroconium. And Morgana. Was that where we were headed?

>>><<<

WE SET OFF north the next morning at first light, following a road I'd ridden before, on both occasions heading south and leaving Viroconium and everything I hated about it safely behind. I wasn't happy to be taking this road again, but at least it was roughly in the direction Arthur had gone in. If we were lucky, we might catch him up and turn out to be of some use before he met the Irish army. We now had a sizeable force of sixty warriors, a small army by the standards of the day.

We made good time. The branch of the minor Roman road we had to follow remained in good condition. Our cavalry spread out to the rough ground on either side whenever they could, as we followed the rising hills north into what would one day be the Forest of Dean. We crossed the river by a sturdy bridge at Blestium, a small industrial township that reeked of the fires required for smelting the iron ore brought in from the mines in the forest.

From Blestium, the road north descended into sprawling river valleys, where marshy ground frequently surrounded the road on both sides. Only the surviving agger lifted us safely above swamps made worse by the persistent summer rain. Horse flies and mosquitoes plagued us in these damp lowlands, biting animals and people without discrimination.

However, no sign appeared of the passing of any other large force of men. No burnt-out farms. No churned-up tracks. No dead bodies. No droppings on the road. If either the Irish raiders or Arthur and his army had come this way, they'd left nothing to show for it, and I couldn't help but worry in case we were on a wild goose chase.

In one of the drier valleys, we made camp for the night in a deserted farmstead, the crumbling walls of the house still standing to shoulder height. This wasn't the work of invaders, though. The growth of stunted saplings and tall weeds pushing between the tumbled stones indicated its inhabitants had been gone a long time. An air of loneliness hung over the ruins, making me wonder at the fate of the people who'd once lived here.

But I didn't have time to speculate. Merlin stood back and left it to me to organize the rota for the night watches. Then the men lit fires and cooked themselves tasty stew with the dried meat Caninus had supplied. Darkness fell, and the sky above us spangled with a myriad of stars hanging above the sleeping world.

I sat on a large rock looted from the farmyard wall, eating the hunk of black bread I'd used to wipe out my stew bowl, while the men passed around a skin of cider. On the far side of the fire Rhiwallon took a long slug from the skin, then, with a grin, passed it on to his friends.

A boy become a man. He even had a few wisps of ginger beard breaking the surface of his spotty chin. How different he now seemed to Llacheu. He'd left his boyhood friend far behind him on this expedition, his journey into manhood. Not long now until Llacheu was the same. A sobering thought. And Medraut and Amhar wouldn't be far behind.

Time was not my friend.

The flames of the fire crackled and leapt as one of the men added wood to it, and motes of red-hot ashes leapt towards the dark sky.

"How far now to Viroconium?" I asked Merlin, trying to distract myself from my sobering thoughts.

He'd perched on the rock beside mine, with his long legs stretched out straight in front of him. He stifled a yawn. "Forty miles, maybe a bit more. I hope we'll catch up with Arthur before we get that far."

I sighed. "If he's even going this way. We only have the word of one messenger that he is. We might be headed in quite the wrong direction." Oh, for cellphones, so I could have just called him. How much easier would that have been? The further we rode, the more Britain seemed to stretch larger, with Arthur ever more distant. My heart ached with an intense longing to see his handsome face again, to have him take me in his arms, to curl naked in bed with him…

Merlin interrupted my reverie, holding out the skin of cider. "Such is life."

Irritated, I took the cider, and putting it to my lips, swallowed a few long gulps. That was better. I passed the skin back to Merlin. "I don't know how you can accept this lack of communication. It makes life so much more difficult than it needs to be. Surely there ought to be some way we can get news from all over Britain a bit quicker?"

Merlin pulled a maybe sort of a face, but didn't say anything.

I frowned, an idea forming. If we set up a messaging network, news of danger would permeate about Britain much faster than it did now, which had to be a good thing. Coel had been forced to send a troop of half a dozen men, old, yes, but armed, to take his message to the High King. Now, because Arthur was away fighting, I was wasting time chasing him around when he should have been heading north to support Coel against the Saxons.

"What about beacons?" I said to Merlin. "Could we set up beacons that are visible one from the next? To light when danger threatens and help's needed?"

Merlin passed on the cider to the next man. "That's an idea. But how would we know what the beacons meant? A light is a light. It can only mean one thing. And it might not always be the message we wanted to convey."

True. I screwed up my face in concentration and waved away the offer of the next skin of cider. Caninus had sent riders out to the east, and they'd swapped tired horses for fresh ones, making their journey faster. What if that extended all over Britain? What if a man could mount a horse in Ebrauc and gallop to the next station, where he could take another fast horse. He'd be able to ride the two hundred plus miles from Ebrauc to Din Cadan at twenty miles an hour. Ten hours or less. Half a day. And one man wouldn't have to do it all. There could be relief riders posted at intervals along with the horses so a message could be carried and passed on from man to man. Like the Old West's Pony Express. That had been superseded very swiftly by the railway, but that wasn't going to happen here.

I turned to Merlin, and began to outline my plan.

Chapter Eleven

IN THE MORNING, the sun came out, chasing away the last of the rain clouds. After a breakfast of hard bread and the cold remnants of last night's stew, that made me nostalgic for toast and marmalade, we mounted up and set off once more along the road. An advance guard rode on ahead, in case danger lay close by, and a rearguard took up position a mile behind us.

We continued due north through the wide marshy valleys of a maze of rivers, most passable by fords, a few by less than well-maintained bridges. On both sides of our road, the drier lands climbed to distant, thickly forested hills, and in the hazy far west, the Welsh mountain peaks rose in jagged teeth.

Grazing sheep dotted the rough grassland up to the dark forest edge, and here and there a few deer ran for cover when we approached. Small farmsteads, like the ruined one we'd stayed in last night, huddled above the marshlands on dry spurs of ground. Only the smoke rising from their thatched rooftops told us they were occupied.

"I thought about your idea overnight," Merlin said, edging his horse in beside Alezan, as overhead a couple of angry crows mobbed a peregrine falcon, intent on driving it away. "They say new ideas are best slept on."

"Unlike that lumpy ground where we chose to camp."

He chuckled. "You seem to have a knack of choosing the spot with the most roots and rocks. *My* bed was very comfortable."

"What conclusion did you come to?" I asked, ignoring his jibe. "Does it still seem to you as useful as it did last night, when you were half drunk on all that cider?"

He snorted with laughter. "I'm never drunk."

As that didn't merit an answer, I waited for him to go on.

"I think it could work, but it requires the cooperation of all the kings. And that you might not get. Some of them are so parsimonious they won't want to have good horses standing idly by to hand over to riders from another kingdom. Meirchion of Rheged to name but one."

We'd had experience of that king's lack of willingness to help anyone else when we'd been fighting along the Wall. Meirchion was one of those kings who unless he himself was directly threatened, would not see danger to others as something he needed to bother about. Probably many of the kings were like that.

"But some of them will think it's a good idea, surely?" I had to rein in Alezan as she took an ears-back swipe at Merlin's horse. Not a team player, she really could be very grumpy with other horses. "And we can persuade them it's in their own interests. They'll see that, won't they?"

Alezan swished her tail in protest and tossed her head, snatching at the bit.

Merlin shrugged. "We can but try. I think Arthur will agree this is a good suggestion." He paused, brows knit. "Is this an idea from your world? Is it how you send messages there?"

I bridled. "Sort of…" I couldn't tell him we no longer needed anything more than a computer keyboard or a cell phone, could I? To bridge the entire planet. Although he'd brought me here from my world, he had next to no knowledge of what it was like.

He flashed me a confident smile. "Then it should work."

If the other kings could be brought into line.

Our way continued across the low-lying borderlands between England and Wales, straight as Roman roads usually are. No gentle curves, just a few angled turns, because their surveyors didn't go in for curves. Too fiddly.

Around midday, in thick forest, we stopped to rest our horses and eat a meal of onions and hard cheese, washed down with warm cider. One thing about long journeys on horseback – most meals, no matter how sparse and plain, tasted like the food of the gods.

We'd just remounted and set out again when galloping hooves sounded. From around the turn ahead of us, two of our scouts appeared, belaboring their horses with the ends of their reins used like whips. In a flurry of kicked up gravel, they yanked their horses to a sliding halt in front of us, the beasts snorting from the exertion, sweat darkening their flanks and flecks of foam adhering to their coats.

"Milady," gasped the first one. "Milord Merlin. Ahead of us. Irish raiders. Their full army. Not far ahead."

A buzz of excitement rose from behind me as the message filtered back as if by osmosis.

"How many? Going which way?" Merlin snapped, staring past the two young men as though he expected the Irish to come running over the brow at any moment.

The young warrior shook his head. "Heading north, same as us. Too many to count. Three hundred – maybe four. All on foot though, as is their habit."

A big army indeed.

"What of the High King's army?" I asked, trying hard to keep my voice calm. "No sign of them?"

He shook his head again. "We saw no one but the Irish. Two miles ahead."

At least that meant we could take a moment to stand and decide what to do without them coming upon us. Four hundred against our sixty would have been terrible odds.

Merlin shook his head as though to clear it. "They've not come by the same route as we have, or we'd have seen plenty of signs of their passing. They must have come along the foothills of the mountains to the west, across country, keeping their feet dry. Maybe they don't know about the old legionary roads."

"Where are we?" I asked. "How far now to Viroconium? Are we even in Powys yet?" The temptation to let the raiders get on with it and attack Cadwy was enormous. Teach the bastard a lesson.

"A good thirty miles to go yet," Merlin said. "But we're in Powys all right." He frowned. "I'd assume their target to be Viroconium, but you never know. With an army of four hundred, they probably think they stand a good chance against Cadwy. The Irish are a contrary race. I once met one who told me it never ceases to rain in their homeland, which is why they keep on coming over here. Looking for a dry spot to live."

That would normally have made me laugh, it being so true of Ireland, but under the circumstances, with a huge enemy army up ahead and only sixty men under my command, it wasn't the place for mirth. "I wish we knew where Arthur was with the rest of the army," I muttered, half to myself and half to Merlin.

"We'll have to call a halt and let them move on," Merlin said. "We can't attack a force that size. And being on foot they'll be slower than us. The last thing we want to do is catch them up. Or let their scouts spot us."

I glanced at the thick forest to either side, an idea forming. I turned to the scouts. "Did you say they're following the road?"

The second young man nodded. "We saw the signs of where they'd joined the road before we spotted them. A lot of freshly trampled ground where it was wet and muddy. They'd come down out of the forest along a rough track that brought them to the road. We knew to be wary, so we took good care as we continued. They don't march like an army, though. They were all over the road, and some of them looked drunk."

The other young man butted in. "If you ask me, they've not long looted someone's villa. Only in a place that large would they find the ale and wine to get so many of them that drunk."

I nodded. "And they think themselves safe enough to do that. So they can't suspect they're being followed – by us or Arthur." I shook my head in frustration. "If only we knew where he was."

The midsummer sun burned down on the back of my neck, and my skin itched under my heavy mail shirt, impossible to scratch. I turned to Merlin. "What lies ahead of them on the road? Isn't there a town coming up soon?" If my memory served me, a small town lay a few miles further on at a confluence of several waterways – with no bridge, but a stone-lined ford.

He nodded. "Maybe ten miles distant. A long-abandoned fort occupies a hilltop to the west, and just after that lies the town of Breguoin on the north bank of the river. Roman once, but all British now. Not a huge population, and not well defended. Easy pickings for raiders bold enough to venture this far from the coast."

I stared down the empty road. "We can't just leave them to their fate. They'll rape the women and take the children as slaves, after they've killed the men." Thoughts of Ummidia and her daughters pricked my heart. Certainty that Irish raiders would be every bit as bad as Saxons made my stomach twist at the images that leapt into my head.

Merlin rubbed his chin. "Even if its walls are defensible, which I fear they're not, we don't have enough men to help them defend their town."

Alezan fidgeted under me, impatient to be off again. I checked her fiercely. "But we're on horseback and the Irish are on foot, and drunk." I pointed at the woodland. "If they can travel through forest, then so can we, and faster than they can." I twisted in my saddle to look back down the ranks of warriors and raised my voice. "Is there any here who knows the paths in this forest? A man of Gwent, perhaps?"

A rumble of muttered conversation ran through the men. Then a rider moved forward, dark haired and helmetless, hardly older than Rhiwallon. "I were born not far to the south of here, Milady," he said, jerking a thumb back the way we'd come. "I used to know these woods well, as a boy."

"Good." I beckoned him forward. "Do you know a way to Breguoin from here? We need to travel through the forest as fast as possible to warn the townspeople, and remain unseen from the road."

The boy nodded. "I do that." His dark eyes danced with excitement – oh for the bravado of youth and excitement at what lay ahead instead of fear.

"What's your name?" I asked.

"Peredur, Milady."

I fixed him with a hard stare. "Well, Peredur, we're relying on you to get us to Breguoin with time to evacuate the town to safety before the Irish arrive. Lead on. Quickly."

With a somewhat out of place grin of delight, the boy took the lead. Glancing over my shoulder, I saw Rhiwallon's equally excited face, where he rode a few horses back with the new friends who'd taken him off whoring and drinking in Caer Went, all of them a year or two older than him. For them this was one great adventure.

At the first small path we came to, Peredur branched off, heading left-handed and uphill into the forest. Just a narrow deertrod at first, it soon widened into a track we could trot and canter along, although the sweeping branches made it impossible to go flat out over the muddy, uneven ground.

Without hesitation, Peredur chose more side paths going off at angles that would have rapidly had me completely lost, had not the weak overhead sun given me a hint of direction. We kept up a steady pace, cantering wherever we could and only walking down the steepest, roughest slopes.

Ten miles is a long way, even on a horse, and a speed of eight miles an hour would have been good, getting us there in an hour and a quarter. By my reckoning we made it in nearer an hour, emerging from the forest on sweat-soaked horses into the wide river valley where the town lay.

All appeared peaceful. Small, fenced-in fields of wheat, oats, and barley lay scattered about the town in a patchwork of ripening shades, interspersed with fields full of delicious cabbages and the leafy tops of root vegetables. Sheep grazed on the open hillsides, and shaggy-coated cattle waded hock-deep in the marshy ground around the river, searching for the sweetest morsels of grass. Smoke rose from the houses sheltered within the tumbledown walls of the town. A peaceful sight. Lying this far inland, the inhabitants probably never in their worst dreams imagined danger heading their way.

Without hesitation, we cantered down the grassy slope, scattering indignant, bleating sheep to right and left, heading for the road and the river crossing. A few barefoot young shepherd boys turned to stare at us, then bolted after their sheep, whistling their dogs frantically. Sixty armed riders could mean nothing but trouble.

Nearer to the town, shirtless men, and women with their long skirts tucked up out of the way, labored in the fields on the south bank of the river. Seeing us, they turned frightened, wide-eyed faces in our direction, holding up their hoes and rakes defensively.

Merlin shouted to them as we passed, "The Irish are coming!" And we splashed through the shallow ford in front of the town. They dropped their baskets and ran.

On the north bank, the road led through what had once been a substantial gatehouse but now was nothing but a ruin, the walls no taller than my head while mounted. The gates had long gone, and the height of the stone curtain walls undulated between almost ground level and the height of a man. Nothing here that would defend the inhabitants from a bloodthirsty army of drunken Irish raiders.

We trotted through the empty gateway into a town made spartan by the loss of houses. A primitive wattle church to the right of center rose a little higher than the thatched rooftops, and between the buildings, more small fields spread out where once houses and workshops must have stood. A farming village, not a military one.

"The Irish are coming!" Merlin bellowed. The people in the street or in their vegetable patches dropped their tools to stand for a moment, staring at us, open-mouthed.

I stood in my stirrups. "Run!"

They ran.

We scattered down the side roads and between the buildings, shouting to the people still inside the houses to get out and run. Chaos. Men shouting. Women screaming. Children wailing. The inhabitants rushed into the streets, faces white with fear, clutching babies to their chests and dragging small children by the hand. Dogs ran everywhere, barking excitedly as though this were some kind of game. And from the lean-to hut beside the church, a tall, thin man in long brown robes emerged, the pate of his partly shaven head gleaming in the sunshine.

A deceitful blue sky burned overhead, as though challenging that this was a day of danger.

"To the forest," Merlin shouted, as people ran past him in all directions. "Go east. Run. Leave everything and run."

A few people were trying to load handcarts. Some, rendered ham-fisted by terror, harnessed nervous bullocks to heftier vehicles.

"You don't have time," I shouted at a pot-bellied, middle-aged man trying to pile all his worldly possessions onto an ox cart. "They're less than an hour away."

The man glared up at me as if I were mad. "I won't leave everything I've worked for to those heathens."

Merlin swung his horse around. "Better to leave them than to leave yourself. They don't take prisoners. Not unless they're young and pretty, which you're not."

Indecision flitted across the man's ruddy face. Then, as his portly wife waddled out with an armful of bedclothes, he grabbed her with no more ado and heaved her into the driving seat. Springing up beside her with amazing agility for his age, he cracked his whip at the pair of rust-red oxen, and the cart rumbled toward the eastern gates.

I trotted Alezan along the main street toward the wattle and daub church where it stood along one side of the small market square. Small hummocks surrounding it marked where Christian burials had been made, all but a few grassed over, one or two even decorated with wilting flowers. The priest stood in the doorway of his church, his bony jaw set, and his face determined.

"You need to get out," I called to him. "They kill all holy men."

He glared up at me, thanks to my helmet probably unaware that I was a woman. "I will not leave my church to their desecration. Leave me be."

Fool. I knew from Merlin's history lessons what foreign raiders did to priests. And women. "Suit yourself," I snapped at him, and wheeled Alezan away. Other more appreciative people remained to be rescued.

Beyond the church, houses stretched up toward the tumbled north gateway, our men hurrying between them, leaning from their horses to bang the pommels of their daggers on the closed doors. Why were people so slow to react? Didn't they realize this was a matter of life or death? Did they think we were joking?

I trotted to the north gateway to find it in a worse state of repair than the south one. In the distance, a group of small boys were playing in the grass with an inflated pig's bladder, just as I'd seen Llacheu and his friends do at Din Cadan. Football, fifteen hundred years before the Premier Division. Setting my heels to Alezan's sides, I urged her into a canter, then pulled her to a skidding halt beside the boys.

They stared up at me in shock, eight sets of eyes fixed on my face, mouths hanging open at the sight of a fully armed warrior.

"Run," I gasped at them, fear robbing me of my breath. "The Irish are coming. Don't go back to the town, go east." I pointed towards the wooded hills, not close enough for comfort. "Run as fast as you can, and hide. They take boys as slaves."

For just a moment they all continued to stare at me, then the biggest of them tugged his shaggy forelock in respect. "Come on," he shouted, and they turned and ran, their football left forgotten in the grass.

I watched them for a moment as they legged it over the grazing lands with more speed than their elders, then swung Alezan back around. Already, people were pouring out of the eastern gateway, heading up the cart track toward the dark line of the forest. A few rode horses, mostly beasts of burden, lumbering at the head of the flight – some with wives or children perched behind the rider.

One or two carts brought up the rear, their drivers belaboring the straining draft animals. And behind them, people on foot ran in dribs and drabs after their fellows. Our men were helping as best they could. Was that Rhiwallon with a girl perched behind his saddle, her arms about his waist?

Touching my legs to Alezan's sides, I urged her back into a canter. In moments I was through the gateway and turning to the right down a side street, shouting to the few people who remained to hurry, that we had no time before the Irish arrived. They ran out into the main street, leaving me alone for a moment.

"Hey," someone shouted. "Over here. I need help."

I swung Alezan into a narrow alley leading off the street.

Something hit me hard in the chest, shooting me backwards off Alezan, arms flailing. As I hit the ground the air shot out of my lungs, my head thumped the cobbles, and everything went dark.

>>>><<<<

HEARING CAME BACK first. Birds singing somewhere far off. A hen clucking to herself, and her feet scratching in the dirt near my head for a tasty morsel. Where was I?

If I moved my throbbing head, it was sure to fall off. Was that light shining through my eyelids? Bright, hot light. Was I in bed?

With infinite care, I opened my right eye just a slit, and closed it again, dazzled by something huge and fiery right above me. It took a moment or two to work out it was the sun.

More feeling returned, and with it the sensation of lying on something hard and knobbly. My fingers stretched out, and the tips touched cobblestones. What was I doing asleep on a road? If I hadn't been worried about the security of my head, and the pain, I'd have shaken it.

A flake of memory returned. I'd fallen off my horse. No, someone had knocked me off her. Fear surfaced – had I broken anything? My neck, maybe? I wiggled my toes and found they worked, shifted one leg at a time, then lifted first one arm then the other, just a little, and stretched my fingers. All of that worked, so hopefully I hadn't done serious damage. Except my head.

I tried to move it and found the back hurt the worst. Gingerly placed fingers found a large swelling where it must have struck the cobbles. My helmet. The straps hadn't been done up. It must have come loose when I fell.

The rest of my memory flooded back. Breguoin. I was in Breguoin, and the Irish were coming. Heedless of the pain lancing through my head as though I'd been stabbed with a red-hot poker, I rolled onto my side and managed to push my body into a sitting position. The world rocked a few times then came into focus. I was lying in a silent, empty street on dirty cobbles. House doors hung ajar, a few chickens scratched about, and a small brindled dog ran past with a joint of cooked meat clasped in its jaws. Apart from him, not a soul was to be seen.

And no Alezan.

Of course. Some ungrateful bastard had knocked me off to steal her for himself and left me to the fate we'd come to rescue him from.

The Irish.

They were coming. I had to get up.

Leaning on the rough wattle and daub wall of the nearby building, I struggled to my feet, and stood there swaying, waiting for the world to stop rotating. Probably I had a concussion, but now wasn't the time to worry about it.

I heaved in a few steadying breaths as nausea threatened, and stood more upright, fighting the urge to let my legs collapse under me. Apart from the carefree birdsong coming from some of the bushes in the abandoned gardens, silence reigned.

I had to get out. Where were my men? Had they all forgotten me? And where was Alezan? Anger surfaced. A vision of the chaos of shouting mounted warriors and screaming running people flashed into my head. Of course. Probably not their fault they hadn't noticed my absence.

On unsteady legs I tottered from house wall to house wall, heading for the end of the street. Surely someone must still be here? Someone who could help me. At the corner of the last house, I leaned against the wall, breathing deeply again as sickness welled up in my stomach. I touched a hand to the still growing lump on the back of my head and winced, hoping I hadn't cracked my skull. No way would I get my helmet back on there again, even if I could find it.

Gathering my courage, I took a peek around the corner. The road gave an unobstructed view past the church on the left to the south gateway. My heart almost stopped beating. Hordes of savage and probably drunken warriors were pouring in through the entrance and over the ruined walls in a rising tide, barging into the houses on either side, their shouts lifting to the skies.

The Irish were here.

Chapter Twelve

TRANSFIXED WITH TERROR, I stared down the Roman road that bisected the town of Breguoin as nearly four hundred Irish raiders began their rampage. At least they weren't in a hurry. But that was a small blessing. It must have been three hundred yards from the north to south gateways, but it might as well have been only thirty, for all the difference that was going to make. Some of the keener ones would reach this end before long, and I had nowhere to hide.

Deep, guttural shouts came from inside the houses, and sticks of furniture catapulted through broken doors to be smashed to splinters in the road by huge double-handed axes. Someone ran out brandishing a burning torch and hurled it onto the nearest thatched roof. It rolled off the steep pitch and hit the road in a shower of sparks. Undaunted, the man picked it up and held it to the thatch's edge until the dry reeds caught. Flames leapt and black smoke billowed upwards.

They were laughing, and most likely swearing, only I didn't understand their shouted words. Gaelic, maybe, but excluded from whatever magic had given me the ability to understand British speech. Huge, bearded men, some already reeling drunk, burst out of houses clutching food and flagons of beer and cider, or waving pots and pans, tools and clothes. The raucous din grew louder by the minute.

Movement by the church caught my eye. The priest. The idiot had come to stand in his little churchyard, defiant, a wooden cross clutched, talisman-like, in his hands. I wanted to run and make him hide, scream at him to get away while he could. But I didn't. Instead, I watched in horrified silence as half a dozen of the ruddy-faced warriors swaggered up to him, flagons in one hand, axes in the other, jeering.

Some of them wore rusted mail shirts, others, leather jerkins that revealed bare, muscled arms. Long hair hung in dreadlocks, and thick ginger beards half-hid their faces. Even from a hundred yards away, I could sense their vicious delight at having discovered an inhabitant too foolhardy to have fled. Throwing aside their flagons of drink, they shifted their axes from hand to hand, almost in time with one another – like grotesque, land-bound synchronized swimmers.

One of them shouted, lips curling back in a snarl, and all his fellows guffawed with ribald laughter. The priest drew himself up taller, arms outstretched as though to protect his little territory, holding out his crucifix in front of him.

Too far away to hear the Irishman's words, or the priest's reply, I was close enough to see the blow that cleaved the tonsured skull in two, scattering blood and brains into the little churchyard to decorate the graves. For a moment the dead man remained upright, before toppling to the ground like a felled tree.

Turning away, I threw up the cheese and onions I'd eaten at our mid-day break, spitting bitter bile onto the paving stones.

I wiped my mouth on my sleeve, panting, tasting the sourness of my vomit. I had to get away before they did that to me – after they found I was a woman and raped me.

A glance over my shoulder showed me the silent side-street. Where was there to hide that they wouldn't find? Perhaps a barn. No, I could end up burned to death. Although might that be preferable to being raped, probably multiple times? Like Albina and Cloelia.

I peered back at the main street. If I made for the north gateway, they'd see me, even preoccupied as they were. I'd have a hundred-yard head start, but that was nothing. They were men, with longer legs and better stamina than I had. And there'd only been grassland, with a few stunted trees, in that direction. Nowhere to hide. If I tried to run east, to the forest, following the townspeople and my men, I'd lead the Irish raiders straight to them.

I pushed myself off the comforting support of the house wall, and stumbled back down the side-street toward the western rampart, thanking God that the town walls were so tumbledown. Ahead of me, the brindled dog sat chewing on his unexpected bounty beside a rickety garden fence. On impulse, I bent and grabbed the meat before he had chance to growl at me. "Come on boy, we have to get out of here." I couldn't leave him for the raiders to slaughter as they'd killed the priest. I *was* English, after all.

The dog ran after me, eager to retrieve his meal, growling a little at my cheeky theft.

I reached the end of the street. Three feet of partly robbed-out wall stood between me and the outside. I hurled the meat over, the dog leapt after it, and I scrambled in his wake.

I hadn't counted on the other side of the wall being at the top of a steep grassy bank. Neither had the dog. We rolled head over heels together to the bottom. He recovered first, snatched the meat, and bolted, abandoning me to my fate. Ungrateful hound.

Winded by a second fall in less than an hour, I lay still, flattened against the bank, struggling to regain my breath. Nowhere to hide. The sheep had done a good job of grazing this bank and ditch – not a blade of long grass as cover. If any of the Irish raiders came and looked over the wall, they'd see me.

My heart thudded and my breath came short and fast. The throbbing in my head made itself known again – the adrenaline of my flight had quite put it out of my mind. I winced, screwing up my eyes against the glare of the sun, trying to concentrate with a brain that could only foggily claw itself out of the well of pain.

I had to be about a quarter of the way down the western side of the walls, at the bottom of the deep ditch that surrounded the town.

Another grassy bank rose between me and the water meadows. If I could get to the far side of that, I might have a chance of staying hidden.

My breath coming a little more easily, I crawled across the bottom of the ditch, which was still wet and muddy after all the rain we'd had, and began my climb to the top of the far bank. I had to claw my way up its steep side, digging my fingers into the soil, hanging onto tussocks of grass. And all the while I was doing it, a horrible itching in the middle of my back had me expecting at any minute to receive an arrow, or worse, an axe, between my shoulder blades.

I didn't. I made it to the top unscathed and rolled down the far side, landing just a few feet from where the water meadows began, running down toward the sparkle of the distant, curving river. The calmly grazing cattle didn't even glance my way, as though nothing could happen to disturb the regularity of their lives.

Flattening myself face down against the earth, I hung on with desperate fingers and toes as though it might buck me off. A deep shudder of relief shook my body, and I kept my eyes tightly closed against a new wave of dizziness.

Minutes ticked by. I rolled onto my side, my breathing steadying, the sun hot on my body.

A shadow blocked the light. I opened my eyes. The huge figure of a man towered on the top of the bank, staring down at me, the sun behind bestowing on him a gilded halo.

I stared back, mesmerized with fear. He must have been over six feet tall – or he seemed it from where I lay. Long red hair hung to below his shoulders in tangled dreadlocks, and a thick dark beard had been stiffly forked with limewater. His sleeveless leather tunic displayed the bulging muscles in his hairy, tattooed arms. In his hand he held a huge axe.

He grinned at me, showing large, yellowed teeth, and spoke a few guttural words.

I didn't understand.

In one bound, he leapt down off the bank to stand over me, legs apart, one hand on his groin. I understood that gesture all right.

I rolled onto my hands and knees, scrabbling away from him, my right hand reaching for my sword. A fist shot out and grabbed me by my long plait, yanking me back so forcefully I crashed to the ground on my back, the air shooting out of me again. I had the sword half out of its scabbard when his other hand grabbed mine, pinning me down as he leaned over me. He said something else and laughed, leering at me from thick lips and lust-filled eyes.

For a moment, fear paralyzed me.

Then he bent and licked my face, leaving a trail of warm spittle across my skin.

His touch sent a shock of white-hot fury coursing through me. No. I was a warrior queen. I swung my knee up and caught him hard between the legs with all my strength.

With a high-pitched shriek, he staggered back, anger contorting and darkening his face. Anger and pain.

I scrambled to my feet and whipped my sword out, every bit as angry as he was. After all, he had no virtue to defend, and I did.

He stood, one hand on the offended organ, gasping and swearing. I should have gone in for the kill, but some vestige of the twenty-first century made me hesitate. Idiot that I was. Never give the enemy a chance to recover. Not one this size and holding an axe, anyway.

Raising his weapon, he advanced. I stepped back, my sword between him and me. Another grimace of pain distorted his face. Good. I'd done him damage.

The axe swung; my sword went up. Like someone swatting a fly, he knocked it out of my hands. I reversed some more, reaching for my dagger. He raised the axe again, blood lust in his sea-blue eyes, now I'd quenched his lust for sex.

He was young, his face barely lined by sun and wind, his nose crooked where someone had broken it for him in the past. Gold rings dangled from the lobes of his ears, and around his neck hung a chain of gold links. All this I saw in that fraction of a moment, as his lips curled back in fury to show his gritted teeth.

He was going to kill me, split my head like a melon as one of his fellows had done to the priest. I'd never see Arthur again, nor Amhar or Archfedd. A strange peacefulness draped itself over me, an acceptance that death was coming. At least it would be quick. Would I meet my father and tell him how I'd married King Arthur, lived my life as his queen? Born his heir?

Wait. What was I thinking?

I shook off the peaceful shawl. If he was going to kill me, then I'd make it hard for him. Knuckles whitening on my dagger, I took a step toward him.

Shock transformed the warrior's face. His eyes bulged wide, his jaw dropped open as a trickle of blood ran down his chin, and the axe slid from his slack hands. For a second, I thought fear of me had done that, then he toppled forward onto the grass at my feet. An arrow protruded from the center of his back, the feathered shaft still quivering.

My eyes were probably bulging too. I stared past him in the direction the arrow must have come from. Galloping across the water meadows came a phalanx of riders, the banner billowing in the breeze showing a rampant black bear. A white horse led the charge.

Arthur.

Legs suddenly unable to support me any longer, I dropped to my hands and knees as they bore down on me. Briefly, I raised my head and met Arthur's angry and accusing eyes, before he swept past on Llamrei, his men in close formation behind him. Beneath my splayed fingers, the thunder of their hooves shook the ground like a mini earthquake.

I knelt motionless, frozen to the spot by that look of fury.

Shouts rose from within the town walls. Weapons clashed. Screams, wailing, roaring. I couldn't move, but sat stunned on the grass beside the dead Irish warrior, concentrating on remembering to breathe. The knowledge that it was best if I kept well out of the way lodged in my head and held me there a long while, even after the strength returned to my limbs.

The sun hammered down, unusually hot even for a British midsummer. My mail shirt sat heavy on my shoulders, the sweat trickling down my back. Within the walls, the fight went on, heard but not seen. Smoke rose in black billows as houses burned. The shouts and screams continued. Horses squealed in pain and fear. My fears for Arthur rose with every long minute I had to wait, sitting on the grass beside the corpse of my would-be assailant.

Eventually, common sense made me get up and search for my sword. When I spotted it, I kept it clutched in my hand rather than stowing it back in its scabbard. Goodness knows where my helmet had got to. Without it, the dead Irishman had no doubt found it easier to work out I was a woman.

Armed and feeling more able to take care of myself, I slithered to the bottom of the ditch again. Using my sword as a kind of piton, I managed to climb back up the other side to stand crouched against the low wall.

No sound came from immediately behind it, so I dared a peek between the jagged stones. Nothing. The side-road lay empty, a couple of the chickens still scratching about as though nothing were going on. No dead bodies. No flames. Beyond the nearest thatched rooftops, though, smoke continued to billow as though more houses in the center of the town had caught fire. And although the noise of battle had diminished, it hadn't died completely.

I stood for a while, straining every sense, fingers hooked onto the topmost stones. Hoofbeats drumming on the turf to my left disturbed my vigil. Swinging around and almost losing my balance, I raised my sword, my other hand still gripping the top of the wall.

A man on a bay horse, carrying a shield – a blue falcon on a yellow background.

Merlin.

I'd half-expected it to be another Irish warrior, though why he'd have been on a horse I had no idea. My common sense had flown out the window with my bravery.

Merlin slowed his horse as he approached the far bank, his gaze fixed on me. Relief drenched me with such force I sat down with a thump and slid into the ditch again in a crumpled heap.

Merlin brought his horse to a halt and dismounted, then held out his hand. On shaky legs, I scrambled to my feet, and he heaved me to the top of the bank. "Are you all right?" His eyes went to the body of the Irishman. "What did he do?" Anxiety laced his words.

"I'm fine. He didn't do anything." I grimaced, angry at the tremble in my voice. "He was going to, but I kicked him where it hurts. That changed his mind for him. He'd just decided to kill me instead, when someone shot him in the back. I wasn't going down without a fight, though."

Suddenly aware my hand was still in his, I snatched it back. "Where were you?" My voice rose in anger, steadying the tremble. "Someone knocked me off my horse, and I hit my head on the cobbles." I put my hand up to the huge bump and winced. "When I woke up, everyone had gone." I poked him in the chest with an accusing finger. "Didn't anyone notice I wasn't there? Didn't *you* notice? I thought you were supposed to be looking after me." Anger was definitely making me less shaky.

He had the grace to redden. "I'm sorry." He tried to take my hand again, but I put it behind my back. "It was chaos. We got the townspeople into the edge of the forest in the nick of time. Everything happened so fast. We saw Arthur and his army arrive and charged down to join him. I didn't even know you were missing until Arthur told me he'd seen you outside the walls." He paused. "He sent me to find you."

"That's not good enough." I was properly furious now, probably a reaction to everything that had happened. "You all just left me!" Unwanted tears squeezed out of my eyes and ran down my cheeks.

Damn it. How not to look like a warrior queen.

I fought to stop them, but failed. A great heaving sob welled up, all self-control gone. "I saw them k-kill the priest." The image of his brains flying out of the great split in his head rose again and the tears flowed faster. I bent over and retched up bile as that was all I had left.

Merlin put a comforting hand on my back as I spat out the bitterness, my nose running.

After a moment, I straightened up, and he enfolded me in his arms, pressing me against his chest, one hand on the back of my head, his touch gentle. "You're safe now. The battle's done. The Irish that aren't dead or wounded have retreated down the road with their tails between their legs."

He smelled of horses, leather and sweat, warm and reassuring. I didn't struggle, but I didn't stop crying. I'd seen death before, many times now, but this was different. He'd left me alone, and I'd stared my own death in the face all by myself. I'd thought that warrior was going to kill me, and no one could save me.

We stood like that for what felt a long time, until at last my tears dried, and all I could do was hiccup pathetically. Suddenly conscious of his physical closeness and the impropriety of letting him hug me, his queen, I pulled away and wiped my snotty nose on my sleeve. No hankies in the Dark Ages.

He stepped back, eyes troubled. "Can you ride?" His words came out as stilted, perhaps made awkward by the amount of time he'd had to embrace his crying queen.

I wiped my nose again. Damned thing wouldn't stop running. A small nod was all I could muster.

He mounted swiftly, kicked his foot out of his stirrup and held out a hand. I set my foot in the discarded stirrup and sprang, his strength pulling me up to straddle his horse behind his saddle.

Oh, the relief of being on a horse again. I set my jaw in an attempt to stifle the hiccups. I was going to bloody well kill the man who'd stolen Alezan from me when I found him.

With my arms around Merlin's waist, we jog-trotted back to the north gateway and paused, staring down the main street. I had to lean sideways to peer around Merlin's body at the carnage. A few houses still smoldered, and so did the church. Corpses lay scattered over the road like broken dolls. Already, in the summer heat, flies buzzed over the mess of blood and brains and ordure. The stink of death filled the air. This was going to take a lot of clearing up.

"Is it safe?" I asked, into Merlin's chain-mailed shoulder.

For answer, he nodded. "They've gone, leaving only their dead behind them."

His legs moved as he squeezed his horse's sides, and she trotted down the main street, stepping with dainty care over the sprawled bodies. As we passed the church, I averted my eyes from the foolish priest, bile welling up in my throat again. I'd seen enough of what had happened to him before.

Arthur sat astride Llamrei in the little square at the center of the town. Sweat streaked her body, and blood too, but not her own. Arthur turned his helmeted head and stared.

"What are you doing here?" His voice held anger, relief, concern – in equal measures.

I loosened my grip on Merlin's waist, setting my hands lightly on his hips instead, no longer needing the support clasping him had given. "Bringing you a message, that's what." If he was going to be angry with me, then I could be angry back. "Only you're so hard to find I had to follow you all the way up from Caer Went. And then you weren't even bloody well here, and the Irish army was."

He glanced at his men, but most were out of hearing, some on foot moving between the dead and dying, finishing the Irish off with swift slashes of their knives. I'd seen the aftermath of battle too many times now. Every time it affected me, and I knew better than to look. Instead, I concentrated hard on Arthur, as around me groans were suddenly cut short.

Don't look.

His face softened, but only slightly. "What is it with you that you always think you can do everything better than we men can?" His brows met in a heavy scowl. "Merlin could have brought the message just as easily as you. More easily. But no, you had to come and nearly get yourself killed when you should be home with our children. If we hadn't seen you, and Anwyll hadn't fired that shot, which was risky as that warrior was so close to you, you'd be lying with an axe in your skull like that priest over there." He waved his hand to illustrate his point.

Don't look.

Telling him how I'd got left behind while we were sensibly evacuating the town, *at my suggestion*, didn't seem like a useful exercise right now. Merlin had probably told him what we'd done already. Anger took over, loosening my tongue more than was wise. "And if you had some kind of messaging system in place, I'd have known where to find you – or even been able to just send you the message without ever leaving Din Cadan."

His eyes flashed. He was angrier with me than I'd ever seen him before. *"Would you?* Are you sure? Or was this just another excuse to come chasing me down? To keep an eye on me because you don't trust me to look after myself?" His voice came out in an angry hiss, but he kept it low, no doubt conscious of not being somewhere private.

His men were keeping away on purpose now, eyeing us both warily from a distance. The fury must have been coming off us both in waves.

"If you *could* look after yourself then I wouldn't have to!" I retorted, getting angrier by the moment, to match him, but also keeping my voice low. This wasn't the reunion I'd envisaged. I let go of Merlin altogether and slid to the ground, folding my arms across my chest, then, when I'd done it, recognizing it a classic defensive posture. "And someone stole my fucking horse."

Llamrei sidestepped under Arthur's too tight hold on her reins, tossing her head and showing the red inside her nostrils. "Fine. We'll get her back. Then you can ride straight back to where you came from. I don't want women with me on my campaigns."

I turned away, biting back the tears that threatened to flow again. How had I messed up our reunion like this? Why was he so angry with me? And why was I so angry with him? That I was being an idiot was obvious, even to me, but so was he. I bit my lip and stayed silent.

Bloody Dark Age men.

Chapter Thirteen

THE AFTERMATH OF a big battle is always dreadful, not the joyous celebration you might imagine. Corpses, already beginning to stink in the hot sun, litter the battle site, and flies gather. The victors have to deal with not just their own casualties but also with disposing of the enemy dead.

Here, in Breguoin, we had to lure back the terrified townspeople to help with the clearing up, and they were nearly as afraid of us as they had been of the raiders. Not a surprise, really. Arthur's warriors must have been as alien to them as the Irish. Soldiers from a different kingdom who'd fought a fierce battle in their town and left houses burned to smoking ruins and countless stinking dead to dispose of, including their priest.

In the end, young Peredur persuaded them to return. As almost a local boy, and with the blush of youth still on him, he had a pleasing presence that calmed the people. As night fell, they came creeping in through the north gateway in dribs and drabs to try to pick up the broken pieces of their lives.

I didn't find the man who'd stolen Alezan. A small boy, no more than eight years old, dark haired and dark eyed, led her back. When asked, he told me he'd found her tied to a tree by her reins. Not wanting to leave her there alone, he'd taken her to his parents, probably hoping he might get to keep her. With little on me to offer as reward, I found a simple, oval, gold brooch, embossed with the dragon emblem of Dumnonia, that I wore sometimes with my gown.

I pressed it into his grimy little hands in front of his wide-eyed parents. "What's your name?"

The boy stared up at me in awe. "Llawfrodedd, Milady Queen."

"Well, Llawfrodedd, this is for you to keep for when you're a man," I said, giving the parents a hard stare. "My horse is worth far more than this to me, and I feared I'd lost her. Keep it safe. It's proper gold and could even buy you a fine horse of your own one day, and a sword. Perhaps, then, you'll become a warrior, like Peredur."

The boy's parents, the mother clutching a toddler by the hand and a snot-faced baby to her breast, stared at me in awe. Most likely they'd never seen gold before.

Peredur, who'd brought the boy to me, grinned, white teeth flashing in his filthy face. "It's a fine life. You could do no better." He gave the boy a jolting slap on the shoulder. "Come to Dumnonia when you're older and fight for the High King, as I intend to do."

The boy nodded, mouth open as wide as his eyes, small fingers clutching the brooch.

Now I had Alezan back, I felt a little less aimless and useless. I took her to the horse lines that had been set up in one of the fields inside the walls and spent a long time grooming and fussing over her, whispering my troubles into her receptive ears.

"Bloody men. So unappreciative. You'd think I'd committed a crime the way he treated me, instead of doing him a favor." I rubbed her forehead. "Bad tempered git. A bit like you." She nuzzled my front, probably hoping I had a treat for her. "Sometimes I wonder why I bother with trying to help."

A few horses down from Alezan, Rhiwallon was working on his horse, as deep in conversation with her as I was with mine. The sight brought a much-needed smile to my face. I'd long since come to the conclusion that each warrior loved his horse as much as or more than he did his wife, and it seemed Rhiwallon was no different. The girl he'd rescued earlier had been hanging around him hopefully, but his horse came first in his affections.

Cei came stumping out of the gathering gloom of evening, leading his tired steed, his eyes roving over the horse lines.

"Father!" Rhiwallon raised a hand.

Cei's face lit up. "Rhiwallon!" For a brief moment, father and son stood gazing at one another, before Cei opened his arms and Rhiwallon ran into them, a boy again, just for now. Cei held his son as the long seconds ticked by, arms tight around him, a glow of pride enveloping them both.

Embarrassed to witness this tender moment, I turned back to Alezan. Out of the corner of my eye I saw them separate, then push the horses apart and make a space where Cei could squeeze his horse in beside Rhiwallon's. I brushed harder, conscious of a lump of solid emotion forming in my chest.

How quickly would the years fly by before Amhar, too, was riding to his first battle? However much I told myself I'd adapted to life here in the perilous Dark Ages, I could never truly leave behind my old life. Would I be able to accept my son riding off into battle with his father with as much equanimity as Coventina had?

I was going to have to. Unbidden, the image of the priest leapt into my head and my stomach rebelled. I bent over, retching as quietly as possible, bringing nothing up but bitter bile. I tried, with little success, to spit it away.

Wiping my mouth on my sleeve, I turned back to the warm comfort of my horse, burying my face in her sweet-smelling mane.

Full darkness had fallen before I finally wandered back to where our campfires burned, their vibrant flames leaping up toward the almost full moon. The already unpleasant bodies of the dead had been loaded onto ox carts and taken outside the town to the meadow where they'd be burned in the morning. And, where they could, the townspeople had sorted out their homes. Those whose homes had burned were sleeping in the church for the night, the roof of which had only smoldered.

In the field beside the horse lines, our men were already cooking supper. The aroma of roasting mutton drifted through the air, making my belly rumble. I'd thrown up my mid-day meal, and breakfast seemed an age ago. But where was I supposed to find a spot to sit?

With a heavy heart, I trudged from fire to fire, searching the flickering circles of golden light for Merlin's friendly face, but there was no sign of him anywhere. Nor Arthur. My anger had finally dissipated during the time I'd spent with Alezan, and I'd been hoping his had too.

"Gwen!" Cei's voice sounded out of the dark. He and Rhiwallon were seated with a group of other men, a few of them just boys. "Come. Sit down here with us. With my brave warrior son."

Rhiwallon bridled like an embarrassed girl. "Father!"

Unable to hold back my smile at his discomfort, I took a seat beside them, perching my bottom on a handy rock looted from the wall. The leaping flames darkened the surrounding night, and the warm glow of the other cookfires made comforting bright circles within the dense blackness. Firelight flickered over the faces of the seated warriors, casting them in planes of light and dark that bestowed on them a spooky, otherworldly appearance.

Cei, a skin of cider in his hands, grinned a welcome to me, eyes twinkling.

Rhiwallon, his face glowing pink with heat and the remnants of his embarrassment, turned to me. "Milady Guinevere, thank you for allowing me to be part of this," he began, his voice now permanently deep, like his father's. "My first battle. Everything I thought it would be." The voice of innocence – happy, excited, proud.

Clearly not the same experience I'd had, then.

Cei clapped him on the back, his grin even broader. "My boy's a man now."

Rhiwallon flushed redder still, staring down at the earth between his booted feet. "Father, no," he muttered.

One of the other boys, sitting across the fire from us, laughed, carefree as a bird. "Same for me. My father would've been proud of me today."

"Would've been?" I glanced across at him. "Where is your father?"

The boy's narrow chest expanded with pride. "He died. At the battle of Celydon Wood. He was a hero."

One of the battles Arthur had fought north of the Wall a few years ago.

I frowned. How did dying when your son was just a child make you a hero? The bitterness returned. Would that happen to Cei, sitting so large and solid beside me? Or to Bedwyr, now downing a large mouthful of the cider? Or to Arthur? Would any of them see their sons grow to manhood?

That lump reformed in my throat, and the tears, that had been so near the surface since the Irish attack, threatened to return. Might I be suffering from shock? I swallowed down the lump and pressed my lips together in an effort to take back control. I had to stop being so emotional. I was a warrior queen now, and I needed to remember it.

Footsteps sounded, and a dark shape loomed out of the night. Arthur stepped into the firelight. He still wore his mail shirt but had discarded his helmet. The orange glow of the fire camouflaged the dirt on his face and hands well, but did nothing to disguise the deep shadows beneath his eyes. He looked exhausted.

He couldn't have seen me at first, because he sat down heavily on one of the lumps of rock the men had dragged into a circle to make seats. As he did so, a deep sigh escaped his lips. Setting his elbows on his knees, he leaned forward and dropped his head into his hands for a long minute. When he looked up, his tired eyes met mine, widening in surprise – and perhaps relief.

I held his gaze, keeping my face immobile, waiting. My anger and bitterness vanished in a puff of smoke, replaced instead by a deep longing for him to take me in his arms and tell me he'd forgiven me, as I'd forgiven him. And a wish to wipe away his tiredness and have him sleep in my embrace.

The reflection of the fire danced in his eyes like a burning heart. My heart. I drank him in. His dark hair, streaked golden by the fire's glow, curled about his grubby forehead, loose strands hanging over his almost black brows. Blood had crusted on his right cheek, just beneath his eye, and on his bottom lip. Several days' growth of beard shadowed his jawline.

God, how I loved him. And how I wanted him. What was it about him that set my pulse racing whenever I laid eyes on him? What made me physically ache for him when he was gone?

The corner of his mouth twitched. Could he read my mind? See the longing in my eyes?

My own mouth did the same.

Hands on his knees, and with a visible effort, he pushed himself to his feet. Two steps brought him to stand in front of me, eyes still fixed on mine.

I couldn't have dragged my eyes away if I'd wanted to. Not that I did, of course. I could have melted into those dark peaty pools.

He held out his hands. Dirty, blood-stained hands. Hands that had killed today. Hands that I loved. Hands that I longed to have hold me, touch me, love me.

Putting my own hands in his, I felt the familiar calluses on his palms, the roughness of his fingers. The hands not of a High King in a palace, but of a warrior who fought alongside his men, who led the battle charges from the front, who ensured his men were fed and cared for before ever thinking of himself.

He pulled me to my feet, and I came willingly.

As he stood a good five inches taller than me, I had to tip my head back to keep on gazing into his eyes.

The twitch at the corner of his mouth became a small smile.

"When will you ever learn to be a proper wife?" But he, too, had lost his anger. His voice, low and gentle, held just a hint of loving mockery. His hands slid up my arms to my shoulders. "I'm sorry I was angry with you. It's because I love you so much. I thought that Irishman was going to kill you, and I was too far away to save you."

Cei snorted. "It's only thanks to Anwyll, and his prowess with a bow, that she's here still."

I took a breath, wanting to kiss the hurt from Arthur's bloodied lip. "I'm sorry, too. I only came because I love you. Not because I want to control you." I paused. "I want to be able to see you for myself – every day. Be with you." I lifted one of my hands and set it on his mail shirt, over his heart. "I…I sometimes feel my time with you is just borrowed."

"For God's sake," Cei said, in disgust. "Give her a kiss and have done with it."

A few shouts of encouragement echoed around the fireside.

Arthur's battered mouth curved into a smile that reached his eyes at last. "Come here then, and kiss your husband. Your men want you to." He pulled me closer and, bending his head, kissed me softly, perhaps a little wary of the hurt on his own mouth.

The men cheered.

"It was her idea to get to the town before the Irish raiders," Merlin's voice said, out of the darkness. "Without her determination, most of the townspeople would have died."

Arthur and I parted, his hand going to the cut on his lip that had begun to bleed again.

Merlin stood beside the fire, grinning. "And she has another good idea she wants to tell you about."

We all sat down again, me next to Arthur, after some judicious juggling of seats – like a children's party game of musical chairs – and Merlin on his other side. Someone passed us plates of roasted mutton and bread. We ate, suddenly ravenous. Then Merlin and I outlined the idea I'd formed about a British Pony Express.

Arthur, and all the warriors around our fire, listened with rapt attention, his arm draped around my shoulders, holding me close, his body warm against mine, stoking my internal glow. After we'd finished, a murmur of conversation arose, as everyone talked at once.

Arthur held up his hand. "She's truly the Luck of Arthur," he began. "And the brains." The men all chuckled, as they continued to pass around the cider. Probably most of them were more than a bit drunk by now, as the supply of cider seemed never-ending.

He turned to me. "The idea's a good one. The Romans had something like this, but it fell out of use long ago. Our only problem will be the number of kingdoms and their difficult kings we have to persuade to join us in this. At least the Romans ruled a single province here – unlike us." He grinned. "But I have the advantage of being High King, and, supposedly, what I say, goes. We can but try. I'll bring it up at the next Council. For now, though, we'll have to bide our time and wait for better communications." He chuckled. "And cross our fingers."

The fire had reduced to glowing embers by the time we all retired to our beds. Arthur took my hand and led me to where he'd laid out his own bedroll, and spread mine beside it. Having taken off our mail shirts, we lay down fully dressed, me on my side, him curled around me from behind, his face close enough to my ear to warm it with his breath. All around us the rest of the men – bar those on guard duty in case the Irish came sneaking back in the dark – lay down to sleep.

Despite the hard ground and how dirty I felt, a veil of contentment settled over me, warming my heart and chasing away the fears I had for everyone I loved in this dangerous world. Arthur's arm draped over my body, his hand cupping my left breast through the rough fabric of my tunic, his body warm against my back. If only my life could continue like this forever, with Arthur as close to me as this, and as safe.

People in my old world, and probably in this one too, often talked about wanting to know the future – horoscopes, palm reading, divination. But the reality of knowing the future was a huge weight to bear. As I snuggled against my husband's warm body, I wished with all my might that I didn't know his.

⇛⇜

THE MORNING BROUGHT another fine day. We had no time to help the inhabitants of Breguoin rebuild their town. Ahead of us, we had a long hard ride to get to Ebrauc.

"I ought to send you back to Din Cadan," Arthur said, as we ate a quick breakfast of bread and cheese together. "But if I do, I'll have to send a sizeable escort with you. There're brigands in this forest, as well as wolves."

"Wolves?" I'd heard them once, a long time ago, at night, but far away.

He nodded. "Didn't you hear them last night?"

I shook my head, eyes wide with sudden fear. "They were here?"

"Yes. If you care to take a look at the pile of enemy dead we stacked outside the town walls yesterday, you'll see there's a bit less of them. A pack came down from the forest in the night, attracted by the scent of blood. You were sleeping so soundly, I suppose you didn't hear them howling."

Thank goodness. With my knowledge of how low the town walls were, I'd never have got back to sleep again if I'd woken to hear that.

"The horses? Were they all right?" I meant Alezan, of course. My special horse.

He swallowed his last lump of cheese. "The men were guarding them, but they were restless. The wolves weren't after live prey, though – not when they had a pile of fleshy bones to pick over."

A shudder ran through me. We'd buried our dead and the priest in a hurry yesterday evening, and now I understood why. I put down my cheese, not hungry anymore.

Arthur picked it up. "Better not waste it." He popped it into his mouth with a grin.

It was an altogether quicker process to prepare an army already on the move to march than it was to get them to set out from Din Cadan. Up at first light, by the time the townspeople emerged sleepily from their damaged homes, we were all mounted up ready to leave. Our fires had been quenched, and very little sign remained that we'd been here, save the ground trampled and manured by our horses and the charred circles in the grass.

We left by the northern gates, Arthur's army nicely bolstered by the addition of the men I'd brought from Din Cadan, and those Caninus had donated. A few of the townspeople came out to see us off – or perhaps to make sure we were really going. Their surly, discontented faces held no look of gratefulness. Maybe they thought it our fault the Irish had come at all, and our fault the town had been fired, and our fault their foolish priest had died.

The little boy, Llawfrodedd, who'd rescued Alezan for me, was sitting on the stony ruins of the northern gate tower, skinny bare legs dangling. When he saw me, he jumped to his feet and waved his arms, a wide grin splitting his grubby little face. I waved back, doubting I'd ever see him again, and guessing that his parents would take his brooch and trade it for something they needed after I'd gone.

The town fell behind us, and ahead, on the road to Ebrauc, lay Viroconium. Viroconium, Cadwy… and Morgana.

Chapter Fourteen

IN THE RAIN-WASHED evening light, the rendered walls of Viroconium reared up grim and well-maintained to their crenellated battlements, where the helmeted heads of a host of heavily armed guards showed above the stonework.

Merlin, Arthur, and I stood amongst a crowd of locals on the wet, cobbled road outside the city gates. All around us, tired men and women were returning from the fields outside the walls, or emerging from the city carrying goods they'd bartered for at the daily market – new tools, bolts of cloth, pots and pans.

We looked just like they did, dressed in rough, homespun clothing we'd acquired from a farmstead in the hills five miles to the north where our army had made camp. Tunics and braccae for Merlin and Arthur, a peasant woman's long tunic for me, and smelly cloaks for all three of us.

Both Merlin and Arthur, with their short growth of beard, had the unkempt look of peasants – if you were generous. Fortunately, the warm summer rain meant we could have the hoods of our threadbare cloaks up over our heads and not look out of place. Arthur carried a grotty bag slung across his back.

We were here for Merlin.

Arthur had given Viroconium as wide a berth as possible. He'd taken the army up into the foothills of the western mountains so as not to be spotted by anyone who might report our passing to Cadwy. As we'd progressed, Merlin had grown more and more dejected, sinking into himself and ignoring anyone who tried to talk to him. Even me.

When we made camp beside a small farmstead in a quiet valley, I'd determined to keep an eye on him and had caught him sneaking away to saddle up his horse. I fetched Arthur, and it hadn't taken the mind of a Hercule Poirot to work out where Merlin was going. Arthur refused to let him go alone, and I refused to be left behind.

"I'm the only one who can get you into the palace unseen," Arthur pointed out. "You might think you know it, but you weren't a boy there. You can hardly walk up to the main doors and ask to be let in to see your child, can you?"

"If you take a woman with you," my argument ran, "then you'll arouse less suspicion than two strange men would."

Of course, they hadn't wanted to take me, but eventually I wore them down with my persistence. Merlin resigned himself to taking both of us with a sigh, but the light of excitement shone in Arthur's eyes – he was a boy again about to undertake an exciting adventure. So much so, he probably didn't think too much about the danger he was about to take me into. Thank goodness.

So here we were, a trio of spies about to enter the lion's den that was Cadwy's lair. All so Merlin could see his child. *Her* child.

"We can't stand here much longer," Arthur muttered. "We'll attract attention if we do. We'd better get inside while people are still going in."

Farm workers trudged past us, tools over their shoulders, nodding occasionally at the people coming out as though they knew them. The dribble of scruffily dressed peasants passing back and forth appeared to be lessening as the sun sank below the hills in the west.

Merlin gave a brief nod. Despite Arthur not having prevented him from going, he'd remained quiet and aloof during our journey astride the three ancient horses the farmer had supplied. They were so pathetic looking that for part of the journey I'd dismounted and walked, feeling sorry for my scrawny mount.

A creaking wagonload of newly cut hay covered by some sort of rough tarpaulin, but still sweet smelling and fragrant, rumbled past. We fell in beside it, all three of us hanging our heads a little and trying to look insignificant. A bit hard when you're a king. Arthur still had the purposeful stride of a warrior, no matter how much he tried to disguise it.

"Limp," I whispered to him. "Walk slower."

He glanced at me, eyes alight with mischief, but he did as I advised. The limp hid his over-confident, martial walk a little. Merlin, slouching along with the air of the deeply fed up, appeared much better at acting than Arthur. If I hadn't known, I'd have thought him just another downtrodden peasant.

Shoulders hunched and back a little bowed, I passed through the gateway under the not-so-close scrutiny of the guards, and so did Arthur and Merlin. We were inside.

Despite the drizzle, people crowded the streets. Lack of refrigeration in the Dark Ages meant food had to be acquired fresh every day. Camouflaged in these itchy, smelly clothes, we fitted in well with the workers returning from the fields, the occasional, slightly-more-smartly dressed merchants, and the farmers with their empty ox carts heading back outside the walls.

Lamplight spilled from open doorways, and the sounds of raucous voices rose as men began the evening ritual of drinking. Not unlike many of the large towns in my old world of an evening, with young people out boozing and clubbing. Carousing voices rose, laughter, shouts, the odd screech. As evening drew on, the city vibrated with life.

In the forum that surrounded the Council hall, where the sword in the stone had once stood, we tied our horses up to now nearly empty rails, the amount of droppings indicating how busy the market must have been.

All around us, stall holders were shutting up their shops, although a few selling hot food remained open, their owners shouting to attract the last customers of the day.

I dragged my eyes away from a stall still selling hot pies, and followed Arthur and Merlin around the edge of the forum in the direction of the royal palace.

"How are we going to get in there?" I hissed at Arthur, as he hurried me along a narrow side street. "It looked pretty well guarded to me, last time we were here."

He glanced down at me, eyes still brimming with boyish excitement. "Don't forget. I was a boy here. I know every secret way in and out of the palace."

Good thing one of us was enjoying this mad escapade.

He'd lived here until he was fifteen, and Cadwy had engineered a fall from grace that had seen him dispatched to govern Din Cadan. A move that had turned out to be fortuitous. Merlin had once told me that if it hadn't happened, Cadwy would have found a way to poison Arthur before he'd got much older.

We arrived at the outer palace wall via a series of increasingly narrow and dirty back streets, where a few bedraggled beggars sat dejectedly in corners, and the detritus of daily town life filled the gutters. Glad I'd not had to see this side of Viroconium before, I trotted along behind the two men, holding my cloak tight about myself for fear of catching anything. Lice. Fleas. Scabies. The sight of rats scurrying across the dirty cobbles and through a hole at the foot of a wall made my skin crawl.

"This way," Arthur said, ignoring the rats and diving into a passageway only just wide enough for us to walk along, pressed up against the palace wall on the left and what smelled as though it could be stables on the right. The stables' blackened, thatched roof overhung the passageway enough to shelter us from the rain, and Arthur threw back his hood, so I did as well.

The end of the passage loomed ahead. A dead end. But it wasn't. In the stable wall, a small wooden door had been jammed in at an angle, only about four feet high and two feet wide, and made of hefty, silvered boards.

I glanced at Merlin, and he raised a single, eloquent eyebrow as though this was as much a surprise to him as it was to me.

Arthur bent, put his shoulder against the door and shoved. "It'll be bolted on the inside. But I can do this." He shoulder-barged it again, and it gave a little with the sound of splintering wood. A third blow, and the door slid open a crack. He pushed it a few inches wider, the bottom edge scraping all too loudly over the ground. It didn't look to me as though anyone had used this particular door since he was a boy.

It jammed. No matter how hard he shoved, panting a little now, it refused to open further. The dark gap revealed was very narrow. Although tall, Arthur wasn't a big man, but no way would he fit through there.

"I can get through," Merlin said, pushing Arthur aside. "I'm thinner than you. Let me try."

"Wait a minute," I whispered, very conscious of the fact we were breaking and entering into a king's royal palace, even if he was Arthur's brother. Well, on the whole, that made it worse. "What if there are people on the other side? Where does it lead to?" I paused. "Things have probably changed a lot in ten years."

Arthur frowned, but his eyes still shone with anticipation. "Into an old shed in the stable courtyard, used for junk. That's all. I doubt anything like that's changed. There's probably something big in front of it. Let Merlin wriggle in and move it."

Without waiting to be told, Merlin bent and jammed his head and shoulders into the gap, pushing with his feet. Arthur gave him a helping shove, and he disappeared completely. An interference fit. I couldn't help but wonder what we'd do if he got stuck, like Winnie the Pooh in Rabbit's burrow. The thought, and nerves, made me giggle.

Arthur gave me an inquiring look, so I controlled myself and shook my head. He'd never have understood that particular cultural reference.

For a moment or two, Arthur and I stood in expectant silence, then the scraping of something large moving carried to us, and Merlin's face reappeared as he pushed the door a little wider. "Come on in. It's still the old store shed."

I crawled through first. Merlin was right. It was a very old store shed indeed, the thick, swathing cobwebs and generous layer of dust proving that. Bits of old furniture leaned against the walls near a cart's broken-spoked wheel, beside odd items of discarded horse harness, a pile of wood gone gouty with age, some broken pots, and an old rug in which a family of mice – or rats – appeared to have taken up residence.

Arthur appeared, brushing cobwebs out of his hair, and straightened up.

"Why would there be a secret door hidden at the back of an old store shed?" I whispered.

Arthur tapped his dusty nose. "I had it put here when I was a boy. One of my friends was the son of the palace carpenter. It's only a cob wall – easy for boys to dig a hole in. We installed it together so we could get out of the palace without anyone knowing and have some fun." He grinned. "As boys do."

I could imagine. "Good thing no one ever found it then."

Merlin crossed to the main door, a contraption made of some very ill-fitting boards that allowed plenty of the remaining evening light to filter into our hiding place. He put his eye to one of the ample cracks. "Corner of the stable yard," he whispered. "Nothing much going on. A few servants out there sweeping."

Arthur sat down on a large wooden box. "Now all we have to do is wait for it to get fully dark."

It was a long, boring wait. And uncomfortable. And dirty. I perched next to Arthur on the box, wishing I could have snatched forty winks. Before long, my bottom protested at the hardness of my seat. I kept a wary eye on the old rug and the mouse habitation as darkness fell, but nothing came sneaking out while I was looking, and then I couldn't even see it. If Merlin hadn't been there playing gooseberry, I could have thought of a few ways to help pass the time. But he remained over by the door, watching what went on in the stable yard. I contented myself with threading my fingers through Arthur's and leaning against his solid shoulder.

At last, Merlin turned toward Arthur and me with a nod. "No one out there. They've all gone off to eat. And it's full darkness now. We should make a move."

Arthur got to his feet, and he and Merlin pushed the shed door open a crack and peered through. Waiting behind them, I couldn't see anything, but presumably it was safe, because they stepped out into the now torchlit stable yard with confidence.

Arthur glanced back over his shoulder. "You should wait here while we go in and find the baby."

I bristled with indignation. "No way are you leaving me here on my own. Waiting and worrying. I'm coming too." I stepped out of the shed and pushed the door shut behind me. At least the rain had stopped.

Arthur led the way on silent feet across the yard, not to the main doors into the palace that we'd used when we'd been here before, but to a smaller, insignificant looking one in a corner, that must be the route the servants used. It opened onto a narrow, dingy corridor, lit only by sparsely scattered, and smelly, clay oil lamps in wall recesses.

Unerringly, he led us through a maze of corridors, across several small courtyards and through a few unused rooms stacked with old furniture. With caution, we passed rooms where busy servants worked, until at last we emerged in the corner of a much more splendid, torchlit courtyard.

Here, the painted walls showed signs of having been touched up, and the pillars around the colonnaded walkway had been patched where the render must have flaked off. The round bed in the center blossomed with aromatic herbs, their scent filling the humid evening air.

In the center of each side stood a single doorway.

I turned to Arthur.

He was staring around himself, eyes wide with something akin to shock. "It's just as I remember it," he whispered, awed. "This is the courtyard where I lived as a child. That was my room, over there. That was Cei's. Morgawse was with our mother in Din Tagel." He pointed to the far side. "Morgana's was there. It won't be now. This was the royal nursery. She'll have moved to better rooms than this, once she was an adult."

Merlin nodded. "Not that I saw them."

How bitter he sounded. I couldn't blame him.

"If this is the royal nursery," I whispered, leaning closer to them. "It'll be where the baby is, won't it?" Although she wasn't going to be that much of a baby. A good eighteen months by now – a few months older than Archfedd.

Arthur and Merlin nodded in unison. "That's what I thought," Arthur said, his eyes traveling around the gloomy courtyard. Long shadows stretched across the flagstones, thrown by the torches on every pillar.

"There'll be a nurse with her," Merlin muttered. "I'd bet Morgana's got her child in her own old room."

We padded around the edge of the courtyard, instinct keeping us in the shadows even though we'd seen no sign of guards. At Morgana's old door, Merlin put his hand on the dark wood and pushed it slightly open. We all peered in.

A woman sat on a bench seat with her back to us, head bent, scarcely visible in the darkened room, the dim light of a single candle flickering over her. The nurse. In front of her a cradle rocked back and forth as the woman sang to the child who must be sleeping in it. A strange song I'd never heard before, the tune haunting, the words ancient.

"Dinogad's shift is speckled, speckled.
It was made from the pelts of martens.
Wee! Wee! Whistling.
We call, they call, the eight in chains.
When your father went out to hunt –"

Merlin pushed the door open wide and stepped into the room. The words of the song cut off short, and the woman leapt to her feet, swinging around to face the door.

Not the nurse. Morgana. Singing her child to sleep.

Eyes widening, her hand went to her heart, as though the sight of her ex-lover had shocked her to the core. But this lasted only a moment. Her hand dropped, she stood up straighter, and her face took on its usual cold superiority.

"You," she spat, her gaze traveling past Merlin to take in Arthur and me behind him, filling the doorway. She looked me up and down. "I see your taste in clothes hasn't improved."

Merlin took a step toward the cradle, and she moved sideways to put herself between it and him. "No." From the crib came the sounds of a child humming to herself, as though the song had meant something to her, and now it had stopped she had to provide it for herself.

I slid my hand into Arthur's and gripped it tightly. Hostility emanated from his every pore. No love lost between these siblings.

"She's *my* child," Merlin said, stiffly. "Get out of my way."

"You think?" Morgana sneered. "You really think you're the only man I've spread my legs for? Fool."

Merlin faltered as though she'd struck him. For a moment, he stayed silent, then he visibly pulled himself together. "Don't lie. I know she's mine. Why would you want a child from any other man?"

Her eyes, black in the dim light, flashed at him. "Don't flatter yourself. I don't need anyone else to help me create a powerful woman. My child will surpass both you and me in her powers."

"Mami?" A little voice, baby sweet, from the crib. "Mami?"

Merlin laughed, mirthlessly. "Condemned by your own words. Get out of my way, and let me see my child."

She stood her ground. "If I scream, my guards will come." She narrowed her eyes. "I'll tell them you're brigands, come to rob me. They'll ask no questions and kill all of you on the spot."

I didn't see Merlin move, but suddenly his dagger glittered in his hand, the point under Morgana's chin. "Try it, then. Don't think I won't do it."

She stared at him over the blade, her cold, pale face seemingly unmoved. Did she care so little for her own safety? Or did she think Merlin incapable of killing the thing he loved?

She didn't scream, though.

Arthur released my hand and strode from the doorway into the room, his own sword naked in his hand, the sword from the stone. His sister's eyes followed it greedily as he positioned himself beside Merlin, and raised the sword until its tip, too, rested just beneath her chin. "Go on," he said to Merlin. "See your child."

Morgana started in fury, and the sword tip indented the skin where her jaw met her white throat. "Don't," Arthur hissed. "He might hesitate, but I won't." Over the sword she glared at him in impotent fury. Good thing she didn't have the power to strike someone dead with her gaze.

Merlin sheathed his dagger and went to the crib. He bent over it, for a moment hovering, uncertain. Then he reached in and lifted out the child.

I left the doorway and moved closer to see her for myself. This Nimuë. This child with a name of destiny that carried such weight.

She wore a long white sleeping gown, her hair a tangle of dark curls. He cradled her in his arms, even though she was big for doing that with, and she gazed up at him out of limpid brown eyes.

A hiss of indrawn breath came from Morgana, and Arthur pressed harder with the tip of his sword. Blood trickled down her pale neck toward her heaving breasts.

I'd have expected a baby of this age to be frightened if a strange man picked her up from her bed and held her in his arms. But this child wasn't afraid at all. Her small, chubby hand came up and fingered the ties on Merlin's grubby tunic front, her mouth a perfect rosebud smile. She was pretty, I'd give her that, with something her mother lacked. Humanity, perhaps. She giggled, gazing up into her father's face, her laughter musical in the tense atmosphere of her nursery.

"She knows me," Merlin said. "She knows her father."

How that could be, I had no idea, but it looked as though he was right. This was the child of two people who possessed the Sight – anything was possible.

Merlin reached into the crib with his spare hand and gathered up her blanket. "We'll take her with us."

Arthur's gaze shot to his face, but the sword never moved from Morgana's throat. "What? Are you mad? We can't."

"Don't you dare," Morgana spat. "She's my child, not yours. She will serve the Mother, not your Christian God."

What?

I looked between their faces. Hers distorted with anger, Merlin's anguished, Arthur's horrified.

"I can't leave her here," Merlin said. "That witch isn't fit to be a mother."

Arthur shook his head. "Think about it, man. We can't take her marching with the army."

Torn, I looked back at Merlin, holding his daughter in his arms, head bent over her. If he knew her destiny, would he still be this loving? Or would knowing it bring it about, as he'd postulated?

Perhaps, even, he *did* know it and that was why he wanted to take her.

Morgana sucked in her lips. "Please," she said, her voice cracking. "Don't take her from me. She needs her mother."

This was a change of tune. But I was a mother too, and instinct told me her pain might be real. Just because she was wicked in some respects didn't mean she didn't love her child. And it had been her we'd found singing the child to sleep, not the nurse.

"I thought we only came for you to see your child?" I said to Merlin. "You never said you were thinking of taking her." I paused, turning back to Arthur and jerking my head at Morgana. "And what about her? As soon as we leave, she'll raise the alarm."

"We'll tie her up," Arthur said, with untoward relish. "Right now." He handed me the sword. "If she opens her mouth to say anything, kill her. I know you've done it before." His eyes met Morgana's. "You'd better stay silent. The Ring Maiden has become a warrior queen."

From the bag he'd been carrying, he pulled out a length of rope and swiftly bound Morgana's hands behind her back. He pushed her down onto the bench and tied her wrists to the back, then her ankles to one of the carved legs. All the time, I kept the sword's tip against her throat, waiting for the moment she'd open her mouth. Luckily for me, she didn't. Either she thought I looked sufficiently ruthless to do it, or she couldn't think of anything to say.

Arthur produced a grimy rag from the bag and stuffed it into his sister's mouth, by the look of him taking perverse pleasure at its state. She coughed and tried to spit it out, but he shoved it further in then bound a second rag around her face, holding the first firmly in place. That was her silenced. Her furious eyes flashed at us from above the gag, and I handed the sword back to Arthur.

Sheathing it, he turned to where Merlin stood engrossed in his child. He sighed and shook his head. "I'd love to let you bring her, old friend, but it would be taking her into needless danger. We have to leave her here, where she's safe. You can't argue that Morgana doesn't love her and won't keep her safe. You've seen her, held her, and now we have to go before someone comes looking for her mother and alerts the palace to intruders."

I stepped closer to Merlin, smiling down at the chubby little girl in his arms. Her eyes flicked sideways to look at me, suddenly sharp and knowing, and her face screwed up in dislike. She opened her mouth to wail. I stepped back hurriedly. Her mouth shut, and she stared back up at her father, happy again.

My mouth hung open in shock. How weird was that?

"In a moment," Merlin said, swinging around so his back was to us, shoulders squared, shutting us out.

A sound that might have been a strangled "no" erupted from Morgana, but I ignored her, with eyes only for Merlin.

For a moment, nothing happened. Then, from the quiet shadows, Merlin's whispered voice echoed around the walls, the words spilling out like a tumbling river in a language I didn't understand. A shiver ran down my back and goosepimples prickled my skin. Beside Morgana, Arthur stood up straight, his body suddenly stiffening.

Magic. The words rolled around the room, sibilating into every impenetrable corner, climbing the walls, pooling at our feet.

Morgana struggled and made furious impotent noises, but the whispering went on.

I staggered back to Arthur on unsteady feet and grabbed his hand again. Around us the shadows seemed to have life, dancing across the walls. What was going on? What was Merlin doing?

Morgana looked as though she was about to have an apoplectic fit. Maybe she knew something we didn't.

The air felt heavy and oppressive, the darkness alive with echoes of the whispered words. *No.* I didn't believe in magic. But what was this if it wasn't magic?

Arthur's hand in mine felt hot and sweaty. I held it tight, afraid of what Merlin's unfriendly conjured shadows might do, my breath coming fast and shallow.

The single candle guttered, the flame leapt upward, then died, plunging the room into total darkness. Arthur pulled me toward the still open door, out of the oppressive air and into the freshness of the night. A moment later, Merlin staggered out, his arms empty. I had the distinct feeling that even if I asked, he wouldn't tell me what he'd done.

"This way," Arthur said, pushing the door closed behind us. We ran back to the servants' door and into the maze of passageways, leaving Morgana and her strange child behind. I longed to ask Merlin what he'd done in those few minutes of creeping magic, but we didn't have time to stop and talk. At any moment, a servant might find Morgana and set her free to raise the alarm.

Our horses were waiting patiently for us in the now empty forum. All we had to do was get out of the gates, and Arthur had a plan for that.

From the bag he brought out a bell, and, leading our horses, we staggered drunkenly down the road toward the gates, schooling our anxious feet not to hurry. He led the way, and as he went, he rang the bell every so often. The sign for a leper. All three of us kept our tatty hoods pulled well forward, hiding our faces just as lepers would. But all the same, my heart hammered harder, the nearer we drew to safety.

With the gates in sight, Arthur rang the bell more often. We crawled slowly closer, shuffling along the cobbles. The gate guards drew back in disgust and fear as we approached. Darkness was our friend. Only a single torch burned on either gate tower, the road a pool of black shadows.

"Lepers comin'," shouted one of the guards.

A door on the walkway opened and a man stepped out, possibly their commander. He peered down into the street. "Get them gates open quick, and let 'em out," he shouted down. "How'd they get in, in the first place, I'd like ter know. What you all been doin' today, sleepin' on the job?"

"You lot keep back," the guard called to us, as he swung one side of the gates open. "Doncha come near me."

Heads down, trudging, Arthur remembering to limp, we plodded through the gates, and they slammed shut behind us.

Chapter Fifteen

Romano-British Caer Ebrauc, that would one day become modern York, stood on low-lying land on the banks of the River Usa, probably prone to just as much flooding as Caer Gloui. But the canny Romans had chosen the slightly higher ground to the south of the river for their city, and to the north had built their legionary fortress. A substantial stone bridge crossed the river between the two, but the fortress had long since fallen out of use, the walls robbed out for farm buildings and field boundaries, the barracks empty shells.

The city walls, however, rose up as high and impregnable as those at Viroconium. At intervals, stout towers pointed skyward, manned by armed guards, their spear tips visible, like a small forest, above the main south gates. Bits of the white render had fallen away in places, but no stone robbing had gone on here.

We approached at nightfall, from the southwest. Having bypassed a number of deserted and ruined Roman towns, we'd crossed eastwards over the high moorland of what would one day be called the Peak District and the Pennine ridge, before descending toward the lower lying, richer farmlands of the east coast. And now we'd come at last to Ebrauc.

I'd been here once before, on my way north to join Arthur at the Wall, when Amhar had been a baby. But my stay had been brief, and in a mansio. I'd not met with King Coel at all, nor even laid eyes on his palace.

As our army was so large, Cei organized a camp outside the city walls on the open grazing lands. Then, with just a small party of ten, we approached the gates. The guards on the walls and towers who'd been watching us, peered over as we drew nearer. But evidently someone had warned the men down below to expect us, because the huge gates creaked open to let us pass inside.

Riding between Arthur and Cei, with Merlin just behind, I stared about myself in curiosity, not having had much opportunity to see the city on my last visit, as it had been dark when we'd arrived and very early morning when we'd left.

The once perfect grid system of roads the Romans had built their houses around had largely been lost as those houses fell into ruin. Many of the grander dwellings seemed to have been divided into smaller units, and their tiled roofs had given way to thatch, in places blackened by age and in dire need of renewal. Open areas marked where buildings, that might have begun by falling down, had been completely demolished to make way for gardens, pigpens, and stables. The smell of the farmyard hung over the city in a heavy pall, and busy hens scratched about everywhere in the waste that lay discarded in the streets.

The tumbledown decay reminded me sharply of Caer Baddan, and yet an air of vitality clung to this city that Caer Baddan didn't possess. The people in the streets, hurrying about their business, or hawking their wares to passers by, seemed more cheerful, better dressed, and had a healthy robustness about them. The raised voices of street vendors, the laughter of children running through the maze of dirty side lanes that opened off the main thoroughfare, and the barking of dogs filled the evening air. Smoke twisted up from a myriad of hearth fires to mingle with the earthy stench of animal droppings and the strong ammonia from the stale urine running in the gutters.

The city stank of post-Roman Britain. If I could have bottled that familiar odor, I would have called it Eau de Ville – town smell. How different from the pervading fug of poisonous exhaust fumes in the towns and cities of my old world. I knew which I preferred.

In common with the practice of many of his fellow kings who'd held onto Roman towns and cities as their strongholds, Coel had taken what remained of the largest house for his palace. It sprawled over the highest ground in a maze of courtyards, corridors, and rooms, and might once have been two or three neighboring properties, for all I knew.

His palace stables occupied long, low, thatched buildings grouped around a cobbled courtyard. Here, we dismounted and left our horses in the care of a crowd of eager servants. Perhaps they knew why we'd come. The news that a large army had set up camp outside the city walls must have flown around the city like wildfire.

A tow-headed servant boy led us along several narrow corridors, across a small, dingy courtyard and finally into what must have been the main part of the palace. Around a wide, paved courtyard, with a huge fountain playing in the center, rows of doors opened off a colonnaded walkway. Much like the palace at Viroconium. In fact, much like most large houses left behind by the Romans. The boy stopped outside the most splendid of the doors and knocked.

The door swung open, and he gestured to us to go inside, bowing low.

A wide room, with a black and white mosaic underfoot, opened up before us. Now evening had fallen, torches blazed from iron brackets, giving each of us the multiple long shadows of a crowd. The frescoed walls told the story of Theseus and the minotaur in the labyrinth at Knossos. This splendid room had to be the king's audience chamber.

At the far end, a platform a couple of feet high held a single elaborately carved wooden throne. On the throne sat an old man.

Not an old man like King Manogan of Linnuis – gnarled and bitter and obsessed by religion and his church. No, this old man resembled nothing if not a silvery lion. He sat upright on his throne, posed as if he'd been expecting us, in rich red robes, the tunic that hung to below his knees decorated with gold thread and jewels.

His mane of thick white hair hung down to mingle with his ample snowy beard, and bushy white brows jutted over sea-blue eyes that fixed us with a gimlet glare. If he hadn't been so stern and imposing, he'd have made a good Father Christmas. But no air of benevolence clung to him, and he'd probably have terrified any child who'd come to him asking for a present.

The words of the nursery rhyme that preserved his memory leapt into my head. *Old King Cole was a merry old soul.* No, he wasn't. That much was very clear.

Arthur strode up the chamber toward the throne, and Cei, Merlin, and I followed in his wake, dragged along like flotsam on the tide. Our accompanying warriors remained standing by the door. Arthur halted just in front of the throne, but didn't bow. He *was* the High King, after all.

Coel regarded him from under those splendid brows as silence stretched between us. Then he set his hands, gnarled like old roots, on the arms of his throne and slowly rose to his feet, the stiffness of his movements betraying his extreme age. His head inclined so slightly I almost missed it. Probably an old king like him felt such a young man as Arthur, unproven as yet in his eyes, didn't merit more than that, even if he was the High King.

Arthur mirrored the nod.

I glanced across at Merlin, but he had his eyes fixed on Coel.

Coel stepped down from his platform and up to Arthur. The two men faced one another – the young man and the old. Most likely Coel had once been as tall as Arthur, but now had shrunk with age. Arthur topped him by several inches.

Coel cleared his throat. "You came."

Arthur inclined his head. "You called."

Now he was standing, the king's great age was even more apparent. He had a slight stoop to his wide, bony shoulders that could have been caused by osteoporosis, and up close a multitude of fine wrinkles fissured his skin. Heavy bags hung under his eyes, and age spots sprinkled his face and hands.

His gaze moved past Arthur to rest on me. I'd taken off my mail shirt and helmet before we left our camp, but still wore my boy's clothing and had my sword hanging at my belt.

"And I see you've brought the Ring Maiden."

Arthur held out his hand to me. "My wife and queen – Guinevere."

I stepped closer, taking the proffered hand and making a bigger bow than either man had done. I was only a queen and knew my place. Or at least, I wanted them to think I did. "My Lord Coel."

When I raised my head, I found his blue eyes, still bright despite his age, fixed on me, a mixture of curiosity and what might well have been admiration in them. "My Lady Guinevere."

A smile hovered on his thin lips for a moment, hinting at the man he'd once been, and I smiled back. Was that a twinkle in his eyes? Did I need to revise my initial opinion? Then his gaze returned to Arthur. "I have had rooms prepared for you and your generals. My servants will take them there." He paused. "You and I have much to discuss. I'll have food brought to my chambers and we'll talk there." His eyes slid back to me. "I think your most unusual wife should join us."

My eyes widened in surprise. Not many men wanted women at their councils. The glint in his eyes suggested it probably wasn't my brains he was interested in, though.

Arthur shot me a quick, appraising glance, then nodded. "My men are tired after the long ride here. Can you arrange for refreshment to be brought to their rooms?"

Coel snapped his fingers. From a door to the left of the throne three servants hurried out. They must have been waiting for his summons. A few quick words to them, and Arthur and I were separated from Cei, Merlin, and our guards.

Worry clouded Merlin's face as he was escorted out, glancing back over his shoulder at me and Arthur. It went against the grain for him to abandon his lord in another king's stronghold. Coel could look and sound like an ally, but the danger that he wasn't remained ever present in this world of petty rivalries and long-lasting disputes.

I swallowed down my misgivings and followed Arthur and Coel through the door the servants had emerged from, into what must have been Coel's suite of private rooms.

The first we came to held a large square table, its surface silvered and smooth with age, with substantial, high-backed chairs scattered around it. Two more servants stood in a corner. A click of the king's fingers sent them scurrying away. My stomach rumbled. Hopefully they'd gone to fetch food.

They had. Half a dozen of them returned laden with platters of delicious smelling meats, and side dishes smothered in rich sauces, which they set down on the table where we'd taken our places. Wine arrived in tall earthenware pitchers, and loaves of bread, with olives and dried figs in beautiful bowls. Coel waved his servants away, leaving us to eat alone, with no one to overhear our conversation.

"Please, eat," Coel said to me. "You look hungry." He'd positioned us one on either side of him, so he'd probably heard my stomach rumbling. Blushing, I took some of the offered venison the servants had already sliced up into thick gobbets, dripping with sauce.

When we were all eating, Arthur turned the conversation to military matters. "You sent for me because you needed help. Perhaps you'd better outline the situation here and tell me how things have progressed since your messengers came to Din Cadan."

My ears pricked, even though I guessed I'd be left out of this. My opinion meant nothing to this king – only my looks and biological function mattered. I'd long ago grown used to Dark Age sexist attitudes. No point in complaining about something that was rife. Besides which, the food was excellent, and I was still starving. I helped myself to more, quite glad I didn't have to talk. But my ears were flapping.

Coel set down his knife. There were no forks. It was strictly knives and fingers in the fifth century, helped by lumps of bread and maybe a small spoon. "The Saxons have been raiding up and down our coast all summer long. Far more than normal. Never in the same place twice, but here and there, where they've drawn their keels up on a beach and attacked the local fishermen. Sometimes they've dared to march inland. A lot of churches have been fired and priests killed. Pagan bastards. I've had to spread my men thin to try to intercept them. My bishop, Exuperius, is at me all the time to strike back at them for their desecration of his churches."

He took a mouthful of wine and scowled. "Just before Cadman rode south to Din Cadan, a whole host of them – a proper army, not just a raiding party – marched inland from the coast. They'd beached their ships near the ruined fort of Praesidium, unopposed, then disembarked and headed this way, leaving a trail of destruction a mile wide behind them, across my richest farmlands."

Was he more worried about his farmlands than his people? I took a swallow of wine to wash down my food.

He shook his shaggy head in what could have been despair. "I've had the same problem all along the length of my coastline. My forces have to be divided. One son rode north toward the moors, the other south to the Humber estuary, chasing bloody will o' the wisps and phantoms. As soon as we had news of this mass landing, I sent out my fastest messengers. My two armies came racing back. We were lucky. They engaged the enemy some eight miles east of the city where an old stone bridge crosses the River Derwent. Only thanks to the narrowness of the bridge did my son succeed in holding them back until both of their armies had united. But they were still outnumbered."

"What happened?" Arthur kept his eyes fixed on Coel's face.

Coel's broad shoulders sagged. "Defeat." He shook his shaggy head. "One son wisely chose to turn tail and run for it, outnumbered and outmanned, to live to fight another day. His brother was killed. Not my heir – a younger son."

For a moment, his eyes clouded, perhaps thinking of the son he'd lost.

Then he rubbed his forehead. "The Yellow Hairs are fierce warriors. My men are brave, but were driven back when the Yellow Hairs waded the river. The only thing my surviving son could do was urge his men to flee, on horseback, faster than the Saxons could follow. If he hadn't, his army would have been decimated. And it'd be the Yellow Hair chieftain sitting in this chamber, holding Ebrauc."

His voice cracked. "I lost a son, but I wasn't the only one to suffer such a loss. Many families in this city and from the farms outside our walls have lost a husband, a son or a brother. Some have lost their entire farms and have fled here to Ebrauc for safety, cramming their families in wherever they can find a space. We're full to bursting with refugees." He shook his shaggy head. "Those heathen Yellow Hairs want this land. They'll not give up until we drive them off it." He paused. "Or until they drive us off so they can keep it for themselves."

I swallowed. This was something the people of every kingdom had to cope with on an almost daily basis – the threat of losing their loved ones in battle, or just in raids. The threat of having their homes burned to the ground around them and their lands stolen. I studied Arthur's somber face, my food forgotten.

"And since?" he asked.

Coel visibly drew himself up straight. "I sent Cadman and his fellows south to find you. They volunteered, despite their age and afflictions." A small smile touched his lips. "And I well know what *that* entails. They're all of them younger than me. Boys when I was already a man grown."

"And now?"

"Since they returned, we've had a lull in the raiding. But it's before the storm to come. The enemy's numbers have swelled with ever more keels landing to reinforce them. I have spies out, watching. The Yellow Hairs have been raiding the farms that abut the coast, knowing there's little we can do to stop them. We never know where they'll strike next. I've sent patrols out every day, led by my sons and generals. When they've come across small bands of the invaders, they've been able to put them to flight, inflicting heavy losses. But we daily live in fear that they'll turn up outside our walls." He gave a bitter laugh. "No legion here any longer to defend us."

Wait. There'd been a legion stationed *here*?

I struggled to remember what my father had told me about York, about the cities that had hosted legions. Only three – Chester, on the border with North Wales, Caerleon – our Caer Legeion gwar Uisc in South Wales, and… a third… York. Of course. One of Arthur's twelve battles as recorded by that obscure monk Nennius in the early ninth century had been the enigmatic Battle of the City of the Legion. Thought to be one of the easier to locate of the battles. However, scholars had long argued about whether it meant Caerleon, whose very name means "city of the legion" or Chester. Most had dismissed York as unlikely, if not impossible.

And yet here we were, barely a stone's throw from the Saxon Shore, with Saxons threatening attack at any moment. This *had* to be the City of the Legion Nennius meant. It had to. All those scholars were wrong.

"I'll send out patrols of my own men to the coast, and maybe attack them there," Arthur said. "I'll need to speak with your scouts in the morning. We need to work out what the Saxons could be planning."

I cleared my throat. "They're coming here."

Two heads swiveled to stare at me. Faded blue eyes and bright young dark ones.

"What?" Arthur said.

I stared him in the eye. "They're coming. Don't ask me how I know because I can't tell you. But they are. There'll be a huge battle right here. You mark my words."

Coel's eyes narrowed, almost sinking into the folds of spare skin around them. "No one told me the Ring Maiden had the Sight."

I opened my mouth to say I didn't, then shut it with a snap, without speaking. Let him think that if he wanted to. Easier by far than revealing how I felt so certain about this battle. How lucky they all believed in magic.

Arthur's eyebrows had shot up, and his tongue darted out to lick his lips, but he too stayed silent. He was going to want to know how I'd come by this knowledge – not being a great believer in magic himself.

Coel nodded his head. "She's seen it. We will wait here for them to come to us. And we will fight them."

※

"Why did you say that?" Arthur asked, as the door to our opulent bed chamber closed behind us, shutting out the darkness of the courtyard. He caught hold of my arm and pulled me around, staring down into my eyes. "You know something. What is it? Tell me."

How right I'd been about his reaction to my prediction.

But oh, how I longed to share my knowledge with someone. And how I longed to be wrong. If I was right, this battle would be a victory, but with every incident that came true, Camlann loomed ever closer and more real. But I couldn't tell him. Instead, I had to find a lie to prove my words. "The Sight," I said, my heart beating hard and fast. "Sometimes I'm given a flash of foresight. I had one of those tonight."

His eyes narrowed, his fingers digging into my arm. "That's not it." He wasn't stupid. "I know when you're not telling me the truth.

You no more have the Sight than I do." He paused. "Did Merlin tell you this? Has he seen something?"

Relieved, I nodded. "Yes. He told me he'd seen them coming here."

He let me go and strode over to our bed. "My men are outside the walls. I'm not happy with that if the Saxons are coming. We need to send out scouts to find out from which direction they'll arrive. Or did he tell you that as well? I'll go and ask him."

He unbuckled his sword belt and threw it on the bed, then turned toward the door into the courtyard. Merlin and Cei had rooms beside ours.

I caught his arm. "He'll be asleep." I wanted the chance to speak to Merlin before he did. Explain why he'd have to lie.

"Well, he can wake up," Arthur snapped. "I'm his king."

I got between him and the door. "No, don't go. It... it wasn't him."

Arthur had never seemed so tall, his face in shadow from the oil lamp that burned behind him. No doubt my own face was thrown into stark nakedness by that same light.

I couldn't see him frown, but I heard it in his voice. "What d'you mean? Did you make this up? Why did you say it?" He shook his head. "Old Coel believed you, and so did I. What madness is this that you think you can order our battle plan?" His voice rose. "How many times do I have to remind you that you're a woman?" He loomed over me, large and threatening.

I'd backed myself into a corner in more ways than one. I licked my lips. "I told you because I *know* it." My voice sounded small and feeble against his angry rant.

He recoiled. "You *know* it? How?"

I swallowed. I'd have to tell him. He needed his army here in York, not riding on a wild goose chase to the coast. "Because it's written down."

Silence filled the room, our breathing loud.

"Where is it written down?" Arthur asked, his voice laden with menace.

"In a book."

"A book?"

I nodded. "A book written by a monk. Probably. He wrote down your battles. A list of them. Lots of scholars don't think they were real."

Arthur caught my arm again and this time pulled me over to the bed to sit on it. Facing me, he stared into my eyes, his watchful and wary, as though perhaps he didn't want to hear this, yet something was driving him on to question and listen. "Tell me about this book."

I compressed my lips for a moment, thinking hard. "I've never read it. My father did, but he only told me bits. I was a child. It wasn't the sort of book I even wanted to read. So I don't know much."

"Tell me what you know."

Inside, a huge part of me felt an overwhelming relief at being able to tell him. The rest of me screamed warnings not to let too much slip. I shoved the screaming to one side. I'd tell him only what he needed to know. No need to elaborate too much.

"Tell me," he repeated, more gently, and this time he took my hands in his, warm and somehow persuasive. His dark eyes were limpid pools, the magnetism of his personality luring me on to disclosures I didn't mean to make.

"There's a list of your battles. I can't remember all of them." Small white lie. "And one of them is at the City of the Legion. Most people think that means Caer Legeion or – or Deva. Do you even know Deva? Does it still exist?"

He nodded. "I know Deva."

"Well, Ebrauc is a city of the legion as well. There were three that held Roman legions. I think it must be here. You'll fight a major battle right here. And win." That was enough. He didn't need to know more.

He stared into my eyes appraising me, making me shift in discomfort. "Is that the only battle you know?"

I tried to stop myself from fidgeting under his compelling gaze. What was he doing? Hypnotizing me? "No. There were others. You've already fought them. With every one you've fought, it's become clearer to me that the list was right. The River Glein, the Dubglas. Bassas. Celydon Wood, Caer Guinntguic, Breguoin. They were all on the list my father told me about."

Arthur's grip on my hands tightened. "And after Ebrauc? What then?"

I stared back into his eyes, willing myself to keep calm, but sinking ever deeper. "I-I don't know."

He studied my face, and I schooled myself not to flinch. I'd told him once that I couldn't tell him anything about my world, but now I'd opened the floodgates, would he be content with the little I'd given him?

His shoulders rose and fell in a deep sigh. "On second thought, I don't want to know." A bitter note tinged his voice. "What man wants to know his future? Only a fool. Don't tell me anything more."

How I wished I didn't know myself.

I, too, sighed, but with relief rather than resignation. I pulled a hand free and caressed his stubbly cheek. "You're right. It doesn't do anyone any good to look too far ahead." I managed a smile. "I only know you need to stay here and guard the city. They'll come to you, if you wait. And you'll win."

He nodded. "I'll find room within the walls for our men tomorrow, even if Coel objects. Either that, or we'll go back outside to pitch our tents with them. I don't want to be separated from my men." His head turned toward my hand, and he kissed it gently. "But I'll think about that in the morning. For now," he nodded at the bed, "we have an inviting bed that's not on the hard ground nor surrounded by other men."

His eyes twinkled, and my mouth slipped into a smile. Men. They have such one-track minds. Had I read once that they think about sex every three minutes? It seemed that was as true in the fifth century as the twenty-first. Not that I was going to complain. I leaned forwards and kissed him on the mouth.

Chapter Sixteen

I AWOKE ALONE in my bed with an Arthur-shaped indentation beside me. Blinking in the light spilling through the unshuttered window high above my head, I reached out a hand to find him missing. Half asleep in that early morning semi-dream state, I'd been hoping for a replay of the previous night, imagining him touching me the way he had when we'd finally got into bed. Even just thinking of it had me squirming. It came as a hard return to reality to find him gone.

I pushed the bed covers off and got to my feet. My clothes lay on the floor where he'd torn them off me the night before. Hugging the memory, I gathered them up and slipped my undershirt on to cover my nakedness in case anyone came to disturb me.

Arthur's clothes had gone, of course. No sign remained that he'd even been here. I'd better finish getting dressed and find out what was going on.

Merlin and Cei had vanished too. The doors of their rooms stood ajar, as if they'd left in a hurry. As with Arthur, no sign remained to indicate they'd been there, apart from rumpled bedclothes. Disappointed, I turned away. In the center of the courtyard a raised bed boasted a spindly bay tree and a lot of leafy weeds amongst the herbs, all growing in what might once have held a fountain. The uneven flagstones badly needed relaying, and the whole place had the familiar air of neglect common to most Roman towns and cities, not enhanced by the dismally cloudy sky.

Sandaled footsteps clacked in the corridor from the main palace, and an elderly woman emerged from the comparative gloom. She wore a long, pale-blue gown, and her almost white hair sat piled on top of her head in carefully arranged curls.

With her face creased in a smile, she halted near the herb bed. "Ah, you're up. That's good. I wasn't sure if I should wake you or not. Your husband told me you were exhausted from your journey."

Well, that and other things. I returned her smile. Who could she be? Well-spoken and a little abrupt, her air of authority hinted that she couldn't be a servant. And her dress, simple though it was, might well have been made of silk, a very scarce fabric. Only my underwear was made of silk – to my own design. Who'd have thought I'd have introduced silk knickers and bras to the Dark Ages?

Dismissing my speculation about her clothing, and conscious of the fact I was still dressed as a boy, I smoothed down my tunic. "Good morning." Best to be polite, especially as I didn't know who she was. "My lady."

Her friendly smile widened. "Tush, tush, tush. I'm an old woman now and the niceties of royal politics are too awkward for me to bother with. If you will call me Ystradwel, may I call you Gwen? That's how your husband referred to you."

None the wiser as to who she was, but liking her, I nodded. "Please do."

Her piercing gaze swept the courtyard, taking in the open doors and emptiness. She tutted. "Have you been served breakfast yet? No? I expect the servants were waiting for you to waken. Your husband was most adamant in his request that no one should disturb you."

Whoever she was, she was very chatty. I butted in. "Do you know where my husband is?"

Ystradwel nodded. "He and his generals have gone out to organize their men and bring their camp inside our walls. My husband has accompanied them."

Her husband? Could she be Coel's queen? Even though she had white hair, she didn't look anywhere near as old as him.

She gestured to the corridor she'd emerged from. "If you'd like to come with me, we can breakfast together."

Mustering as much grace as I could, which was difficult considering how I was dressed, I bowed my head in acknowledgement and accompanied her.

My guess turned out to be right. She was indeed Coel's queen, and had chambers near to his. We sat at a small circular table and consumed a breakfast of dried figs and fresh rolls spread with thick, golden butter. We washed the delicious meal down with some kind of fruit drink that didn't taste alcoholic, but might have been deceptive.

"I married Coel when I was just a girl," Ystradwel told me, as we got to know one another over the food. "My father, Gadeon, was King of Rheged, my mother from Dumnonia. I should think I must be distantly related to your husband."

Intrigued, I waited for her to go on. So many of the kings of Britain were related to one another, finding suitable wives and avoiding inbreeding must have been quite difficult.

"I had an older brother, but he died young. My nephew rules in Rheged now – Meirchion. They call him 'the Lean' but not because he's thin – more because he's so mean."

I had to smile. Arthur and I'd had dealings with her unhelpful nephew before. But I warily held my tongue rather than reveal my own opinion. You never knew whether people would take offense.

She took a bite of bread, and chewed thoughtfully. "When I was young, Coel chose me to be his queen because I was beautiful, although to see me now, you'd not believe it. Ystradwel the Fair, they called me. Many young princes fancied their chances."

"You're still beautiful," I said, an opinion I felt brave enough to share, as I studied her high cheekbones and perfectly oval face. "You're just old. Being old doesn't make a woman ugly."

She chuckled. "Spoken by a young woman in her prime. One day you'll not be able to count the wrinkles that have multiplied on your face. It comes to all of us."

Not to women in my world – plastic surgery, face lifts, and Botox saw to that. But I didn't tell her. Something intrinsically elegant and glamorous hung about her, making it easy to imagine how the young Coel must have fallen in love with her. No wonder she'd had the epithet "the Fair."

When we'd finished eating, Ystradwel took me on a tour of the palace, ending in the royal nursery where two little boys were playing with a pair of wheeled wooden horses, riding them at each other like a pair of warriors, under the watchful gaze of a rotund nursemaid.

"My great grandsons. This kingdom's future," Ystradwel said, a hint of sadness in her voice. "The bigger one is Bran, the younger Cyngal."

"I won," shouted Bran, a sturdy, dark-haired child, as his brother took a tumble from his horse, a beast someone artistic had rendered dapple gray. "That's three times I've beaten you. That makes me king for today."

Cyngal scrambled to his feet, his lower lip jutting rebelliously.

A pang of sadness seized my heart, and I had to swallow the lump in my throat. How like Amhar he was. The same age, similar dark hair, arms and legs still round with the chubbiness of babyhood.

Ystradwel touched my arm. "I'm sorry. Has this upset you?"

I swallowed again but the lump wouldn't go. "It's just that I miss my children."

She nodded. "They're not ours long enough, are they? Especially not the boys."

Especially not the boys.

"I had eight children." Ystradwel lowered her voice, probably so the little boys, who'd remounted for a second charge, wouldn't hear. "Two girls and six boys. Now I have only two sons left living." She shook her head in sad resignation. "One of my daughters entered a nunnery and died there of the wasting sickness. The other married well but died young, birthing her first child." She put her hands on her hips. "Not made like me with hips for birthing, you see. Too young, too young..." She shook her head.

I thought of Coventina and the Caesarean section Donella and I had performed on her. Not for the first time I wished I'd arrived here in the fifth century with something useful I could contribute. Yes, the army were touchingly convinced I brought them luck, but that wasn't true, and I'd rather have had some practical skill. Medical knowledge beyond a first aid course would have been helpful.

"And your sons?" I asked, sensing the old queen wanted to tell me more.

Ystradwel sank down onto a cushioned bench at the side of the room, eyes still on the two children. "My first born, Tegfan, named for his grandfather, caught a chill one winter before he was even five. He was gone in less than three days." Now her gaze stretched beyond the boys, as though looking back in time to when her own children had played here in this nursery – perhaps with the same wooden horses. "Garbaniawn is my second born, always a strong lad. He's these boys' grandfather."

She chuckled. "He's fat and bald now, and looks older than his father. I sometimes wonder if my grandson, these boys' father, will follow my husband as king instead of our son." For a long minute she stared ahead of herself, lost in her remembrances, before continuing. "As to the others, Ceneu is a priest, and Dwfwr fell long ago in battle. Urban died fighting the Saxons a few short weeks ago. Eudos fell from his horse as a young man, out hunting, and was kicked in the head. I sat with him a week, hoping that God would bring him back to me. God didn't listen to my prayers. My youngest and best son died without ever opening his eyes again."

She sighed. "I'm sorry. I shouldn't be telling you my troubles. I'm lucky, really – I have Garbaniawn and his son and grandsons. I love my little ones."

The boys had given up on their horses and were lining up rows of wooden warriors, gaudily painted simple conical figures, facing each other across an imaginary stone-flagged battlefield. Indoctrinated from birth, one day these little boys would be as fearsome warriors as the men who fought for their great-grandfather. Unless, like the unknown Ceneu, they entered the church. And even that wasn't safe, as I'd seen firsthand at Breguoin.

―――

BY EVENING OUR army had squeezed itself within Ebrauc's walls. No mean feat as there were so many warriors and horses. But luckily, plenty of gaps existed between buildings where horses could be tethered and bivouacs set up. As night fell, campfires sprang to life all over Ebrauc's small, intramural fields, but with little of the usual carousing the men liked. Mindful of my warning that the Saxons were on their way, Arthur had given orders that no man was to get drunk. And they were to keep the noise down, in the hope the Saxons, should they arrive, would not know a new, and large, army had reinforced Coel's own battle-depleted force.

That night, Arthur and I dined in the king's hall, a long, thatched building cobbled onto the side of the predominantly Roman palace, as so many kings' halls were. Although not quite so big as the hall at Din Cadan, it was impressive, nevertheless. A wide high table occupied one end, where Arthur and I were seated to either side of Coel and Ystradwel. The remaining seats belonged to Garbaniawn, a man as fat, bald and elderly as his mother had described, and Exuperius, Bishop of Ebrauc, a short, scrawny man in clergyman's robes, with a continuous drip on the end of his long nose.

Cei and Merlin had to make do with seats in the body of the hall with Garbaniawn's warrior son, a well-built young man still in possession of a fine head of hair. The snowy head of Cadman, and some of his fellow messengers, stood out amongst tables closely crowded with ranks of Coel's foremost warriors.

I'd seen a number of kings' halls during my time in the fifth century, so this one came as no surprise. Rushes from the nearby riverbanks covered the flagstone floor, and sigil emblazoned shields festooned the walls. Despite the summer's warmth, a huge fire burned in a central hearth, sending smoke curling up to hang among the blackened rafters and filter through the thatch. No chimneys this far back in history, and definitely no smoke holes – that would have made the draft so vicious the chance of the roof catching fire would have been enormous.

Torches burned in iron brackets along the walls, insufficient to light the hall well, but enough to add to the general fug of smoke, sweaty bodies, food, and a slight undertone of urine wafting up from the rushes.

Coel had set me on his right-hand side, with Arthur to the left of Ystradwel, so I had no chance to talk to my husband. As the night progressed, the old king's reason became clear.

He was a charming man, a leonine silver fox, showing few of his probable eighty years, and it took him no time to make it obvious he liked me a lot. A bit too much, in fact.

"Do you like to hunt?" he asked, as I put my hand over my goblet for the sixth time to stop the servant hovering behind me from filling it up. He had to nearly shout to make himself heard above the din of voices from the body of the hall.

"Not really," I said, which was true. "I like the riding, the galloping, but not the kill. It turns my stomach."

He grinned, showing me his yellowed teeth – remarkably all present as far as I could see, if a trifle wonky. Well, not a lot of sweet things to rot them. His eyes held a twinkle a younger man would have been proud of. "And yet your reputation goes before you. You have killed more than one man. Quite the warrior queen."

Not exactly an accurate reputation, it seemed. I shook my head. "Just the one. And I helped a friend kill the other, or he would have killed her." For something to do with my hands, I pushed a lump of tough meat I hadn't been able to eat around my plate. "But how do you know?"

He shook his shaggy head, his eyebrows waggling at me like fat white caterpillars perched precariously just above his eyes. "The Wall is not so far. We get all the news down here. I even know that it was you who suggested snatching the scaling ladders when the foolish Dogmen left them outside Vindolanda's walls." He smiled again. "I trust the luck you bring will be evident here as well, when the Saxon army you predicted arrives."

Not really anything I could say to that. A bit like when someone tells you you're clever, or pretty, or some other flattery. What are you supposed to reply? Thank you, and sound smug? I took a tiny sip of wine – golden, unwatered, and a little bitter.

He smiled. "What *do* you like to do, then?" His hand slid beneath the table and touched my thigh. I'd put on a gown for the evening, and the heat of his hand radiated through the thin fabric, intimate and invasive.

I froze. What to do? He was our host, another king, and my husband's ally. I could hardly slap his face. Instead, I removed his hand and set it firmly back on the table. "I like to be with my husband."

He guffawed out loud, making Arthur, who'd been talking to Ystradwel and Garbaniawn, turn his head to stare.

"It's all right," Coel barked, full of good humor despite having been rebuffed. "Your wife's just put me in my place."

A puzzled frown creased Arthur's brow, so I smiled radiantly back at him. The last thing I wanted was trouble between him and our ally, and Arthur could be very touchy where I was concerned.

I was saved from having to further fend off the old king's attentions by the hall doors bursting open. Heads turned, conversation faltered, and the noise receded as everyone craned their necks to see the source of the interruption. A youth in a mail shirt stumbled through the gap between the tables and into the narrow aisle.

For a moment he paused as if orienting himself. The firelight flickered over his drawn face, dancing across the links of his chain mail. With a huge effort, he drew himself up to his full height and on unsteady feet, staggered toward the high table.

Complete silence fell. Every eye followed his progress.

His boots dragged in the rushes, halting and unsure.

I stared. Long hair hung in rat tails around an ashen face streaked with blood, and he carried his right arm across his body, clutching his chest. This very action served to make him bend forward, robbing him of the height he'd tried to give himself.

Forgetting me, Coel rose to his feet. Arthur too. The juggler who'd been entertaining us scurried to the shadows at the side of the hall, and the young man limped unopposed to the foot of the platform the high table stood on. Hunched, he seemed slight and vulnerable and scarcely older than Rhiwallon.

"Yes?" Coel asked, his deep voice booming out over the heads of his people to carry around the hall. "What news do you bring?" His brow furrowed with impatience.

Nothing good, by the look of him.

The young man dropped to his knees in the rushes. "My Lord King…" His voice trailed off as though he'd used up all his strength to get this far and had none left for speaking. Parchment-pale skin glimmered in the torchlight, making a ghost of him already.

"Speak, man," Arthur said, his voice, too, tinged with impatience.

The urge to shout at them to let the poor boy rest was huge, but I bit my lip and stayed silent. No one in this hall would take kindly to me interrupting, queen or not.

The young man raised his head. "They're coming." His voice barely rose above a whisper, and in their seats the suddenly alert and watchful warriors craned their necks to hear his words.

"Where?" Arthur snapped. "From which direction? Spit it out."

"The south." The young man's breath rasped like a rusty saw. "Toward the Humber estuary. We came upon their scouts… I mean… they came upon us." He coughed, bloody spittle running down his chin. "Twenty miles from here, as evening fell. There was a fight – a skirmish." He coughed again. "Only I escaped." He heaved another rasping breath, the arm clutching his chest tightening. "My commander ordered me to flee and bring you the news." He faltered, barely breathing, as though every inhalation racked him with pain. "They have bows. An arrow hit me as I fled." Every word was run through with anguish, his eyes dark with sorrow. "My friends…"

He toppled face down onto the rushes, the broken shaft of an arrow protruding from his back.

Oh God, no.

Bitter experience had taught me that any arrow lodged in someone's body would be almost impossible to remove. The arrow's fierce barbs would hold it tight in the flesh. Only where you could push it all the way through did you have a chance – and that wasn't possible with an arrow that had pierced the young man's ribcage. Nothing would save him now, and he must have known it.

Cei pushed back the bench he sat on with a clatter and leapt to his feet. Merlin, at the other end of the table, was already standing. All over the hall, men did the same, food and bonhomie forgotten.

"We have to reinforce the wall guard," Arthur called to Cei and Merlin as he skirted the high table and leapt from the platform. "We join our men – now."

Without waiting to speak to Coel, the three of them hastened down the hall to the doors and out into the night, the poor young messenger sprawled forgotten in the rushes.

A buzz of noise arose as everyone spoke at once. Coel raised his hands, and stood waiting until silence fell again before he spoke. "Warriors, to the walls. We stand watch tonight. They'll be here by morning. Go."

Garbaniawn struggled to his feet as best he could, being so portly. "I'll get my armor."

Coel shook his head. "No. I want you here, seeing to our arms supply. Your sons can do the fighting. You and I are old men now."

Anger flashed across Garbaniawn's heated face, but he must have seen the sense of his father's words. Without argument, he hurried from the hall, as his warriors hastened to arm themselves.

Without a backward glance, Coel followed them.

I stayed seated, with only Ystradwel and Bishop Exuperius for company. Down in the hall, a few women remained, exchanging silent, fearful glances. They must be used to their men going off to fight by now – but also used to not all of them coming home again. Just as I was. One of them bent over the body of the young messenger, shaking her head in resignation.

Ystradwel heaved a sigh. "And so it begins," she said, weariness edging her voice. "We women know our place – and that's waiting. Whatever you accomplished at Vindolanda, Gwen, waiting is our lot, while our husbands, sons and brothers march into danger."

Chapter Seventeen

WITH ALL THE men, young and old, departed from the hall, we women dispersed to our sleeping quarters. Before entering my chamber, I stood for a moment in the quiet courtyard, breathing in the comforting scents of lavender, sage and rosemary. From outside the walls of the palace, the sounds of the nighttime city wafted to me – a dog barking, a few shouts, the slamming of a door or two. The sounds of peace.

Only it wasn't peaceful at all. Not really. A current of tension sizzled through the night air, making the little hairs along my arms prickle upright. The atmosphere felt so thick, I had to deliberately push the air in and out of my lungs.

Later, lying in bed, hot and uncomfortable in just my undershirt, I waited for Arthur to come, but he didn't. Part of me hadn't expected him to and accepted that where battle was concerned, I had to come second. But the selfish part of me longed to have him beside me, warm and alive and unharmed, holding me, my head on his chest with his reassuring heartbeat loud in my ear.

I must have slept eventually, because I woke to a watery early morning light filtering through the window. My head ached, and my eyes felt gummy from lack of sleep. I rubbed the back of my hand across them, blinking in the comparative brightness, and sat up.

Silence. No birdsong. No dogs barking. No voices. No sounds of battle, however distant. Foreboding crept up my back, and my skin prickled. Nothing could have been more ominous than that silence.

I jumped out of bed and dragged on my tunic and braccae as fast as I could, topping them with my mail shirt and pausing only to slip my feet into my boots and buckle my sword belt around my waist. Outside, rain fell in a soft mist, bestowing a dark shine on the patches of exposed stonework on the palace walls. My soft boots made next to no noise on the wet flagstones as I crossed the courtyard to the corridor then threaded my way to the main palace.

No guards on doors. No servants to be seen. My heart began to hammer, and sweat sprang out down my back, not just from wearing a mail shirt in the humid summer heat.

I ran across the center of the main courtyard, past the fountain, where the cool water splashed musically as though no danger threatened, and the thin rain had bedewed the bushes so they sparkled with tiny jewels. Two guards stood alone in the atrium, gray haired, wrinkled, watching over the main doors.

"Where is everyone?" I asked, breathless from nerves as well as running.

The guards, old but not lax, saluted me. "On the walls, milady. The Saxon army's fast approaching. Every man's been called to arms. Only us left here to guard the palace."

The patter of running footsteps sounded behind me. The two little boys, Bran and Cyngal, galloped into the atrium with Ystradwel in hot pursuit, a much younger woman following. Both boys carried their wooden swords and shields.

"Open the gates for us, Boden," Bran called out. "We're going to join the battle."

"We're warriors!" piped up Cyngal, waving his sword about. "Grandfather needs ev'ry warrior he c'n get."

Ystradwel and the younger woman came puffing into the atrium, as damp as the children. "Boys," the girl called, her voice betraying her anxiety. "I told you already, you can't go."

"But we're warriors with our own swords," protested Bran. "Grandfather said – we heard him. He needs ev'ry warrior." He stamped his small, booted foot. "An' that's us."

Ystradwel got her breath back. "I'm sorry," she said, half to me, half to the guards and probably half to the two little boys, even though that made three halves. "They got away from us when we weren't looking." She managed a strained smile. "Gwen, this is my grandson's wife, Fianna." She paused. "Fianna, Queen Guinevere."

Fianna was a slight young woman, scarcely more than a girl, whose sandy-brown hair tumbled down her back in unruly curls, as though perhaps she'd been dragged early from her bed to cope with this crisis in childcare. She bobbed a quick bow. "Milady. I'm sorry if my boys have disturbed you."

"Call me Gwen," I said. Not the time to insist on protocol. "And I don't mind at all. I have a boy myself, about Cyngal's age, at home in Din Cadan." I couldn't't help but smile as an image of Amhar's face popped into my head, and the thought that he, too, would have been there offering his help if danger threatened his home.

"Come now, boys," Fianna said. "Back to the nursery."

They set up a wailing protest. "We want to fight."

"We're soldiers now."

"We've bin practicin'."

The guard, Boden, squatted awkwardly down on his haunches to face the boys. "I can see you have indeed been practicing," he said, his voice gravelly with age. "But your great-grandfather wants you to guard your mother. In her rooms. That's the job he did tell me he wanted you to do, just afore he left for the walls. He did say as you was the bravest of the boys in the palace, and you'd know what to do if danger threatened."

The wailing ceased. The tiny warriors exchanged glances. "We do..." Bran's voice wavered as though he suspected he might be being conned in some way. "But we oughta be helpin', really."

Fianna clasped her hands, meeting Ystradwel's eyes over their heads. "You can't leave me on my own. I'll be too frightened. I need my personal guards."

Bran glanced at his little brother.

Cyngal raised his eyebrows and gave a shrug.

Perhaps resigning himself to the role of protector and not warrior, Bran heaved a heartfelt sigh, and took a firm hold of his mother's hand. "Come on then, Mother, this way. Me 'n' Cyngal'll take good care of you, 'speshully if those dirty Saxons gets in here."

With a quick smile that didn't quite reach her eyes, and did nothing to hide her trepidation, Fianna let her sons lead her away. Boden straightened up, heaving a groan as he did so. "Not so easy to get down on me haunches nowadays, miladies. Nor to get up from there, neither."

Ystradwel put a gentle hand on his arm. "That was well done, Boden. Now, let Queen Guinevere and me out so we can go to the walls. Quickly."

A frown of hesitation crossed his face. "Should I be doin' that?"

I stepped forward. "Yes, you should. I'm the wife of the High King and you have to let us out. If the Saxons are not yet here, then we'll be safe."

His gaze slid between our faces. "I'm not sure as I should…"

I put my hand on the doors. "If danger threatens, we'll come back. I promise. Neither of us have a death wish, but we want to watch the battle if we can."

With a look of indecision on his face, Boden held open one side of the double doors for us to step through. "You'll need to head to the south gates. I'm told the scouts seen them a-comin' that way."

Outside, the wet streets were deserted, and the chill of early morning sent another shiver of foreboding down my back. At least the lack of people made our progress to the town walls easy. Where were they all? Hidden indoors or out manning the walls?

"What about the side of the city that faces the river?" I asked Ystradwel as we hurried along the old Via Praetoria, the main Roman road. "And the bridge?"

She glanced sideways, drawing her cloak about her, brow furrowed. "Unless the Saxons have got boats, they won't get in that way. No walls, but the river's too deep to ford. And the bridge is narrow and easy to defend. It's to the north, and Boden said they were coming from the south." She shivered. "Let us hope he's right."

I peered down the many narrow side streets as we passed, searching for any sign of where Arthur had billeted his army. Nothing. Where was he? Had he already ridden out to meet the enemy?

Ahead, the tall towers of the main south gates rose, imposing and massive. On either side of them a huge earthen bank reinforced the inside of the city walls, with steps set in it at intervals leading up to the long, stone wall-walk. Along the run of the wall stood further towers, projecting out, and they, like the double gate towers, bristled with armed men.

The warriors manning the walls had been augmented by the townspeople, armed with whatever they had in their houses: woodaxes, hunting bows, hoes, spades, even piles of rocks to hurl. As with Vindolanda, women and older boys were up there too, prepared to defend their homes. Archers held their bows at the ready, each with a plentiful supply of arrows.

We climbed the nearest rain-slippery steps to the wide wall-walk, Ystradwel with some difficulty in her long gown. The nearest warrior spotted us and stood respectfully back to let us peer between the crenellations.

The valley of the Usa stretched wide and comparatively flat in all directions, the distant western hills veiled by heavy cloud. Not many buildings existed beyond the walls – ruined pagan temples, rows of old tombs beside the road, farms in the distance. Cattle still grazed unperturbed, and further off the white dots of sheep showed against the green of open pasturelands, as though nothing bad could be coming.

"Where are they?" I asked the warrior. "I don't see them."

He leaned closer, the hot stink of his body strong in my nostrils. "By there, milady. Look. You see all that smoke? They be in that low bit beyond the trees. A-burnin' of a farm. The heathen bastards." Bitterness edged his voice, and he spat. Perhaps he wanted to get out there and fight them off right now, instead of waiting for them to come to the city walls. Perhaps he knew the farm. Inaction is never the warrior's friend.

He snorted in disgust. "They must've crossed the river to the south of 'ere by the looks of that. Or they'd've come upon us from the east."

Ystradwel squeezed into the narrow crenellation and peered out beside me. Sure enough, a dark column of smoke rose from beyond a distant stand of trees, and even as we watched, a shadow tinged the brow as if from a mass of marching soldiers on the road.

"Miladies!" A voice I recognized. I swung round.

Cadman stood on the wall-walk, his helmet hanging from his gnarled fingers, staring at Ystradwel and me. "This is no place for queens."

I'd heard all this before. "We're safe enough here for now," I snapped. "If danger threatens the walls, I'll get the Queen back to the palace as quickly as I can." I tapped my hip. "And I'm armed."

The old warrior ran a hand through his wet white hair, eyes troubled, probably unimpressed by my claim to be able to defend myself. "That's as may be, but it's my duty to keep every woman and child within these walls safe. And standing up here isn't that."

"Good heavens, man," Ystradwel barked. "The enemy are nowhere near the walls as yet. We're staying here. Look about you. There are other women here, too."

He stood his ground. "They're not queens. But if you're staying, then I'll stop here with you. At the first sign of danger, I'll have you down those steps and escorted back to the palace, if my men have to carry you over their shoulders."

I compressed my lips for a moment and inhaled deeply. "If danger threatens, then you won't need to waste a man escorting us. We'll go by ourselves if you tell us to. You have my word."

He nodded, jamming his helmet on over his wet hair. "Thank you." One-handed, he fastened its buckle, but intent on his mission as guard dog for his two queens, he didn't leave us.

I took another peek through our crenellation. The dark shadow of a throng of warriors was drawing nearer, the march of hundreds of booted feet heading our way. Where was Arthur? Were we going to sit here and wait for a siege? Would it be like Vindolanda, with scaling ladders and fire arrows? My memories of that battle surged back, making my empty stomach twist with fear. But this was a much larger city. Could they hope to besiege us successfully? Surely not? Hadn't Cadman told us Saxons had no heart for siege warfare?

A clattering of many hooves filled the city streets. Down the Via Praetoria, a mass of several hundred mounted warriors approached the gates. Coel, helmetless, rode at its head, his thick white mane glowing like a beacon.

Ystradwel drew a sharp breath. She must have seen him the moment I had. "What's he doing?" she whispered. "He's too old to lead his men into battle." Her hand went to her heart. "The old fool." But her eyes glittered with pride.

I touched her hand. "If he's an old fool, then he's a brave old fool."

She met my eyes. "He's riding his old warhorse. Old Morthwyl. I'd know that animal anywhere. He's been semi-retired himself these past ten years, just ridden for ceremonial purposes. For a horse, he's as old as my husband." She drew herself up taller. "We breed them brave here in Ebrauc."

And she didn't mean the horse.

The warriors standing along the walls and towers abandoned their defensive posts and rushed down the steps to join their king, filling the streets around the gatehouse. A loud creaking told me both gates had swung open wide.

Eyes fixed ahead of himself, Coel urged Old Morthwyl, a big, black beast with flowing mane and tail, under the arches of the gatehouse and out of our sight, his men surging out behind him.

Ystradwel and I rushed back to the crenellation and leaned out to watch her husband ride proudly onto the plain before his city. Morthwyl stepped out as if this were his first battle, almost prancing with excitement, as conscious of the occasion as any human warrior. Close behind the king, the cavalry followed in tight formation, the infantry on their heels, spreading out to either side of the road to face the oncoming Saxon army.

Coel made an imposing figure, with his white hair blowing out behind him, one hand on the reins, effortlessly controlling his spirited mount, the other balancing a short lance tucked under his arm. Not one of his men could miss him.

"He's done what he wouldn't let us do," Cadman said, shaking his head. "He told us to man the walls. That we were too old to fight."

Ystradwel nodded. "Ever a man to lead by example, but also to want to protect others."

Cadman leaned over us, looking out. "I don't feel like I need protecting, milady. I'd rather be out there with my king than in here with the women and children, like a coward. Even if it means being struck down by a Saxon axe."

The horses jog-trotted off the road, heading left to let the men on foot take the lead. Coel kept the riders close together, in a solid section to one side of the ranks of his foot soldiers.

The crash of the closing gates reverberated through the towers. There'd be no retreat.

Three hundred yards out, the ranks of the infantry came to a halt, spears ready in their hands. Coel and the mounted warriors continued left, cantering up onto a ridge of slightly higher ground, most likely so they could make a charge when the Saxons arrived. Still no sign of Arthur. Anticipation twisted my insides. That he had something planned was obvious.

The Saxon force drew ever nearer. In amongst the dense, dark shadow their ranks made, the pale morning light reflected off their chain mail shirts, helmets, and huge axes.

Ystradwel took a rosary from the small bag on her belt, where it hung beside a bunch of large keys, and began praying as she slid the beads between her fingers. Much good that would do her. As Arthur had once said to me, the outcome of a battle has precious little to do with God, and everything to do with the decisions of men.

I glanced along the city walls. Just older warriors, like Cadman, remained, beside the townspeople with their sickles and hoes, the young boys with their hunting bows, the women with their wooden washing dollies, a baker with his peel. Some of the women were as powerfully built as the men, and I wouldn't have liked to have received a whack on the head from one of those dollies. But hopefully it wouldn't come to that.

In dreadful fascination, we watched the Saxon army spread out across the road maybe a quarter of a mile from Coel's force, too far for me to make out much detail, but close enough to see they outnumbered the old king's men.

For a few long minutes, both sides stood staring at one another. Almost like a game of chicken. Of course, neither of them gave way. Coel had a lot to defend, and the Saxons hadn't marched this far from the coast to turn back now, especially not when faced with a less numerous foe, led by a man as old as Coel. Would they have known his age? Did they have spies amongst the citizens of Ebrauc?

You could have cut the silence with a knife. It felt as though we watchers on the wall all held our breath, the rain suddenly increasing and pressing down on us, a fellow feeling linking every one of us.

My skin itched with sweat under my heavy mail shirt, and warm rain trickled down my neck. Cawing raucously, a bevy of crows swept across the sky, perhaps sensing there'd soon be carrion for them to feed on. Maybe they followed armies around like strange camp followers.

As one, the Saxon army raised a mad hollering that ripped through the air, the noise eerie and terrifying after the silence of the morning. They waved their weapons above their heads, banged them on their shields, and the hollering increased. Then, just as suddenly as they'd started their war cries, they broke into a run, charging toward Coel's foot soldiers. His men, outnumbered, bravely held their position, a forest of spears ready to repel the enemy charge.

"That's it," Cadman muttered next to me. "Let the bastards tire themselves out running all the way to meet you. Wise move."

Coel's warriors stood their ground. The tide of Yellow Hairs thundered across the turf toward them, still yelling, waving their axes and swords as they ran.

Coel's men set their shields, locking them together, perhaps a remnant of remembered tactics from the Roman legions. Spears bristled in a hedgehog of death. The Saxons cannoned into them with an audible crash. Surely some must already be dead? Swords flashed, their blades catching the sunlight, men shrieked and bellowed.

Movement to the left caught my eye. Coel's small cavalry charged down from the rise where they'd been waiting, crashing into the right flank of the enemy.

A battle horn rang out. Once, twice, again.

"Look!" Ystradwel cried, pointing toward the corner tower of the city's western wall. I followed her finger.

Around the tower, thundering through the rain-washed fields that surrounded the city, came Arthur's combrogi, his brotherhood of warriors. The white horse at the center led the charge, as they galloped toward the Saxon's left flank.

"Yes!" Cadman punched the rain-washed air. "A pincer movement. Attacking from both sides, and on horseback. They won't have been expecting this."

Each wedge-shaped section of mounted warriors rode with short lances tucked under their arms, their horses' hooves beating a drum tattoo on the ground. Arthur galloped at the front, too obvious by far with the only white horse there. Without thinking, I grabbed Ystradwel's hand, thin and bony in mine. She clutched me back with a strength I'd not expected from one so old.

Arthur's charge crashed into the enemy's left flank, scattering Saxon foot soldiers like spilled barley. At the same time, on the opposite flank, Coel's cavalry hacked at the enemy with solid determination, his white head visible for a moment in the fray. The Saxons, caught between two ferocious armies, fought like demons.

Chaos reigned. Impossible from where we stood to see who was where, to tell friend from foe, as the clouds thickened and the rain fell ever more heavily in solid sheets. On the walls, we stood like drowned rats, the water sluicing down our faces, soaking our clothes.

I'd seen battles before, many times now, but this was the biggest, the most chaotic, the most frenzied. Perhaps these Saxons were a more determined foe. Though how it would have been possible to be worse than the Dogmen from north of the Wall, I didn't know. But our British warriors were also more determined, fiercer, angrier.

My knuckles whitened on the cold stone parapet as I leaned out, straining to watch through the falling rain. Ystradwel did the same beside me, and Cadman, standing behind her, stared out over our heads.

Time stretched out; the rain fell ever more heavily. The battlefield churned with mud and bodies, blood and death. The screams of horses rose above the shouts of men, the shrieks of the dying. Nowhere could I see Llamrei or Arthur. Coel's white mane of hair had vanished. Like a scene from Dante's *Inferno*, hell was reenacted before my eyes on the plain before Ebrauc.

I couldn't watch a minute more. Desperate, the fear running through me making me braver than I'd ever been, I swung round on Cadman. "We need to help them." I waved my hand along the city walls. "The old men, the young. Get them out there. We can't stand by and watch them die."

Cadman met my eyes, his faded eyes alight with something wild and young, a rekindled memory of his youth, perhaps. "You're right." He drew his sword. "My king wouldn't have me stand by like this." He turned and bellowed along the wall. "To me, to the gates. Now."

Releasing Ystradwel's hand, I ran after him, down the slippery steps to the road, as the old warriors, the men, and even some of the women, clattered down behind us. At the bottom, I drew my own sword, and followed him toward the gates.

Some sixth sense must have told him I was there. He spun, his face contorted with fury. "What are you doing? Get back to the walls. If *they* were no place for a queen, then this is worse. You're not coming with us."

"I can fight," I snarled back at him, swiping my wet hair out of my eyes. "That's my husband out there. You can't stop me."

"Can't I?" he roared, as the warriors from the wall crowded round us: stiff old men, young boys, townspeople. "I've heard tales of the High King's wife, but I never heard one that said she was mad."

The guards on the gate were swinging one side open.

Cadman reached out to the baker with his peel. "You, hold her tight. You're not coming."

The baker, a huge man with a massive belly and arms like hams, scowled back at Cadman, but grabbed me by the shoulders and dragged me out of the way. "I'm sorry, milady. I has to do what Milord Cadman says."

I didn't struggle. He was too strong for me. Cadman's reinforcements charged through the gates, and the gate guards slammed them shut. I sagged in the baker's arms, defeated.

He loosened his hold. "Best get ourselves back up onto the walls, milady. T'see what happens."

He was right. I ran, and he lumbered, up the steps to the wall again.

Our meager reinforcements ran toward the fray, slipping and sliding in the mud churned up by all those feet and hooves. And all that bloody rain. But the battle had shifted. Now the fighting was further from the walls. Damn this rain. I couldn't see at all.

Ystradwel caught my hand. "Where did you go?" Her voice rose in panic, her grip like a vice.

I didn't answer but leaned out through the crenellation, desperate to spot Llamrei's white coat.

Nothing.

A young boy peering out of the neighboring crenellation, no older than Llacheu and armed only with a sickle, raised a thin arm and pointed. "Look, they're on the run. At the back there. I sees it."

I strained my eyes, swiping the rain out of them on my already soaked sleeve. "Where? I don't see."

"There, milady. Right there. I sees 'em runnin'."

He was right. If the enemy were on the run, surely it was nearly over?

But not quite. Our army appeared to be following them. Mounted warriors, the only ones I could be sure were ours, ran them down. Even the men on foot struggled through the mud in pursuit. At least, I thought they were our men. The thick rain swallowed them up.

Left behind them on the plain, a morass of mud, as deep and wet as the Somme itself must have been, remained. Bodies sprawled in that mud, dead horses made mounds, here and there *things* moved. Cries rang out, plaintive and terrible. And down came the crows, settling on the corpses and the not quite dead without discrimination. A farmer friend had once told me how crows will take the eyes from living newborn lambs, while their mothers are distracted. I had to look away.

Ystradwel turned to me, the flesh on her face sagging, suddenly loose and old, her eyes full of fear. "In all my time as queen," she whispered, "I've never been present at a battle. This… this is the most terrible of sights."

I nodded. "Every battle is terrible." I bit my lip. Where were our men? Nennius had dismissed this battle in a few short words – the Battle of the City of the Legion. Words that did nothing to carry the enormity of what had happened here. Nothing could convey how dreadful a battle was.

Nothing.

Chapter Eighteen

For a long while, Ystradwel and I remained on the wall, in the rain, waiting. Eventually, the baker, taking his responsibilities to heart, persuaded us into one of the tower chambers. But we both paced between the rickety chairs around the central table and the windows that overlooked the battlefield, unable to rest with our menfolk not yet safely returned. We weren't alone in our vigil – the tired townsfolk, the women, the children, the lame, still crowded the walls, cloaked, expectant, afraid. Just as we were.

At last, our men began to appear out of the misty rain in ghostly dribs and drabs. Trudging, mud covered, exhausted, but victorious. As they neared the gates, their shoulders straightened, and they stood taller, walking with the pride of men who have vanquished a savage foe. On the battlements, the waiting townspeople set up a ragged cheer.

Arthur's men, unhorsed for some reason, might well have been amongst their number. Knowing that, I searched in vain for faces I knew, but they were unrecognizable. The shields slung across their backs were crevassed and filthy, and red-rimmed, exhausted eyes looked out from grimy faces. But when the townspeople ran out of the gates to offer help, the warriors refused. With ramrod straight backs, they marched into the city and up the Via Praetoria to find their billets.

The night had passed, and the first pale light of dawn was peeking over the eastern skyline, before Coel's cavalry and Arthur's combrogi returned on their exhausted horses. I heard their hoofbeats before I saw them. A long and winding column of riders trailed up the shadowy road, as dirty and wet as the men on foot had been, their horses slathered in mud and blood. Severed heads, hooked on by long yellow hair, hung from saddle horns, proof the Romans had not succeeded in extinguishing the old ways, even after three hundred and seventy years of occupation.

Where was Llamrei, with her easy to spot white coat?

Nowhere.

Leaving the baker sleeping propped against the wall in a corner of the tower, Ystradwel and I descended the wooden staircase to the lower level, emerging into the gateway recess as the first of the riders arrived. My anxious eyes roamed the ranks of warriors, still seeking Llamrei, but finding nothing, no glimpse of white amongst the muddy coats. Only dark horses, made darker still by the mud and the dried blood that had run down their flanks from the gory trophies hooked on their saddle horns.

I recoiled in shock. These were not the shining warriors who'd ridden so nobly across the plain in perfect wedge formation at the start of this day. These were creatures I couldn't recognize, things from a fevered imagination's worst nightmare. Not men I knew, but ferocious, unkempt warriors, savage as wild beasts, rank with sweat and the blood of the enemy. Scratch the surface of a Dark Age man, and this was what lurked beneath.

One of them slid down from his horse and turned toward me, as behind him, the rest of the riders filed silently past. He took off his helmet.

I stared.

His hair hung in filthy rats' tails, his handsome face nearly hidden by dirt and blood and other things I couldn't identify and didn't want to. But out of that nightmare face, familiar dark eyes stared at me, holding my gaze for a long, pregnant minute. Then they slid past me to where Ystradwel stood, leaning against the gatehouse wall for support, as though her inner core of strength had finally given way.

Arthur shook his head at her in silent apology.

An anguished gasp escaped her lips. Her hand shot to her heart as she staggered under the blow, her other hand groping for the wall, fingernails scratching at the cold, uncaring stonework. In the flickering light of the torches, still burning smokily in the gateway recess, her face drained of all color. Age sagged her cheeks; despair bleached her eyes.

"I'm sorry." Arthur's voice spoke out of that bloody, mud-covered face. Broken, desolate. "I couldn't save him. I tried. He died a hero."

Ystradwel's legs collapsed under her. A little cry escaped her lips, and she sank to the cobbles like a broken marionette. "Oh God, no. No, no, no."

I took an uncertain step toward her, hand outstretched, my gaze flicking between her and my husband, where he stood, staring out of eyes as anguished as hers.

The tower door crashed back on its hinges. Our baker emerged, his gaze flying from Arthur to Ystradwel to me, shock and horror written on his large and homely face. He must have overheard Arthur's words.

I drew myself up straighter, a deep breath steadying my shattered nerves. "Good baker, the king, *your* king, is dead. Please carry the queen back to the palace."

Needing no other urging, and accepting that today a humble baker would be called upon to carry a queen, he bent and swept Ystradwel up into his arms, as though she were a child to be comforted. Her head lolled against his broad chest as tears ran down her stricken face. On sturdy, reliable legs, the stalwart baker set off up the Via Praetoria toward the palace, as the morning shadows shortened.

I turned back to Arthur.

Inside, unspoken, I was thanking everything – God, the gods in general, fate, my prayers, my luck – that it was Coel who'd died and not my husband. Heartbroken as I was for Ystradwel, relief that I wasn't in her place swept over me. My heart rose as I gazed at Arthur. Regardless of the dirt that covered him, I wrapped my arms around his body, laying my face against the rough links of his mail shirt.

For a long moment he stood stiff and motionless, a statue of a man, before he at last lifted his own arms and laid them awkwardly across my back, as though this were an action alien to him.

"I love you," I whispered into his mail shirt, too quietly for him to hear. "Thank you, God."

THE DOOR INTO our chamber closed, shutting out the servants, who, on my orders, had brought the bathtub and buckets of hot water to our room. Arthur still stood where he'd been since we'd come in from the stable yard. His face had a fixed, distant look, as though in his mind's eye he were far away, reliving that dreadful battle.

Tired, no, exhausted as I was after twenty-four hours with no sleep and nothing to eat, I concentrated my whole being on him. I'd never seen him like this before. So utterly out of it, he didn't seem to care about the state he was in.

I touched his hand, where it hung limply by his side. "Your bath's ready."

Nothing. No reaction.

Taking a deep breath, I reached for the buckle of his sword belt, to undo it.

His hand came down on mine in a vice-like grip, hot and rough.

I raised my eyes to his face. At least now he was looking at me. Interacting. But the desperate pain in his eyes nearly sent me reeling backward.

I bit my lip. "You need to get undressed. Once you're clean you'll feel better." That I was spouting lies wrenched my heart. How could anyone who'd taken part in that bloodbath, that maelstrom of mud and death I'd watched from the walls, ever feel better? I didn't think I could myself, and I'd only viewed it from afar.

He removed my hand, and both his own went to his belt. They were shaking.

Compressing my lips, I stood back as he finally got the buckle undone, letting belt and sword clatter to the mosaic tiles.

"Let me help you with your mail shirt." My own voice quavered. The sight of him like this tore at my heart, bringing tears perilously close to being shed. Tears of both sympathy and shock. This was my bold, brave husband standing here, hands shaking so much he could hardly undress himself.

He remained silent as I pulled his mail shirt over his head and dropped it to the floor beside his sword, in a muddy heap. Underneath, a second belt secured his tunic at the waist. I waited while with still shaking hands he fumbled with the buckle, taking several attempts to get it unfastened. That, too, fell to the ground.

His tunic, at least, was cleaner than the rest of him as it had been covered by the mail shirt, but the cuffs and neckline were stiff with a mixture of mud and blood, and beneath the tunic so were the extremities of his cream undershirt. With still trembling fingers, he undid the laces at his neck, and I helped him out of the tunic.

"Sit down on this chair," I said, common sense keeping my voice gentle and low, as though I were speaking to a child.

He sat. Like an automaton.

I knelt and pulled off his filthy boots. He must have fought on foot at some point for them to have got this badly caked with mud. The question rose again in my head. Where was Llamrei? The horse on which he'd returned had been bay beneath the dirt, not white.

I had to ask. "Where's Llamrei?"

"Gone."

My heart twisted for him. He'd loved that horse. *All* the warriors loved their horses – some more than they loved their wives. A warrior's horse was part of him: his partner, his servant, his faithful friend. To lose that horse would be as big a wrench for him as losing a child, almost.

And yet I sensed that was not the reason for his – what was it? Shellshock? Battle fatigue? PTSD? Surely possible even in a time when no explosives existed. But he was a veteran of many battles – so what had made this one so different? The urge to enfold him in my arms and kiss away his horror nearly overwhelmed me, but the same sense that told me it wasn't caused by the loss of his horse, told me to bide my time.

I touched his shoulder. "Let's get your shirt off."

He let me pull it off. Underneath, his skin was marked with red blotches across his chest and back and down his arms, that by tomorrow would be purpling. A sword fight doesn't just result in cuts or stab wounds – blows from the flat of a sword, from a spear butt, or from the edge of an opponent's shield, could leave a warrior black and blue. I'd seen him bruised so many times. But never like this after a battle – shut off, silent, brooding.

"Braccae. You'll need to stand up."

He did as he was told, but brushed my hand away as I went to undo the lacing. His hands still shook. He heaved a deep breath, fisted his hands, stretched his fingers, tried again. The second time, he got the laces undone and slid out of his leather braccae to stand naked before me.

"Into the bath."

In silence, he stepped into the short, linen-lined tub and sat down in the hot water, knees bent. I picked up the sponge the servants had left and sluiced the water over him, starting with his head and filthy, mud-encrusted hair. Fresh blood ran down his face where I knocked the newly formed scab from a cut, and a new worry about mud in wounds and the possibility of tetanus raised its ugly head. I shoved it away. No time to think of that right now, and nothing I could do about it, anyway.

He sat still, shoulders hunched, as I washed him clean of the mud, and the blood that mostly wasn't his, thank goodness. Apart from the bruises, he only seemed to have the one cut high in his hairline on his forehead, not bad enough to stitch. As I worked, he sat with his hands clasped together – to still the shaking? I watched him closely, afraid of what I was seeing, the fleeting relief at having him back safely, vanished.

At last, when the water had turned a murky brown, he stepped out to stand dripping on the mosaic floor. As if he were a child, like Amhar, I took a rough linen cloth and toweled him dry, while he stood as though not even noticing my presence.

That something terrible had happened, I didn't have to ask. Something worse than just the battle. He hadn't said a word since his apology to Ystradwel.

"Bed," I said, my hand on his naked, still damp back, pushing him toward it. He sat down on the edge. I pushed him again, and he lay down, hands fisted by his sides, staring up at the ceiling. Instinct told me what he needed was the familiar, and here in Ebrauc that was me. I took off my tunic and boots and lay down beside him in just my undershirt and braccae.

He lay still, staring without seeing.

I waited in silence for a while, afraid to touch him, perhaps hoping he'd close his eyes and sleep, but he didn't. Eventually, I took the plunge. "Do you want to tell me about it?"

He blinked. Were those tears sparkling on his thick dark lashes? I'd never seen him cry.

I put my hand on his balled fist. "Talking can help, you know."

He turned anguished eyes on me. "Will it bring them back, then?" His words came out hard and accusing, as though he thought it my fault the dead were so.

What answer was there to that?

I shook my head, fear for my friends gripping me. I'd only seen the few warriors who'd been with him when he rode through the gate, and had eyes only for him. Until this moment I'd not even thought to ask – too concerned with the state he was in. But where were Merlin, Cei, Drustans, Rhiwallon and the other men I knew? "Who-who do you mean?" My own voice shook.

"The dead." His voice came in a hoarse whisper. "The unquiet dead."

A shiver ran through me, icy fingers tickling my skin. "*Who* is dead?" I had to ask. I had to know. Not Merlin, please. Not Cei. Don't let my friends be dead. An ache of fear gripped my chest, and my breathing quickened. "Tell me."

"Geraint."

What? Who?

I stared at him. "Who is Geraint?" Not one of our men, that was for sure. But I knew the name from somewhere my terrified brain refused to let me access, my thoughts flicking everywhere, unable to settle.

A memory flitted past me. A story from Arthur's boyhood recounted to me by Merlin. I grabbed it and held on tight.

When Arthur was a boy, his mentor had been his much older cousin – Prince Geraint, the man who'd then had command of Din Cadan. Arthur's father, and the already adult Cadwy, had been absent in the west. When a messenger warning of Saxon raids in the south had arrived at Viroconium, Arthur, just a boy of thirteen, had led the remnants of his father's men to Din Cadan to join with Geraint before the battle of Llongborth.

That same Cerdic of Caer Guinntguic who now sat on the Council of Kings, but at that time fighting alongside his mother's people, had killed Geraint before Arthur's eyes. And only some clever ruse of

Merlin's had snatched Arthur to safety, before he too could be killed. But that was fifteen years ago now.

"My cousin," he whispered to me. "Those bastards killed my cousin." He blinked away the tears. "And now they've killed my nephew too."

I'd read in books when people said their blood ran cold and thought it fanciful. Now, I suddenly realized it wasn't. A chill settled on my heart at his words, clenching around it in an iron fist and stifling its beats. "Rhiwallon?" I could hardly choke the single word out. A boy, a child, on his first campaign. No. It couldn't be. He must be here, alive, somewhere.

Arthur nodded, and now the tears ran down his cheeks. He turned toward me, and I put my arms around him, nestling him against my breasts, holding him tight as he sobbed, his body wracked. It was a long time before he quieted, and I thought he might have gone to sleep.

He hadn't. "I killed him," he whispered against my shirt.

I tightened my hold, in a bid to reassure him and show him how much I loved him, a fruitless attempt to make him feel better. "You didn't kill him. It wasn't your fault he died. He was a warrior born." The words came out in a rush, tumbling over themselves as I sought for words of comfort and no doubt failed abysmally. I wasn't good at this. "No one could have kept a boy his age kicking his heels at Din Cadan any longer. Not when his friends were marching to war." I remembered the conversation I'd had with Coventina, my heart heavy as a lump of lead in my chest. "If it was anyone's fault that he was here, it was mine and his mother's. We let him come."

He shook his head, not raising it to look me in the eye. "You don't understand. *I* killed him." His hands began to shake again. He clasped them tight, and I covered them with one of mine, stroking them in an effort to calm the shake. I might as well not have bothered.

I had to ask the question, though. "What do you mean?"

For a long moment he remained silent, then his body went rigid. "A Saxon twice his size. The boy was fighting him. Outmatched." His voice shook. "The man gutted him."

My treacherous stomach heaved, and I struggled to prevent myself from retching. I'd seen enough dead and dying men now to know what that meant. Horror curdled in my heart.

"I killed the warrior, but I was too late to save Rhiwallon." He shifted his head so he could look up into my eyes. "I cradled him in my arms as he lay dying." The tears ran down his cheeks. "He was so frightened and so brave. He looked into my eyes and asked me to tell his father he loved him." The words came choking out. "Then... then he asked me to end it for him."

I stared into eyes that brimmed with self-disgust, words flown. Nothing would comfort him for this. In Vindolanda two years ago I'd administered an overdose of poppy syrup to end the suffering of a terribly injured child, but this was different. Rhiwallon was a boy I knew, a boy I'd seen grow to the cusp of manhood, a boy we both loved. Cei's son. That icy hand renewed its hold. Did Cei know?

Arthur swallowed. "He-he could see his own entrails hanging out. He knew it was the end. The-the pain..." He hesitated. "I couldn't let him suffer."

I pulled him tighter against me, holding him as close as I could, my face against his, our tears mingling.

Rhiwallon, playing at being a warrior with Llacheu on the day I met them. Long legs dangling from a too small pony. Rhiwallon, disgusted by the sight of Merlin and Morgana kissing – thinking girls were awful. Rhiwallon, sitting around the campfire swigging cider from the skin being passed around. Rhiwallon, arm-in-arm with his new friends, off to the fleshpots of Caer Went to become a man.

Rhiwallon lying dead on a battlefield far from his home.

Coventina weeping for a son she'd never see again.

We cried ourselves to sleep.

Chapter Nineteen

I AWOKE ALONE. Arthur had gone, and the room felt sad and empty without him. I pushed myself up and blinked in the dim evening light, battling to pull myself together and unfog my mind. I felt as though I had a hangover.

Rhiwallon.

I jumped off the bed and pulled my boots on, leaving my tunic lying on the floor where I'd discarded it this morning. As I reached the door, a wave of dizziness washed over me, and my stomach growled its protest at thirty-six hours without food. A mouth as dry as sandpaper told me I needed something to drink. Now.

Out in the warm courtyard the shadows of evening had already lengthened, and the sun had dropped below the palace walls. The oppressive quiet unsettled me. The kitchens. Drink, and then food, were what I needed in order to function properly. Only then could I deal with the fallout of what had happened yesterday.

I found the kitchens at last, and barged in without ceremony. The half-dozen servants froze, arrested in their work at the sight of me.

"I need something to eat and drink," I said. "Quickly, please."

They scurried to do my bidding. Being a queen had its benefits. Within minutes they'd provided me with a large beaker of weak cider and a hunk of bread and cheese. I devoured them ravenously, and held out the beaker for a refill. Then, having thanked them, I took more bread with me and hurried back out into the corridor.

By the time I reached the stables the extra bread had followed the first lot, and my head had stopped spinning, although the two beakers of cider had made me light-headed in a totally different way. A way I liked. I needed some kind of prop this evening.

Already, a few torches had been lit in the iron wall brackets, chasing the last of the daylight away. In the long, thatched stable building, the rear ends of many horses showed, where they'd been tied in their stalls with their rations of oats and armfuls of hay. Good reward for their service in battle. Amongst them must be Alezan, who'd stood idle while her fellows had ridden out.

All the horses looked clean, the mud of yesterday groomed out of their coats, their tails untangled. Warriors know their horses are more than just a means of riding into battle, the equivalent of young men in my old world with their fancy souped-up cars. Each warrior would put his horse before everything but a fellow warrior.

Their horses cared for, the men sat around, cleaning their harness, polishing the brass, rubbing oil into the treasured leather of bridles and saddles. Without that, the leather would soon crack and harden, with danger of it breaking in battle. These were men in synchronization with their whole way of life, to whom war and fighting came as naturally as breathing. They, too, were cleaner, although not quite as clean as their beloved horses and tack. Faces, that only this morning had seemed alien and wild, had returned to staid normality.

I hesitated on the threshold. A few of our men seemed to be here, but mainly the stables held the remains of Coel's cavalry. No sign of Arthur. Our main force would be out somewhere in the city, camped in the intramural fields.

By the trough in the center of the stable courtyard, Merlin sat on an upturned bucket, head down, working at his reins with an oily rag.

With hesitant steps, I approached. Clad only his undershirt and braccae, he'd confined his long hair in an untidy braid.

He must have seen my shadow, or heard my footsteps over the

subdued conversation in the stable yard. For a moment or two he kept on rubbing at the reins. Then he raised his head and met my gaze. "Gwen."

I sucked in my lips for a moment, squeezing them between my teeth. "Merlin."

He looked undamaged. Clean… ish. No visible wounds. But then, Arthur's wounds weren't visible, either.

He picked up the rest of his bridle and buckled the reins to the bit. "Done," he said, as though nothing mattered more than having clean tack. "Finished." He got to his feet. He stood taller than me by a good four inches and I had to look up.

"Do you know where Arthur is?" I asked.

He walked over to the stables and hooked his bridle onto the horn of his saddle, where it sat on the wooden wall between his horse and the next.

I trailed after him.

"With Cei." He didn't look at me as he spoke, but the bitterness in his voice told me he knew what had happened. The sound of many horses masticating their hay seemed loud in the musty warmth of the stables. A few flies buzzed. Up the line, a horse staled with a hiss and froth of urine on cobbles. The conversation from outside muted.

I stood with one hand on the low wooden wall, running a fingernail along the grain of the wood. "He told me what happened."

Merlin turned around, his eyes every bit as anguished as Arthur's had been. "Should I have seen this coming?" His words spilled out. "Should I have foreseen Rhiwallon's death? Could I have saved him, like I did Arthur when I snatched him from Cerdic's blow at Llongborth?"

I stared at him. How could I answer this? He had the Sight. Perhaps he should indeed have known Rhiwallon was riding to his death. Who was I to say?

His eyes narrowed. "Did *you* know?"

My mouth fell open. For a moment I floundered, searching for words, drowning in the sensation that perhaps I *should* have known. Wondering why I hadn't paid more attention to my father's research. Was there somewhere a mention of a boy called Rhiwallon? A boy who died at the Battle of the City of the Legion? Should I have known this, and if I had, could *I* have saved him?

I shut my mouth and shook my head. "No. I didn't know. If I had, I'd never have let him ride north with us. Never." Merlin's horse stamped its feet. From further down the line came a few snorts.

Llacheu. Did he have a death like this waiting for him? Somewhere in the none-too-distant future? And Amhar, following on so close behind. Just a little boy now, but in no time, he'd be a warrior like Rhiwallon.

I swallowed. "How... how did Cei take it?"

Merlin shrugged. "How do you think? Rhiwallon was his only son."

I glanced over my shoulder at the warriors in the torchlit stable yard. They were talking quietly, with none of the exuberance you'd expect from victors. "Who else is dead?"

Merlin sighed. "A goodly number. Coel fell a hero. As did many of his men. But there were more deaths amongst the Yellow Hairs than in our ranks. We drove them hard, right back to their ships. If we'd had fire arrows, we'd have set their ships alight to speed them on their way. They ran before us, driven like sheep, and we picked them off as they ran. Our horses gave us the advantage."

He paused, ruminating. "That was how it happened."

I waited for him to go on, but his eyes had taken on a faraway look, as distant as Arthur's had been. The horse beside me lifted his tail and did a dropping, the slap of it hitting the cobbles loud. Steam rose from the pile. A snort came from further down the row. Hooves stamped. Outside in the stable yard night had nearly fallen.

Merlin cleared his throat and spat into the straw underfoot. "We were fording a river. A deep river. The current took Rhiwallon and dragged him and his horse downstream. A Saxon straggler must have knocked him from his horse as he struggled onto the far bank. Perhaps he meant to steal the horse." He paused. "The boy had no chance. The Saxon was a monster – he must have seen his opponent was nothing but a stripling. He took his time, letting the boy tire, nicking him here and there to make him bleed... to cause him pain... to taunt him."

He heaved a heartfelt sigh, setting his hand on the quarters of the horse beside him. His horse. "The boy fought bravely. Arthur and I saw the current take him. Once we were across, we rode to find him. We weren't quick enough..." He fell silent, staring at his feet.

I waited, wanting to hear more but also not wanting to. Dreading the words that would come out of my friend's mouth.

He straightened up, but didn't look at me. "The bastard Saxon saw us. His ugly face – I'll see that in my dreams. He looked at us and sneered, seeing his own death coming, and ripped his sword through the boy's stomach. He made sure to mark the boy for death before he died."

It had grown very dark in the stable, the flickering light of the distant torches throwing Merlin's face into grotesque shadow, made worse by his expression of horror. "Arthur rode him down too hastily. The Saxon used his axe and Llamrei fell, the axe in her chest. But Arthur was quick. He took the man's head – with the sword from the stone – even as Llamrei fell."

"Is she... is she dead?" Perhaps I'd been nurturing a hope that Arthur had just lost her, that she was out there somewhere looking for her master.

Merlin nodded. "I had to finish her off."

Llamrei, with her shining white coat, her flowing mane and tail, her large dark eyes with the perfect white lashes. Strong and proud, and trained as an extra weapon to fight for Arthur. Dead. Beside Rhiwallon. The tears flowed down my cheeks afresh – for everything that had been lost. For youth, for beauty, for innocence.

"And Rhiwallon?" My voice sounded small in the quiet stables.

Merlin swiped a hand across his eyes. Rhiwallon was a boy he'd taught. A boy he'd prepared for this life – the life that had killed him. Did he feel guilt? Most likely. "He'd fallen to the ground. His... his belly had been ripped open." He shook his head. "There was nothing we could do. Nothing could have mended that... that gaping wound. He could barely breathe."

I stood still, unable to think of anything to say that wouldn't sound crass.

Merlin sniffed hard, his hand returning to his eyes. "Arthur took him in his arms. The boy was still alive, but he knew his end had come. He called out for his mother."

Somehow, when I'd heard the tales of Arthur and his knights from my father, I'd never bestowed human emotions on them, never thought of them as being affected by the deaths of their companions. They'd been stories, but this was real, and even men accustomed to violent deaths had feelings. And where a stripling boy was concerned, a boy they'd known from babyhood, they were like anyone else. Deeply affected.

Merlin picked up the reins he'd been oiling, twisting them in his fingers. "You get used to death when you're a warrior. Every time you ride into battle it could be the last... your last... but when a young warrior dies, a boy in his first campaign... it's different."

I licked my dry lips.

He shook his head. "A boy like that has all his life ahead of him. Or he should have done. A life of fighting, whoring, drinking, hunting. A wife, perhaps, and children. To have it snatched away in such a manner... not in battle... in spite. That Saxon killed him out of spite, because he could, careless of the consequences to himself."

He gave the reins a savage jerk. "You expect deaths in battle. You expect to lose men. Sometimes many. But not this way. And not

Rhiwallon. A man should not outlive his children."

He fell silent. Behind him, his horse swished her tail, and the contented rhythmic masticating of the animals seemed to grow louder in the quiet.

I dug my nail into the wood, not wanting to ask the question forming on my lips. But I couldn't keep it in. "Did-did Arthur *kill* him?"

Merlin nodded. "He had to. The boy was in terrible pain. It was the kindest thing to do. Just as I did for Llamrei. As he held him close, he slid his knife up under the boy's ribs into his heart – the surest way."

Tears overflowed and ran down my cheeks. Tears for a future Rhiwallon would never see. Tears for his mother, all unknowing of her loss.

"What did you do with his body?" Surely they hadn't left it out there on a distant river bank for the crows, or worse?

Merlin must have guessed my thoughts. "We brought it back. He'll have an honorable burial. Here, outside the city, after the Roman fashion. All our dead will."

I nodded. Shock had numbed me, but part of me was screaming inside that this could be Amhar in ten years' time, that someone could be bringing me news of my son's death, just as we would have to bring our news to Coventina.

I clenched my fists in an effort to stem the tears. "Do you know where Arthur's really gone?"

Merlin shrugged. "To see the men. That's what a good leader does. He rises above the losses, squares his shoulders and carries on. Arthur and Cei both know that." He set down the reins. "Does this not happen in your old world?"

Did it? My instinct was to blurt out a hurried no. But that wasn't true. I thought of the young men who'd died in Afghanistan and Iraq, and all the other wars that still were fought in my old world. Needless deaths, all of them. Was any death in war truly necessary? Why were men so aggressive and acquisitive? If women ruled, would we be like this? Always coveting what our neighbor had?

I gave myself a shake. "Sort of. The world is bigger in some ways. More people. More pressures. And smaller in others." I sought for words. "Here, this feels like we're the only people in the world. That outside of Dumnonia and Britain, nothing else matters. But in my world, everywhere is connected, and people fight needless wars between far-apart countries." I frowned, thinking of the nuclear threat most powers thought they needed, worse by far than the hand-to-hand combat I saw here. I couldn't explain any of that to Merlin. Instead, I managed a watery smile, setting my hand on his arm. "I much prefer it like this."

"With all this death?"

I nodded. "It's a part of your world. Of my world now. I see that every king has to defend his territory and his people. But our armies don't take the fighting across the sea to the Saxon homelands. We just fight them off right here. It's defense, not aggression. We don't want to share any more land than we've already ceded to them. But they – they want more than we're prepared to give."

Merlin nodded. "You have it right there. I've tried to look, but I don't see the end of this. Man's nature is to fight. When I do look, I see rivers of blood and dying men. So I don't look anymore." He gave himself a little shake. "It frightens me."

I moved closer to him and put my other hand on his where it rested on one of the horns of his saddle. "Me too. I have so little knowledge, and yet I also have so much. This is my past I'm living in, but it's a past about which no one in my old world knows much at all. Everything is garbled, confused, uncertain. There's little written down apart from a long list of moans written in forty years' time. Then nothing. The only things we have about these battles, and about Arthur, are books written hundreds of years from now. And no one knows if what's in them was made up, or stolen from some other source, or could possibly be true."

He turned his hand over and took mine in his. "Knowing the future is a burden, not a blessing. If you would share it?"

The calluses on his palm felt rough on my skin, but the contact with another human being warmed my heart. "My friend," I said, keeping my voice down low. "You don't want to know what I know. I couldn't burden you with that."

Outside in the stable yard, one of the men had begun a song – a sad and lilting lament, about a long-ago battle, the words rising toward the star-sprinkled sky. When he reached the chorus, the other men joined in, their low, melancholy chant echoing in my heart.

We stood, handfasted, listening to the melody.

Merlin shook himself like a dog. "We need to eat. Come with me to the camp. The men have fires lit and stews cooking. Arthur and Cei will be there. With the men."

"How is it I'm hungry when I'm so sad?" I asked, wiping the tears from my eyes. "I feel I shouldn't be. It's wrong. Disrespectful of our dead. Disrespectful of Rhiwallon."

Merlin put an arm around my shoulders, the comfort of his touch wrapping itself around me like a warm blanket. "Life goes on. You and I know that. The dead are dead a long time, and we have but a short time on this Earth. You need to eat, and so do I. Come."

Chapter Twenty

ARTHUR'S MEN HAD made their camp in the eastern quarter of the city in fields sandwiched between the high walls and the riverbank. Their tired horses stood tethered to rope picket lines set up under the walls, and small fires dotted across the dark fields shone like stars.

Groups of men huddled around each fire, their heads turning as Merlin and I passed. Did they still think of me as their luck bringer? Maybe. They had won, and still lived. But at what cost? I hadn't brought luck to Rhiwallon, had I? Nor to the other dead lying waiting to be buried.

"They're with the dead," young Drustans of Caer Dore, a bloody bandage around his head, told us, when we came upon him sitting beside a fire, eating a plate of brown stew. "Cei wanted to sit up with his son until morning. There are feral dogs about... and wolves..."

At least the wolves wouldn't be able to get inside the city walls, though.

I nodded, my eyes seeking Merlin's face. "Should I go to them?"

He shook his head. "Leave them to their grief. It's best. A warrior grieves in his own way. Cei needs to mourn and Arthur with him. Tomorrow there's work to be done." He indicated some empty seats, just lumps of wood, pulled near to the fire. "Sit down and eat. You're good for nothing without food inside you. Can't have you fainting."

The bread and cheese felt a long time ago. I sank down beside

Drustans. He set his plate of food on the ground and leaned forward to fill a couple more plates from the cauldron hanging on a trivet over the fire. The stew was thick and meaty, its aroma setting my guilty saliva running. He passed the plates to Merlin and me, and picked up his own again.

We sat and ate the savory stew in silence for a while. On the far side of the fire, Bedwyr, Anwyll, Gwalchmei, and a few other warriors, watched us from across the flames, eyes wary. Gwalchmei had his left arm in a rough sling. None of them looked clean – no baths of hot water out here for our men. Maybe tomorrow they could bathe in the river. Maybe some of them already had.

The sound of the wind rustling the willows down by the water's edge carried over the crackle of flames and the muted voices from around the other fires.

Hunger made us scrape our plates, and left my shrunken belly feeling bloated. Bedwyr passed round a skin of wine, and we all drank too much of it. Maybe I was hoping it would make me forget Rhiwallon for a moment and push aside all thoughts of how to tell his mother about his death. Burying him here with the other warriors would mean she'd never even have a grave to mourn beside. The thought had tears running down my cheeks again, unstoppable.

The flames died down. "Time we all slept," Anwyll said, his voice so gruff, I suspected he, too, might have been near to crying. Perhaps not just for Rhiwallon. Many men had died in the battle – brothers, sons, fathers, friends. I'd always thought that after a battle the victors would feel – what? Celebratory? Happy? Victorious? Proud? But in reality, after a battle the result is often as bad for the victors as the losers. Men have died on both sides, men who would never wield sword nor shield again.

Why, then, did men continue to fight? Why did they seem to enjoy riding off to war? Eternal optimism that they and their loved ones would not die, perhaps. Pride in what they did. The urge to defend and protect their homes and families. Probably a multitude of reasons. At least here they weren't interfering in far-off overseas wars.

Merlin interrupted my philosophical musings. "I've spread your blankets beside mine. Come and lie down."

I had a bed in the palace, but I didn't want it. I couldn't bring myself to be near Ystradwel and her grief. Not even kicking off my boots, I lay down on the blanket beside Merlin, under the starry sky.

With a sigh, Merlin pulled another blanket up over his legs. The night was growing chilly. All around us the other warriors spread out their bed rolls.

Wiping my watering eyes, I rolled over to look at Merlin where he lay on his back, showing me his profile. "I hate war," I whispered, trying not to disturb the other men.

He turned his head, eyes golden in the firelight. "It's a necessary part of life." He, too, kept to a whisper.

I drew my knees up into a fetal position. "Why? Why do we have to have it? It's not fair that all those men – those *young* men – are lying dead. For what?"

He rolled onto his side to face me. "For Britain. For all the kingdoms here. For all the people – the women, the children, the sick and the old. It's our duty to protect the weak and vulnerable. To save them from the Saxon hordes."

My tears kept on running. How could I tell him it would all be in vain, that his Britain would end up being called England whatever he did – named after a group of the invaders he so vehemently wanted to repel – the Angles. That we might as well give up and let them come. Save the lives of all these brave warriors – save the lives of boys like Rhiwallon.

I didn't tell him, of course. I couldn't. The burden of knowing the future sat ever more heavily on my body, pressing me down into the hard ground, and the tears flowed faster.

He shuffled closer. "Come here." His voice was gentle.

I moved into my friend's embrace, his comforting arms around me, my face against his chest. And for the second time that day, I cried myself to sleep.

>>>•<<<

I WOKE EARLY. Impossible not to. The sound of wolves howling outside the walls had disturbed me a few times in the night, but I'd fallen back into a troubled sleep that hadn't lasted long. Merlin gently extricated himself from my embrace, and went to prepare us some breakfast. I pushed my blanket off, sat up, and wiped the sleep from my eyes with a grubby hand.

With the sun still low in the eastern sky, the warriors began their day's work. Horses had to be fed and watered, fires stoked hot enough to toast stale bread on the ends of daggers, work parties organized.

Still no sign of Arthur and Cei.

After breakfast of the toasted bread, and cheese washed down with cider, still cold from the night's chilling, I followed Merlin to the lesser southern gateway of the city, close by our camp. We trailed behind the men, all now armed with tools for digging. Did they carry them with them? I'd never noticed. Maybe they were like army entrenching tools from World War One? I'd seen one in a museum on the Flanders battlefields when my father had taken me there. More young men who'd gone out all bold and brave and never returned. I swallowed the lump in my throat that refused to go away.

Just beyond a ruined pagan temple, and a hundred yards outside the city walls, half the men began digging out a trench to bury our dead. Further over, the rest set about building fires to burn the heathen corpses. No grave for them. And they'd not been protected overnight by city walls – even just a cursory glance showed me that bits of them were gnawed or completely missing. The wolves I'd heard must have had a feast last night.

"I need to help," Merlin said. He walked away, leaving me standing in what would one day be a busy street in modern York, the trampled grass around me still pocked with hoofmarks, the battlefield a morass of mud a little further away. Crows perched on the fallen horses, pecking. Was that happening to Llamrei? Beautiful, noble Llamrei. Somewhere on a far-off riverbank. That bloody lump rose again, choking me. Tears ran afresh down my cheeks. Would I have any left to shed?

Even though a lot of men labored on preparing for the burials, it took most of the day to dig the pit and burn the Saxon corpses. I watched it all. These men, the living and the dead, deserved my gratitude. My honoring. Without their sacrifice where would we be? Dead or Saxons slaves.

Day was drawing to a close when the main gates opened, and the funeral cortege began. Black smoke still billowed from the funeral pyre of the hated Saxons, tainting the evening air with the stink of their burning flesh.

On foot, Arthur led the way, dressed all in black as was his habit, unadorned, plain, a crow amongst a flock of birds of brighter plumage.

Walking behind Arthur came the new king, Garbaniawn, somehow shrunken in upon himself, a smaller man than I remembered from the feast in the hall, head down, shoulders slumped. He must have loved his father, a rare quality to be found in a king's heir. A simple gold circlet adorned his hair, but Arthur went bare headed.

Behind the two kings strode the scrawny old Bishop, Exuperius, in his formal robes of office. A long, pale gown adorned with rich embroidery swept the muddy ground, a cloak of rich green draped his shoulders, and a heavy gold crucifix rested on his chest. Small boys in long cream tunics followed, swinging incense holders, chanting psalms.

Behind the boys, an oxcart carried the old king's body. And behind that walked Ystradwel, supported on both sides by her women. Was one of them Fianna, the mother of those two bold little boys?

The remainder of the dead followed, three to a cart, swathed in pale shrouds. Beside the first walked Cei, one hand resting on the cart's side, every step leaden. I thought of Merlin's words. Sons aren't meant to die before their fathers.

In a long column behind the laden carts came the townspeople, silent, respectful, wretched, many of them bereaved themselves, no doubt. The warriors, who'd dug all day long, drew back to form a wide honor guard, eyes fixed on the wrapped corpses of their comrades. Every man here mourned.

From their ranks, Merlin came to stand beside me, filthy from his work. Careless of the dirt, I slid my hand into his.

"Should I be there?" I whispered. "Walking in the procession beside my husband?" I peered up at Merlin's haggard face. "Walking with Cei beside Rhiwallon's bier?"

He leaned close, the smell of sweat about him strong. "Possibly. But you can just as easily pay them your respects from here. No one will object. It doesn't matter."

I closed my eyes, offering up a silent prayer, but to whom I had no idea. Was God even listening? Did he not care that so many had died? A child amongst them. But the words Arthur had spoken once resonated in my head – *"Battles have nothing to do with God, and all to do with man."* How right he was.

As the cortege reached the burial pit, the carts lined up side-by-side. A ramp had been constructed leading into the wide pit. The drivers and mourners took turns to carry the bodies down on flat boards, where they laid them in regimented rows, with Coel's body at the front on its own. Too many by far.

"Does he not get a tomb of his own?" I asked.

Merlin shook his head. "His wish was to be buried with his men."

When it came to Rhiwallon's turn, Arthur left Garbaniawn and went to help Cei carry his son. Taking an end of the board each, they bore him down the ramp to his place with his fellows with as much care as if he still lived. For a moment the two men stood still, heads bent and Arthur's hand on his brother's shoulder. Maybe they were praying, although I couldn't imagine Arthur doing that. Then, together, they turned away and walked back up to stand looking down into the pit, close by Garbaniawn and Ystradwel.

A shadow of her former self, shrunken and bent, the old queen showed every year of her age. Had she hoped her husband would die peacefully in his bed with her by his side? But which was better? To die honorably fighting for your kingdom, or to succumb in the end to the ravages of age? I had no idea. The fear of what lay ahead for Arthur before old age reached him, and for me, rekindled in my stomach. I regretted the food I'd eaten that morning.

The long prayers for the dead began. I hung my head, too distraught to look at the sea of mourning faces. Never had I felt the sense of being on the outside looking in so strongly. This was their world, not mine, no matter how much I thought I'd come to be a part of it. My first twenty-four years of living in the twenty-first century had spoiled me for that.

AFTER THE FUNERAL was over, as night fell, I walked back with Merlin to the palace, unsure where Arthur would choose to go. Once in my chamber, I sent a servant for hot water and had the bath refilled. I'd just settled into the warm water when the door swung open.

Arthur stood on the threshold.

He was drunk. Easy to see because of the swaying, and the fact he was leaning on the door lintel.

I sunk my shoulders down into the water, acutely aware someone might see me through the open door, even if it was only Cei or Merlin.

For a long moment, he stood staring at me, before he came in and let the door slam shut. He wove his way over to the table, where a jug of wine stood beside the bread, cold meat and olives a servant had brought me, and sat down heavily on one of the chairs. Uncertain whether to continue with my bath, I watched him, wary of his drunkenness.

With an unsteady hand, he slopped wine into a large goblet, lifted it to his lips and gulped it down. Some of it ran down his bristly chin. He refilled the goblet.

That was enough of that. I rubbed myself down with the sponge as quickly as I could, and climbed out of the bathtub, reaching for my linen towel. I'd been meaning to wash my hair, but that would have to wait.

"Don't," he said.

Hand on towel, I froze. "Don't what?"

"Don't cover yourself up." His gaze ran over my body in a way I didn't like and didn't understand. This wasn't my beloved husband looking at me. This was a stranger. A drunken stranger. I drew the towel in front of myself, as the water pooled by my feet.

"Have a drink with me," he said, slopping more wine into another goblet. The table swam with wine.

I wrapped the towel around myself, glad it was big, and came and sat down in the other chair. "I'd rather have some food." I reached out and pulled the plate of cheese toward me.

His hand shot out. "No. Drink with me. Both of you."

I met his gaze, as he blinked myopically. Where had he got this drunk? I'd come straight back to the palace after the funeral, so where had he gone? And why, when he was mostly a sparing drinker, had he got like this? I'd only ever seen him this drunk once before – after the deaths of Ummidia and her daughters. Perhaps it was his way of coping.

I picked up the goblet and took a tentative sip. "I'm hungry. I haven't eaten since breakfast."

He drained his second goblet. "Yes. Where were you? You should've been with me. Walking in the funeral procession. Showing respect for the dead." He slurred his words, having difficulty getting them out, more drunk than even after the women died.

"I was with Merlin. He was looking after me."

He snorted. "Hah. Merlin. Thought he could worm his way in with you, did he? Now he doesn't have Morgana."

I bristled at the implication, but heat rose to my cheeks as I remembered how I'd slept in his arms, for comfort only, when Arthur hadn't been there. "Merlin and I are friends. Just as you and he are."

Another snort. "Really? Then if he's my friend, why didn't he do something to save Rhiwallon? Why did I have to slide my dagger into that boy's heart? Eh? Tell me. Why?"

Oh, how I wished I could. And how I wished I could undo my decision to bring Rhiwallon with me when I'd followed Arthur.

He put the goblet to his lips again and drained half of it in one gulp.

"You're drunk," I said, as gently as I could. "Don't drink any more."

He would have stood up if he could, but luckily, he couldn't. Instead, he leaned across the table toward me, his face distorted with a mixture of fury and pain. "Don't tell me what to do. I'm your king. Your husband. You can't tell me what to do."

I sat rigid, staring at him, a nugget of fear in my heart. Not fear of him, but fear *for* him. I reached out and touched his hand. "Why don't you come to bed?"

His mouth worked as though he wanted to say something, but his brain wouldn't connect. He must have had an awful lot to drink before he'd arrived here, and now he'd drunk the best part of a bottle of wine in less than five minutes.

I got up and stepped around the table to his seat. "Come on," I whispered, my heart breaking for him. "Let me help you up. Come and lie down beside me."

He was hard to get across the room to our bed. His legs didn't appear to want to obey him, and he leaned heavily on me, dislodging my towel so that when he tumbled onto the bed, I was stark naked. But his eyes closed as his head touched the pillow, and not even if I'd done the dance of the seven veils in front of him would he have shown any interest.

I pulled my undershirt on over my nakedness and lay down beside him, wondering if Cei was in a similar state.

>>><<<

ARTHUR'S SHOUT WOKE me in the middle of the night to total darkness. The candle I'd left burning had gone out, and oppressive, warm night pressed in all around.

"No!" He shouted again, thrashing back and forth in the bed beside me. "No! Leave him alone!"

I sat up, leaning over him, my heart pounding in fright. "Arthur. Wake up. You're dreaming." I put a reassuring hand on his chest, and found it drenched in sweat, his heartbeat galloping under my touch. "Wake up!" I shook him with both hands.

His thrashing lessened. Finally, he lay still, panting. Had he been dreaming of Rhiwallon's death?

I stroked his face. "It's all right. I'm here. You're in your bed, with me." I kept my voice low and gentle, a mother soothing her child after a nightmare.

"Gwen?" How vulnerable and young he sounded, how unsure. Not the determined, powerful king I knew and loved. But somehow, I loved this version of him all the more – the boy he'd once been, afraid of his nightmares. The man who needed me.

I bent and kissed his forehead. "I'm here."

He lifted his hand and touched my face. "I have a terrible headache."

I smiled, but he wouldn't have been able to see. "I'm not surprised, the amount you must have drunk." I touched his clammy forehead. "I think you needed to do that, though."

"My mouth feels like a dusty road," he croaked. "I need a drink."

"Not that strong wine. You've had enough of that. I think there was some watered wine as well. I'll find it."

"No." His hand closed around my wrist. "Don't get up. I'll manage. Hold me."

I lay back down next to him, my arms around him. "I'm here."

For a few long minutes we lay in silence, before he spoke again. "I dreamed of Llongborth."

I stiffened. His first battle, where Prince Geraint had died. "You did?"

He nodded. "I've never told you about it, have I?"

"No, but I know about it. I know about Geraint."

I felt him shake his head. He groaned. "Ow, that hurts. I doubt you were told the full story."

I bit my lip. I wanted him to go on, but part of me recoiled from yet another tale of death. "Go on, then," I whispered, shuffling closer.

His warm breath tickled my neck. My heart bursting with love for him, all I wanted to do was kiss away his demons. But I couldn't.

"I led part of my father's army south to Din Cadan to join Geraint. We rode together to Llongborth. I felt like a god, riding at the head of our combined armies, beside my cousin, as though I were a general, like him. He glittered in the sunlight. All I wanted was to be just like him."

The stubble on his face felt like sandpaper under my fingers.

He swallowed. "We came to battle. My first. I'd learned all the tricks, the theory, ridden at the targets with my spear. But nothing could have compared to being in a real battle." He paused. "I was terrified, but I loved it. Geraint stayed by my side, and I tried to copy everything he did. Glorious, brave, handsome. My horse fell, a spear in its chest, and I was trapped under its body. Geraint saw and leapt off his own horse to pull me out." He paused. "Then Cerdic came."

He fell silent, maybe conjuring that long ago day inside his head.

I waited, my hand against his cheek.

Arthur heaved in a steadying breath. "We were on foot. Cerdic did to Geraint what that Saxon did to Rhiwallon." The words tumbled out in a hurry.

Oh God. No wonder he'd been so badly affected by the boy's death. I leaned over and pressed my lips against his cheek, tasting the salt of tears.

His chest rose as he drew in another deep breath. "He'd have done the same to me if Merlin hadn't snatched me away. I don't know to this day how he did it, but one moment I was facing Cerdic, and the next I was somewhere else." He paused. "But we'd abandoned Geraint to his fate."

He shuddered. "It takes a long time to die from a wound like that. It's why they do it. They want to inflict as much suffering as they can, and put an enemy out of action, and maybe the man who goes to help. They're barbarians."

"They are." No wonder he hated Cerdic with a vengeance. No wonder it had been so hard to face him at the Council of Kings.

He moved his head, his mouth close to mine and our breath shared. "I dreamed I was on the battlefield at Llongborth, with Geraint, fighting Cerdic and his men." His breath smelled stale, of the wine he'd drunk, but I didn't care. My fingers were in his hair.

He touched my face. "Then, when I looked, it wasn't Geraint lying gutted in the mud. It was Rhiwallon, staring up at me out of terrified eyes. Eyes that knew his death was come upon him." He hesitated. "And just as with Geraint, there was nothing I could do to save him. My brother's son. But then Merlin whipped me away, before I could help Rhiwallon. I didn't want him to, but he did. I had to leave the boy there, trying to shove his guts back inside his belly."

I kissed his salty lips, cupping his face between my hands. "It wasn't your fault. None of this is your fault. At least you were with Rhiwallon to do what you did. That will be of some comfort to Cei and Coventina. I know it will."

He kissed me back, his lips soft and gentle. "I love you, Gwen. I'm sorry I behaved so badly when I was drunk. I shouldn't have spoken to you like that."

I kissed him again, my own tears mingling with his. "Don't worry. I understand. I love you, too. I couldn't bear it if anything were to happen to you." I kissed him a third time. "I love you so much, Arthur Pendragon."

Chapter Twenty-One

ARTHUR WAS ALREADY pulling on his mail shirt when I woke. As I sat up in bed, memories of last night flooded back.

He picked up his sword belt from the floor and buckled it around his waist. Only then did he look in my direction. "You're awake. Good. No time to lose. We march south today. You'd better get up and eat something. I'm going down to join my men, so I'll see you in the stables shortly."

I opened my mouth to reply, but he was out of the door and gone, as though the night had never happened. Maybe he was choosing to forget it, to hide his vulnerability beneath a veneer of practicality. Abandoning my pseudo-psychology, I swung my legs out of bed.

Yuck. Even I thought my clothes smelled, and I'd got used by now to not having clean things to wear every day. But with an army on the march, I was lucky to get clean things every week. I pulled them on, regardless of the stink. No one would notice as we all smelled the same.

As I emerged into the small courtyard, so, too, did Merlin. And Cei. My step faltered as my gaze fixed on my big bear of a brother-in-law. Dark circles ringed his red-rimmed eyes, as though sleep hadn't come since the battle, and a haggard, haunted look clung to him. But as he saw me, his face lit up, and he held out his arms. "Gwen."

I didn't hesitate but stepped into his embrace, wrapping my arms around his solid body, holding him tight against my own. "Cei. I'm so sorry," I mumbled into his mail-clad chest. A platitude, but what else could I have said? He was such a kind and gentle man, my heart ached for him with a pain as deep as a sword thrust. Underneath his usually bluff exterior beat a heart of solid gold. It hurt me afresh that this suffering had fallen on his shoulders, broad as they were.

He buried his face in my neck, having to stoop to do so, his body shaking for a moment before he had it under control. "He was just a boy," he whispered, mouth near my ear. "Just a boy." Blinking back my own tears, I stroked his back with one hand, the links of the mail rough under my touch, much as I'd have done with Amhar if he'd been hurt.

He made no effort to free himself, so I stood there holding him, offering the only comfort in my power, as time ticked by. Eventually, though, his grip on me loosened, and he stepped back, tears pearling on his ginger lashes. His Adam's apple bobbed. "He died in battle, as every warrior should. A son to be proud of." Was he trying to justify his son's death? Could anything ever justify the death of so young a boy?

I nodded, unable to speak. If he said anything else my resolve would break, and I'd be sobbing. Again.

Merlin put a hand on each of us. "Come. We need food, and then we'll get our horses. Arthur's orders were to hurry."

His words snapped us both out of whatever it was we were in. I nodded, swallowed the lump in my throat, and the three of us set off in search of food in Coel's hall. I wouldn't think about Rhiwallon.

I wouldn't.

⇛⇚

ALEZAN, HAVING BEEN confined to her stable since we arrived at Ebrauc, danced on her toes like a skittish two-year-old as we rode down the Via Praetoria. At the gates we joined the army, mounted men filling every street from wall to wall.

As if the battle were just a forgotten nightmare already, the townspeople hung out of upper floor windows to wave us off, cheers rising every so often along with shouts of encouragement and ribald remarks. The mood was no longer somber. The dead were buried. The living would continue. We'd remember the casualties of war, but that was all they'd be – memories.

I should have been shocked. In my old world, when death comes, it's not expected as inevitable before people reach their eighties. When someone dies, especially someone young, there's great sadness, and that sadness isn't swept away with stoicism. Mourning continues, people reflect on their loss, they spend time at graves, show sympathy. It's a long time before bereft families recover – if they ever do.

Here, with death so constant a companion, I'd seen before how life was expected to go on, unchanged, after the burials. People died. Women in childbirth, children before they left babyhood behind, from diseases that in my old world would have been remedied with antibiotics, warriors in battle, farmers from accidents. If you reached old age and died in your bed, you were lucky.

A funeral marked the end of mourning, not the start. The dead were honored, buried, gone. Never forgotten, but not dwelled upon. In this life there was no time for that.

The double gates swung open, and the army moved off, Cei, Merlin, and I bringing up the rear. Alezan swished her tail and pranced, eager to get going, and I had to put both hands on the reins to keep her under control. Cei and Merlin wisely hung back, aware that in this mood she might well kick out at their horses – or them. We were the last out through the gates and heard them thud shut behind us.

I didn't look back. I couldn't. Instead, my gaze was drawn to the still smoking, and still stinking, funeral pyre to my left, not far from the bare mound that covered our dead. What was that poem from World War One about a corner of a foreign field being forever England? True here as well. Our warriors were far from their homes, sleeping beside Coel's men, and poor Coventina would never lay her eyes on her son again, nor even her son's grave. Just like the mothers of all those eager young men who'd died in Northern France and Belgium.

My eyes slid sideways to find Cei. He was staring at the mound where his son lay buried, his mouth a thin compressed line, and his whole body stiff with what I could only suppose was the effort required not to succumb to his grief.

Unable to keep on looking, I put my heels to Alezan's side, and she burst from a walk straight into a canter, surging across the trampled, muddy grass at the side of the road to catch up with Arthur.

He rode at the front, astride a fine bay horse I didn't recognize. Maybe a gift from the new king, Garbaniawn. I reined in Alezan next to him, and he shot me a grin, although his dark brows were heavy. Could he have been restored to normal? Could you just do that? Push everything away and shut it in a closed room inside your head? Even if he could, I couldn't.

"We're taking the road south, to make sure they're not still lurking along the banks of the Humber, near the remains of Petuaria," Arthur said, pointing off to the southeast. "I don't want them thinking that because I've returned to Dumnonia they can establish new settlements this close to Ebrauc. I want them gone. With their tails between their legs, and yelping like the curs they are, for preference."

I nodded. "And then we'll go back to Din Cadan?"

He grinned again, so much like his old self I could hardly believe it. "I'd hope so. I've had enough of campaigning for this year. I have an urge for simpler things – for helping with the harvest, hunting, sorting petty disputes, playing with my children." But the grin didn't reach his eyes. Was this all an act?

My turn to smile, this time for real, as I thought of Amhar and Archfedd. "Me too. Especially the last bit. I can't wait to see them again."

Our road south led through what had once been rich, rolling farmland. Now, the fields we passed had been trampled by the feet of countless men and horses. Many had been burned, leaving nothing but blackened soil where once a crop of wheat or barley had stood, nearly ready for harvest. There'd be hardship this winter in the north.

Ahead of us, where a clump of charred chestnut trees had once provided shelter, the still smoking ruins of a farmhouse came into view. Only tumbled walls and a few blackened roofbeams remained. The leaves on the trees had curled and crisped in the heat, and the barns and hayricks had burned to cinders. The smell of soot left a bitter taste in my mouth, and I had to turn away at the sight of a single corpse curled pugilistically in the doorway. The urge to vomit nearly overwhelmed me.

But where were the rest of the family? Inside, perhaps.

"Will no one give them decent burial? Shouldn't we stop?" I asked, as we rode past. "Or will they just be left there for the scavengers?"

Arthur shrugged. "Theirs won't have been the only farm burned. Their neighbors might come, I suppose, if they still live. But such is the fate of war casualties. We give our warriors decent burial, but the small people must take care of their own. We can't stop and bury every corpse we find."

Somber words. I fell silent for a while, reflecting on the inequalities of life.

Beyond the farmhouse, we turned off the main south road to take a smaller, less well-maintained road heading east. "A shortcut," Arthur said.

Potholes full of muddy water from the heavy rain pocked its rough surface, and to either side, the ground had been churned to a quagmire. But for now, the summer sun decided to bless us with its heat. Not a pleasant heat – more a muggy, clammy heat that made the sweat gather between my shoulder blades, sticking my shirt to my skin. A British heat, bringing with it swarming flies.

Eventually, this track in turn brought us to a better road, where we were able to turn south again.

I smelled the dead before I saw them. This must have been the route Arthur had taken as he followed the Saxon horde to the coast. A few lay sprawled close to the road, their look of humanity vanished with their souls. Just heaps of jumble-sale clothes, some of the bodies half eaten by wolves or foxes, they'd been dragged about into positions that gave them the appearance of carelessly discarded puppets and robbed them of every vestige of dignity. And more burned-out farms.

With no sympathy for the raiders, I kept my eyes averted from their bodies where I could, but the stink seemed to follow us as though we were drawing it along in our wake. We rode in a cloud of death and damp soot all the way to the barren coastal marshes where the town of Petuaria had once stood.

Nothing but more dead greeted us there, some scattered amongst the ruins of the long-abandoned town. On the salt flats of the foreshore, the blackened skeletons of two Saxon ships lay beached, exposed, now the tide was out. Beyond these marine corpses, a wide expanse of mud and stones made a grim foreshore leading down to where the opaque, brown waters of the River Humber flowed, at least a mile wide even with the tide out.

"Good. They've gone," Arthur said, shading his eyes to stare east toward the distant, invisible sea. "I'd feared they might not have. If we've suffered after this battle, then my one consolation is they've suffered worse. I'd hope they've run back to their homelands, licking their wounds and vowing not to return. Telling their countrymen that Britain is well guarded."

Merlin brought his horse in beside us. "What now? Do we try the ford?"

Arthur nodded. "I've no desire to tackle the pest-ridden marshlands to the west. Far too difficult. The tide's on the ebb, still, so we have plenty of time to get across."

A ford? Across this wide river? A shiver of fear ran through me and Alezan danced sideways under my suddenly heavy hands on her reins.

The river, and its mud flats, stretched a good two and a half miles from where we stood. Was Arthur sure this was a ford? It didn't look anywhere near as inviting as where we'd crossed the Clyde to the east of Dun Breattann, and I hadn't liked that much.

"Is there a stone-built causeway?" I asked, trying to keep doubt, and terror, out of my voice and most likely failing. There'd been one at Dun Breattann, built by the Romans when they'd been trying to annex the lands north of the Wall as their own.

Arthur jerked his head. "Just to the west of the old town. Come along. We'll find it."

A rough track, not worthy of being called Roman, led us past the ruined town walls and along the edge of the salt marshes, where sea couch and lime grass grew tall and rank, their dry seed heads rattling in the breeze.

A hundred yards further on we came to where a mud-encrusted paved roadway led down through the marshes directly toward the river, thick green weed adhering to the flat stones and probably making it dangerous and slippery. *This* was our safe passage? The only thing it was better than was passage by leaky ferry. And it came a very close second to that.

"Keep close by me," Arthur said, and started down the road. "See that post? We aim for that to make sure we stay straight, and our horses don't fall off the causeway into deeper water."

Not a statement guaranteed to make me feel better.

He grinned, irrepressible in the face of what looked like grave danger. "There used to be marker poles right across the river to follow, but they've long since been washed away." He winked. "Let's hope none of the causeway went with them."

Thank you for that.

I strained my eyes. What post? Oh, that tiny matchstick on the far side of the furthest marshy bits on the other side of something resembling the mouth of the River Amazon in spate. Easy. *Not.*

Little waves, caused by current and the wind, rippled the surface of the murky water stretching away in front of me. Alezan skittered sideways, not liking the slippery weed under her unshod feet, and I tightened my reins, my heart thudding, which only made her skitter more, tossing her head and snorting.

Maybe I could ride on Arthur's horse, my arms wrapped tightly around his waist, my eyes just as tightly shut. Or maybe not. How would that look to the men? I was their luck. I couldn't show my fear… my absolute terror. If they could be brave in the face of hordes of savage Saxons, then surely, I could be brave in the face of an expanse of water…

The causeway rose a good two feet higher than the surrounding marshes, on a typical Roman agger, and no doubt was the same all the way across. If Alezan were to shy sideways when we were in the water, and fall off it, mid-stream, I'd be washed away. As our horses splashed into the river, I edged her up beside Arthur, pressing close for comfort and security. No shame in being afraid. I just had to make a huge effort not to show it to the men.

Arthur glanced at me, his face suddenly sympathetic, much more the Arthur I loved than he had been for days. "I know you don't like it, but it's far better than the alternative. Days fighting our way through marshland. Mosquitoes, mud, impassable tracks."

I forced myself to smile and nod, although the lure of some mud and a plague of mosquitoes seemed undeniably attractive right at that moment. Far better than a mile of water that might be deeper than we thought.

Back in my old world, I'd once ridden a horse that hated getting its feet wet and refused point blank to enter water, even puddles. Alezan had no such reservations. Half of me wished she had, then I'd have had to go the other way, or ride clinging onto Arthur. But she must have been well used to water by now. For myself, I was heartily fed up with all the precarious river crossings we had to make to get about Britain. Tarmacked roads and nice solid bridges had never looked so appealing.

Trying to breathe more slowly, I ploughed on into the river.

The tide must be about to turn by now, with that few minutes of slack water just before it happens stilling the small waves. We were about a quarter of the way across, splashing up a storm behind ourselves, the water now nearly reaching my feet. Could it get deeper? The impulse to turn Alezan and head back to the shore and the nice safe marshlands grew ever stronger.

Arthur reached out a hand and covered mine, as though he'd read my mind. "It's safe. I've been this way before with my father, when I was a boy. Stop worrying."

His touch did a little to steady my heart rate, but nothing to lessen the sweat springing out all over me. "I know," I managed, between gritted teeth. "I can't help imagining the worst."

"I won't let anything happen to you. Stay this side of me." He looked over his shoulder at Merlin. "Can you come up here and ride on the other side of Gwen? We need to keep her safe."

Merlin urged his horse forward, splashing my legs as it came, and pulled in so I was jammed between them in a comforting horse sandwich. That did make me feel a little safer, but my anxiety transferred itself to them, primarily to Arthur, riding on my left, the most dangerous side. Now I needed to worry about him riding off the edge of the causeway by mistake, instead of me. Not helped by being unable to see the bottom thanks to the murky water, and only having that tiny and very distant post to aim for.

We splashed onward. No going back now, as the tide began to flow upriver, lapping at the tops of our horses' legs disquietingly.

"We'll be across soon," Arthur said, one hand still on mine, the other keeping his horse pressed up against grumpy Alezan's side. The bad-tempered baggage wasn't enjoying being the filling in their sandwich.

Arthur jerked his chin toward the far side. "Once the Romans had a harbor here, but I don't know what goods passed through it. You can see the remains at low tide, poking through the silt."

I tried to concentrate on his touch and what he was saying as the water lapped over my booted feet. Alezan, however, seemed unmoved by being asked to virtually go to sea.

"Ships used to come in here from the Middle Sea," Arthur went on, clearly determined to distract me as best he could. "I never saw them, of course, and neither did my father. He wasn't brought up here in Britain. Over the sea in Armorica. I believe they still have Roman ports over there. Unlike up here. Too many Saxon pirates roaming the waves this far north." He laughed, but it was forced, as though he thought that if he sounded happy, I might be convinced this was a safe undertaking. I wasn't.

I'd been staring steadfastly ahead, eyes fixed on that tiny post, but now I dared a quick glance to my left, over Arthur and his horse, at the vast stretch of the River Humber heading out to sea, small wavelets rolling toward us as the salty tide came in. Bad idea. I whipped my head around, back to that still faraway wooden post, mouth and lips paper dry.

Slowly, oh so slowly, the post drew nearer. At last, the paved causeway appeared, leading out of the water and across the mudflats on the south shore of the estuary. Beyond the flats, tall marshland grasses waved their feathery heads in mocking welcome. The water depth lessened. Alezan was now only knee deep in the brackish water, and it was possible to spot the paving stones under her feet, large and flat, that long-ago legionaries had somehow laid.

At last, we emerged on the south side of the river, without having had a single man washed away, and followed the roadway up a gentle slope into the marshes.

Where the land became drier, we came to a cluster of low, weed-infested stone ruins surrounded by a grassy bank. Small brown sheep grazing there scattered as we approached, and a young boy ran after them with a shaggy dog at his heels.

"My father told me this was once the town the harbor served," Arthur said, with a grin, possibly of relief that we'd all made it across unscathed. "We'll make camp here, as I did in my boyhood, and set lookouts to watch the river, in case some foolish Saxon dares to set his sail in this direction." It sounded as though he hoped they would. Maybe he was itching for another fight. Maybe all those losses only made men yearn for revenge.

I dismounted, glad to have my feet on dry land, and Alezan rubbed her head against me. Maybe she felt the same way, despite her bravado and annoying skittishness.

Arthur jumped down from his new horse and threw an arm around my shoulders. "My brave warrior queen."

Now I was on dry land, the terrors of the river crossing had receded. I chuckled. "I'm never doing that again, warrior queen or not. If you want to come this way in the future, you'll be coming on your own."

He pulled me into a clumsy one-armed embrace. "That's the idea. You're supposed to stay at home, not come trailing after me like some camp follower."

What a good thing I loved him, because that remark deserved a slap. Instead, I took my revenge by pressing myself against him and sliding my hand down to his braccae in the most provocative way I could, hidden from the view of anyone else because of the way he was holding me.

He caught his breath, as well he might, and looked down at me with a quizzical frown on his face. I grinned back up at him, and gave him another squeeze. That'd teach him to call me a camp follower – and leave him frustrated.

He leaned in closer. "I know what I'd like to do with you tonight."

I ran my tongue around my lips, intent on teasing him as much as possible. "Me too."

Merlin tapped him on the shoulder. "No time for that. Horses before pleasure."

We parted, me satisfied that I'd left him with an unfulfillable desire. Not that I didn't feel a little like that myself, but he would find it harder to tolerate.

Evening was drawing in by the time the horses had been fed and watered. With no firewood to be found, the meal tonight would be a cold one – of dried meat, cheese, onions and skins of cider. But I was hungry, and plain dried bread would have tasted like a feast.

I sat between Arthur and Cei on a stone robbed from the tumbledown walls, with Merlin on the far side of my husband. Arthur had put a protective arm around my shoulders as soon as we sat down, and now, most of the food eaten, I leaned against him, my earlier annoyance at being called a camp follower gone, my eyelids drooping.

Gwalchmei fished his lyre out of his saddlebags and played a few rippling notes, his fingers dancing over the strings. It seemed the arm he'd been carrying in a sling since the battle had improved.

"Go on," Bedwyr said. "Let's have a song."

Gwalchmei bowed his head over his instrument, silent for a moment as though thinking. Then he raised his head and stared across at Cei. "A song for dead heroes." His fingers plucked the notes and the beautiful sound rose toward the darkening sky. Closing his eyes, he began to sing. He possessed a beautiful voice, higher than his speaking voice, clear and pure. All around, the men ceased whatever they were doing, moving closer to listen to the paean.

"Men in minds, youthful in years
Gallant in the din of war;
Fleet, long-maned chargers
Ridden by our brave heroes.

Bearing shields, light and broad,
On swift and slender steeds
Their swords blue and gleaming,
We celebrate your praise in song.
You who have gone to the bloody bier,
Sooner than to a marriage feast;
You who were food for ravens
And a swelling sorrow rises
Where fell in death the only son of Cei."

In the dark of evening, I leaned against Arthur as the tears ran down my face, remembering how Llacheu had once told me he wanted men to sing tales of his exploits around their fires. Rhiwallon had that now.

Chapter Twenty-Two

Just over a week later we arrived back in Din Cadan, none the worse for our long journey. A hypocritical bright summer sun shone down on us, as though on a day like this we couldn't be the bearers of bad news to so many women – to the wives, mothers and children of the warriors who'd died. It was with a heavy heart that I negotiated the curving road up to the gates.

The first day was the worst. Some of the young men who'd died had come to Arthur five years ago as volunteers from other kingdoms, and some were local; men from the scattered villages and farms of Dumnonia. But even those from other kingdoms had laid roots down either inside Din Cadan itself, or in the village at the foot of the hill and the farms closest to the fortress – with friends, wives, and babies.

They were all there, waiting when we returned, our army most likely having been spotted from a distance by the dust cloud we were kicking up. Fathers, mothers, wives, and children, their faces anxious, excited, expectant, lined the walls. Others clustered at the edges of the cobbled road where it climbed the slope from the gates toward the great hall, eager faces searching for their menfolk. Some whose fragile hopes would be shattered.

The lucky warriors who'd returned, spotted by their families and friends, dismounted to embrace them, and walked the rest of the way to the stables with their arms tight around their loved ones. Wives planted grateful kisses on bearded faces, touched forming scars, kissed the wooden crucifixes around their necks, as though believing God had brought their men back safely to them.

No, not God, and not Arthur, either. Luck. And not the luck they thought I brought.

Coventina and Morgawse stood waiting on the platform outside the Great Hall with Maia and Keelia, just as I'd done so many times. Maia balanced Archfedd on her hip, and hung onto an impatient Amhar's hand. Keelia had charge of Reaghan, leaving Coventina empty handed, the fingers of her right hand clasped about the crucifix she, too, wore around her neck. Only hers was gold.

Standing a little apart, Morgawse rested a restraining hand on Medraut's dark head, as he stood squarely in front of her, arms folded and scowling, probably having refused to hold anyone's hand. A distinct look of his uncle Cadwy clung to him.

My heart, that I'd been ignoring as much as I could on our journey home, ached anew at the sight of Coventina, dread of the confrontation to come curdling my insides. Instinct told me how she must be feeling – that poignant mixture of relief that your man was home, mixed with the anxiety of not knowing if he was unharmed. The search for his face amongst the crowd of warriors, the delight in spotting him at last. The soaring joy when he came striding toward you to take you in his arms.

Or the bottomless pit of despair when he wasn't there. This had never happened to me, of course, and Arthur had always come riding home, but my imagination could supply me with how it must feel to suddenly realize your worst nightmare had come true. I averted my gaze from Coventina's hopeful figure, as she strained to study the crowd of returning warriors.

At the stables, Cei dismounted, squared his shoulders, and silently passed his horse's reins to a waiting servant. My gaze drawn as if by a magnet, I had to watch. With heavy footsteps, Cei began the short walk uphill to the Hall. How he must be dreading what he had to do, every step he took laden with doom, drawing him closer to having to tell his wife she'd never see her child again.

A kind of fatal fascination kept me watching, the horror of what Cei had to do burning like a hot coal in my insides. A wide smile of relief blazed across Coventina's homely face as she spotted her husband. Then she must have seen his expression. Her own faltered. The smile faded, dropping away. Her eyes flew wide as she let the cross slip from suddenly slack fingers. Her mouth hung open.

Finally, I dragged my eyes away. This was too raw, too private. Not my place to watch. The thought that one day this would be me, without any doubt, gouged its way into my heart, a wound that refused to be denied and could never be healed.

Slithering down from Alezan onto shaky legs, I shoved her reins into the hands of a passing servant. Should I go to Coventina?

Without waiting for Arthur, I hurried after Cei.

He'd halted in front of his wife. He must have spoken, told her. She collapsed into his arms, fingers clawing at his body, and a low, unearthly wail rose into air that had become oppressive in that instant. Heads turned, Keelia's hand went to her mouth, Reaghan and Archfedd began to cry. Amhar looked up at Maia in concern, his lower lip beginning to wobble. Only Medraut was unmoved, a sly smile creeping across his cherubic face.

Cei swept Coventina, who wasn't small, up into his arms as though she was a child, and, leaving everyone else standing on the platform, strode into the courtyard beside the hall and kicked his front door open. It swung shut behind them with a bang, but the terrible wailing continued, scarcely muffled by the walls.

Below the hall, more wailing rose in concert, as other women discovered their men had not returned. Children cried. Even a dog joined in and howled.

I reached the platform and, bending down, scooped a surprised Amhar into my arms to hold him tight against my chest, breathing in his grubby, small-boy smell. Never would I agree to him going to war. Never. The grief of losing a child was something I could never bear.

Footsteps. Running footsteps. Llacheu came galloping up the road from where he must have watched our arrival from the wall-walk, his eyes wide with shock as he looked from my face to Maia's and Keelia's stricken ones.

"What is it?" His voice rose in panic, his head swiveling as he searched our faces. "Where's father? Is it him?"

"No." I held out my hand. "It's not your father. He's in the stables."

Keelia shoved Rheagan into Maia's arms. "I have to go to the mistress." And she was gone.

Llacheu stared with wide, frightened eyes, but he didn't take my offered hand. "Then what is it?"

"Come inside, and I'll tell you there. In private."

He shook his head, his long hair rattling with the beads someone had threaded into it. Not his mother. She no longer lived here inside the fortress. Maybe Coventina, unable to do that any more for Rhiwallon. "No. Tell me here. Now."

I tried to take his arm, but he shook me off.

A furious glare settled on his face, disconcertingly like a smaller version of his father when angry. "What *is* it?"

More footsteps. I swung around. Arthur appeared by my side, and Llacheu's accusing gaze leapt from me to his father. "Why will no one tell me what's wrong?"

Llacheu was eleven now, and over five feet tall. Arthur didn't need to bend down to talk to him any longer. Instead, he put his hands on his son's shoulders, holding him firmly as he faced him.

"You're nearly a man, Llacheu, and with manhood come responsibilities and things you have to face. Like a man."

The face glaring back at Arthur was not a man's, though. Soft still with the lines of childhood, no teenage acne, no fine down on his upper lip or chin. His lower lip wobbled. A child.

Arthur's fingers had him tight. "We fought a battle. To keep Britain, and all the kingdoms in it, safe. Many of our men gave their lives, fighting for this cause. Brave men. Heroes. Rhiwallon amongst them. He's not coming home. He's dead."

Llacheu's face crumpled, his mouth twisting in something between fury and despair. "No!" he cried, writhing in his father's grasp. "You're lying. He's not. He can't be." He glared at his father in impotent rage. "He's my *friend!*"

Arthur gave him the smallest of shakes. "Stop it. You're my son. Everyone is watching you. You must face this like a man."

I moved toward them, but Arthur turned his head and fixed me with a glare to rival his son's. "No. Leave this to me. He's nearly a man grown and needs to behave like one."

I bit my lip, holding Amhar closer to me, his baby cheek pressed to mine. Eleven was *not* nearly a man. This was a child, a bereaved child. Unable to hug Llacheu close, I enfolded Amhar in his place, tears running down my cheeks.

Llacheu turned his head, desperation on his face, his eyes fixing on me again. "Tell me it's not true." A plea. A child facing the death of someone close for perhaps the first time in his life. Yes, he'd have grown up knowing death existed – seen it every day amongst the livestock, known his mother had lost babies after his birth. But this was his friend, his cousin – the boy he'd spent his childhood with. Boys didn't die – they had their lives ahead of them stretching off to the unseen horizon of old age. Like the young in my old world, death must have been a thing that happened to others, not to boys like Rhiwallon.

"It's true." My voice came out taut and gruff. "I'm sorry, Llacheu."

He gave another convulsive twist and Arthur let him go. Without a word, he fled, diving down one of the side alleys between the buildings. Gone.

Arthur heaved a sigh. "He needs time by himself to get used to it, as do Cei and Coventina. Rhiwallon won't be the first friend he loses." He sounded tired. With another deep sigh he caught my arm. "Come, let's go inside."

※

RETURNING HOME RENEWED the mourning we'd spent more than a week trying to forget. For all the wives and mothers of the men who'd died, their loss was fresh and raw. It was a somber company who ate that night in the Great Hall, with no entertainment save Gwalchmei with his mournful paean for the dead as the meal drew to a close. We all sat in silence, as the words of his beautiful elegy rose toward the rafters, every one of us with someone lost held close in our hearts.

Neither Cei nor Coventina came to the hall. And although some of the older boys of the fortress were present, Llacheu was conspicuous by his absence. I longed to go and find him, to hug him and try to make him feel better, even though instinct told me nothing would. With his mother married off and no longer living in the fortress, who else did he have but me? Now Rhiwallon was gone.

When the paean's last words were still echoing round the lofty hall, I rose quietly and slipped off to our chamber, unable to contain my grief. Not just for Rhiwallon, but for all the warriors we'd lost. Him, mostly, though.

A couple of oil lamps on the table created a circle of warm light, throwing the rest of the room into deep shadow. On the far side, our big, fur-strewn bed rested up against the wall, between the chests where Arthur and I kept our clothes. A sense of peaceful quiet pervaded the room, in sharp contrast to the sorrow that had drenched the Hall, as though this were a different world to the one of loss without.

A tap on Maia's door, where she slept with the children, Rheagan too tonight, brought her hurrying to help me out of my gown, which had inaccessible lacing down the back. She worked with deft fingers and soon had me stepping out of the soft, pale-blue gown and into a clean linen undershirt.

"'Ow'd it happen, then?" she asked as she brushed out my waist-length hair for me. "If'n you don't mind me askin'?"

I shook my head. "How does any death in battle happen? By accident. By being in the wrong place at the wrong time." Bitterness laced my words. She fell silent, and as soon as my hair was re-braided, crept back to her small charges.

I brushed my teeth and thought determinedly about them to keep my mind from straying back to Coventina. As most people appeared to have reasonable dentition, perhaps this regime worked, although that might also have been thanks to the lack of sweet things available to eat. My father had once told me the Romans used to rinse their mouths with urine, Portuguese being thought the best. Thank goodness that habit hadn't been adopted by the population of post-Roman Britain. Small mercies.

I climbed into bed and snuggled down, listening to the fast-diminishing noises in the hall carrying over the partition wall, and still battling not to think of what Coventina must be going through right now. Although sleep seemed far away, I must have eventually dozed off, because the sound of the door from the Hall opening woke me.

The still flickering oil lamps cast their light over Arthur as he set down a jug of wine on the table and pulled out one of the chairs. With unsteady fingers he unbuckled his belt and threw it on the floor. His tunic followed, then his boots, as though he were preparing to come to bed. But no, he sat down heavily in the chair in just his undershirt and braccae, and with shaking hands filled a goblet to the brim.

Oh no. Drunk again. Since we'd left Ebrauc he'd had little opportunity to indulge, as we didn't carry enough alcohol with us on the march. But now he was home... was he going to make a habit of this drowning of his sorrows? I sat up in bed.

"Go back to sleep," he said, without looking at me.

I pushed the covers back. "I can't."

"Then that makes two of us." I'd lain beside him every night in our camps, and seen for myself how sleep had eluded him. When it came, it brought nightmares, from which I had to shake him awake before his men heard him shouting. I'd not had much sleep myself on the journey back from Ebrauc.

I set my bare feet on the wolf skin beside our bed and stood up. "Come to bed. I need you to hold me."

He shook his head, leaning his elbows on the table and still not looking in my direction. "No. Not yet. I've drinking still to do." He drained the goblet and poured a second.

I padded across the floor to the table. "Drinking won't chase away your demons."

He stared fixedly at the goblet in his hands. "Who says I have them?"

I wanted to take him in my arms and do the chasing away myself. Instead, I put a gentle hand on his shoulder. "I do. Drinking will only make your nightmares worse, not better."

"Not if I drink enough." He drained half the second goblet in one gulp. "Then their dead faces might not come to reproach me every night."

If only I'd studied psychology instead of bloody English. Of all the subjects least likely to be of use in the post-Roman Dark Ages, English must have capped the lot.

I took a breath. "Today you told Llacheu he had to face things like a man. You asked a child to do something you're not willing to do yourself. If you were, you wouldn't be drunk right now." I rubbed his shoulder as he stiffened under my touch. "You have to accept that sometimes you'll feel grief. That sometimes you can't do anything to change things. That you're not responsible for Rhiwallon's death…

nor Geraint's."

He set the goblet down, still holding its ornate, twisted stem and not looking up at me. "I see their faces every night, Gwen, staring at me out of their dead eyes." His voice faltered, filled with desperate hopelessness. "Sometimes they don't even *have* eyes – the crows have been there first." He shook his head. "Why? Why now? I've seen men die many times before. Why do I feel like this now? Why is Geraint back inside my head after being so long forgotten? Why won't Rhiwallon's shade leave me in peace?"

I put my other hand on his back, bending low so my face was close to his. He didn't look up. "Because you wrongly think it's your fault he died. And it's not. That was just one of the many battles you've fought. Men have died in all of them, with more to come. Rhiwallon was born to be a warrior – to fight in battles for his king and to *die* a warrior. Just as his father was, and you. You couldn't have denied him that." I couldn't hide the cracking in my voice as I realized what I was saying. "It's not your fault."

His hair smelled of woodsmoke. Hopefully, I'd chosen the right things to say and wouldn't make everything worse with my own incompetence. "You're no more guilty of their deaths than you are of the deaths of any of your men. Rhiwallon's death has opened up your memories of Geraint and how he died. You were just a child then, yourself, not a warrior. A child should never see things like that."

He was staring down at his hands, clasped about the stem of his goblet. "I'm guilty of all their deaths. I'm their leader. I lead them into battles they wouldn't be involved in if it weren't for me."

I slid my hands down his arms toward his wrists, pressing my body against his back in an attempt to gain as much physical contact as I could, something telling me that was what he needed. "You defend this island, Arthur. You're the only thing standing between all of us and the pagan Yellow Hairs."

I could feel the rise and fall of his ribs as he breathed. I breathed with him, our bodies synchronized. "In my old world," I began, my voice low and almost singsong, whispering in his ear. "Fifteen hundred years from now, the whole world knows your name. The other kings are forgotten, but your name lives on in glorious legend. You're the most famous king Britain has ever had. You'll hold back the Saxons with such great defeats that you'll create a golden age that will never come again. You're Britain's savior."

Yes, I was being economical with the truth, but this was what he needed to hear.

"People will write hundreds of books about you. Some speculating about who you were, some works of fiction with you as the hero. People will study you, write about you, make films about you…"

"Films?"

"Pictures that move."

He shifted under me, turning his face to try to peer into mine. "This is *true*?"

I nodded, loosening my hold on him a little. "And all your warriors will be remembered as heroes. Every one of them. The men who held back the Saxons and brought peace to Britain."

He turned in his seat until he was facing me.

I took his face in my hands. "Everything you do leads to this." I kissed his forehead. "Everything you do is right. No other king will ever equal you."

I couldn't tell him how I felt, how alien this all was to me. I couldn't help destroy him and drive him deeper into self-disgust. No matter how I felt about how he'd treated Llacheu, about the deaths I'd seen, I had to keep him following the path that would lead to legend. It was my destiny.

He pulled me onto his lap, my legs straddling his, holding me against his chest with his head on my breasts. "None of this was your fault," I whispered into his hair again. "The Battle of Ebrauc was on the list I've read. You had to fight it because history said you did. For me, this has already happened. I'm living the history I know, and I don't think I could change it even if I tried. And nor can you."

"And what happens next?" he asked, voice muffled against my breasts. "Where do we go from here?"

I shook my head. "I don't know." My fingers tangled in his hair. "I just don't know." Should I tell him? It was in my power to and never had I longed to more. I licked my lips. "All I know is that there's an even bigger battle than Ebrauc coming. And it'll be the one that brings the peace. It'll be at a place called Badon."

There. I'd done it. What harm could it do?

He lifted his head, alert and awake in a moment. "Badon? Where is that? And when?" The drunken slur had vanished.

I shook my head. "No one from my old world knows the answer to either of those questions."

His eyes had lost their hopeless look, washed away by the few words I'd spoken. Now they blazed with an excitement I'd not seen since before Ebrauc. "Why not?"

Staring into his eyes, I felt my heart give a leap of joy – and of desire. Too weighed down by sorrow, I'd not felt like that for a while. Now, with the old Arthur gazing back at me, I felt a stirring in my stomach that moved rapidly downwards. I had to deliberately gather my thoughts to answer him. "Because it was never written down. There're no records at all of where it was, and only a few mentions that mostly can't be verified."

How difficult was it to concentrate on talking about battles, when a burning desire for his body had just kindled itself deep inside me?

He nodded. "So, if I can find it, I should bring the Saxons to battle there, confident of a victory." Not a question – a statement. Had I just done to Badon what I'd once done to the sword in the stone story? Made it real because I knew its name? And if I had, was it such a bad thing?

He put a hand on my bare leg, sliding it upward under my long shirt. "The Ring Maiden has many talents."

He was right. I did, and this might well be the medicine he needed. Without hesitation I lifted his shirt and ran my hands up his torso to his chest, then round to his back, digging my fingers into the muscles, pulling us closer together.

He gave a little groan of pleasure, and lifted his head to mine. I kissed him, tongues meeting, desire coursing through me like a fast-burning wildfire.

He tugged at my undershirt. "Can you get this off?"

Panting, I dragged it over my head, then leaned forward to lock my lips on his again. When we could drag our mouths apart, he tore his own shirt off and flung it to one side. His hot mouth explored my throat, descending to my breasts, as one hand groped blindly with the laces of his braccae.

We didn't make it to the bed.

Chapter Twenty-Three

I SLEPT LATE the following morning, waking to sounds of activity and childish laughter in the Hall, and climbed groggily out of a bed empty of Arthur. My head ached as though it had been me who'd been drunk the night before. Pulling on my workaday dress over my undershirt and gathering it at the waist with a woven belt, I pushed open the door and stepped into the Hall.

Morgawse and all the children were in there, with Maia, who was carrying a hefty woven basket. The children, from sturdy five-year-old Medraut down to toddling eighteen-month-old Archfedd, were running up and down the central aisle in an energetic game of chase. The motes of dust they were kicking up danced in the sunlight streaming through the open doors. None of them could catch Medraut, who was skipping about between the tables and shouting taunts, mostly at Amhar.

Morgawse turned to me with an excited smile. Rhiwallon's death seemed not to have touched her, even though her own son was closest to becoming a warrior himself. "Gwen. I was just wondering whether I should come and waken you. Arthur took all the warriors, first thing, to help with the harvest. We women are to take down food for their mid-day meal."

"We're goin' to the village!" sang Medraut, climbing onto one of the tables. "We're goin' to have a picnic."

Amhar came running up to me, panting breathlessly and closely followed by Reaghan. "Mami! A picnic! We're goin' outside!"

"Can we take Seren?" Medraut shouted at me from the tabletop. "Can I ride her? I want to ride Seren."

I held up my hand, glad of this chaotic distraction, this normality brought on by our children. They couldn't be expected to mourn. "Seren can carry the picnic," I said, in my firmest tone. "You children can walk. Only the youngest need to be carried by Seren. Certainly not you, Medraut, with your long legs. Nor you, Amhar."

Two sulky faces regarded me, but not for long. "Race you to the gates," Medraut shouted to Amhar, leaping down off the table with amazing agility for one so young. He bounced up, but Morgawse managed to grab him by the back of his tunic and haul him back. "No, you don't. You stay with us. No racing off and leaving us to search for you. Neither of you." She turned her gaze on Amhar as well, too easily led astray by his older cousin. "If you come, you both have to promise to behave and stay with us."

Amhar stared at her, wide-eyed, awed by her tone. "I promise." He meant it.

Medraut stuck out his lower lip. "Do I have to?"

His mother nodded. "You do. Or I'll leave you here. Under guard."

"In the lockup?" suggested Amhar, brightening at the prospect of his friend being locked in that stinky hole.

"Not the lockup!" Medraut's eyes widened, and his voice rose in panic. "I promise to be good."

Maia moved closer to whisper in my ear. "She wouldn't really, would she?"

I had to laugh. That was what this day needed – laughter and children. I shook my head with vehemence. "What? Her little prince in the lockup? Not likely. But luckily, he doesn't know that."

Once Seren had been caught, quickly groomed, and the basket of picnic food transferred to her paniers, along with Archfedd, who was too small to walk, we were ready to leave. It took us much longer than

I'd expected – organizing four small children was like herding cats.

With Maia leading Seren and in charge of Archfedd, that left Morgawse and me with three boisterous youngsters to keep an eye on, which, despite the promises made by the boys, was not an easy task. And Reaghan was not behind the door at following their lead. With Medraut as leader, this was not always in the desired direction.

We descended the sloping road to the northern gateway and took the steep and stony track down into the village at the hillfoot. The morning by now was late on and warm already, with scarcely a breath of breeze. The branches of the few trees that stood around the small, white-washed, wattle-and-daub church hung lifeless in the still air, and the hum of flies over the village midden carried to us clearly.

We weren't the only ones on a mission to take food to our menfolk. In dribs and drabs, the women of the fort were following the same route, meandering down the steep path with laden baskets slung over their arms and small children running rings around them. Some sang, the cheery harvest verses rising up to where hopeful pigeons circled, waiting for the bounty of the harvest. What a contrast to the horrors of battle – the rhythm of the seasons acting like a soothing balm on the hearts of tired warriors and sorrowful womenfolk. At least, that was how it was working on me.

In her pannier, Archfedd dozed.

A winding dirt track threaded its way between the small houses, past pig pens huddled next to verdant garden plots and tatty chickens scratching in the dust. A farmyard smell of middens, pig shit, and old soot hung about the village – a smell as familiar to me now as Hugo Boss perfumes had once been.

Harvest was a community task. Only a few of the oldest and least able of the villagers had remained behind – like the wizened, white-haired crone sitting in a wicker chair by her front door, rocking her grandchild's crib as she strained rheumy eyes to stitch a garment. And the old man sleeping in the sun beside an equally ancient, gray-whiskered dog, whose deaf ears didn't even twitch as we passed.

A fine-feathered cockerel strutted proudly on the thatched ridge of one of the houses, pausing every now and again to crow his superiority to any would-be rivals. Down below, a fat black and white cat sunned herself and her kittens on the stone sill by an open cottage door.

The kindly morning sun warmed my back as I strolled beside Morgawse, our children running on ahead excitedly amongst the crowd of other youngsters, but so far, wisely keeping within shouting distance. The threat of the lock-up must have loomed large.

A feeling as warm as the friendly sunshine burgeoned. This was how life should be – children playing together regardless of their rank, the sun shining down on a chubby baby sleeping in her pannier, a rustle of longed-for wind in the treetops, wheat and barley standing golden in the small fields, a harvest meal carried with us. Not fighting mired in mud, boys dying horribly with their innards hanging out. I shoved that unwelcome image away, not wanted on this day of tranquility.

We found where the men were working. None of the fields were more than an acre or two, enclosed either by stone walls, prickly hedgerows, or grassy banks in an effort to keep out the free-roaming livestock. Moving clockwise from the outside in, a dozen men worked in each field, stripped to their waists, their tanned and muscled backs bent as they swung their sickles in perfect rhythm with one another.

Each man took a clump of wheat in his left hand, sliced through the dry stalks just above ground level, then moved on to add to his bunch. When his hand was full, he laid the sheaf on the ground behind him. Boys followed the men, picking up the sheaves, banging their bases on the ground to level them, and twisting around a rope made of wheat stalks to secure them. Behind them followed the women, standing the sheaves of cut wheat up in groups to make stooks, seed heads uppermost, to allow the wheat longer to dry.

Amhar came running back to me from his friends. "Where's father?"

I scanned the field, searching for Arthur, a king laboring by the side of his people. It didn't take long to spot him working near Merlin, both of them naked to the waist just as the other men were. Their field was nearly finished, dotted with neatly stacked stooks, and only a small portion of the wheat still uncut in the center.

I pointed.

"Father!" Amhar sprinted through the narrow gateway into the field. He galloped across the short, freshly cut stubble, little legs pounding. "Father!"

Arthur straightened up, his face breaking into a wide grin. As Amhar reached him, he dropped his sickle and swept the excited little boy into his arms, lifting him high into the air above his head. I couldn't help the smile that leapt to my face. A day for family, a day for the bounty of the harvest, a day to forget the horrors of war.

They were close enough for me to overhear.

"Have you come to help me?" Arthur asked. "I've need of someone strong. We've nearly finished here, but that last bit looks really difficult."

Contented, I leaned on the grassy bank that surrounded the field to watch, as Seren helped herself to a snack beside me. Archfedd remained sleeping in her panier, her chubby thumb firmly ensconced in her mouth.

With Arthur downing tools, all the men in his field had done the same, their rhythm disrupted. They didn't seem to mind. A few more children raced through the gateway to find their fathers, all the men as pleased to see their offspring as Arthur had been.

Medraut strolled through the gateway by himself, staring around with the air of a monarch surveying his subjects, then spotted Arthur and trotted toward him.

Morgawse, who'd come to stand beside me with a tired Rheagan in her arms, chuckled. "My son has poise, I'll give him that."

I glanced sideways at her, certain I wouldn't have wanted Amhar to behave the way his cousin did. Not sure poise was what I wanted to see in a five-year-old. But she was watching Medraut's progress, pride glowing in her eyes.

Arthur set Amhar on the ground as Medraut picked up the sickle Arthur had dropped. It must have been heavy for so small a child, but he hefted it like an expert. "I can do this," he announced, and took an energetic swing at the remaining wheat stalks. He was close to Amhar. Too close. The blade swished through the dry stalks toward my son. Morgawse gasped. I opened my mouth to shout a warning, my heart leaping into my throat, and my legs suddenly too weak to hold me up as my fingers dug into the turf on top of the grassy bank.

Arthur grabbed Medraut's arm. "Thank you." His voice was icy calm.

The deadly blade stopped inches from Amhar's legs. Even from where I stood it was obvious Medraut didn't want to let go of the sickle. Arthur had to pry his hands off it. But Medraut wasn't looking at his uncle – his eyes, so like his Aunt Morgana's, were fixed on Amhar, his thin black eyebrows lowered in a frown. A cold shiver ran down my spine.

Setting the sickle down out of harm's way and taking a boy in each hand, Arthur walked over to the gateway where we stood. "You've brought food? Good. We'll get this field finished then come over and eat. Better keep the boys out of the way unless you want them going back home minus a limb." His tone was light.

Had he not seen the look on Medraut's face? This wasn't a joking matter. How close had my little boy come to being seriously injured by another child? Perhaps on purpose.

What was I thinking? *On purpose?*

The thought had leapt into my head unbidden. I clamped my lips together in case it leapt out of them fully formed. No child could be guilty of that. Could they?

I grabbed Amhar's hand and pulled him close to me, making him whine that I was hurting him, as Arthur returned to his fellows.

Maia tied Seren's leading rein to the stone gate post, and we lifted the still sleeping Archfedd out and laid her down on the plaid blanket we'd brought to sit on. Medraut skipped off to join a group of other little boys kicking an inflated pig's bladder football about across the stubble in the next field. Amhar tried to wriggle his hand free, but I held him firmly. "You're not big enough yet. You'll have to stay with me and your sister."

Lower lip jutting, he sat down next to Archfedd and gave her a hard poke. She woke up with a whimper.

Maia scooped her up for a cuddle and I gave Amhar an angry stare that brought hot color to his cheeks. Good. For his own safety he needed to learn that he had to do what I said.

There I went again. The idea that playing with Medraut was not safe for my son resurfaced. What was I doing? Surely it was my imagination and knowledge of what I thought, only *thought*, Medraut would one day do, that had made me so suspicious? But I couldn't rid myself of the fear. My fingers tightened round Amhar's hand, and he gave a whimper. I had to force myself to slacken my grip.

It wasn't long before Arthur and Merlin came bounding over like a pair of playful colts to join us, punching each other's arms and laughing. They flopped down onto the blanket, still laughing. How good to see Arthur light-hearted again. Hopefully with genuine joy.

"What've you brought?" Arthur asked, reminding me more than ever of his sons, whose main reason for living seemed to be to eat. "I'm starving."

We had pies, cold meat, cheese, onions, the first of the season's small rosy apples, fresh bread, and cider to wash it down. And elderflower cordial that Maia had made with clean spring water for the children.

Regretting that being a woman meant I had to wear a dress on top of an undershirt and stockings most of the time, I wiped a strand of hair off my hot forehead and watched Arthur eat, envious of his state of undress. He'd not been lying when he'd said he was starving. And Merlin was the same. While we women and children ate sparingly, Arthur and Merlin put away all the rest of the food, only crumbs remaining. Might that mean the end of self-recriminations and nightmares?

The sight of Arthur doing something so different from fighting, and so obviously enjoying it, gladdened my heart. He'd caught the sun, and it did cross my mind to wonder whether working shirtless in such heat was a good idea. When Amhar asked to take his tunic off, I wouldn't let him, even though some of the other children were by now running about naked, in and out of the shallow stream that ran along the edge of the fields, down by the sweeping willow trees.

He moaned at that, of course, but Arthur fixed him with a hard stare that silenced his complaints. He knew better than to cross his father.

All too soon the men had to return to work, and we loaded Seren up again with Archfedd in one pannier and a tired and sleepy Reaghan in the other, both clutching wilting bunches of flowers and corn dollies Maia had twisted for them.

Medraut returned from paddling with his friends, and Morgawse enfolded him in a hug he plainly didn't appreciate. "I'm tired," he whined. "I need to ride back up the hill on Seren as well."

Morgawse glanced across at me. She must have guessed what I'd say to that one. Medraut was older than Amhar, and not only was Seren my son's, but Amhar wasn't moaning about being tired. Mind you, he had been sitting quietly with us while Medraut played with the other children.

I smiled sweetly at Medraut. "Well, maybe you shouldn't have run about for such a long time playing football with your friends. This will be a good lesson to learn. Save some energy for getting home. Seren's only small and has enough to carry with the two girls. You'll have to walk."

The long trek back was made worse by Medraut's constant moaning. He complained about everything – about not wanting to walk, about how his legs hurt, about the stones he kept getting in his shoes, about being too hot and too thirsty, about needing to pee, and about it not being fair that the two girls got to ride when he didn't. Morgawse, her face like thunder as she clearly thought I should have given in to him, stayed stonily silent. Which in turn I could tell made Maia angry.

Then, as we started up the steep track to the south gates, Medraut managed to push Amhar over and make him cry, which set Archfedd to wailing as well, in sympathy with her brother. On top of that, the climb made me sweat in my far too thick clothes, and the horseflies came out in strength to try and bite us. A frustrated and tetchy group finally reached the gates in the height of the afternoon's heat.

"You take the children," I said to Morgawse and Maia. "I'll go and sort Seren out."

Morgawse, whose face had grown ever more fed up as Medraut's constant complaints rose, threw me a dirty look and stomped off dragging a still moaning Medraut after her. I had a moment of smugness that for once he hadn't had his way, and she'd had to get cross with him, before turning back to Maia.

"I'll take 'em to your chamber, shall I?" she asked, lifting Archfedd down from her panier. "Get them playin' nicely?"

I nodded as I lifted down Reaghan, already halfway decided I was going to abandon Maia with them for a while. I'd had more than enough of moaning children today, and what was the point of having a maid if you couldn't palm your children off on her when you got fed up with them? My old friend Sian would have been shocked at how spoiled I was getting.

Maia, who never lost her patience, set off up the road to the Great

Hall, walking slowly so Archfedd could toddle at her side. As for me, I hurried Seren through the maze of narrow passageways that would take me to her pen, a sense of guilty relief blossoming in my heart. Seren went gladly – maybe she was as fed up with children as I was.

She shared a paddock with Llacheu's beautiful black cob, Saeth, and, as soon as he saw her coming, he trotted up to the slip rail, nickering a welcome. Little Seren, only the size of a modern Welsh Mountain Pony, nickered a greeting back, small gray ears pricked.

Having divested her of her panniers and shoved the over-eager Saeth back out of the way, I maneuvered his friend through the slip rails. With her bridle removed, she tossed her head and cantered off on a circuit of the paddock, Saeth running behind her. She might have been much smaller than him, but she wore the trousers in their relationship. At their dusty rolling spot, she sank to the ground to rub off the sweat of the day's work, short legs waving in the air.

As I replaced the slip rails and bent to pick up the panniers, movement caught my eye. The large, open-fronted barns overlooking the horse pens were almost full of new hay for the winter, and, from high up in the one nearest, a pale face regarded me – Llacheu. A pile of loose hay on the floor marked where he'd climbed up. If anyone caught him, he'd be in trouble. No baling machinery in this world – the hay came in loose and had to be forked many times over and carefully stacked. Anyone who messed with it once it was stored was in for severe punishment.

I hooked the panniers on the fence and looked up at the sullen little face staring down at me. "You'd better come out of there before anyone else sees you," I said, setting my hands on my hips.

He was about three feet above my eye level, right up under the low rafters and lying on his stomach with his chin on his folded arms. He scowled at me. "I don't care who sees me."

"You will if you get a beating for messing with the winter's hay," I retorted. "I wouldn't do that, but your father might. Come down."

"Don't want to."

I sighed. "Have you been up there since yesterday?"

He nodded.

He must be starving. "If you come down now, we could sit and talk."

His mouth worked for a moment as though he were trying to get the words out. "Don't want to talk."

Just like his father. Well, just like most men. Not many of them even in my time wanted to talk about their feelings in depth. Real men suffer in silence. Huh. "Well, how about a hug then?" I asked, smiling at him. "You look like you could do with one."

He blinked at me, chewed his bottom lip, frowned, then retreated into the barn. A moment later his booted feet appeared, and he slithered to the ground in front of me, bringing a lot more loose hay with him.

I held out my arms. "Come here."

He threw himself into them so hard he nearly knocked me over. I wrapped him in a tight hold, pressing him close, one hand on the back of his hay-snared head.

His body shook as he gave in to tears. No, sobs. I held him for a long time while he cried and cried, making my shoulder and the front of my gown wet. No one came and disturbed us, although after a bit I heard an inquisitive snort from Saeth or Seren.

I waited until his sobs began to subside before I gently extricated myself from his embrace. Then I set my hands on his shoulders much as Arthur had done the day before, and held him at arm's length, studying him.

An unlovely spectacle: puffy red eyes, a runny nose, and not only his hair but also his clothes covered in bits of hay. He wiped the snot off his face with the back of his hand, then wiped his hand on his braccae, leaving a long smear. He followed this up with an enormous sniffling snort, and peered up at me.

"There," I said, keeping my voice firm. "Does that feel better now?"

He shrugged, then must have thought better of it and nodded.

I smiled. "A good cry always helps you work things out of your system. It's not the right thing every time to force yourself to be a man and not cry." I paused. "Shall I let you in on a secret?"

He nodded again and snorted a second time. His nose must be very blocked from all that crying.

"Your father cries sometimes." Not wise to tell the boy it had been over Rhiwallon. It might set him off again.

"He does?"

"Yes. Real men do cry when they have to. It's knowing when it's all right to do it that's hard. And this was an all-right time. You're with me. No one else is around. You can be yourself and grieve. Holding it all in is really bad for you." I let my hands drop.

And you're too young to get drunk and try to forget your sorrows that way.

He wiped his nose on his sleeve this time. "He was my best friend."

"I know."

"Even though he got to be a warrior and train with the other older boys, he was still my best friend." He paused, fingers knotting themselves together. "I didn't see him so much once he'd done that, but soon, I'd've been there with him."

"You would."

He rubbed his eyes with the backs of both hands. "How – how did he die? Do you know?"

Be honest or lie? Which to do? This was a case, if ever there was one, where a lie was needed. I didn't hesitate. "Like a hero. It was quick, and he didn't suffer."

A watery smile appeared. "Th-thank you."

I slid down, leaning my back against the haystack, my bottom nicely cushioned on all the hay he'd managed to kick out. I patted the ground beside me.

He sat down, the sun warm on our faces, the ponies grazing peacefully close by their gate. I leaned my head back against the sweet-smelling stack and closed my eyes, glad of the peace after the kerfuffle the children had kicked up. Beside me, Llacheu did the same.

After a bit, I broke the silence. "It's hard for me, too, you know. This whole life here is so different from where I come from. At fourteen, Rhiwallon would still have been in school. But here, life's nothing like where I was born."

I put an arm around his narrow shoulders. "I know you want to be a warrior like him, but if you wanted, you could go to the Abbey like Gildas, and learn to be a monk. Then you'd never have to fight in battle like Rhiwallon did. Never risk dying. You could do what Gildas intends to do – write down the stories of the battles. The history." It was worth a try.

He gave a snort of contempt, pulling away. "That's not what I want to do, though. Just because my friend died doesn't make me afraid to fight. I still want to be a warrior like my father."

I tried again. "But you don't have to. No one, no matter who their father is, should let someone else decide their future. You can choose, you know, between being a warrior and being a scholar. I know you can read and write, which is a great skill. It wouldn't be hard for you to learn the things Gildas learns. It's quiet and peaceful there." I wanted to say "safe," but held my tongue.

He shook his head, defiant, determined. "No. I want to fight. I always have, and now I want to even more." He set his jaw and looked me in the eye. "I have Rhiwallon to avenge."

I sighed. It had been a faint hope. He was Arthur's son in more ways than one. I pulled him toward me. "Come here for another hug, then, before we go back to the Hall and find you some food. You must be starving."

He moved in to snuggle up against me, a little boy once more. When we stood up, he would be a fledgling warrior with a score to settle. The little boy would be gone.

Chapter Twenty-Four

Nothing disturbed the progress of our harvest. The corn stood in stooks while the seed heads dried out further, and then was stacked, heads innermost, on wagons that brought it back to make stacks by the winnowing barns. A good proportion of the wagons wound up the hill to the fortress's western entrance, others unloaded on the farms.

Blackberries ripened in the hedgerows and apples in the orchards, onions were pulled up, dried, and strung in long plaits to hang from rafters. Pigs were slaughtered, cured, and smoked, ready for the coming winter.

Every day Arthur brought his men down to help with gathering in the bounty the season offered, and unwittingly, by doing so, the men repaired their war damaged souls with the balm of nature. Morgawse, Maia, and after a while Coventina, came with me and the children to pick basketfuls of fat blue-black berries to eat fresh, turn into wine, or cover in honey to preserve for the winter.

Over on Ynys Witrin the monks must have been busying themselves with their cider, as before long, wagonloads of barrels arrived from the lake village to be stored in the fortress. The forest lost its rich dark hues as gilding tipped the leaves, and before we knew it, the view from the fortress walls was one full of the golden tints of autumn, painted by nature's hand in all her many colors.

No time to dwell on those lost this year.

But with autumn came a messenger from Caninus, in his capacity as seneschal to the Council of Kings, akin perhaps to a company secretary, calling Arthur to a meeting. It had been more than two years since the last one, when the Council members had ratified Arthur in his position as High King. Maybe Caninus had been waiting for every kingdom to have brought in their harvest, an even more important part of Dark Age life than battles.

"You can't come," Arthur said, forestalling my question that night in bed, on the day the messenger had been received in the Hall. I'd waited until we were alone to pose it, as I didn't intend to lose. But he knew me too well and no doubt had been expecting my request.

I bristled. "Why not?"

"Because of how dangerous it is in Viroconium."

I pursed my lips, prepared for this. "You let me come with you when you sneaked in there with Merlin to see his child." I prodded his naked chest. We were in bed and had just made love, always a good time to get my own way. "That was far more dangerous than this will be."

"Cadwy wasn't expecting us then. He will be this time."

I regrouped. "All the more reason for me to come. Someone needs to make sure you stay safe."

"Merlin's job."

"Surely you're not taking him back there again? Where he'll see Morgana?"

He put an arm behind his head to support it. "I don't care about Morgana. He'll be there to advise me, not mope over her."

"Pfft." I tapped his chest again. "I don't think he should go. Too dangerous for *him*. He's still in love with her, and we all know how devious she can be."

He fell silent. I was snuggled in the crook of his arm, so I fiddled with the dark hairs on his chest for a moment or two, knowing how much he liked that. "And Cei will want to stay with Coventina, won't he?"

Arthur, who'd been almost purring like a cat, shook himself to wakefulness. "No. Cei's coming with me."

That surprised me. "Oh. Well, if he's coming too, then you should definitely take me. You're both going to need my... tact."

He slid the arm that was around my shoulders down and tapped me on the bottom. "Are you saying I lack tact?" He chuckled. "Or rather that you have more tact than I do? That's funny. Since when did you develop *tact*?"

I ignored the insult. Why rise to it? "What about Theodoric? Is he coming?" We hadn't seen him all summer long, as he'd been off with the fleet at Caer Legeion, and out to sea chasing Saxon and Irish pirates. He pretty much did as he wanted when he wasn't either in his home port or here. Since Uthyr died, he'd hardly been back to Viroconium where he'd once been stationed.

Arthur shook his head. "I've not been able to get word to him for some time. If he meets up with us in Viroconium, then all well and good, but if not, it won't matter."

I ran my hand down his concave stomach, feeling his muscles tighten. "You'll miss me if you don't take me with you. I'm not a queen who stays home and twiddles her thumbs while her king's away." My hand crept lower.

He chuckled again. "Don't I know it. In your own way you're as much of a witch as my sister." His voice hitched. "You think *this* will make me change my mind?"

I grinned, slithering down the bed. "Yes."

"Damn it," he muttered, as I reached my goal. "You might be right."

WE SET OFF the next day a little after first light. We would have been away earlier, only a repeat performance of the night before had been required to convince Arthur he needed to take me with him. Which had been a fun way to start the day.

Autumn mist, promising good weather, swathed the plain, giving it the appearance of a soft white sea, with isolated trees and high ground poking up out of it like islands. Far in the distance, the tall hump of the Tor stood out like a beacon. A beautiful day to be setting out.

Riding down the curving track around the hill plunged us into the mist, the cool damp air beading on our horses' manes and in our own hair. We passed almost silently through the village where the people were beginning to stir – with threshing to be done and their vegetable patches waiting to be dug. Hairy pigs had been turned out in the stubble fields to root, manuring it at the same time, and by the little stream a small boy, as early a riser as we were, sat fishing with a long pole and a string of plaited horse tail.

Merlin fell in beside me as we approached the edge of the forest. I'd not succeeded in persuading Arthur to leave him behind. "How did you get him to let you come?" he asked.

I grinned and tapped my nose. "We women have our ways."

He frowned, perhaps remembering how Morgana had so easily lured him. "Well, no acts of bravado required. You'll need to keep your head down and out of the way of certain people."

I chuckled. "You mean Morgana, don't you?" He'd ridden close enough for me to tap his leg. "And you? Will you be keeping out of her way?"

He sighed. "How can I? I want to see my daughter."

Of course. How hard must it be to know she was there but not be able to have any contact with her. An argument for establishing modern access rights. Fat chance of that.

Alezan, full of the joys of autumn, skipped sideways as a pheasant flew out of the undergrowth and flew noisily away, carking as it went.

Bloody birds. Weren't the Romans responsible for introducing them to Britain?

We rode in silence for a while longer as the forest thickened, following a track that in bad weather would have been nearly impassable. Lots of low-lying wetlands lay to the north of Din Cadan. Ahead, Arthur rode alongside Cei, talking to him volubly, his voice carrying back.

Eventually, Merlin broke the silence between us. "I don't want her growing up not knowing her father." He paused. "Like me."

He so very rarely volunteered any information about himself, my ears pricked with interest. "Did you never know your parents?"

He shook his head. "They abandoned me in a monastery as a baby. Well, I say *they*, but most likely it was my mother who did it. She'd have been unwed, and I'd have been her shame, I imagine. That was what the monks told me, anyway. Nearly every day. But they might have been lying out of spite. You never know."

The sadness of this statement washed over me. I'd never really imagined Merlin as having had a childhood – he seemed more likely to have sprung ready-formed into existence as he was today. "When was that? Where was the monastery?" If he was going to open up, then I was going to ask him questions while I could.

He shrugged. "I don't know when. And I couldn't tell you where, either. All I remember is being a small child in a cold monastery on a windswept cliff, and being punished. Every day."

"Punished? How old were you?" Alezan took a sideways swipe at Merlin's horse, and I had to shorten one rein to keep her head turned away. She could be such a cow with other horses.

He shrugged again. "I don't know. Pretty young. The circuitor didn't like me much."

"The what?"

"The circuitor. He was in charge of discipline. He particularly took it upon himself to instill discipline in me." He grinned. "Didn't work."

"Is that where you learned to read and write?"

He nodded. "I was a precocious child, advanced for my years. They put me with boys much older than me, and, amongst other things, they didn't like me being better at the lessons than them."

"Like Gildas?"

He wrinkled his nose. "I suppose so. But he's not like me. They didn't dislike me for who I was – I was no one, and some of them were nobly born, just as Gildas is – or even just for how clever I was. They disliked me because I had the Sight."

"Even as a small child?"

He heaved a sigh. "From birth, I suppose. Perhaps my unknown mother had it too. The circuitor liked to tell me I'd been begotten on her by a demon, as he tried to beat the Sight out of me. Maybe I was. Maybe that's where the Sight comes from – evil. Although that circuitor had plenty of evil in him." He rubbed his chin ruefully. "I fixed him, though."

Fascinated, I leaned on the horns of my saddle, eager to hear more. "Go on."

He chuckled. "At every meal someone had to stand on a platform and read from the Bible on a lectern. I worked out when it would be the circuitor's turn. That night, I sneaked from the boys' dormitory and loosened or removed every nail in the platform and on the lectern. He stepped onto it, opened his mouth to speak, and the whole thing collapsed. He landed on his skinny arse." He laughed out loud. "We boys had such trouble not laughing we got belly aches. Even some of the monks were stifling their laughter."

"Did he know it was you?"

He nodded. "No one else would have dared, but the beating was worth it. The next night I ran away. I've never been back there since."

Rust-red leaves carpeted the path ahead of us, others drifting down to join them. A smell of autumn forest filled the air, of mushrooms, damp earth and the sharp scent of a fox who must have passed through here a while ago. "And how did you find your way to Guorthegirn's court?" I asked.

"By a twisted route. I traveled alone for a few days, but as a monastery boy I wasn't much good at fending for myself. My luck held, though, and a band of traveling players found me before I starved to death. They soon discovered my skills and turned them to good use – Merlin Emrys, the Child Seer. That was how they marketed me in every village we stopped at. But people don't really want to know the truth. I learned that very quickly."

He shook his head, eyes faraway as though conjuring the scene in his mind's eye. "I saw a woman heavy with child. A black cloud hung over her. I saw her dying as she gave birth. And the child, too. I was a child myself and lacked the experience to hide what I'd seen. Telling her wasn't a good idea. We were chased out of that village by her angry family. After that, Herne the Giant, who led the troupe, advised me not to tell people anything bad. To stick to seeing tall dark strangers coming into the lives of single girls, to profit for farmers and merchants, long life and happiness for all."

I smiled. "That's pretty much what fortune tellers tell people in my old world. All good things and everything generalized. I doubt any of them truly have the Sight, like you. Maybe it's died out because they don't need it any longer."

"That would be a sad thing because it has its uses." He smiled as well, shaking his head, perhaps at the thought of a world without magic. "But what you want to know is how I ended up nearly being sacrificed by Guorthegirn, isn't it?"

Mind reader.

I'd heard this story before, but not all of it could be true – after all, it involved dragons, and they weren't real. Were they? It would be interesting to hear the truth. "Yes please."

"Years had passed and I wasn't so much the child seer anymore. Still half a boy, but growing fast. We'd been working our way around

Gwynnedd, aware that trouble was brewing between the High King and his Saxon allies, but as it didn't affect us, we didn't care. Until we came to the fortress Guorthegirn was trying to build so he could hide from Hengest, his wife's father.

"Then it wasn't called Dinas Emrys as it is now. Then it was just a hill where the walls of a fortress kept falling down overnight. He had his wise men all around him: long robes, dirty white hair and beards, mad eyes, all of them. They told him the walls would stand if he sacrificed a boy with no human father. I was in the wrong place at the wrong time, performing in the village at the foot of the hill. His guards' attention fixed on me."

He swatted a late-season fly away from his face. "Someone had told them I had no known father. Herne liked to give his audience a hint that I wasn't of this world. It brought him more money. The guards seized me and dragged me before the king."

I had to find out. "What was Guorthegirn like? You must be one of the only people living who's met him."

He chuckled. "Nothing special, but he was a beaten man when I clapped eyes on him, running from the men he'd made his allies, whom he'd come to fear. Scared, old... friendless."

"And what did you do?"

He flashed me a smug smile. "You want to know if there really were dragons, don't you? Well, what do you think?"

"Dragons don't exist. Not really."

"They do in people's minds. I made them see them. They believed they saw them. For them, the dragons were real."

"How? How did you do that? Could you make me see one right now?"

He shook his head, laughing. "Probably not, because you don't think they're real. The people I showed them to did. I told them what was there, and they saw it. I put it inside their heads."

I still didn't understand how he'd done that, but however it had been achieved, it had worked. Some sort of mass hypnotism maybe? Auto-suggestion?

He went on. "I guessed bad foundations over water, and possibly an underground cave, were at the root of the fallen walls, and sure enough, they dug down and found a cave with a suitably large pool in it. A little suggestion, and they all saw what they wanted to see. A red dragon fighting with a white. I didn't get sacrificed and the old advisors were given their marching orders."

"But Guorthegirn built his fortress and then burned to death in it, didn't he?" I said, struggling to get my head around what he'd told me. "How come you didn't die with him?"

This made him laugh so loudly Arthur and Cei turned their heads to look at us. "What point would there be in having the Sight if I didn't use it to save my own life? I don't have a lot of control over what I see, but I spotted that one coming a long way off. Even as I explained the meaning of the two dragons to the old king, the unbuilt fortress rose before my eyes, swathed in flames. I saw his ending in its beginning. I didn't stay to find out if I was right."

"So you went to join Ambrosius?"

He nodded. "Herne and his wandering troupe had abandoned me to my fate. Probably afraid they'd be next on the sacrificial list. They didn't stay long enough to see the dragons. That would have impressed them. Guorthegirn got his fortress built, settled himself into it, and I sneaked away one night. Further down the valley I met Ambrosius's army, fresh from a victory over the Saxons and hungry for more blood. I needed no persuading to join them. The next day Dinas Emrys and everyone in it burned. Guorthegirn, his wise men, his groveling followers. Some Saxons too."

What a story. If only scholars in the future could hear it, could know what I knew. Then no one would doubt the truth and try to say King Arthur and Merlin had never existed. But nothing survived – no written records, nothing. Perhaps they had been made, but lost. My father had told me how he and his fellow scholars suspected older records had once existed. Told me that the writers we knew of, in the three to eight hundred years after Arthur, had used these now lost records to write their histories. But none of these earlier works had survived to the twenty-first century. Only the later ones, and most of what had been written in them was suspect.

But did this need to be so? *I could write. I* knew the history. *I* had sources to question firsthand. What was to stop me writing my own history of the Dark Ages? One to rival that of Gildas. Excitement boiled up in me. Yes, that was what I'd do – I'd write an account of everything I'd discovered, of Arthur's life and reign, of the history that came before him. And I'd stow it somewhere safe, where one day some lucky archaeologist would find it. I already had a title for it. *The Book of Guinevere.*

Chapter Twenty-Five

As High King, Arthur was not expected to have his men make camp outside the walls of Viroconium. Instead, he sent Cei ahead to announce our arrival and demand accommodation. Those were the exact words he used – no pretense of politeness here, and probably none expected. Cadwy, with a touch of unexpected irony, or maybe spite, allocated us Euddolen's old house, the Domus Alba.

Arthur seemed unmoved by this, but a shiver of foreboding raised every hair down my back as we passed under the archway into the domus's stable courtyard, half expecting to find it tumbledown and abandoned, with none of the luxuries due to us as Britain's senior kingdom.

However, I was pleasantly surprised. Five years had passed since Euddolen fled the house, and either Cadwy had ordered an extensive refurbishment or someone else had been living there in the interim. Whoever he was, very little sign of him remained, and the genteelly shabby rooms seemed, on first sight, to have been washed clean of all traces of Euddolen's tragic family.

Showing admirable caution, Arthur marched the whole of his force inside Viroconium's high walls. The Domus Alba possessed extensive stabling and accommodation, but not enough to support the huge number Arthur deemed it wise to bring. Our warriors and their horses had to spill out into the surrounding properties and fields, probably to the great annoyance of the neighbors. But who cared? We had our army with us, and I could look forward to sleeping safely at nights. Something I wouldn't have done if we'd brought a smaller force.

"I'm not stupid enough to come in here with the half-dozen bodyguards he thinks I ought to have brought," Arthur snapped, as Cei set off to organize billets for all our men. "Nor to stay within his palace walls." This was what Cadwy had first offered, couching his oily words in silken phrases of wanting only to honor the High King's rank. Not personally, of course. He sent Archbishop Dubricius as his errand boy.

Merlin snorted. "I've a feeling the other kings will feel the same. No one really trusts Cadwy. I doubt many of them will set up camp within his city walls." He glanced over his shoulder as though suspecting Cadwy might come sneaking up behind him wielding a dagger. "I'm not at all sure *we* should have."

I felt pretty much the same myself. And to cap it all, we were staying where the ghosts of a once happy family probably still walked. I couldn't help but shiver again as I remembered Euddolen's two lovely, carefree daughters when I'd first met them. And how dead they were now. Thanks to Cadwy. I didn't often let myself think of them, but when I did, anger rose afresh at the waste of those young lives.

Arthur shook his head. "On the contrary. We're safer inside the city walls with all our men than we would be camped outside. If we'd done that, then we'd only have been able to bring a fraction of our force into the city for the Council. This way, we have our entire army here, with us, ready for any eventuality." He grinned, dark eyes twinkling. "I'd like to have seen Cadwy's face when he realized we'd done that."

Put like that, it did sound like the wisest move. However, I wasn't at all sure about the servants we'd been supplied with. Cooks, maids, stable hands, and cleaners. At first glance, they'd seemed a sorry group of downtrodden cast-offs from Cadwy's palace. Until I passed the kitchen doors and peered inside, my nose twitching at the aroma of cooking food.

"Karstyn?"

The elderly woman engaged in kneading dough at the table lifted her head to look up. Steel gray hair had been scraped back from a face as doughy as the bread she was making, and her familiar, lumpy body still had the appearance of an over-stuffed sack someone had tied a string around at approximately the right level for a waist.

For a moment, the woman hesitated, before her round face creased into a smile. She wiped her floury hands on her grubby apron, and hurried to the door. "My Lady Guinevere!" She bobbed a hasty bow.

I took her hands in mine, overjoyed to see a familiar face. I'd only known her for a short while five years before, but the ordeal we'd shared, of incarceration in the palace kitchens while Morgawse gave birth to Medraut in the middle of a fight for supremacy between Arthur and Cadwy, had bonded us indelibly.

Dropping her hands, I threw my arms around her and hugged her squishy body to mine. "I never thought to see you here. This is wonderful." My fears of poisoned food made by a cook in Cadwy's employ flew out the window.

"'Tis wonderful to see ye here an' all." She wheezed as I let her go. "And fine tales I've heard o' ye these past years. An' that handsome husband o' yourn."

I laughed, the relief of finding a face I knew in a house with so many sad memories lightening my heart. "What on earth are you doing here?"

She waggled her head from side to side. "Not in favor no more, thass what. I got sent over here a year or so back. This is where the king houses guests he don't like. As far from his palace as he can get 'em." She sniffed. "Folks do say as this house be haunted. I'm thinkin' he must've heard those tales."

I managed an uneasy laugh. If any house could be said to harbor ghosts, surely it was this one. "I don't believe in ghosts." Not really true, but I was trying to convince myself and saying it out loud seemed a good idea.

Karstyn glanced over her shoulder as though she feared an on-the-spot manifestation. "Thass what I thought..." she mumbled.

I held up my hand. "Enough talk of ghosts. If we're not careful, we'll convince ourselves we can see them. And they don't exist."

She raised a single quizzical eyebrow, which, accompanied as it was by a knowing smile, did nothing to soothe my nerves. Damn the woman. Now I couldn't get the thought of unquiet specters walking the corridors of the Domus Alba at night out of my head.

She turned back to the table. "I'd best be getting' on wi' makin' this bread then. There be a whole lot o' ye to feed. I b'lieve there's other kitchens in other houses atakin' care o' the men what didn't fit in this here house. I did hear as how young Arthur has brung all his army with him this time." She chuckled. "A wise precaution, I'd say."

The Domus Alba kitchen was a long, high ceilinged room with stone cooking troughs down two of the sides. These already glowed with hot coals, making the room as sultry as the interior of a volcano. A few large cooking pots, responsible for the alluring aromas, sat on tripods over the heat, with large, leaf-wrapped parcels resting on top of the coals. The bread Karstyn was preparing would go to the ovens set in the earth banks against the city walls. Not many houses cooked bread at home as it was such a dangerous undertaking.

"Something smells good," I said, peering into the nearest pot and risking getting my eyebrows singed off by the heat of the coals. The rich smell of the cooking stews mingled with the acrid, eye-watering stink of woodsmoke. Working in a kitchen long term, or even in a great hall with its huge open fire and smoke-filled rafters, couldn't be good for the lungs. Did people here die of things like emphysema and lung cancer? Or did they die of some other cause before those things developed?

As if to illustrate my thought, Karstyn coughed long and deep, then hawked and spat onto the flagstone floor beside the cooking troughs where her globule of mucous sizzled on the hot stone. I'd never get used to the casual disregard for hygiene common in this time.

"Oyster stew," she said. "We did get a deliv'ry from the coast this mornin'. Shucked 'em already, I have, and popped 'em in wi' the beef." She sighed. "That were the Lady Morgawse's favorite. I did cook that for her right often." She looked up from her kneading. "Have ye seen owt of her at all?"

I filled her in on what had been happening to me and Morgawse in the last five years. She'd started on a second batch of bread by the time I'd finished, and a row of neat round patties of dough sat on a tray covered by a linen cloth, ready to be carried to the nearest oven.

A pimply boy staggered in, hefting a lumpy sack, and threw it down on the terracotta floor tiles. He wiped his nose on the back of his hand, and his curious gaze traveled to me. As soon as we'd arrived, and conscious of the part I had to play as wife to the High King, I'd put on a pretty, pale-blue gown and redone my single braid with gold thread woven through it.

He bobbed a bow and tugged his forelock in deference. "Milady."

"Off you go, Nyle, and take this tray o' loaves to the oven. But mind as ye stay an' wait for 'em, lest that oaf of a baker sends ye back wi' the wrong ones."

Good. I didn't want poisoned ones coming back.

With a wary look for me out of his curiously pale eyes, as though I were some kind of weird alien creature, the boy bolted with his load, leaving the kitchen to Karstyn and me.

She sighed. "Can't get the help nowadays. Boys're bone idle. Girls no better. Weren't like that when I were a youngun. That boy, he dreams o' bein' a warrior, not a cook. Foolish boy. Soldiering ain't for the likes o' him."

I forbore from commenting, and instead, turned the conversation in the direction I'd been wanting it to go in all along. "Do you know anything about the Lady Morgana's child?"

Karstyn's gaze sharpened, and she stopped kneading. "I might."

Good. For Merlin's sake, after hearing his sad story of a fatherless childhood, a determination to discover what I could had become one of my priorities. "She's well?"

Karstyn nodded. "She is. Thrivin's what I hear."

I sat myself down in the one chair at the table, back straight as befits a queen, hands folded in my lap, conscious of keeping up appearances. "If you've been sent here, how is it you know?"

She smiled, setting her own pudgy hands on the table and leaning her weight on them. "I've a dear friend what works in the palace still. She be a waitin' woman, and also a midwife. 'Twere she what d'livered the babby. And she do wait on the Lady Morgana still. And the babby."

"Oh." Useful bit of information. "Has she told you much?"

Karstyn narrowed her eyes. "Well, that the babby's mami seems smitten by her. That the Princess Morgana do be'ave more like a proper mother'n you'd'a thought she could."

I nodded. "You're right about that being strange. I wouldn't have expected her to have one ounce of maternal instinct, and yet when we sneaked in here earlier this year so Merlin could see his child, it was Morgana singing her baby to sleep, not a nursemaid."

Karstyn grinned, starting her kneading again, thumping the dough down on the table. "I did hear a fair bit about *that*. Talk o' the palace it were – talk o' the town too. Soon got out. Can't keep a secret like that." She chuckled and her ample bosoms shook. "'Twere my friend what found the lady Morgana, all bound up and fair aboilin' wi' rage. My friend were right scared to untie 'er, lest she took it out on her. Turned 'er into a frog, or summat like that. Ye never know with her sort."

I chuckled. Whatever powers Morgana had, turning people into frogs probably didn't feature on the list. But it felt good to know the small people thought it did. "Do you know when she found her?"

"When she come to help with the child, first thing in the mornin'."

Brilliant. Morgana must have had to sit tied up and gagged like that all night long. I couldn't have asked for more. Our fears that she'd raise the alarm before we were well clear of Viroconium had been unfounded.

Now to the nub of the matter that had been bugging me for a long time – since the name of the child had been revealed, in fact. "Does she... does the child show any signs of... of having inherited her mother's powers?" And her father's, of course. Debatable as to whose powers were the greater.

Karstyn stopped her kneading, her eyes narrowing. "I can't rightly say, milady, seein' as I haven't seen the littlun for meself. But..." She leaned across the floury table toward me and lowered her voice. "My friend do say as she thinks there's somethin' queer about her. Somethin' that she don't quite like. A feelin' that a child that age shouldn't be givin' her looks like she do. Knowin' looks. An' she not even two-year-old yet."

Disquieting.

A shadow blocked the doorway, and I looked up, half expecting it to be the boy Nyle back with the cooked bread. But it wasn't. Arthur stood there, looking in, silhouetted by the sunlight.

"Milord." Karstyn bobbed a bow, wiping her hands again, eyes twinkling.

Arthur hopped down the three steps into the kitchen, a grin on his face. "Karstyn, it's you. Well met, because I'm hungry. D'you have any of the delicacies here you used to once make for me?" He put a hand on my shoulder. "Apart from my wife, that is."

Karstyn beamed at him. "I've honey cakes right here. Just like when you was a nipper." She turned to a wide shelf at the back of the kitchen.

Wait? Arthur had known her when he was a boy? He'd never mentioned that to me before. Mind you, the last time we'd seen her, other things had been much more pressing – Morgawse and her newborn baby, his rivalry with his brother, getting us all to safety.

Karstyn whipped a cloth off a tray of honey cakes and carried them to the table.

Arthur pounced on it, picking up a flat cake in each hand. "My favorites. You have to make them every day while we're here." He beamed at me like a schoolboy, as though he didn't have a care in the world and wasn't within the city of his hated brother. "Karstyn was the best – and nicest – cook in the palace kitchens." He chuckled. "How kind of my brother to let us have her here." He popped a whole cake into his mouth, with very little difficulty, and made a valiant effort not to spit crumbs everywhere.

"And you've not changed a bit." Karstyn chuckled, pushing the tray toward me.

I took one and bit into it, tasting the sweetness of the honey that was all but outweighed by the nuttiness of the cake. More like large biscuits, really, as they hadn't risen as you'd have expected a cake to.

"Is there milk?" Arthur asked, perching himself on the table, bottom in the flour and legs dangling. "I remember how when I used to come to the kitchens, it was always you who gave me milk and honey cakes, right from when I could first escape my nurse. Seeing you's transported me right back there."

Karstyn poured him a horn beaker of milk from a jug on the side and he took a long swig that left his mouth mustached with white. Just to prove that even a king can revert to being a child without much encouragement.

<hr />

THE COUNCIL BEGAN two days later, under a clear autumn sky, a delay having been caused as we waited for some of the more far-flung kings to arrive. According to Merlin, both Lot of Lleuddiniawn and Caw of Alt Clut had turned up, not together, of course, and thankfully set up camp outside the city as far apart as they could get. Each king had brought a sizeable force as though expecting trouble.

"Will we propose the system of messengers?" I asked Arthur, as we prepared to ride to the Council Hall, along with the twenty warriors allowed to accompany us. The riders, and a number of servants on foot, made the stable courtyard appear overcrowded. Knowing Arthur, the rest of our considerable force were probably already strategically positioned either in the hall's upstairs viewing galleries or around the forum amongst the waiting crowds.

"I will," Arthur said, hands on my waist. With no apparent effort, he lifted me up onto the flat pad that had been fixed behind Merlin's saddle, and which I was expected to balance on as I was wearing a long gown of fine blue wool. No women in braccae allowed into the Council Hall. I was expected to dress and behave like a queen – the High King's queen, at that.

Arthur turned away, and as Merlin's horse side-stepped, probably under the unaccustomed extra weight, I had to put a steadying hand on Merlin's waist, tucking my fingers into his belt. "What does he mean, *I*?" I hissed. "It was *my* idea. Not his."

Merlin twisted to peer at me. "Women are not allowed to speak at the Council."

Well, not a surprise. No rights for women in this world. But very annoying. And the fact that Arthur hadn't told me earlier made me bristle with anger at my own stupidity. He'd probably kept quiet so he didn't have to face an argument, which was quite definitely what he'd have got. Too late now. He was mounting the horse Drustans was holding for him, too far away for me to speak to unless I shouted, and I wasn't about to make a spectacle of myself by doing that. Besides which, it would get me precisely nowhere.

I had to content myself with shooting him a glare.

With the escort ready now, and Cei beside him, Arthur led the way out of the courtyard.

To my surprise, many of the townspeople had lined the narrow streets to the forum to watch us pass. The Council only occurred every couple of years, and although at the last one Arthur had been created High King, presumably it hadn't been the same as the spectacle of actually having a High King already in place. And we made a splendid sight.

Arthur, astride the bay horse Garbaniawn had gifted him, wore his customary dark clothing, but his tunic had gold embroidery in a thick, elaborate band around the neck, cuffs and hem and was of the finest wool. His short riding cloak was his one nod to color, dark on the outside but lined with a rich, deep red. From the madder plant, and one of the most difficult colors to obtain so the most unusual. On his head he'd set the gold circlet of his rank, hopefully sufficiently jammed down that it wouldn't dislodge on the ride to the Hall.

I'd cheated with my own gold circlet, and had the timid girl who'd been waiting on me stitch it in four places to my hair, which hung loose in a rich chestnut veil to my waist. That thread was going to be fun to get out later. If I ended up with four short tufts, I was going to be very cross.

With my hand still tucked into Merlin's belt, as this wasn't the most secure way to travel, I surveyed the faces of Viroconium's townspeople as we passed. Tradesmen, artisans, the old, the young, men, women, children, even a few mangy dogs. They might have been Cadwy's people, but Arthur was a homegrown hero to them, a boy many of them had watched grow up. They cheered him as he passed, and they cheered me, too.

"The Ring Maiden. God save the Ring Maiden."

"Long live the High King."

"Uthyr's boy."

"They love him like their own," I said into Merlin's ear, as we approached the very British thatched Council Hall where it stood in the old forum amongst the remains of broken columns and ruined Roman porticos.

The market stalls surrounding the hall were already doing a roaring trade in takeaway food with all the crowds of people. The stone that had once held Arthur's sword stood forgotten and played on by children. Such is the fate of legend. For a brief moment, it crossed my mind to wonder if in my old world that stone still lay beneath the fields at Viroconium, waiting for some archaeologist to discover it. And if they did, would they even recognize it for what it was?

One of our men was detailed to guard the horses we tethered to a rope picket line, another to take charge of all our weapons. Even Arthur had to relinquish his sword this time.

Arthur strode over to Merlin's horse, and I slid down into his waiting arms. For a moment, he held me tight against his body, his face in my hair, before releasing me. Boyish excitement glinted in his dark eyes before he schooled his face to calm. Then, side-by-side, with Merlin and Cei just behind us, we walked into the hall at the head of our strongest warriors.

I knew the drill by now, this being the third Council I'd attended, and let Merlin guide me toward the section of the Hall where we were expected to stand in silence to watch the Council proceedings. Despite there being no hearth-fire, the heat was suffocating.

The hubbub in the Hall lessened as Arthur strode with purpose to the biggest seat at the huge round table, the High King's throne, which up until now I'd never seen filled. For a long moment, he paused, looking down, perhaps considering the momentousness of the occasion. Perhaps the showman in him was waiting for all eyes to be on him. Last time he'd not even touched the throne. Everything important had taken place outside, in the forum.

Silence fell in the Hall, as though, without being told, every man and woman there had become suddenly aware of the occasion. No one needed to ask them to stop talking.

Arthur turned his head and met my eyes, mouth twitching in a smile. My heart swelled with pride as I returned that smile, pride for what he was about to do, but also an immense pride that he was my husband and I loved him, and he loved me back. The moment had come. Still with his eyes fixed on me, he took his place on the throne.

What would my father have said had he known his daughter would end up as queen to the man he'd dedicated his life to studying? I cherished the hope that, if there was a heaven, he could see me now and know.

A gasp hissed around the Hall. I had to bite my lip to stop the tears that were close to running down my cheeks. This was his destiny, and mine was to be his queen.

Oh Dad. Look at me now.

Arthur tore his eyes away from mine to gaze around the table at the other kings, who were now nearly all seated in their places. I did the same, at faces now familiar to me.

On the far side of the table the great bear shape of Cadwy sat hunched in his own seat, glaring at his younger brother. If looks could have killed, then Arthur would be lying dead right now, slumped forward over the table, a metaphorical dagger between his shoulder blades. How galling it must have been for Cadwy to see his hated brother rise to such heights when he'd been bypassed. Old, over the hill, and fatter, with more gray streaking his unruly dark hair and beard than two years ago.

People began to talk again, mainly the townspeople crammed into the viewing galleries above the main body of the Hall, the noise rising to a crescendo. Amongst them I recognized faces of warriors I knew, alert and watchful. The last of the kings came in – not Manogan this time, but Beli, his oldest son. Could the old king of Linnuis be dead?

Morgana stood behind Cadwy, at the forefront of his faction, beside her brother's shadowy wife, Angharad. The five years since I first met Morgana had done little to age her flawless beauty, and her stomach was as flat as ever in her figure-hugging white gown, despite having borne a child. She must have felt my scrutiny, because her eyes flicked in my direction: cold, hard, calculating.

I stared back. If ever there was a woman to hate, it was her. The familiar longing to give her a bloody good slap rose in me, and I had to force my fists to unclench themselves. A punch on the nose would reduce her good looks a bit.

A smile hovered on her lips, as though she'd read my mind, before her eyes flicked sideways to rest on Merlin.

I glanced at him as well, but he had his attention fixed on the back of Arthur's head. Perhaps deliberately. I allowed myself a tiny smug smile as I glanced back at Morgana.

A few seats down from the throne, Caninus of Gwent rose to his feet. Gradually the silence fell once again. When, finally, you could have heard the proverbial pin drop, Caninus spoke.

"Let the Council begin."

Chapter Twenty-Six

"YOU WANT US to have our best horses available, left in wayside inns so riders from other kingdoms can just *take* them?" Meirchion of Rheged was standing, hands on the tabletop, bushy gray brows jutting ferociously as he glared around the table at the other kings, and principally at Arthur.

"Yes," Arthur said, glaring back at him just as fiercely. One thing you could say about Arthur was that he could do as good or better a glare than he got.

"At whose expense?" thundered the deep voice of Lot of Lleuddiniawn. "This won't be a cheap or easy undertaking, as I've already pointed out. More than once. Horses are an expensive asset."

Young King Cynfelin of Cynwidion rose to his feet. "Surely this is of more benefit to the kingdoms in most danger?" He glanced at Lot. "Like yours." Was that a hint of a sneer? The young often show lack of respect for their elders – unsurprising to find it the same here as in my old world.

White-haired March of Caer Dore, Drustans' father, lumbered to his feet. "Aye, that's true. The kingdoms of the east coast would be the winners here, sending their men through the territory of others to steal their horses. What good would it do such as me, off in the far west?"

What about the Irish?

He seemed to be conveniently forgetting about them – and it

would be the west they struck, not the east. And you couldn't get much further west than Cornubia.

A rumble of protest rose to the rafters, not just from the kings but also from their supporters, and from the watching crowd in the gallery. They must have been as fed up with all this as I was.

I met Merlin's troubled eyes. The kings had been arguing about Arthur's, or rather my, idea of a Dark Age Pony Express for some time now, getting nowhere and just going over and over the same arguments. Proof that governing by committee was not something guaranteed to result in a decision. All the kings thought it a good idea, in principle, so long as none of them were to be made out of pocket by it.

"A good horse is a man's most valuable possession," Merlin whispered to me. "A king prides himself on the standard of his war horses. They won't want to give up even one, despite this being such a good cause and potentially so helpful for them all. Bloody minded, penny-pinching idiots." He spat onto the flagstones at our feet.

"How can they be so stubborn?" I whispered, tired of standing for so long while no ground was gained, and fed up with the hot, stale air inside the Hall.

Merlin shrugged. "That's people for you."

He was right. People the world over and throughout time have only thought money worth spending when it could directly benefit them. Trying to get these kings to cough up help, even if it was in kind and not in money, was like getting blood out of the proverbial stone. Banging your head against the wall of the Hall might have been a better idea, for all the good it would have done.

I heaved a sigh. If they didn't hurry up and decide on this soon, I might give up and edge my way to the back of the crowd to see if I could find somewhere to sit down.

Arthur held up his hand to stop the argument. The kings fell silent, and after a minute, so did the crowd. The standing kings sat down.

Etiquette required them to give way to the High King when asked.

"I have horses," Arthur said, his deep voice carrying around the Hall as well as any Shakespearian actor's at Stratford-on-Avon. "I will begin this system by setting up a line down the center of Britain with horses stabled at intervals ready for messengers to use. And I will employ young riders – young because they are lighter than full grown men – to carry messages for *us*." He paused, surveying the many hostile faces amongst the kings. "*For us*, I say. Not just for me – for all of *you* as well. Because if one of you falls, then so do the rest of us. Only if we work together can we defeat our enemies. Divided we will surely fall."

He looked at Lot of Lleuddiniawn. "You, King Lot, should know at firsthand how much a system like this would have helped you."

Lot nodded his grizzled head. A short man, like his son Gwalchmei, with the same nut-brown skin that suggested a hint of foreign blood flowed in his veins. The Romans had not all been from Rome – detachments had come to Britain from all over the Empire, and stayed when they retired. Who knew what blood any man here might have in their ancestry? "Aye, you're right about that. But not all of us have the horses to spare."

From across the table a low growl rumbled, emanating from Lot's geographical neighbor and sworn enemy, sandy-haired Caw of Alt Clut. Both kingdoms were situated beyond the Wall, with a long and somewhat flexible border running between them.

Arthur turned to look at Caw. "And you, Caw of Alt Clut, are also a member of this Council. You will have the right, as will every king here, to send a rider to the line I intend to establish – with the support of this Council or without. That rider will find horses and messengers ready to take his message south, or into the next kingdom, at speed, to get help if you require it." He swept his gaze over the other kings' faces. "And help in our fight against those who wish to steal our lands will come to any who ask."

Caw glowered at him from hostile eyes, his hands gripping the table as though it might have been the only thing stopping him from leaping up and attacking Arthur. Not a man to forget a grudge. Well, that had been part of the problem in the north – the feud between him and his neighbor, Lot. A feud going back generations and likely still simmering.

Arthur moved on to Cerdic of Caer Guinntguic. Their eyes met. "Help will come to even those with Saxon blood flowing in their veins. We are not just men of Dumnonia or men of Alt Clut or Caer Guinntguic. We are all British here, united as one kingdom in our fight to resist those who seek to invade our island. Be they Saxons, Angles, Jutes, the painted Dogmen from beyond the old earth wall, or the Irish of King Ilan from across the western sea. If we stand united then we will succeed, and drive the invaders back to where they came from."

Cerdic got to his feet. Not unlike Arthur in appearance, he was tall and slim, his dark hair confined in a single braid, and his rather sallow skin offset by the intense blue of his eyes, perhaps a legacy from his Saxon mother. "I stand with the High King," he said, his accent guttural, probably due to his upbringing with his mother's people. "On the rich grasslands of the downs around Caer Guinntguic we breed good horses. I will supply horses, if need be, and boys to ride them."

From where I stood, it was difficult to see all of Arthur's face, but I could sense the rigidity in his stance. This was the man who'd killed Geraint before his eyes. The man to whom he'd been forced to cede the throne of Caer Guinntguic after the battle that had led to Natanleod's death. As bad as Caw and Lot in his own way, Arthur was not a man to forget a past insult, grudge, or aggression.

Arthur's shoulders rose as he took a deep breath. "I, too, have good horses I'm prepared to send. But I need my young men for my army." He glanced toward where Garbaniawn of Ebrauc sat, his bulk filling his seat more effectively than the other kings. "I have lost many men in the last few years, and can't afford to lose more and still be able to defend these shores."

Cerdic fixed Arthur with an appraising glance. "I have young men for your army. It is a cause I wish to support." A smile hovered on his lips. "As you say, I'm a British king now, as was my father, Elafius. My people are British, and my throne is British. On the south coast, I fear we'll have great need of the High King's help in times to come. I do not wish to share my lands with any invaders, not even my mother's people."

My eyes widened, the idea of sneaking off to sit down at the back forgotten. Was this the hand of friendship? Or at least an olive branch? Cerdic must know how Arthur felt about him – they'd been on opposing sides in battle more than once. Although perhaps he might not even remember the angry boy who'd watched him kill Geraint all those years ago. Perhaps for him that event was done with and forgotten. Unlike for Arthur.

A rumble of disapproval ran around the table. Cerdic was new to the Council, he had Saxon blood, and he'd caused the death of a fellow king. The watching townspeople leaned over the railings of the gallery, hanging on every word.

Cerdic ignored them. "I pledge a dozen men and horses to the High King's army, and a dozen of my fleetest horses with boys to ride them to the message system."

What would Arthur do? I held my breath.

Cerdic's seat lay a third of the way around the table from Arthur's throne, giving me a perfect view of him. For a long moment, Arthur did nothing. Then he pushed back his heavy seat, its feet scraping on the flagstone floor, and walked, on measured tread, around the table to where Cerdic stood.

I held my breath.

They were of a height. From four feet apart they stared into one another's eyes. Enemies. Used to being on opposing sides. Prepared to fight to the death for what they wanted. But were they still? I thought of Arthur's nightmares of the day he'd seen his cousin die, and swallowed. Was he wise enough to accept the hand of friendship, or was he still young enough, and hot-headed enough, to want to hold a grudge and build a feud? A feud that would do no good for the united Britain he wanted to forge.

Arthur looked Cerdic up and down. The king of Caer Guinntguic had dressed himself with care, in rich dark blue, his tunic heavily embroidered, and his wrists, neck and ears bedecked with solid gold jewelry.

Possibly everyone in the Hall was holding their breath just like me. The silence sizzled with electricity.

Arthur held out his hand to Cerdic.

Without hesitating, Cerdic took it, clasping Arthur's forearm.

No longer enemies, but allies.

BACK IN THE Domus Alba, after hours standing in the Council Hall, I flopped onto our bed in relief, my legs and back aching from so much standing.

Arthur unbuckled his ornate belt. "Thank God that's over," he said, plonking the belt on the table beside his sword, which he'd retrieved as soon as we emerged into the forum. "Managing that lot is a nightmare. Like herding chickens."

Lying flat on the bed, I chuckled at his description of his fellow kings, as well as at the luxury of at last being comfortable. "It went on forever. I thought they'd never come to a decision about the messengers."

He wriggled out of his tunic. "Nor sending more men to my army. They'll be glad of it if they get trouble with raiders, but until that point, they're bloody unwilling to help and will stay that way." He shook his head. "A case of I'm all right, so why should I bother if my neighbor has problems. A total lack of foresight."

I kicked off my boots and wiggled my stockinged toes, which felt wonderful. "You need chairs in there for the audience. You were all right with your nice big throne." I groaned. "I need you to rub my back for me." I rolled onto my front, and tried to look inviting.

He came and sat on the bed and set both hands on my back. "Where?"

"Just there. A bit lower. Ooh, that's perfect."

He kneaded my stiff muscles. "Difficult through your clothes. Shall I undo your laces?"

Smothering a grin, I nodded, and waited while he fumbled with the ties down the back of my dress, something he'd never been all that good at. In too much of a hurry to get them unlaced most of the time.

Once he'd undone them completely, he continued massaging my back with his strong fingers, and I relaxed, head down on the bed, luxuriating in his touch. With my face pressed against the bedclothes, I mumbled, "Don't stop."

He chuckled, his hands working up and down, easing out the tensions caused by so long standing.

I sighed. "You should have been a masseur."

He stopped. "A what?"

I wiggled to make him keep going. "A masseur. From my old world. Someone who does what you're doing. Mmmmm."

"What I'm doing?" His hands were sliding down inside my dress, over my bottom, under the silken panties I'd had Cottia and her daughters make for me.

I chuckled. "Maybe not *quite* what you're doing. But don't let that put you off."

A knock on the door broke into what might have been going to happen. Arthur pulled the back of my dress together and got to his feet with a sigh. "The work of the High King's never done, it seems."

Cei and Merlin were at the door.

I turned onto my back so they couldn't see my state of semi-undress. Not that they'd have cared, but a girl does like to preserve her modesty.

"Cerdic's in the atrium," Merlin said, averting his eyes from me. "Come to call on his new ally."

I sat up, immediately curious, holding my now loose dress up.

"Who's he with?" Arthur asked, reaching for his tunic on the floor where he'd discarded it.

Cei pulled a face. "No one. It's just him."

Silence stretched between the three of them. Probably they were all thinking the same as me – that it was very odd for a king to visit another king without at least a few of his own warriors in tow. Very trusting.

Arthur cast a glance back. "Tell him I'll be with him in five minutes. And take him to Euddolen's old office. I'll see him there."

Cei and Merlin departed, and Arthur pulled his tunic on in haste, then grabbed his ornate belt. But not his sword belt.

I got up, having difficulty keeping my dress decent. "No sword?"

He shook his head. "If he's come for a reason other than friendship, I'll rely on Cei to protect me."

"Shall I come?"

He shook his head. "No. I'll see him alone." He must have seen my frown. "You're a woman. He's half Saxon – they don't see women in the same light we do – I do. You're a chattel, not an equal. To him. Not to me." He probably added that last bit when he saw the look in my eyes. "You know you're not my chattel. Don't act offended. I have to see him on my own. I'll have Cei and Merlin waiting by the door. If he's come armed, I'll have them inside the office with me. Don't worry."

"How can I not? But it's not because I'm worrying that *he'll* hurt *you*. I'm frightened you might hurt him and ruin your new alliance. His support could be valuable to you. Very."

He cocked his head to one side as he buckled his belt. "You know something about him, don't you?"

I compressed my lips. "Nothing much. He's as much a legend in my old world as you are. Nothing I can be sure of. I'm quite surprised he turned out to be a real person, to be honest."

He wrinkled his brow. "But you think this alliance is a good one?"

I nodded. "Yes. I do. I think he'll be a strong king, and good to have on your side. You don't want him as an enemy."

For a moment, he stood deep in thought, as though pondering my words and the decision he was going to have to make here. I watched him in silence.

Finally, he gave a shake of his head as though to clear it, and stepped up to me. A smile strayed across his face, as he gathered me into his arms. "I don't know how long I'll be. I cherish my time with you and resent every interruption we get. Can you hold this moment? I'll come back and we can continue where we left off – if you'd like that?"

I smiled up at him. "Yes, I would like that."

He kissed me hard on the lips, released me, and was gone.

I stood for a long moment staring at the closed door.

Cerdic. I hadn't been lying when I'd told him how surprised I'd been that Cerdic existed. Back in my old world most of those who now peopled my life were known only in legend or from documents written much later than this, and of very uncertain provenance.

Cerdic. Founder of Wessex, putative ancestor of the British royal family. Probably of most of the population of the U.K. If you went back far enough there weren't enough people for everyone to have their own set of ancestors. Hadn't I read somewhere that most Western Europeans were descended from Charlemagne? So quite possibly Cerdic might be one of my own ancestors, if I thought about it.

Cerdic. Offering the hand of friendship to Arthur. Good or bad? I'd told my husband good, but could I be sure? Could Arthur really form a lasting alliance with the man he'd hated nearly as much as Cadwy for most of his life? I hoped so, because instinct told me this was something that needed to be done. That perhaps King Arthur's golden kingdom might be able to morph into Cerdic's Wessex one day, and from that into the Britain I'd grown up in.

Chapter Twenty-Seven

A HAND CAME down over my mouth, hot and suffocating. Terror surged through me, and my eyes flew open to find only darkness. A rigid band seemed to be holding me down as I fought to free myself, bucking on the mattress and kicking the tangling bedclothes away.

"Hush," a voice whispered in my ear, so low I almost couldn't hear it. "It's me."

Arthur. I stopped fighting him and lay still, heart pounding, breath coming hard through my nose. The arm he had pinned across my body relaxed. The chill of a November night settled over my body.

"Don't make a sound." His voice was barely above a breath.

I nodded, and he removed his hand.

My breath came heaving in, panic making me gasp for it. I pushed myself upright, staying silent, my eyes straining in the darkness. What was this? Why had he woken me in this frightening way?

The bed creaked as he moved. I reached out my hand, my fingers finding empty air. He wasn't there. I sat still, ears straining more than my eyes, trying to work out where he was from the sounds of movement. There were none.

A swish. Was that him drawing his sword? My eyes gaped as wide as I could get them, but still the darkness remained impenetrable. I wanted to call out, ask him where he was and what was happening, but common sense kept me quiet. If he needed his sword, then danger threatened, and he also needed stealth.

A faint click sounded, as a catch lifted oh so quietly. A rectangle of lighter darkness outlined the door as it opened a few inches onto the courtyard, then stopped. Cold air rushed in, and silence fell again. How had he even realized something was going on when he'd been lying here beside me, asleep in bed?

The answer came the moment I'd framed the question. Footsteps – not outside in the courtyard, but on our roof. Too heavy for birds or even a cat. Human feet, trying to be silent, making the roof beams creak and the tiles clunk.

The door slid open wider. Arthur's silhouette momentarily blocked it, then he was gone.

Whatever nefarious reason our intruders had to be creeping about on our rooftops at night, it wouldn't be good. And they'd most likely be searching all the sleeping chambers on this courtyard. If they found me alone in the dark, they were likely to strike first and ask questions later.

I scrambled out of bed and pulled my undershirt on over my nakedness as fast as possible, then groped for my saddlebags. Finding them, I pulled out a pair of braccae and yanked them on, then rummaged for my dagger. My sword should be on the table where I'd left it.

Clutching my dagger, I felt my way, barefoot and arms outstretched, toward where I thought the table must be. Feeling like Clarice Starling in *Silence of the Lambs*, I missed it in the dark and my fingertips found the far wall instead. I stood still, leaning my weight on it for a heart-thudding moment. Then, gathering my courage, I peered back toward the pale oblong of the doorway to find my bearings. I was about to head back in the direction of the table, when a black shape obscured that sliver of lighter darkness.

I froze, instinct telling me it was not Arthur. The door swung wide to reveal the silhouette of a man, hooded and cloaked against the cold and facing into the room. Outside, the moonless sky sparkled with a million wintry stars, their feeble light just enough to show me the vague outline of the furniture. I flattened myself against the wall, my breath catching in my throat, heart pounding so fast a heart attack could well have been imminent.

On silent feet he stepped into our room, heading for the bed as though he knew where to find it.

Don't look at me.

As he reached the bed, he raised his sword. I could barely see, but the movement of his shadowy figure caught my eye, and a glint of metal. Enough for me to guess his intention. The sword flashed, stabbing into the mattress, again, and then again, the noise of the blows and the small grunts of the assailant crystal clear. He couldn't have known whose room this was. Could he?

I slid sideways along the wall, deeper into the room and the camouflaging darkness, my fingers creeping across the smoothly plastered wall. Then, nothing. My fingers had found the recess that held the unlit oil lamp, and before I had time to stop it, the lamp went flying. It crashed to the ground with enough noise to waken the entire house.

The man spun around. Either my eyes had become more accustomed to the darkness, or somehow it had grown lighter, or maybe terror had sharpened my senses. His dark shape loomed, the sword held high. Starlight caught the shine of metal.

I had the barest moment to decide what to do. Stay rooted to the spot in the suddenly cramped bedchamber, hoping he wouldn't find me. Not good. Or run for the door and the open space of the courtyard, with the pillared portico, Arthur, and hopefully Merlin and Cei as well.

No contest. I ran.

I nearly made it to the door. The intruder dived for me, tripped on my saddlebags most likely, and went crashing to the ground. Iron fingers closed around my ankle, and I, too, fell, outstretched hands grasping for the door post. My fingers closed around the wood, and I hung on tight, the dagger still in one hand no help.

From outside came the sudden clash of swords, muffled shouts, a scream that turned into a gurgle. I kicked out hard with my free foot, but without boots, had little I could damage my attacker with. My bare foot collided with something hard. His face? I hoped so. From the grunt he made it seemed likely I was right.

Hanging on to the doorpost with both hands, I kicked out again, and felt his other hand grab for my free leg, sharp nails raking across my skin. No. I had my dagger.

I let go of the doorpost. He felt me do it and yanked me hard toward him, as with a huge effort I rolled onto my side. Twisting, I kicked out. He grabbed for my leg. I let him get it. Then, using his hold to pull myself into a sitting position, I lunged toward him, stabbing blindly down with the dagger, right where his hand had hold of my ankle and praying I wasn't about to stab myself.

The blade found its mark, biting into flesh, grating between bones. Horrible. My reactions betrayed me, and I let go of it before I could stop myself.

My assailant screamed and released my ankles. I scrabbled back away from him, daggerless now and defenseless.

Get up and run. But I was between him and the doorway and he'd see me. Did he even know I was a woman? Crab-like, I scuttled backwards into the courtyard, desperate to get away from him, unable to see anything in the dark cavern of my bedchamber. Aware only that a wounded assailant lurked inside.

A dark shape leapt over me, making me cower in fear. Someone landed just inside our door, invisible, breath heaving. The pale starlight sparkled on the blade of a sword and on a naked torso. I scrabbled further back, across the palisaded walkway, and bumped into something warm and solid lying on the ground, my hands and bottom in a wet and sticky puddle.

I bit back the scream bubbling in my throat, fighting the wave of nausea that threatened to overwhelm me. Grunts and crashes came from inside my chamber as whoever was in there knocked the furniture flying.

"Gwen?" A voice hissed through the darkness.

"Merlin?"

A figure loomed, and a light flared, dazzlingly bright after the cloying dark. Merlin's face appeared, lit from underneath like some pantomime villain. He reached out a hand and hauled me to my feet, out of the pool of blood I'd been sitting in. "Where are you hurt?" His voice rose in panic.

I shook my head. "Not me. Him."

Merlin directed the lamplight over the corpse lying in the walkway. A stranger's face stared up at us, slack, unseeing, definitely dead. I'd seen enough of death not to be mistaken. Nausea threatened again, and I turned away.

Cei staggered into view, holding his left arm above the elbow, blood oozing between his fingers. "Got the bastard, but one of them escaped the way they came. Over the rooftops."

Bedwyr and young Morfran of Linnuis, who'd been guarding the entrance to our courtyard, ran into the pool of light, faces grotesquely distorted by the leaping shadows. "Anwyll's followed the one that got away," Bedwyr said. "But I doubt he'll catch him." His eyes went to Cei. "Let me see your arm."

Cei held it out to him, blood dripping dark splodges onto the pale paving stones.

"Where's Arthur?" I asked, snatching my hand back from Merlin's too-tight grasp.

"Here." A dark shape emerged from our chamber. Arthur, barefooted as I was and wearing only his braccae. He grabbed my arm. Like Merlin, he must have seen the blood I'd had a liberal roll in. "Are you hurt? What did he do to you?"

"Nothing. It's his blood, not mine." My eyes went to the shallow cut across Arthur's chest, blood oozing freely. "You're hurt, not me. Let me see." My voice trembled and my body began to shake. It was bloody cold standing outside in my bare feet in the middle of the night.

"It's nothing. A scratch, that's all." He took hold of my shoulders. "I thought he'd hurt you." His voice cracked with emotion. "I'm sorry I left you. I had to wake Cei and Merlin. There was more than one intruder."

I touched his hand, annoyed to find I couldn't stop the shaking. "I'm a warrior queen, don't forget. You'll find my knife w-wedged in his wrist." Despite my bravado, shock was taking over. I willed myself to stop trembling and failed dismally.

The anxiety in Arthur's eyes lessened. "I will? I can see I should have remembered that." He shook his head, the hint of a smile showing. "I'm still not accustomed to a wife who can look after herself the way you can." He leaned closer. "Are all the women where you come from as adept as you?"

How could he be so casual about what had just happened? We'd nearly been killed in our beds. I wanted to slap him. But at least being angry lessened the trembling.

"No," I whispered back. "Not quite all of them."

"Assassins," Merlin said, kicking the body in whose blood I'd rolled. The metallic smell came creeping up my nostrils. I bit my lip, suddenly acutely aware of the sticky wetness on my undershirt and braccae, but determined not to puke. The inclination was there, though, making my stomach do unhappy somersaults. I needed to get out of these clothes. Fast.

Arthur nodded. "You're right. But whose assassins? That's the question."

Cei sat down heavily on the stone bench outside our room, face drained of color, his hand still clutched to his upper arm, and Bedwyr helped him out of his blood-stained undershirt. Fresh blood ran down his arm from a deep sword-cut between elbow and shoulder. Bedwyr balled the discarded shirt and pressed it to the wound, looking up at me. "Can you hold this?"

I nodded and sat down beside Cei. He gave me a pasty-faced grin. "I'm sorry. I know you don't like blood." He looked dangerously near fainting. Well, he could join the club, because I was pretty near that myself having to hold this blood-soaked shirt to his wound.

I shook my head and lied. "I'm getting better." I managed a small smile. "It doesn't always make me retch." I pressed the shirt against the wound, putting as much pressure on as I could, hoping I was right about not retching. Cei might not be impressed if I threw up over him.

Cei leaned his head back against the wall. "Big bugger got me with his dagger. Didn't see he had one – thought he only had a sword." He grinned again, paler still, but that might have been the poor light. "I got him, though." He chuckled. "He won't be sneaking around trying to kill people in the middle of the night again."

"Just be quiet," I said as gently as I could. "The bleeding's stopping a bit, but you've lost enough to make you light-headed. Breathe steadily. Stop panting or you'll hyperventilate."

Cei raised his ginger eyebrows, probably wondering what hyperventilating was, and gave me a half-hearted smile. "Yes, Mother."

My gaze slid back to Arthur, the lamplight shimmering over his naked chest, where he stood over the dead man. For once he was right and his cut was just a scratch, maybe from the tip of a sword or dagger. The blood was already drying on the wound.

He stared at Merlin. "They meant to kill us all, whoever they were."

"Could've been sent by anyone," Merlin said with a shake of his head, as he held the lamp over the body and peered more closely at the dead man. "Difficult to say from what he's wearing. But as those are plaid braccae he has on, I'd say he's from the north. They're fond of plaid up there."

I couldn't help my gasp of horror. "You mean they are *actual* assassins?" I glanced between the stony faces of my menfolk. "Not burglars?" For some ridiculous reason I'd been thinking they were thieves. Clearly, I lacked common sense when disturbed in the middle of the night. "Someone sent assassins here – to kill us?"

Was it so difficult to believe? With all the kings at each other's throats so short a time ago, and not many of them liking being ruled by so young a man as Arthur, was it any wonder one of them, or maybe more, had decided to open up a vacancy on the High King's throne?

"I'll fetch the one I killed in our chamber," Arthur said. He vanished inside the dark room and a moment later emerged, dragging the man who'd attacked me by his feet. Sure enough, my dagger sat firmly wedged between the bones of his wrist, like a crucifixion nail. That must have hurt like hell. Good. Only he wasn't feeling it now. His wide-open eyes stared sightlessly up at the starry sky, and his shirt was black with his own blood. His body left a wide, bloody smear across the tiles in our room out onto the flagstones in the walkway.

Arthur dumped the man's legs. "Plaid braccae as well."

Cei opened his eyes for a moment. "I'd say they *look* like Caw's men." He shut them again, probably feeling dizzy. I felt dizzy with shock myself.

Bedwyr, whom I hadn't notice leave, returned with bandages and took over from me. He'd brought a flask of spirits, with which he liberally dosed Cei's wound, then offered it to Cei to drink. Cei took the bottle like a man dying of thirst and downed several huge gulps.

Not sure what to do with the blood-soaked undershirt, I dropped it to the floor, my fingers sticky with drying blood and smelling strongly metallic. I sat on them so I wouldn't have to look at them. I'd just made up my mind to say alcohol wasn't the right thing for shock, when Merlin spoke. "How do we know the plaid isn't a disguise?"

The sounds of something heavy being dragged came from the

darkness in the courtyard, and Morfran arrived, dragging a third body by one leg. Also in plaid braccae. The one who'd wounded Cei, presumably.

Arthur nodded. "You could be right. If you were going to send assassins after the High King, or any king for that matter, then you'd not want any sign of your men's origins on them, in case the worst happened, and they were caught. You'd be a fool to mark them as your own."

Cei opened his eyes again, a little color back in his cheeks now Bedwyr had the bandage round his arm. "And how did they know which courtyard to come to, or even which house? Caw's men are all camped outside the walls. If they were his, they'd have had to get inside the city's closed gates after nightfall – impossible – and then inside our walls. Ask yourself. Whose servants are working in this house?" He grunted and closed his eyes, lips compressed.

Merlin nodded, his eyes glowing almost golden in the lamplight. "And we're well guarded at every entrance. They knew to come in across the rooftops. Knew which courtyard to come to."

Arthur chuckled. All right for him, he hadn't been as terrified by this as I had. I clenched my fists to still the shaking that had come back with a vengeance. Never mind Cei suffering from shock, I probably was myself. And cold. November was not the time for sitting outside and discussing assassination attempts.

"They could have come inside the city during the day and stayed," Bedwyr said, tying off the bandage on Cei's arm.

"True," Merlin said. "But I think we're being deliberately misled. These men aren't Caw's. He's not that stupid. But maybe whoever sent them wants us to think it was Caw – it might suit his purpose."

"Well, who do *you* think sent them?" I asked.

Silence.

Without opening his eyes, Cei spoke. "I think we all know who."

Footsteps sounded on the roof, all our heads swung around, and

Anwyll dropped down into the courtyard. "I'm sorry. I lost him on the rooftops. Too dark to see where he went. But I did spot low points on this house where the walls are easily climbable from outside."

"So he's still inside the city walls somewhere," Merlin said. "Three guesses where."

Arthur gave a snort. "I don't need even one guess. I know."

Bedwyr straightened up. "Let me put a bandage round your chest. That's got to sting."

For a moment it seemed Arthur might refuse, but then common sense must have taken over, because he gave a shrug and nodded. He stood fidgeting impatiently while Bedwyr expertly sloshed alcohol onto the narrow wound, then applied a bandage.

Anwyll looked down at the three bloody corpses. "What do we do with them?"

Good point. Not to mention all the blood.

Merlin chuckled. *Men.* I had the distinct impression they were treating this like some kind of game.

He gave the nearest body a kick. "Well, whatever they intended, they've failed. I very much doubt anyone'll be back tonight. That last assassin's probably run home to tell his master the plan went wrong, or he's legged it – afraid of the trouble he'll be in for failing. Let's put the bodies in that storeroom in the corner for now, and get some sleep." He peered up into the sky, that seemed to be lightening a little in the east. At last. "We've an hour or two left before dawn."

Arthur yawned. "We'll get the servants to clear this mess up in the morning. And we'll get to the bottom of who told them how to find us." He caught my hand. "Bed."

Bed? He wanted me to go to bed and forget all this until the morning? As though it hadn't happened, and we didn't have three dead bodies stuffed in a store shed?

Merlin nodded to Anwyll and Morfran. "Best stand guard right outside the king's door."

Pulling me to my feet, Arthur slung an arm around my shoulders. His body was as cold as mine. I shivered, and he tightened his hold. The thought of sleeping in the bed that had been stabbed so many times did *not* seem attractive, and nor did that bloody smear our assassin had left in our doorway.

"Come on," Arthur said, voice suddenly gentle. "Rest's what you need. And warmth." He gave himself a shake. "It's bloody cold out here."

He lit a candle at Merlin's lamp and nodded to Morfran and Anwyll as they took up their sentry positions on either side of the door. Still holding me close, he ushered me back inside our devastated room. The circle of flickering candlelight revealed broken chairs and the table lying on its side, and plunged the corners into unquiet shadows.

Averting my eyes from the threshold as Arthur shut the door behind us, I pulled my blood-stained clothes off with alacrity and threw them on the floor. The cold inside the room bit at my naked body but I couldn't get into bed until I'd sponged myself off with a cloth. Even cold and dirty water was better than getting into bed covered in someone else's dried blood.

Arthur found me a clean undershirt and we lay down on the bed, him still in his braccae, holding me tight against his body. Slowly, warmth returned to my limbs, and the trembling lessened. But I couldn't sleep, and plainly neither could he. Morning was a long time coming.

Chapter Twenty-Eight

"You can't let him get away with it again," I said, hands on hips and glaring at Arthur and Merlin. We were in the center of the courtyard while our horrified servants carried the bodies away and cleaned up the rather copious amounts of blood. We'd done a head count of the villa staff that morning, and only one was missing – the cook's boy, Nyle, who harbored ambitions to become a warrior. Perhaps a giveaway that he'd been somehow involved. The city magistrate, a man named Leudocus, was already on his way.

Arthur glared back at me. "What do you want us to say to Leudocus, then? That we think his king sent these men to kill us? To murder me, the High King?"

I nodded. "Yes. You should say it. Because you know it was him."

"And what proof do we have that it was?" Merlin asked, more gently than my husband. "What proof will you show Leudocus when he arrives?"

I heaved a breath. "But we know it was him. He's tried before. You said yourselves it wasn't Caw."

Arthur gave a wry grin. "True. Apart from anything else, Caw isn't likely to have used sneaky methods like nighttime assassins. If he wanted me dead, he'd come right out with it, and attack us outside the walls. But I doubt he'd do that as it goes against the agreement we've all signed up to – our pact of non aggression at the Council."

"Cadwy clearly doesn't feel bound by it," I snapped. "And unless he's punished, he'll try again."

"Punished?" Arthur's dark brows rose. "How do you envisage punishing him? A king? He's the law here, whatever you think his magistrate stands for. Leudocus is Cadwy's man, and he'll do what Cadwy says. And besides, I don't want us to be at each other's throats. It's not good for Britain."

"But you're the High King," I protested, seething at the injustice of this. "Suppose you'd been killed? What would have happened then? That's what he wanted. Why he sent those men here. One of them nearly killed *me*, for God's sake. Their aim was to kill you."

"If I'd been killed, then there'd have been a Council held and someone else would have claimed my throne, and perhaps my sword. I doubt Cadwy would have got it. He'd have been the most obvious suspect."

I walked away from them, fists balled by my sides. How could they be so matter of fact about this? I'd spent the few hours we'd had in bed going over what had happened in my mind and how close we'd come to death. And now there seemed to be little we could do to punish the man behind these would-be assassins.

Anwyll appeared from where he'd been stationed guarding the doors into the courtyard. "Leudocus, Milord King." He stepped back, and a small, spare man in a below-the-knee cream robe stepped into the courtyard.

About fifty, with a long, lugubrious face and a not-very-successful comb-over, he advanced on Arthur, rubbing his hands together like Lady Macbeth trying to get that "damned spot" off them. Intent on washing his hands of our problem, most likely. And us, too.

"Leudocus," Arthur said, with a nod. "Good to see you again." By his clipped tone I had a pretty good idea this wasn't true.

Leudocus made a very low bow, revealing the extent of the shiny bald patch his comb-over was meant to hide. "Milord King."

"Get up, man," Arthur snapped. "There're three dead bodies that have been sent to your office for you to examine. The fourth attacker escaped. No doubt he's left the city by now, even though I sent a message first thing requesting the gates to remain closed."

Leudocus licked his thin lips, his eyes darting about in an effort not to look Arthur in the eye. "Unfortunately, Milord, I didn't receive your message until after the gates had been opened. Your escapee will be long gone, I fear."

How convenient.

Merlin snorted. I would have done so too, if my mouth hadn't been hanging open. Talk about aiding and abetting. But as Cadwy was this man's king, what else could we expect?

"Well, you'd best take a good look at the three bodies you have," Arthur said. "See if you recognize any of them." He fixed Leudocus with a hard stare, daring the man to demur. "Here's a hint – they're more than likely locals."

Leudocus's mouth opened and closed a few times. "I'm sure I w-won't," he floundered. "They sound like brigands to me – a band of brigands out to rob you. Not locals at all. No. Not locals."

I met Merlin's gaze. He raised one eloquent eyebrow.

"Brigands?" Cei spluttered, emerging from his room to join us. "Who're you trying to fool? Those weren't common brigands out to rob us." He had his arm in a sling but looked otherwise returned to normal, his face flushed a healthy pink with anger. "They came here for one thing only – and it most certainly wasn't to rob us."

Leudocus's shifty eyes traveled swiftly around what must have looked like a sea of hostile faces. "Ch-chance," he stuttered. "Bad luck. You-you disturbed them, and they turned nasty. Brigands are wont to do that... so I'm told."

It sounded as though he didn't want us to think he had even the merest passing familiarity with brigands and their habits.

"And how do you think these 'brigands' got in here?" Arthur asked, tapping his leg, a sure sign of his anger. "Did your gate guards allow them inside the city walls? Are they, perish the thought, *incompetent?*"

Considering how easily Arthur, Merlin and I had got in and out of here a few months back, this might well have been a valid accusation.

Leudocus shook his head, flabby cheeks wobbling. "The guards are most efficient. No undesirables can get into this city through any of the gates." As soon as the words were out of his mouth, his eyes shot wide as he realized how he'd just refuted his earlier statement.

Arthur pounced. "So, in that case they *must* be city-bred brigands."

Leudocus's mouth worked overtime, but no sound came out. A puppet, a yes-man, a servant of his king, now tying himself in ever tighter knots. "N-no," he managed, incredulous. "Surely not? They couldn't have been…"

Merlin edged closer to me and leaned in so he could whisper in my ear. "This man knows nothing of the attack. He's a lickspittle only, not privy to the inner workings of his king's mind."

I'd come to that conclusion myself, and now it looked as though Arthur had as well. He waved his hand at Leudocus. "Well, you'd better get off and take a look at these brigands and see if their faces ring any bells. They should. And you can tell your king, that before I go, I'd like to see him – *here*." He paused, eyes flashing. "In fact, tell him these exact words – the High King requests his attendance at the Domus Alba in one hour – alone. No packs of guards. He can leave them at the doors." He turned his back on the poor man, who was really only doing the job he'd been appointed to. "Be off."

<hr>

ARTHUR SAT ON a high-backed chair at one end of the largest room in the Domus Alba, the dining room, on a platform hurriedly constructed by the house servants. All other furniture had been cleared away to make a makeshift audience chamber, apart from the stool on which I sat, a little to one side. Merlin and Cei, minus his sling but nursing his arm, stood behind Arthur's makeshift throne like a pair of sentinels, feet planted wide apart, intimidating frowns on their faces.

I'd chosen my gown for this occasion with care. In rich dark blue, with its long sleeves trimmed with fur, it clung to my curves everywhere it touched and matched Arthur's own dark tunic and braccae. Gold circlets of rank sat on our heads, necessitating a very upright posture. We must have made an imposing picture, like something out of a medieval manuscript illustration.

A minute ago, Morfran had told us of Cadwy's arrival, and his protest at having to leave all of his huge contingent of warriors at the doors. As Morfran left by a small side door, Arthur glanced at me, and I saw with a start the glint of mischief in his eyes. He was enjoying this.

I was about to ask him what he had planned, when the opening of the door at the far end of the room forestalled me. Anwyll, in full armor, stepped through it, then stood to one side. "King Cadwy of Powys," he announced.

Arthur's eyes lost their boyish sparkle and hardened. I followed his gaze.

Cadwy sauntered into the room. By himself. Not that our guards on the doors of the Domus Alba would have let any of his men inside. He had the air of someone who didn't care that he was alone in the territory of the man he'd just tried to have assassinated.

He glanced about himself, taking in the room. More than likely he'd never been in here before. Why would he have? Euddolen had never been his friend, even though he'd been his father, Uthyr's, seneschal.

The dining room was not large, for a throne room, and Cadwy's presence seemed to fill it. As tall as Arthur, if not Cei, he possessed twice the bulk of either of them, enhanced by the thick black bear pelt he wore over his tunic, secured with a wide leather belt. His sword hung at his hip, and a dagger sat in a sheath at his waist. Armed and formidable – he clearly saw himself as inviolate, even in the den of his enemy.

My eyes slid sideways to peek at Arthur, but he sat impassive, watching as Cadwy strolled almost nonchalantly up the room toward us. Ten feet away, he halted. Corpulent would have been too good a word for him. If he reminded me of anyone at all, it was of renditions of Henry VIII by character actors in my old world – heavy, piggy-eyed... overweight. His dark hair, liberally streaked with gray, hung in greasy curls down his back, thick dark brows tufted above his eyes, and his grizzled beard had the appearance of housing part of his last meal, with his thick, greasy lips like two slugs buried amongst the hair.

The thought that but for Arthur I might have had to marry him made my toes curl with disgust.

Arthur sat silent, staring at his brother, waiting.

Cadwy faced him, hands on his hips, defiant. Oh yes, he was aware that we knew what he'd done, and could do nothing about it. Had he agreed to come here so he could gloat?

The silence stretched. No noise came from outside. The sound of my heart thudded in my ears. The tension in the air sang.

It got to Cadwy first. "Well," he growled. "Why have you requested my presence?"

Arthur's wry smile didn't reach his eyes. "To call a truce."

What? I couldn't stop my head whipping round to stare at him.

Cadwy looked as surprised as I was. His eyes went to Merlin's face, perhaps suspecting him of being behind this. "A truce?"

Arthur's hands on the arms of his throne tensed. "Yes. A truce. I am High King, and you are not. Nothing you can do will change that." He paused, presumably to let the implication sink in. "But there is something you can change."

Cadwy's piggy eyes narrowed in his fleshy face. "What?" Suspicion, aggression, anger, scorn – that one word held everything he felt about his younger brother.

I gripped the arms of my chair, holding my breath.

"Britain is an island," Arthur said. "Once, it was a province ruled by Rome. The legions protected it, ruled it, united it. When they left, it fell apart into countless small kingdoms. Now, we are independent and have the Council of Kings, whereas before we had the iron rod of the distant rule of Rome. But what good is a council of any sort if the members fight each other instead of the common enemy?"

Cadwy's brows lowered even further, shadowing his eyes.

Arthur tapped the fingers of his right hand on the arm of his throne. How close was he to showing his true feelings and losing his temper? "If you and I fight, then we set a bad example to the lesser kings. You are one of the most important kings in Britain. As am I. We must lead by example – show the rest that personal vendettas have no place if we are to protect our island from invaders."

I studied Cadwy's face, but it was impossible to divine his feelings about this statement. Would he see sense and agree? Was he man enough to accept the olive branch Arthur was offering? He stayed silent.

Arthur sighed. "I know it was you who sent assassins to this house in the early hours of this morning. You hoped to rid yourself of not just a brother you've always hated but a High King you have no desire to accept. I understand. It's natural in a man to want more than he has."

What?

For a moment Arthur set his teeth on his bottom lip as though to prevent himself saying something he might regret later. I did the same, wanting to shout out loud and accuse Cadwy of being a would-be murderer many times over. But a king was the highest authority here, apart from the High King, and it seemed you couldn't accuse him of any crime.

Cadwy shifted uneasily, perhaps wishing he'd insisted on bringing in some of his men. The fingers of his left hand, still on his hip, touched the pommel of his sword as though he'd like to draw it. Outnumbered four to one, he didn't.

Arthur leaned forward in his throne. "I have no love for you, Brother. No more than you have for me, I suspect. But we fought a fair fight for this sword." He touched his own blade's hilt. "And I won. And with it came the High Kingship that was foretold for me even before I was born. I am the red dragon, Brother, the hammer of the Saxons. It is I who will drive the invaders back and bring peace to our island, as it was long ago prophesied." He reached out a hand and touched my shoulder. "I have the Ring Maiden by my side. I have the Sword of Destiny in my hand. I have the High Kingship. But what I want, and need, is an alliance with you."

I schooled my face into equanimity, my hands clasped tightly in my lap. Was this a wise thing to ask of someone as sneaky and underhanded as Cadwy? But there was that old adage – keep your friends close and your enemies closer still. Was this what Arthur wanted? Cadwy as a close ally?

Cadwy finally spoke. "An alliance?" His voice rumbled out, gruff and deep, and slightly accusatory.

Arthur nodded. "We are both powerful kings. You have a central position here at Viroconium, sheltered from most incursions made by raiders, safe from the threat of colonization by Saxons in search of new lands. At least it is for now. But how long will it be before they reach further west? How long before your lands, like parts of Coel's, are annexed by the Yellow Hairs?"

I bit my lip at his prophetic words. That he guessed what was inevitably to come tore at my heart.

"My kingdom is safe," Cadwy said. "My city walls will keep invaders out."

"For how long?" Arthur asked.

For answer, Cadwy glowered at him.

Arthur sighed again. "I don't want to fight you, Brother. I want to fight the enemies of Britain. I want to defeat them and send them packing, tails between their legs. I need you on my side, not against me. Just as Cerdic now is." He paused. "What do you say?"

Cadwy glanced over his shoulder at Anwyll by the door, then back at Arthur. "And if I don't agree, what then? Will I walk free from this room, or will you have your men kill me? Be warned, I won't go down without a fight." His right hand touched his sword hilt in threat.

Arthur shook his head. "If you don't agree, you will walk free from here." He smiled ruefully. "I'm not you, Brother. I didn't call you here to threaten you, but to ask you for your help in defending our island. I hope you will agree."

Cadwy lowered his hand. "And what assurances do you demand?"

"None."

Behind me Merlin fidgeted as though he wanted to say something, and I glanced over my shoulder at him. He had his lips pressed firmly together to keep the words inside. Cei's face was poker straight, eyes fixed on his stepbrother's bloated face.

Cadwy sneered. "No assurances? Then what makes you think I'd stick to any bargain I make with you?"

Arthur tapped his fingers on the arm of his throne. How close was he to losing patience? "Your word will be sufficient."

The word of this man? I wanted to tell Arthur not to be a fool, and from the look on Merlin's face I could tell he wanted to do the same. Cei remained silent and impassive.

"And what is in this for me?" Cadwy asked.

"My trust," Arthur said. "The opportunity to call my army to your aid. You know the Irish invaders made it as far as Breguoin this summer, before I stopped them. They'll be back, mark my words. They already have a strong foothold in the far west, and your lands here are rich and fertile – and prosperous. Don't think they'll be happy to stick with the rough lands in the mountains."

Trust? What was he talking about? I wouldn't trust Cadwy any more than I'd trust a viper. Him and that witch of a sister of his. I dug my nails into my hands to stop myself from protesting.

Cadwy shrugged. "Perhaps I'll agree then."

Arthur got to his feet and stepped down off the platform. Four steps brought him face to face with Cadwy, five feet between them. He held out his right hand.

Cadwy looked down at it for a long moment, his face every bit as hostile as it had been when he walked in. The silence stretched between the brothers. Then he lifted his own hand and took Arthur's. They clasped forearms, sealing their alliance.

"For Britain," Arthur said.

Cadwy nodded. "For Britain."

The legends had never mentioned this. Nothing in what I knew of Arthur's story had prepared me for Cadwy. Was this a good thing or a bad one? I had no idea. But at least it was nothing to do with me – not an event I'd inadvertently provoked into happening. In fact, if I'd been able to, I'd have actively discouraged it. But it was done. These warring brothers had made some kind of pact.

But which brother would be the first to break it?

To be continued...

Author's Notes

First of all, I'd like to thank you, the reader, for buying and reading my book. Then I'd like to add all the people who've helped to make it possible. There's my publisher of course – Kathryn Le Veque of Dragonblade Books, my agent, Susan Yearwood, and my wonderful editor, Amelia Hester, who has been so supportive throughout my journey.

However, I mustn't forget how the Guinevere series started out, which was on the amazing writers' website Critique Circle, and all my friends on there who added little nuggets and suggestions to the story as I wrote it. Special mentions to Stacesween, Michelle5, Montavon, Magnusholm, Mistymarti, Ml2872, Rellrod, Oznana, Aventurist, Maryleo, Fitzfan60, Dorothea, Fran, and last but not least Kevinc. I hope I haven't missed anyone out.

You probably don't know, but I have Asperger's syndrome, as do two of my sons, only mine was late diagnosed. My diagnosis answered a lot of questions for me, not least why I've been obsessed with all things Arthurian for most of my life. The Guinevere series is the fruition of a lifetime of research that's still ongoing – my magnum opus if you like. I feel deeply attached to it and probably always will.

The events in all six books are loosely based around the early ninth century monk Nennius's list of Arthur's twelve battles, about which there is no corroboratory evidence. This gives any writer carte blanche to twist the story in almost any way they want, and I've taken advantage of that. I have my own theories about where the battles were fought, and in this book I took the decision to make one of the more easily located battles – the Battle of the City of the Legion – take place at York. There were three legionary cities and most people like to think this battle took place at one of the other two – Chester or Caerleon. But I think that if it was against the Saxons, it would have been in the east, not the far west of Britain.

I've tweaked some of the characters out of their proper historical time and pulled them a little forward in time, but they remain for the most part real historical characters. King Coel really existed, as did his wife Ystradwel the Fair, his sons and his great grandsons – the two little boys playing with their wooden horses. Although I imagined his heroic death in battle at a great age.

Throughout the books I've tried to use as many "real" characters as possible. Most people are unaware that Arthur had children, but the names I've used for these come from legend. Llacheu was his son, as was Amhar, both with legends attached to them, and Archfedd, although less well-known, was probably his daughter. Hence her rather unwieldy name.

Cerdic was "real" and is thought to be the ancestor of the British royal family. Cadwy was a prince of Dumnonia after whom several hill forts in the West Country are named. Prince Geraint did indeed die at Llongborth – its location also unknown, but in my head it's at Portchester Castle near Portsmouth, a Roman fort.

Most of all, thanks to my extensive research, I've tried to create a believable world for my characters to inhabit, setting Gwen's adventures in hillforts, crumbling Roman towns and in places that really exist and can be visited in the present day. I've stood where my characters stand, visualized what they could see when they looked out over battlements or from hilltop forts, walked the paths they walk in my books. I've loved every minute of the research I've done and even now am still doing.

If you have liked my books and would like to be kept in touch with further releases, then you can go to my website at filreid.com/contact and join my MailChimp mailing list. And if you want to contact me, you can do so at filreid@outlook.com and I'll be happy to talk to you.

Thank you again for reading my books. I don't think I'll ever get over the novelty of having people I don't know read my books and enjoy them. So please tell your friends about them if you get the chance, and if you have time, leave a review on Amazon or Goodreads.

Fil Reid
2023

About the Author

After a varied life that's included working with horses where Downton Abbey is filmed, riding racehorses, running her own riding school, owning a sheep farm and running a holiday business in France, Fil now lives on a widebeam canal boat on the Kennet and Avon Canal in Southern England.

She has a long-suffering husband, a rescue dog from Romania called Bella, a cat she found as a kitten abandoned in a gorse bush, five children and six grandchildren.

She once saw a ghost in a churchyard, and when she lived in Wales there was a panther living near her farm that ate some of her sheep. In England there are no indigenous big cats.

She has Asperger's Syndrome and her obsessions include horses and King Arthur. Her historical romantic fiction and children's fantasy adventures centre around Arthurian legends, and her pony stories about her other love. She speaks fluent French after living there for ten years, and in her spare time looks after her allotment, makes clothes and dolls for her granddaughters, embroiders and knits. In between visiting the settings for her books.

Social Media links:
Website – filreid.com
Facebook – facebook.com/Fil-Reid-Author-101905545548054
Twitter – @FJReidauthor

Printed in Great Britain
by Amazon